Postcards from the Past

Linda Leffler

FrenchLady Books

This is a work of fiction. Names, characters, places and incidents are either products of the author's imagination or are used fictitiously. Any resemblance to actual events or locales or persons, living or dead, is entirely coincidental.

As you read my novel, you will encounter foreign terms. Translations can be found in the last section.

www.lindaleffler.com

Cover design by Jen Leffler.

Find her at www.artbyjenleffler.com

For Wally

PROLOGUE

They'd raced across France in pursuit of the treasure, following the enigmatic postcard clues. They'd even dodged bullets for the quest.

But to make the elusive treasure theirs, they needed to understand the story of three brave souls whose lives were embedded in the World Wars.

Finally, they possessed it.

The greatest hoard of its kind in history.

Lucie shook her head slightly as she turned to the man next to her - she still found it hard to believe. Her lover grinned, leaned over to kiss her and raised his glass to hers. As they enjoyed the wine, Lucie's mind drifted back to that impossibly crazy first day.

The one that led to *the greatest adventure of her life.*

CHAPTER 1

September, 2007

The cab lurched off the main road and almost sideswiped the open iron gates that marked the entrance to the estate. Lucie, who was being flung from side to side in the back seat, made another attempt to communicate with the cabbie, but none of the languages she spoke had any effect on him. She was being propelled at breakneck speed down a formal drive of half a mile, and a blur of stately, mature trees whizzed by before the mansion suddenly appeared.

She gasped at the sheer size of it. They had almost flown past the front of the building when the cabbie downshifted, missed two gears and slammed on the brakes. The vehicle skidded on the pebbly driveway and screeched to a halt as Lucie braced herself, then escaped as quickly as possible from the potential death trap.

All thoughts of strangling the cabbie vanished, however, as she stared at the imposing façade of what appeared to be a château built in pure Renaissance style, astonishing even in this Gold Coast area of Long Island.

Three stories were embellished with beautiful gray stone, graceful and elongated windows armed with shutters, and sentry-like dormers that jutted out from the top floor. The entrance, as high as two men head to toe, was fronted by a crunchy driveway that snaked past in a semicircle.

As the cabbie dumped her luggage on the driveway, Lucie heard a woman's voice roar "*Bruno! Come back here!*" Then she caught movement in her peripheral vision and turned: two entities were racing in her direction from the side of the château. The second was a tall, water-logged man running flat out and waving his arms - probably the gardener, judging from his grubby attire – behind what had to be the Hound of the Baskervilles.

Water flew from its fur like hundreds of tiny missiles as it hurtled toward Lucie. The cabbie gazed in horror, yelled something like Aieeeeee and jumped back into the cab. The tires spun, throwing shrapnel everywhere, and Lucie shielded her face while shouting COWARD at the rear of the car.

She stood there, rooted to the spot, with no chance of getting to the front door before – aaagggghhhhh! As the huge animal leaped in an awkward arc, she realized in a flash that the beast had been bounding ungracefully, legs flailing, back end not quite synchronized with the front. But this puppy was the size of a pony, and suddenly she was flat on her back, fortunate, at least, to have landed on the thick carpet of grass instead of the driveway's rough surface. Except that it must have rained recently.

The pup/pony was now joyously slurping every inch of her face; she moaned, half-opened her eyes and saw George Clooney leaning over her, hands propped on his knees, breathing hard. No, wait, she blinked, her contacts shifted and Pierce Brosnan appeared.

He peered down at her and she suspected he was dripping on her, although with a soggy dog on her stomach, it was hard to tell.

Using the only name available to her, Lucie groaned "Bruno, get this – this - *horse* off me!" Trying to avoid the scrub-brush-sized tongue. Not succeeding.

"That (he pointed) is Bruno. Had trouble getting out of the pool and needed my assistance."

She blinked again and decided that the gardener, who had dark hair and intense, amused eyes, was definitely a clone of Brosnan in his cool fifties. With a little Cary Grant nonchalance thrown in. In other circumstances, Lucie would have been interested, but this guy, with that shitty grin on his face, was actually enjoying her predicament. Seriously rude.

"Well then *you* get, ugh, Bruno off me!" The dog shifted its weight. Another groan. "Unhh, please." She tried to squirm out from under the animal.

"Bruno likes you." Suddenly, something occurred to the gardener; he stopped grinning and bent closer to Lucie, clearly worried. "You aren't gonna cry, are you?"

Lucie shrieked, "*THAT'S* THE PART YOU'RE WORRIED ABOUT? **REMOVE THIS BEAST, NOW!**"

Grinning again, the gardener dragged the dog from its new friend and held on to its collar as Lucie pulled herself up on an elbow and ran her fingers through her hair. She felt leaves, grass and what she hoped was mud.

Then she saw her shoe. Her beautiful, used-to-be-a-pair Jimmy Choo sandal. Her $475 (on-sale) favorite black travel shoe. Her formerly sleek but now sad little extravagance, dangling like a dead animal from Bruno's mouth. She narrowed her eyes and let her gaze travel from the shoe to the gardener. With one raised eyebrow she threw down the mental gauntlet.

The look did not escape the man, who quickly retrieved the muddy, slobbery shoe from the dog and extended it to Lucie. She ripped it out of his hand and sputtered, "For your information, that *dog* is a female."

"I know that, but Jeffrey didn't when he named her."

Lucie wondered how old Jeffrey was; this was a lot of dog for a child.

He interrupted her thoughts with "He's twenty-eight."

And then it hit her: Jeffrey was the first name of her new employer. She flopped back down on the grass and gazed up at the sky. Great. Just... great.

***

The day's events were flashing a giant, neon Bad Omen sign in Lucie's brain when a phalanx of worried-looking natives emerged from the house. The gardener suddenly lost interest in the wet, muddy woman on the grass and seized the dog's collar.

"Come on Bruno, let's go get you dried off." As he pulled the dog away with him, his broad shoulders shook with silent laughter. Clooney, Brosnan and Grant evaporated.

Glaring at the gardener's back, Lucie sat up and snarled, "Yeah, right, let's get the DOG dried off, by all means."

She was assessing the damage to her clothes when the phalanx reached its objective and peered down at her: an older man in dirty khaki, a thin-faced woman with graying hair, dressed in dark blue efficiency - probably in her late sixties - and a tallish, brown-haired buttoned-down twenty-something male with a vapid expression reminiscent of a 90s Boy Band. Except for the pointy sideburns. Lucie was beginning to feel like a zoo exhibit.

The young man's innocuous demeanor turned

surly as he began, “You’re not - ”

The woman interrupted, “No, she’s not, but I’ll explain later.”

He put his hands on his hips and frowned. “Well, whoever you are, you do *not* have time to play with the dog: you have a lot to do before Mr. Sautier (he pronounced it Sawter) arrives.” A semi-snarl curled at one side of his mouth and he stalked off.

That was it: no offer of help, no greeting. And from his lack of intelligent behavior, Lucie suspected she’d just encountered the gender-recognition-impaired Jeffrey. Her employer for the next week.

As she stared in disbelief, the older woman helped her to her feet and introduced herself as Mrs. Harris the House Manager.

“And that was Mr. Ethelbert-Meicklejohn – Jeffrey, that is, - and you should just ignore him, he always makes a bad first impression.”

Lucie couldn’t tell if she were joking or not, but a quick glance at the woman’s face assured her that Mrs. Harris didn’t easily suffer fools. As Lucie plucked some leaves and grass from her damp black knit pants and tunic and tried to wipe dog spit off her face, Mrs. Harris turned to the older man, who was blatantly staring.

She pointed at Lucie’s bags and raised an eyebrow. He grabbed the luggage and was gone in an instant.

“I’m Lucie Richards and - ”

“Yes dear, I know, you’re our chef for the week of the acquisition and you’ve arrived precisely on schedule.” Then she smiled.

Lucie grabbed her purse, started to hop in an effort to put her shoe back on, lost her balance and wound up back on the grass.

“I don’t freakin believe this! So far today a lunatic cabby tried to kill me, then I got savaged by

BrunotheWonderDog - the dog part's debatable, by the way - and now I'm a – a soggy mess!" Lucie's voice had risen in proportion to her exasperation.

Mrs. Harris helped her up again and said, "There, there, let's just get you inside."

Lucie took several deep breaths, brushed off some more debris, straightened her back, raised her chin and hobbled determinedly toward the building and through the arch of the open door. Then she stopped so suddenly that the housekeeper bumped into her.

Lucie gaped at the magnificent marble staircase that rose in two L shapes on either side of an entrance hall so enormous that she felt herself shrinking in comparison.

Suddenly a shrill voice startled her: "Shawly you're nawt taking the main stahrcase." A statement, not a question. And in a terrible parody of a British accent. "It has just beeeen cleaned, you knohw."

Lucie stared at the source of the snottiness. A tall, gaunt, pinched-nose man in a suit was pursing his lips in disdain at her bedraggled condition. She was noticing his thinning hair, which made him appear even more severe, when he put his hands on his hips at her.

Wrong Move. Lucie snarled, "That does it!" She threw down her purse as a real gauntlet this time and shouted, "I have had it up to here with bad-mannered, foul-tempered -" She started toward him, fist clenched, but Mrs. Harris pulled her back and frowned at the man. She informed him that they most certainly *were* going up the main staircase and suggested what he could do about it if he didn't like it.

He opened his mouth to retaliate, managed an indignant 'Well! I nevah!', clamped his mouth shut and turned on his heel.

"What is it with the men around here? I know I look scary, but that is not my fault. And what's with the accent? That's the absolute worst fake –"

"That's Roland the butler. Pay no attention to him: he's in love with Anthony the cook and Anthony the cook wants nothing to do with him, so Roland's in a perpetual snit. The horrid accent is the result of one of Mr. Max's wives' desire for a proper English butler. We couldn't find one who would put up with her, so Roland volunteered to, um, pretend. The wife is gone, the accent stayed." Mrs. Harris rolled her eyes. "He is *such* a twit."

"Plus, he thinks he runs the place." She snorted and Lucie grinned. She liked a woman who could snort when provoked.

"Be careful you don't slip on the marble, dear." As they trekked up the glistening staircase on the left, Mrs. Harris explained that Lucie would have direct access from her suite down the back stairs to the kitchen. She apologized for the climb and Lucie replied that she didn't mind, she needed the exercise. Mrs. Harris nodded approvingly. The last visiting chef had been an irritable, pompous ass and the dog hadn't even touched him. This one, on the other hand, would do very well. Very well indeed.

CHAPTER 2

Mrs. Harris deposited Lucie in a lovely suite that featured a canopy bed, a padded, delicately carved bench at its foot and a sitting area with a small table and wing-backed chairs. French doors provided light and led to a balcony that extended the length of the back of the house.

She quickly unpacked, then wandered into the large, marble bathroom and found it stocked with high-end toiletries and her favorite soaps: finely-milled bars by Roger et Gallet.

Lucie grinned at herself in the mirror and decided that this crummy day was starting to improve after all. Piercing blue eyes looked back at her, but as she turned sideways to admire her blonde hair, newly cut in a short style, she saw the muck that still adhered to the back of her head. She gagged and quickly stepped into the shower.

Lingering under the hot water, Lucie thought about what had brought her to this place in time: teaching in a public high school provided only a meager salary, so she sought a second income almost immediately. Lucie loved to cook, so she studied at a local culinary institute in the evenings, began to work part-time as a sous-chef in a restaurant, and started her own week-end catering business.

Lucie was soon earning more in the food business than in education, so since she had pretty much learned all she could from the kids, she quit her day job; in the meantime, two husbands drifted in and out of her life, proof that you *can* have it all, just not *all at the same time.*

Her present situation was the result of being in the right place at the right time. She'd mentioned to her friend Michael that her catering business was attracting a lot of foreign clientele: her menus appealed especially to the French, who were buying into all kinds of businesses in her area. That she schmoozed with the clients after the meal turned out to be an additional asset.

Michael had remarked that he could use her skills with a particularly difficult client, but that the job required an on-site chef for several days, starting immediately. That would mean quitting her full-time job as sous-chef and losing her benefits.

In the end, however, Michael was very persuasive on several different levels and Lucie accepted his offer. Word of Michael's – and Lucie's – success got around, and soon she had to turn down one-shot catering jobs in favor of extended, personal chef gigs in the rarified world of Big Business. She'd found her niche, and a lucrative one at that.

Lucie was at a good, solid place in her life when she arrived at the château.

***

Hair dried and makeup applied, Lucie noticed the entire staff's extensions on a card by the phone. She called to see that the kitchen crew could meet her in several minutes and slipped into her chef's uniform: white chef's coat, black tank top and black cotton slacks.

She strode down the back staircase and peered into the lower hallway to see if Bruno had house privileges, and when an attack didn't materialize, entered the kitchen.

Determined to make a good first impression on the people she'd be working with, Lucie decided on an air of authority, mitigated with a slight smile. Apparently, however, news of the Bruno episode had spread, because no one seemed at all impressed. The woman and two men staring at her were definitely smirking, albeit surreptitiously.

"Which one of you is Anthony?"

They glanced at each other. Cute. Finally the woman pointed at the short, dark-haired Hispanic-looking man who then crossed his arms and leaned back against a counter. He proceeded to check Lucie out, his eyes traveling over her body in a slow, head-to-toe journey.

"Did you receive my fax about the menus?"

"Yes."

Lucie squinted and shifted gears; she had previously encountered problems with established kitchen staffs who resented visiting chefs, so considering that her fee was quite high - and she'd been paid in advance - she could afford to buy some bonhomie on this job.

"Okay, tell you what." She put her hands flat on the island, leaned in at them and raised her eyebrows, "You all make my life easier for the next few days and there's a bonus in it for you. From me, in cash." At this point she named a sum that was not large enough to suggest that their present salary was insufficient, not small enough to insult them.

"So are we good?"

They evidently were, because the atmosphere in the kitchen changed instantly. And the look she was now giving Anthony, plus the tone in her voice, left no question as to who was in charge.

"I want to check the equipment that I had sent here, especially my knives, and I want to examine the food that should have been delivered. Now."

She didn't notice the gardener by the doorway; his gaze had also traveled up and down, but mostly he watched her handling the staff.

***

Lucie was amazed as she glanced around the kitchen: the enormous refrigerator was just short of a walk-in and the commercial-grade range was top of the line. There were four ovens: two in the stove and two in the wall, one of them a microwave-convection oven, plus a warming drawer underneath. Lucie was in heaven.

The audience outside the arched doorway changed and Roland was now lurking there, arms crossed, looking disgusted. But looking disgusted was his usual demeanor, so when Mrs. Harris happened by, she didn't notice that his mood was worse than usual. Roland had to resort to aheming, followed by, (dreadful accent not in evidence) "Do you *see* the way Anthony is fawning all over that woman? It's positively *disgraceful.* And *so* beneath him. He - "

Mrs. Harris sensed the approach of a snit, so she diverted him. "Did you get the memo from Mr. Max?"

He stopped abruptly, mouth still open, and looked puzzled.

"Really Roland, you ought to check your messages more often. The guests' quarters have changed because Mr. Sautier is bringing his wife after all: they'll go in the front suite on the ground floor. Put his associate in the adjoining suite and the French lawyer goes in the guest room upstairs. And make sure Julia's office area is ready."

Mrs. Harris thought briefly about Julia, the family's accountant for the last two decades. A bitter, rabid fundamentalist, she disapproved of just about everything, but saw nothing impious about her constant attempts to seduce Max. Her already-unpleasant personality had inexplicably turned downright nasty in the last few years, and only her über-efficiency kept her on the payroll. That, and Max's odd refusal to fire her. Mrs. Harris sighed. Another high-maintenance employee.

Roland interrupted her thoughts with his pseudo-posh accent: "Of *cohrse* I knaow about those mawdifications." Then scurried off so abruptly that she knew he'd been too busy spying on Anthony to do his job.

Mrs. Harris shook her head: Roland, Julia - and Jeffrey, whom Max had placed in charge of the current business transaction, as his trial-by-fire. Jeffrey, the man who managed to alienate almost everyone he met.

She was encouraged, however, when she saw Lucie in her full-on professional mode. No more bedraggled dog cushion, this woman was obviously competent and enjoyed what she was doing, including getting the upper hand with Anthony. "Don't touch my knives, **I** will unroll them!" made the man jump and when Lucie's eyes met Mrs. Harris', they were amused. The sisterhood of intelligent women. The housekeeper smiled. Lucie's presence would go a long way to make up for Jeffrey's social inadequacies.

Lucie walked over to the older woman and explained, "I always work with my own cookware, cutlery and spices. Cuts down on the variables."

She turned to Anthony and moved in close to him with a sheet of paper. "Some of what was delivered is unacceptable, you know how it is, they put the freshest items on the top. Anthony, please have someone get me exactly what's on this list. You know people, right?"

Her conspiratorial tone and implied confidence in him would assure that he'd see to the list personally, not wanting to disappoint her. That she had just castigated him about her knives would keep him guessing. Perfect.

***

As Anthony hurried off, Lucie turned to Mrs. Harris. "I assume you're the person to thank for getting back to me about the client's food allergy?"

"I am."

"I always inquire, but surprisingly few people take the time to check with their guests."

Mrs. Harris raised her eyebrows in surprise as Lucie continued, "You mentioned earlier that I'll have access to an impressive collection of wine, so could I see the cellar?"

"Of course. How about right now?" The older woman motioned for Lucie to follow her to the butler's pantry. There was an intricate wrought iron gate in one side of the passageway and when Mrs. Harris had swung it open, the two women descended the stairs.

They crossed a small vestibule and Mrs. Harris unlocked one of the doors, explaining that the other one led to a media room. As they entered the wine cellar anteroom, she handed the key to Lucie.

"That really isn't necessary," Lucie began, but Mrs. Harris made it clear that this, one of only three keys in existence, was temporarily Lucie's, as per Mr. Max's directive.

"It's a spare, but don't say anything around Jeffrey. He doesn't have one." She grinned.

"And Mr. Max is...."

"Jeffrey's father."

Lucie considered that as she glanced around the anteroom, admiring its efficient design: it contained a bar sink, a small refrigerator and a microwave. Plus an enormous collection of corkscrews.

With a bit of a flourish, Mrs. Harris pushed open the door to the cellar proper, a truly breathtaking room that included a tasting area. But Lucie only had eyes for the myriad of bottles that sparkled like jewels in a crown. Mrs. Harris explained that the cellar was maintained at a constant fifty-three degrees and described the geography of the room to Lucie, proudly pointing out the location of each varietal and its neighboring blends.

"Mr. Max's father collected wine for investment, but he's gone now. I took over for him, but several years ago Mr. Max told me to stop buying. He decided that since wine is a living, breathing entity, it should be enjoyed while *he's* a living, breathing entity – although some of the vintages haven't lived up to their promise."

Lucie laughed and asked which wines were off limits.

"None of them at all."

Lucie involuntarily sucked in her breath. "None?" She had spotted some very, very expensive labels.

Mr. Max wants you to select whatever you need to enhance your meals: this is Jeffrey's first foray into the real world of business, and his father wants to help him make a good impression."

"ANY wines?" Lucie still couldn't believe what she

was hearing. "Your Mr. Max sounds very interesting. When do I get to meet him?"

Mrs. Harris looked puzzled. "Formally, you mean? Probably tonight at dinner, if he puts in an appearance."

***

Lucie returned to the kitchen to check on ingredients for the meal she'd be serving solely for Jeffrey's family: because the elderly French client had decided at the last moment to spend time with a Manhattan relative, he would not be present that night or the next. No matter, she was hired for as long as it took to close the deal, and she did need to check on the staff's serving skills.

Then, although Anthony had assured her that everything in the kitchen was in working order, Lucie checked for herself. That accomplished, she began to prepare for dinner, and as she looked around for some bowls, a voice remarked, "You clean up well."

She turned to see the gardener leaning against a wall just inside the doorway. He wore an amused expression, which annoyed Lucie immediately, but she couldn't help noticing that he was tall and very masculine. On closer inspection, he still resembled the actor: shaggy and unkempt, but a fiftyish Brosnan.

Lucie raised one eyebrow and looked him up and down; his clothes were still messy and looked damp. And seeing him brought back the morning's humiliations. She made a face.

"You, on the other hand, do not."

He grinned, damn him, and she frowned. "So, earlier, what was that? You just standing out there, laughing, instead of getting that –that- *dog* off me?"

"Oh but I *did* remove Bruno from your, uh, person." She was still frowning. "And besides, you obviously weren't afraid: you weren't crying or screaming. Ok, that was the funniest thing I've seen in months and I couldn't help myself."

Lucie narrowed her eyes at him. "Was that an apology?"

"No. An explanation."

She turned back to hunt for the bowls. "Hunh."

He chuckled and turned to leave, tossing "Top cabinet to your left," over his shoulder.

Without thinking, Lucie reached up to open the cabinet and found the bowls she was searching for. She whipped her head around at the empty doorway in amazement. "What the?" Good thing he hadn't heard her thought about his resemblance to the actor.

Then she could have sworn she heard a faint voice from the hallway beyond: "He looks like me, not the other way around." She dropped one of the bowls.

***

Lucie was finishing her prep work for the evening meal when she heard someone enter the kitchen behind her. She turned and bumped directly into Jeffrey, who remained where he was and glared at her.

She took a step backward and noticed that, at close range, Jeffrey bore an unnerving resemblance to a ferret: beady eyes, protuberant mouth and nose. Plus his build was, well, spindly. Lucie frowned slightly. She only liked guinea pigs in the rodent family.

She pushed the image from her mind and began, "I'm glad you're here. I wanted to introduce myself."

He moved even closer and snarled, "I want the key to the wine cellar."

Lucie blinked several times in disbelief: a man who was about to conduct a multi-million dollar deal was actually attempting to intimidate his personal chef over a key. Thinking that there must be a really good reason he wasn't permitted to have one, Lucie kept her voice neutral and said to the face that was now invading her space, "You'd better ask Mrs. Harris about that."

Jeffrey continued to glower at her, but when Lucie held her ground, he grew tired of the Mexican stand-off and stomped out of the kitchen.

Lucie thought she heard him growl as he left and she distinctly heard the word Bitch from the hallway. Great. Just... great.

CHAPTER 3

In the lull before dinnertime, Lucie found the rear entrance to the château and headed outdoors to walk off her annoyance with Jeffrey. She admired the still-blooming flowers in a large, formal garden, then continued past a stand of tall trees. And almost fell into the swimming pool: its placement was unannounced, an anomaly in the otherwise elegant surroundings.

Lucie, for whom swimming was an infrequent luxury, gazed at it longingly. The setting sun was changing the color of the water, and as the familiar scent of chlorine wafted up to her nostrils, Lucie smiled: right up there with new car smell.

Her reverie was interrupted, however, when a voice bellowed BAAAARUUUUNO! She quickly scanned the area and decided that now was a good time to choose the evening's wines.

***

Dinner was ready, and mouth-watering aromas of garlic, tomatoes and sautéed meats floated up from the kitchen, through the butler's pantry, and into the dining room, where six people - some of whom had been coerced - waited to be practiced upon. Conspicuously absent were Mr. Max, who had yet to surface, and his mother Kate, who was not willing to forgo her favorite TV show.

The evening's 'wait staff' consisted of a maid called Stella and Anthony's assistant John, who'd been hired because Roland insisted that Anthony should have an assistant. Lucie told them they'd be dealing with three courses and to start with the first wine.

As she watched John, a nervous young man with close-cropped sandy hair, shakily pour a crisp Pinot Grigio, Lucie crossed her arms and shook her head. The scene before her was scarily similar to a high school class in a too-warm May.

At one end of the table, Jeffrey was trying to impress Jessica the Maid. Mrs. Harris had told Lucie she was a recent hire and that Jeffrey was all over the girl: tall, with long, over-streaked hair, a nasally twang to her voice, and hoochy-mama boobs highly visible in a low-cut top.

Jeffrey had one arm extended over the back of his chair and gestured with the other while he bragged about having met the coach of...blah blah blah. He seemed convinced that merely talking about sports gave him entrée into the world of athletes.

Jessica's response was to giggle, remove one shoe and play footsie with him, attempting a dialog in her own language. That prompted Jeffrey to lean over, ogle her chest, and say loudly enough for everyone to hear, "You know, dear, one of the family names, Meicklejohn, is Scottish for Big Johnson. And Ethelbert means famous."

Jeffrey looked smug. Mrs. Harris choked on a sip of water. Jessica giggled again. Lucie reflected that her initial assessment of the man stood: snotty, immature, testosterone-driven. Her employer for the next week.

Owen, the chauffeur, sat next to Jessica. And Owen was squirming: he'd been forced to remove his chauffeur's cap and felt himself at a grave disadvantage. He glanced about nervously, running his hand through his hair and searching for a means of escape. When none presented itself, he began to poke at the forks, visibly distressed at the multitude of cutlery on the table, not to mention the presence of two wine glasses.

At the other end of the table, Mrs. Harris kept a watchful eye on Roland, who, having achieved a full-blown snit, was making small huffing noises. And finally, beside him, sat Margaret. An elderly woman who had started out as Kate's personal maid, failed miserably at that, and was promoted to companion, she wore a perpetually vacant, slightly loony expression.

Tough crowd.

When John finished with the wine, Lucie told Stella to serve the first course, comprised of thin slices of Italian salamis, smoked cheeses, sprouts and quince jelly. Everyone except Jeffrey and Owen raved about the sensational combination of flavors: Jeffrey, because he was obnoxious, and Owen, because he was suspicious. The chauffeur peered at the appetizers, cast furtive glances left and right, then pushed the food around on his plate until the main course arrived.

Lucie fervently hoped the food service would flow along seamlessly, and what happened next did involve flowing - but it was the spaghetti bolognaise and not the service. She heard herself scream "Nooooooooo" as a domino-effect disaster cascaded across the dining table.

John, who was trying to get Roland's attention and

not entirely focused on the task at hand, had shoved a large plate in front of Jeffrey, who was in the process of trying to reach Jessica's thigh under the table.

Jeffrey sat up abruptly, turned and crashed right into his food, which became air born. He roared and jumped up, knocking over his chair as well as the wine, a Brunello di Montalcino. He flung his arms out and one caught Jessica in the head; she yowled and upended a plate of bolognaise, which landed on her wine, which flew across the table at Roland, who squealed.

Owen, a taciturn man not given to any kind of socializing - let alone brawls- looked horrified, took advantage of the mêlée and ran for it.

Stella shrieked. And went on shrieking.

Anthony burst out of the kitchen and yelled, "¡Madre de Dios! ¿Qué pasa aquí!?"

Roland immediately forgot about his stained clothes, put his arm around Anthony and hurried him away from the scene of the accident.

Jeffrey maneuvered Jessica out into the hallway and told her they needed to get out of their spaghettied clothes. Together.

Lucie, who had encountered some flying food when she tried to intervene, sat down heavily on one of the chairs and stared at the table. She put her hand to her head and discovered not only sauce, but a few strands of pasta. Great, just... great.

When the debris from the Food and Wine Explosion finally stopped oozing and trickling, Margaret turned her vacant smile on Mrs. Harris and declared that what had just occurred was one more portent of the End of the World.

Lucie snapped back into focus and leaned across the table at Margaret: "No, dear, this -" she waved her arm at the room "- ranks on the Annoyance Scale, not the Total Disaster Scale. *This* we can fix. As to the End of the World..."

Mrs. Harris suddenly shook her head and shot her a look that cautioned, 'Don't go there if you want to retain your sanity.'

Lucie blinked several times and told John and Stella to serve the survivors. But John was too distraught to function: clearly miserable, he wrung his hands and mumbled to the carpet that he'd let Roland down and could only imagine how ashamed the Head of Household would be of his protégé.

Mrs. Harris raised an eyebrow and informed him that she, the Head of Household, was not at all ashamed of him, that he'd actually done quite well, that what happened was Jeffrey's fault. But John was still lamenting his failure as he dragged himself out of the dining room, leaving Stella to deal with the carcass of the meal.

Lucie resurrected some pasta and sauce for the two women, who were starved and didn't seem to mind eating in the War Zone, especially when she opened another bottle of wine. Margaret drank more than her share and Mrs. Harris repeatedly remarked that this wine was so much better than what was usually served. What was up with that? They had a world-class wine cellar at their disposal.

No one was interested in dessert, so an exhausted Lucie finally dragged herself to the kitchen. She bumped right into the gardener, who was absconding with a food container and seemed oblivious to the havoc of the last hour. He was still scruffy-looking, but she noticed that he wore an expensive scent: sort of a visual and olfactory oxymoron.

"I've got to let Kate taste your bolognaise, it's fantastic! I knew you'd be competent but I didn't expect anything like this." She was about to respond when his gaze shifted to her hair. He made a face and said, "Um, you seem to be wearing some of the spaghetti."

And then he thought about laughing.

Lucie narrowed her eyes, emitted a low growl, and pushed him out of her way. Given the day she was having, he was lucky she didn't slug him. Lucie wondered again about his access to the entire house, not to mention the first-name familiarity with Mr. Max's mother.

***

Lucie had removed her stained chef's coat and was cleaning her knives when Jeffrey appeared. Clutching her menus for the next few days, he looked around the kitchen, squinted with the effort of thinking, and abruptly asked, "Are you on one of those cooking shows?"

That surprised Lucie. "Nope."

"Well, do you know any TV chefs?"

"I am a personal chef. Occasionally I cater single events. I don't need or want the public exposure that goes with being a TV personality, and quite frankly, some of those shows are a bit much."

Jeffrey looked shocked; there, apparently, went her cachet, because things went pretty much downhill after that.

He frowned and said peevishly, "Then why didn't you consult *me* about the meals?"

"That's not how I work. I create menus based on the client's - "

"Whatever, you should have checked with me first. Sometimes I like seafood and I don't see any shrimp or scallops or mussels anywhere." He poked at the papers he was holding.

"Is that what you want me to serve M. Sautier?" Lucie turned and gave Jeffrey a shrewd look that unnerved him.

"Who? Oh, um, yes, why not? I want you to change the menus."

"And will you be accompanying M. Sautier to the hospital?"

"WHAT?"

"Shellfish can cause a life threatening reaction called anaphylaxis in some people. M. Sautier is highly allergic to shellfish."

Jeffrey was first aghast, then suspicious. "How do you know that?"

Lucie's patience was wearing thin. "That's what you're paying me to know."

Jeffrey shoved another menu page at Lucie and snarled, "If you're so worried about peoples' health, then what about the cream in this dish? You'll clog everyone's arteries."

Lucie narrowed her eyes at him. She couldn't imagine him being concerned about anyone's arteries.

"Because you can't make Bifteck au Poivre, Cognac et Crème, without the crème. Bifteck au Poivre is a Provençal dish. M. Sautier comes from Provence."

Jeffrey looked confused. "I thought he was French."

Lucie sighed. "Provence is a part of France. And don't worry about the crème. It washes out with the red wine."

Jeffrey looked confused again.

Lucie sighed again.

"Ever hear of the French Paradox?"

"Pair of what?"

"Never mind." She was *really* regretting this conversation.

"Well then what about..." Frustrated, Jeffrey began

to pace around kitchen, picking up pieces of equipment; when he got to her knives, she politely asked him not to handle them.

Defiantly, he pulled several from the block; Lucie's reaction was quick – she immediately took them from his hands and replaced them. She checked their order in the block, touching each one... ok, she admitted to herself that she was anal about her knives, but they were her prize possessions and she'd spent a fortune on them.

Then Lucie made her last attempt at a civilized exchange: "Since you're interested, I'll tell you about them: this one is a Misono, Japanese, great for precision slicing. That one," and she pointed, "is a Sabatier, high-carbon steel with bite and balance."

But Jeffrey was paying no attention and began to pull the chef's knife out of the block. In one swift movement she slammed the knife back into its place and spat "Don't touch my knives!"

"Oh really? Don't touch? Do – Not – Touch?" Childishly he poked at the knives, one by one, taunting her.

Lucie looked disgusted and pointed at the doorway. "We're done here. You need to leave."

Jeffrey suddenly pushed her against the refrigerator. He shoved his hand up under her tank top, squeezing her left breast as he thrust his face in hers to kiss her. Problem was, he'd stuck his tongue out in anticipation, so when she pushed hard against his chest, propelling him backward into a cabinet, his teeth snapped shut before he could retract the tongue. He yowled, "Thunoba!" put his hand to his mouth and quickly withdrew it, checking for blood.

Lucie lowered her voice and said, "Bad move, slick."

Jeffrey ignored her and pretended to brush off his

sleeves, trying to look nonchalant, but wincing with tongue pain. "Oh don't get all bent out of shape, it's not like you never fooled around with your boss before and you weren't my first choice anyway and with the salary I'm paying you..."

That did it. Lucie grabbed the chef's knife and twirled it in midair. She caught its handle and started toward him. "Let's see now, what part of your body should I start with?" She looked down at his crotch.

Eyes wide with fright, Jeffrey reached around to the counter behind him, hoping to connect with a weapon of his own. Instead, his hand caught the edge of a pan and sent it crashing onto the floor, costing him an embarrassing shriek when the noise exploded right beside him. Staring at the large knife that was still aimed at him, he stuttered "You're fired! How - how dare you point that thing at me? That's a weapon!"

"I am not fired and you know it. We have a contract." Lucie took another step toward him and slowly rotated the knife. "Now then. You ever try something like that again, they'll never find what needs to be reattached. You got that? *Now get the hell out of this kitchen!*"

Jeffrey screeched and ran, arrogance in shreds. Lucie slammed the knife into its home, straightened her tank top and kicked a lower cabinet. Then she savagely attacked a perfectly clean counter with a scrub brush and raged at the kitchen, "I do not have to put up with this kind of crap!"

Suddenly Lucie stopped and looked around. She was clearly tempting fate by ignoring the huge list of All-in-One-Day Bad Omens; obviously, she should pack up and leave. So why wasn't she? Lucie really didn't need the money, good as it was. Something she did not understand was holding her back, and that made her even madder.

Probably it was just that Michael was involved, and she did owe him; come to think of it, though, there had been an odd look on Michael's face when he proposed the job to her. She guessed now that she should have been suspicious when they'd voluntarily doubled her usual fee.

Lucie had to vent and because it was too late to walk it off outdoors, she shouted, as though Jeffrey could hear the postscript. "Sonofabitch, asshole, dickheadbastard!" She sputtered before she got to the Really Bad Profanities, this, after all, being a job site.

Meanwhile, Mrs. Harris, who'd been working in the butler's pantry, overheard the altercation from the 'do not touch' part. So did the gardener, who had been enlisted to remove several heavy serving pieces from the cabinets. He started through to the kitchen, but Mrs. Harris held him back, whispering, "Let her put him in his place. We can't have him behaving like this all week."

When they heard Jeffrey yowl, though, Mrs. Harris peeped into the kitchen. She drew back slowly, eyes wide. "Wow. She's *really* good with a knife."

"Should we…?"

"Definitely not."

"What if she quits?"

"Won't happen. She's a pro, and she can hold her own."

When they heard Jeffrey leave and Lucie's subsequent diatribe, the gardener raised his eyebrows, nodded appreciatively and looked down at Mrs. Harris. "Cusses like a sailor, too."

"Indeed." Mrs. Harris grinned at him. "Told you she could handle Jeffrey."

As she turned to leave, she added, "Oh and be careful what you say to her." She raised one eyebrow for effect. "This one is smart."

The gardener interrupted Lucie when she was considering dire and permanent curses in Spanish and Italian. She turned on him, pointing her scrub brush at his chest. "Well what do *you* want?"

He warded off her anger with his hands, palms out, "Nothing. Not a thing."

"So what the hell's his problem, anyway? That meal was superb, it wasn't my fault he decided to fling his plate and his wine and clobber the floozie next to him, it wasn't my fault his dog sat on me - come to think of it, that was probably the high point of this sorryass day – and anyway, why pay the rates I charge if all he wants to do is criticize and maul?"

"He did what?" A look of concern crossed his face.

Lucie waved it away with her scrub brush. "Felt me up, forget it, I dealt with him. He's not the first employer to take liberties."

"Well, I think Jeffrey's being more obnoxious than usual because you aren't younger, with bigger, um, you know." (He was making round gestures in the vicinity of his chest.)

"WHAT?" Lucie involuntarily glanced down.

"Thing is, none of the local caterers will have anything to do with Jeffrey, so he tried to hire a female cook from a steak house. Mrs. Harris intervened and put the word out that we needed a personal chef who moves in big money circles, someone who - and this was the deal maker – could manage Jeffrey."

He smiled at her and finished, "You came highly recommended, and of course, Jeffrey isn't happy."

"Younger?" Lucie was frowning.

"My guess is the girl in the steak house is barely twenty."

Lucie rolled her eyes. "This is so not worth the aggravation."

The gardener shoved his hands in his pockets. "If it makes you feel any better, I think you handled the situation with remarkable restraint."

Lucie raised an eyebrow. Restraint? She'd threatened to slice off Jeffrey's junk.

"You're not going to leave, are you?" It was the same tone with the same worried look as 'You aren't going to cry, are you?'

"Of course I'm not going to leave." So much for heeding the Bad Omens. "I was hired to do a job – "

Suddenly she folded her arms over her chest and narrowed her eyes at him. "And just how would you know how I handled the situation? You were lurking somewhere, and listening. Weren't you?"

He mentally measured the distance between the knives and her right hand, and, thinking that he might have to deflect something, removed his hands from his pockets.

"We – I – uh, it's that just *telling* Jeffrey to treat people with respect has no effect, he has to be threatened into it, and by the person he's mistreating. Only way it works." He paused, keeping the knives in his peripheral vision. "Look, I'm sorry, I probably should have intervened."

His unexpected remorse caught Lucie off guard; she blinked several times and relented, too tired to figure it out.

"Not a problem, I can take care of myself. And thanks for letting me vent." Her anger had ebbed, so she put away the last of the cleaning materials and mumbled to herself, "Maybe I'll just put some ExLax in his food."

The gardener chuckled, then laughed out loud. Lucie noticed that his sense of humor extended to his eyes – always intense, they were now twinkling mischievously. "Not bad for an old guy," she thought to herself, "not bad at all."

"Fifty something is not old."

Lucie flinched. This was becoming embarrassing. And she still didn't know how he did it.

He was smiling as he walked over to a counter, grabbed an open bottle of Brunello and two glasses, and motioned for her to follow him. "Come on, we deserve a nightcap."

"Chef's policy, don't help yourself to the client's wine."

"House policy, get rid of partial bottles at the end of the night, either in food or in us. I vote for us."

Lucie looked skeptical.

"Trust me, neither Mrs. Harris nor anyone else will object."

Articulate, for a gardener. She frowned at the liberty he was taking, but the wine beckoned.

He stopped at the archway, turned and inquired, "Are you coming?"

Lucie hesitated, but finally gave in with a begrudging, "Oh... all right." She reluctantly followed the tall figure outside, to the patio and a small round table with some café chairs, wondering why he was still on the grounds: it was almost midnight. Then again, his arrangement with the family was none of her business.

"By the way, Kate sends her compliments on dinner."

"Thanks. I'm glad she wasn't in the dining room; that was embarrassing."

"Wasn't your fault."

Lucie glanced over at him and noticed that he had changed into a long-sleeved, powder-blue shirt, sleeves rolled up, and clean jeans. Jeans that fit rather well.

Then he leaned over to extract a strand of pasta that was still hidden in her hair – an intimate gesture -

and Lucie noticed that he still smelled expensive. But there was that scruffy, three-day beard and something annoying about his generally nonchalant attitude. That, and he turned up just about everywhere. Like a bad rash.

Conversation wasn't needed for a while, so they enjoyed the night air and drank the wine in companionable silence. Eventually he spoke.

"Mrs. H tells me that you were in education for a while. Why'd you quit?"

"Pitiful salary, mostly. And not being able to teach effectively because of bullshit government policies. I do miss the kids, though, because you don't learn what's cool from adults." She had no idea why she was sharing personal information with this stranger, but it seemed natural.

"Oh, yeah, and then there was the year they revised the Student Handbook to include a penalty for cock-slapping."

He choked on his wine.

Lucie sighed. "You don't want to know."

He grinned at her. "You always this funny?"

She thought she heard derision. "You always this annoying?"

His retort was lost when a female voice bellowed, "BRUUUNNNOOO" from somewhere inside the house. The gardener sighed and said, "'Scuse me, gotta go find the beast."

As he disappeared through the patio door, Mrs. Harris appeared on the stone steps that led to the terrace above and paused to study Lucie for a minute. She remarked that she'd passed Jeffrey upstairs and that he seemed upset. She looked pleased about that, then noticed the wine glasses and nodded approvingly before turning to leave.

Lucie shook her head as she grabbed the wine

glasses and empty bottle and headed for the kitchen; she had landed right in the middle of a crazed parallel universe. But her energy reserves were flashing on empty, so she grabbed one of her knives and headed up the back stairs to her suite. Pondering the crazies would have to wait until tomorrow.

CHAPTER 4

Lucie woke up later than usual, confused in her surroundings. Then she saw her chef's knife on the night stand and remembered the previous, unbelievably bizarre day.

She flopped back on the pillow, groaned and stared at the ceiling. Surely, today couldn't be any worse. Then she winced and thought, yeah, actually it could – but got up anyway.

After throwing on some makeup, a long sleeved tee shirt, shorts and sports sandals, Lucie went downstairs for breakfast provisions and returned to her room to email her daughter. She opened a French door, sniffed the fresh air and settled down on the bed with her laptop.

She'd just finished typing and was enjoying her coffee when she heard scratching at the hall door. When she opened it, a white streak crossed the length of the room in a second, leaped (what was it with the animals around here?) onto the bed and immediately tromped on the keyboard.

Lucie knew the little Bichon wasn't more than a year old, if that, because she owned one herself; she caught the busy little fluff ball, hugged her, and got her face licked in return.

Suddenly the puppy tensed, wriggled away from her and shot out to the balcony that stretched the length of the back of the house. Lucie ambled out after the dog, but immediately yelled and flattened herself against the building: the gardener was crouching behind one of the large, tropical plants that stood sentry on this upper level. And pointing a gun at the lawn below. The little Bichon wagged at him and took off again.

He hissed, “Be quiet for heaven’s sake.”

“What - are - you - doing?” she squeaked, inching her way back to the room and thinking about her knife on the nightstand.

“It’s called behavior modification. You know all about that.” He had explained without turning toward her, intent on the grounds beyond. Lucie hesitated, unsure whether escape was really called for, and took a closer look. He was holding what looked like a pellet gun with a scope. She relented. This was just too weird to miss.

Still pressed against the wall, Lucie crept back over, peered out past the greenery and saw Jeffrey and Bruno. She gasped, “You’re not going to shoot Bruno! All she did was sit on me, ok, she ruined my Jimmy Choo, but - ”

He finally turned and looked at her, indignant. “Not the *dog*.” He shifted his gaze back to the lawn. “Jeffrey.”

Lucie made a sputtering noise.

The gardener muttered disgustedly, “He’s out there the same time every day, doing the same damned stupid things. He just had to get that pony because somebody told him that the size of a man’s dog was in direct proportion with his...”

Lucie interrupted with “Ahhggg” and put her

hands over her ears. The last thing she wanted to hear was 'Jeffrey' and 'penis' in the same sentence.

"Would you look at that?" Exasperated, he pointed at Jeffrey, who was yelling at Bruno and shoving her every few seconds. "His idea of dog training. I warned him about mistreating animals, but as usual, he ignored me, so I'm using a non-verbal means of modifying his rotten behavior."

Lucie was interested in spite of herself. "You any good at it?"

"Watch." Jeffrey yelled and Bruno responded in kind: barking was obviously today's lesson. When he started to hit the dog, the gardener took aim and popped him on the rump. Lucie's mouth fell open in astonishment, and when Jeffrey waved his arms around and began to smack his back end, she laughed out loud.

"Doesn't he hear the shot?"

"Nah, you can't hear anything over Bruno's barking - it's a wonder we don't have to do something about noise abatement. Now watch, when he's done swatting away what he thinks are giant mutant insects, he'll start again, but his dog training sessions get shorter each time I plunk him." He grinned, visibly pleased with himself.

They watched in silence for a moment, then Lucie asked, "So he really believes there's a horde of insects attacking him?"

The gardener shrugged. "Jeffrey's an MBA."

"Oh." That explained a lot.

When Jeffrey returned his attention to the dog, the gardener looked sideways at Lucie. "You want to try this time?"

Lucie was shocked and a little indignant. "No! I am not going to shoot at somebody, even if he is a schmuck. Why would you even think..." She ran out of steam and frowned at him.

His smile was of the shitty variety. "Yeah, right. Can't hit the side of a barn, can you?"

"Not even on my best day." Lucie bit her bottom lip. It would be grossly unprofessional, but after all, it only involved pellets and Jeffrey *did* try to maul her.

She took the weapon and peered through the scope, but wound up blinking a lot. So the gardener put his arms around her to adjust her aim and noted that she was not wearing a bra. For a fleeting moment he enjoyed wondering how often she went braless and then shook himself back to the task at hand.

As he touched her and she felt his cheek close to hers, something like an electric shock went through Lucie's body. She jerked the gun and he looked at her questioningly.

"Sorry, it's um been a while since I... um... held a gun." Lucie did not want to deal with an intensely personal reaction to this man. Her life was blessedly uncomplicated at the moment, plus she had a hard and fast rule about not fraternizing with clients – or fellow employees.

So Lucie buried the feeling and returned her attention to the weapon. She held her breath and succeeded in zapping her employer on the ass, then turned to the gardener, elated: "That was GREAT!"

He laughed and they enjoyed the moment: it was pleasant on the balcony, a breeze wafted through the assorted greenery, the sun was shining and Jeffrey was rubbing his butt. Not a bad state of affairs at all.

"So, what kind of dog is Bruno?"

"A Great Dane mix."

"Mixed with what, a wooly mammoth?"

"Guess we'll know when she's fully grown." They watched as Jeffrey swatted at the unseen invasion of insects and Bruno bounced all over the lawn, jumping and flailing, and then flopped down, legs straight up in the air.

"Maybe not..."

***

Back in her suite, Lucie reflected that shooting Jeffrey had been deeply and troublingly satisfying, and wondered if the owner of the château knew that his gardener was taking potshots at his son.

She shook her head and dialed Mrs. Harris' extension. Lucie figured the housekeeper, despite her ear-splitting bellowing, was probably the most lucid person in the household, and she wanted a guided tour of the spectacular mansion before the clients arrived.

Mrs. Harris said she'd be delighted to show her around, and when they met at the bottom of the front stairs, Lucie noted that, like yesterday, she was dressed in an exquisitely-tailored navy pants suit. The older woman caught the look and told her, smiling, "It's an authority thing. Easier to keep the natives under control when I look like I'm wearing a uniform."

Lucie smiled back but thought 'Yeah, right, an *Armani* uniform.' She followed her into the Grand Salon, where groupings of sofas and chairs formed genteel conversation areas, all crowned by an enormous, sparkling Baccarat chandelier. What caught Lucie's eye, however, was the magnificent carpet that lay underneath.

Mrs. Harris followed Lucie's gaze and commented, "An antique Savonnerie." She waited to see if Lucie recognized the term. When her mouth fell open, Mrs. Harris continued. "They look similar to the Persian Kermans, and are more foot-friendly than their cousins, the Aubussons." It sounded as though the housekeeper were describing someone's family tree.

They continued through a maze of the mansion's public rooms, finally arriving in the huge dining room, which was mercifully devoid of any reminders of Recent Catastrophic Events.

Lucie pointed to a tiny wrought iron cage in the corner and said, "Didn't notice that last night, is it a real elevator?"

Mrs. Harris nodded, "It connects to Miss Kate's apartment above the garage. She's quite a character, that one: rides up and down in it when she gets bored. Mr. Max had wanted his mother to live in one of the main house's suites, but Miss Kate treasures her privacy."

The housekeeper had just motioned for Lucie to follow her into the hallway when her cell phone trilled. She answered, rolled her eyes and intoned, "I'll be right there."

She pointed across the hallway and told Lucie, "Check out the library, it's magnificent, and upstairs, let's see, Mr. Max's suite is opposite yours and if you need me for any reason, I live in the guest house at the rear of the property." She rushed off before Lucie had a chance to ask where the gardener stayed, if he did.

An inveterate bibliophile, Lucie was drawn to the library like a junkie to drugs. Mrs. Harris hadn't exaggerated - the room *was* magnificent, in the style of the Biltmore Estate's library, complete with a wrought iron spiral staircase to the second level. Lucie suspected that there were as many first editions in this room as there were vintage wines in the cellar.

***

She was surprised, when she returned to the kitchen, to find Anthony preparing an Hispanic lunch of stuffed chiles and a pork dish that was eaten with tortillas. He proudly offered her a taste of both, and when he asked her opinion, she enthused and asked for more.

Requesting a refill put Lucie way over the top, and Anthony beamed. He promptly told her she could call him *Antonio*, but not without - and there was another surprise - JessicaTheMaid hovering and fawning over him. And rhapsodizing about the food, licking her fingers suggestively. Lucie wondered if she had dumped Jeffrey to move up the evolutionary chain.

Antonio, however, was focused on Lucie's compliments and ignored Jessica, who eventually rolled her eyes, huffed and stomped out of the kitchen.

Meanwhile, no one noticed Roland, who was eavesdropping in the butler's pantry, wringing his hands in despair; had anyone looked closely, they would have detected tears welling up in his eyes as he witnessed not one, but two women fawning over his Tonio, as he privately called him. When he could no longer bear it, he trudged back through dining room, totally engulfed in misery.

***

Lucie, with no obligations until dinnertime, headed for the library. She'd just stepped through the open door when she ran smack into a tiny old woman, who yelped.

Lucie grabbed her to prevent a fall, and apologized, "Oh good grief, I am so sorry, I hope I didn't hurt you!"

The shawl-wrapped figure wobbled and retorted, "You'd better watch where you're going, girl!" But the voice wasn't angry.

Lucie smiled at her. "Thanks for the Girl."

"Well, Jeffrey's dog sat on you, so I suppose we're

even." The old lady's eyes twinkled as she motioned for Lucie to follow her to a sofa. "Come on, then, we'll have a nice little chat."

When they were seated, the woman, whose silver hair was expertly coiffed in a sleek, flattering style, held out her hand to Lucie and introduced herself. "You're Lucie the Chef and I'm Kate Meicklejohn." Lucie shook the hand, which was surprisingly firm.

"Mr. Max's mother. Nice to meet you."

"Hamish, yes."

"Hamish?" Lucie looked puzzled. "Who's...oh my, is that his real name?"

"Yes it is, and it's a perfectly good name, but for some odd reason, he prefers to be called Max. Something about objecting to a nickname."

"Yeah, well, I can understand that." Lucie almost grimaced. Ham.

"Actually it's Hamish Tuathal Ethelbert-Meicklejohn. Let's see, that's Hamish: just because we liked the sound of that. Tuathal: Ruler of the People. Ethelbert: noble/bright/famous, and Meicklejohn: Large John, as opposed to small John, as in father and son. The hyphenation was Hamish's grand-mother's idea. It isn't traditional Scots, but then neither was she." Kate paused and grinned. "A real pistol, that one."

Lucie grinned. "Signing checks must be a pain."

Suddenly Kate tilted her head and scrutinized Lucie, who gazed right back at her until the old woman smiled. "Would you join me for some tea?"

"Tea?" Lucie scrunched up her face. "Don't you have any gin?" It was out of her mouth before she could stop it, a regrettably regular occurrence of late. But Kate just laughed.

"Of course I have gin. Go over to that Victorian drinks cabinet, there, beside the fern. Ice bucket's full, there should be some fresh limes – just remove the tray on top - yes, that's it, get the Tanqueray and tonic, dear. Truth is, I hate tea, but everyone around here thinks that's all old people should drink. Damned boring, tea."

Several drinks later, Lucie discovered that Kate was not only lucid, but very good company: no typical elderly lectures about sickness, suffering and memories that you don't share. Nope, Kate was one cool old lady.

They'd been discussing their lives as vital women and Kate's widowhood when she asked, "So how'd you manage two divorces?"

"Guess I just buried it all in the emotional graveyard and hoped it would stay there. Speaking of buried, one of them is dead, so I have pretty good closure there, anyway." She looked over at Kate, who had raised an eyebrow.

"What? ***I*** didn't kill him. Anyway, the other divorce, that was my fault: turns out I married outside my species."

She waited until Kate stopped laughing to continue. "Thing is, what always saved me was my daughter and the jobs. Teaching, if you do it right, is exhausting. And the food industry, well, that's a 24/7 proposition. And of course you can never invest too much time in your offspring."

"So you're happy now?"

Lucie considered that for a moment and nodded, "Yeah, as a matter of fact, I am. I figured out what I want, I get to do what I'm passionate about, I'm fairly well off, I have no biological time clock ticking, and - " she took a breath – "I have my health."

Kate reached out with her drink. "Then here's to health." They clinked glasses and the older woman smiled hugely, thinking she hadn't met anyone this well-adjusted for a long time.

"I wish my son shared that conviction about investing time in your offspring. He was never home for Jeffrey, and look at the mess *he* turned out to be." Kate looked disgusted.

Lucie did not want to discuss Jeffrey with his grandmother, so she stood and said, "Well, Kate, I have things to check on. Thank you very much for the tour of your family."

Then Lucie bent over and kissed her on the cheek: Kate had invited her into more than just the library.

***

Lucie had every intention of starting to prep for dinner, but magnificent weather beckoned and when she heard voices coming from a huge, overgrown hedge near the rear terrace, she went out to investigate.

She discovered two gardeners, one of whom was a compact, elderly Japanese man wearing a pith helmet. The non-Japanese man introduced himself as George, and pointed at his sidekick.

"This here's George, too. He don't speak no English and since none of us talks Japanese, we don't know what his real name is. So we call him George Too."

Lucie bowed slightly and said "Konichiwa, George Too San."

His facc lit up and he bobbed in rapid bows as he returned the greeting, then went back to pruning the mini-jungle. When Lucie asked George if she could help, he handed her pruning shears and told George Too that he had an assistant. In English. George Too looked pleased and answered in Japanese. Lucie blinked several times in astonishment: uh-huh, crazed parallel universe.

She had just finished a small section of the hedge when she heard a joyful puppy yelp and saw Bruno dragging the gardenerwithnoname in her direction. He barely managed to keep the huge animal from jumping on Lucie and panted with the exertion. "What are you doing?"

"I'm helping George Too."

"Who?"

"You know, George Too, this other gardener." She poked at the elderly man, who giggled.

"You're helping the gardener." Puzzled.

She gave him a "duh" look and said, "I love to prune stuff and George One said I could work with George Too."

He looked from Lucie to the small Japanese man, who grinned and nodded at him, and back again.

"I don't - "

"George Too. You know, like l'autre Fauvent in Les Misérables." One of her eyebrows rose. "Well do *you* know his real name?" She was thinking that except for Mrs. Harris, he didn't seem to associate much with the rest of the staff.

He squinted. "I don't...think so."

Lucie frowned at him and turned her attention back to the hedge. When she whacked a section very near his nether regions, he jumped and muttered, "Note to self: never, ever make her really angry."

Bruno, bored that no one was paying her any attention, started to drag him away, but he managed to ask, between tugs, "Would you like to see my vegetables?"

"What!" Lucie looked suspicious, as though he'd offered to show her something altogether different.

"I have a greenhouse and we grow vegetables year-round."

"Oh, fresh vegetables. Yeah, sure, ok." She was now toying with the idea that he was some kind of head gardener, probably worked his way up.

"Right now we have - " He was interrupted by a shrill whistle coming from the direction of the château. He dug in his heels to halt Bruno's forward motion and told Lucie, "That'll be Mrs. Harris. She's angry that I don't have my cell phone on me, so she pretends it's high school gym class. Hated those damned classes. Never was any good at team sports."

Bruno suddenly resumed the tug of war and won, jerking the man almost off his feet. Lucie watched them zigzag across the lawn, following a scent that the huge animal had detected. She shook her head and went back to her pruning buddies.

CHAPTER 5

When Mrs. Harris found Lucie in the kitchen, she noted the changed-out black chef's coat. Lucie grinned at her. "Impending mess insurance."

The housekeeper told her that the French contingent would definitely be in attendance for a business lunch and dinner tomorrow, and added, "Feel free to send An-tooooh-nio (she drew the word out for effect) out for whatever you need. He's still extremely pleased with himself about today's lunch and word around here is, he'll do absolutely anything for you now."

As Lucie began to prepare for the evening meal, Mrs. Harris lingered, watching her fluid movements. "So, how many courses tonight?"

"Four: it's what I'd be serving the client, and because he's elderly, I'm sticking to food he's probably comfortable with."

Mrs. Harris nodded.

"We're having a tomato gratin starter, then Truffle Surprise – the surprise is that it's a ball of foie gras with truffle slices on top – then squab in wine sauce with pasta, and chocolate mousse to finish."

Mrs. Harris' eyes widened. "That sounds spectacular; I'll try to get Mr. Max to the dinner table tonight." And left.

As she worked, Lucie wondered about the reclusive owner of the château. She was forming a mental picture of the man who had sired Jeffrey, but her imagination would have to suffice, because once again, Mr. Max chose not to dine en famille.

***

The cast of diners was identical to the previous night, except for Owen, who could not be located. Roland had insisted that Anthony take his place and fussed over him throughout the meal. In his exaggerated fake accent. Anthony began to inch away from Roland, smothered.

Lucie watched with amusement at first, then felt sorry for them: Roland was painfully enamored and Anthony was clearly uneasy. Lucie remembered his scrutiny of her when they first met- definitely that of a predatory male – and wondered how Roland could have so completely misread the signals. Whatever, just so they kept it to themselves for the next few days.

Jeffrey ignored her completely and took advantage of his proximity to Jessica, as expected, but paused several times to glare at Roland and Anthony.

As Lucie fought the urge to slap him, her attention was drawn to Margaret, who, with her elderly-woman tight perm and benign-but-vacant smile, could pass for anyone's grandmother. But Margaret was staring at Jessica's untouched wine glass. When the girl turned to Jeffrey, Margaret deftly exchanged her own empty glass for Jessica's full one and gulped it down. Lucie shook her head. You just never know.

The staff acquitted themselves nicely, if not

flawlessly; they would at least not embarrass anyone the following day. And when Jeffrey turned a peculiar shade of green upon learning that he had ingested small pigeons instead of what he'd thought was chicken, they behaved like seasoned professionals and waited until dinner was over to laugh about it.

Lucie was in the kitchen, poking at her finger with a pin when the gardener arrived as anticipated. She held up a hand to ward him off.

"Get back, I have a splinter."

"Why? Is it dangerous?"

"Get *away* from me."

"Does this mean I don't get to eat?"

"You're - in – my - light! How am I supposed to get this thing out if I can't see it?" Duh.

The gardener hastily moved to one side, afraid of jeopardizing his chance at dinner. "Sorry."

"See, the whole thing about splinters is that they're insidious. They sneak under your skin and then don't want to leave without a lot of jabbing with something that hurts, and if you leave them in there, they fester, kinda like the baobabs in the Little Prince." She looked up at him. "There's a whole Splinter Gestalt, only not too many people realize it."

Dinner was getting cold.

"Um, can I help with that?"

She narrowed her eyes at him. "You never read the Little Prince, did you?"

"Got thrown out of my one and only language class."

"So you don't get the allegory."

He sighed. "You've spent a lot of time thinking about this, haven't you?"

She frowned at him and went back to poking at her finger.

"I get a lot of splinters."

***

The gardener eventually got his meal, took a tray of food for Kate and quickly returned to the kitchen, where Lucie was hand-washing some expensive wine glasses.

Suddenly Jeffrey burst into the kitchen and announced, “Somebody needs to do something about the nest of really nasty bugs out back.” He paused to rub his thigh, wincing slightly. “Because they’re still biting or stinging or something.”

Lucie struggled to suppress an outburst of laughter, but wound up making a snorting, choking noise. She glanced over at the gardener, who winked at her. The glass she’d been holding shattered when it hit the floor, and Lucie stared at him: that was One. Sexy. Wink.

The noise startled Jeffrey and his eyes darted to Lucie’s knives in a flashback. He slowly backed out of the kitchen, as though he could erase his presence.

When the gardener bent down to clean up the broken glass before Lucie could get to it, she told him, “Here, let me do that, I broke it. I’ll replace it before I leave.”

“No need, there are several cases of them somewhere around here.”

Lucie looked dubious as he dumped the remains of the glass in the waste can.

“What? Ok, ask Mrs. Harris if you don’t believe me.” He studied her face for a moment, then reached for the bottle of wine and filled two glasses.

Lucie hesitated, then took one and preceded him to the patio table. He made a mental note: the chef likes to lead.

“Have any family?”

“Of the immediate kind, yes, my daughter Sophie.”

Lucie suddenly smiled at her name and added,

"We're close."

"And is she also close to her father?"

"Don't know, she doesn't talk about him and I haven't seen him for years. Suits me just fine."

Well, well.

"Last few months, I've been trying to connect with my son, but it's like pulling teeth: he just doesn't want to be bothered." He turned to Lucie. "Ever wish you had more than one?"

Without thinking, she answered, "No, one good one was enough. The pregnancy was a nightmare, so after the second divorce, I had my tubes tied."

Her eyes widened, her face turned red and she clamped her hand over her mouth.

The gardener's eyebrows shot up, but before he could comment, Lucie stood and fanned herself. "Um, it's *really* warm tonight."

The gardener rose with her and asked, "Want to go swimming?"

Lucie looked hopeful. "Pool's heated, right?"

"You betcha."

Lucie grinned, "It'll only take me a minute to get my suit."

As she ran inside, the gardener shrugged and said "If you insist", but was careful not to let her hear him. Already wearing swim trunks under his jeans because he often swam on warm evenings, he grabbed some towels from the small room that served as the pool storage area and waited for Lucie's return.

Lucie shook her head as she changed in her room: with very little encouragement, she'd once again spilled her guts to this gardener/dog-wrangler who appeared at the château very early and left inexplicably late. If he left at all.

Five minutes later he was putting their towels on a lawn chair as Lucie inhaled deeply, entranced by the chlorine smell and the steam rising from the water.

The gardener kicked off his sandals, shed his shirt and unzipped his jeans as he walked to the edge of the pool. Lucie threw up her hands and yelled "Hey whoa wait just one minute there, nobody said anything about skinny d- "

Without turning, he said "No worries" and threw his jeans on a chair. He dove in easily, and even though Lucie hadn't stopped sputtering, she managed to notice his well-toned legs and muscular upper torso.

When he surfaced and swam the length of the pool, she thought, 'Don't go there, girl' and dove into the deep end, where she remained, treading water.

Literally and figuratively.

When she finished, the gardener swam over to her, stood, ran his hands up over his face and hair, then put his arms up on the edge of the pool, next to her. He was careful not to let her see him checking her out, and when he looked away, he allowed himself a mental whistle: she looked really good in very little.

All of a sudden a white streak shot across the lawn, and when it reached the cement that surrounded the pool, tried to stop, but skidded toward the water instead. Paws flailing and toenails fully extended in a desperate attempt to save itself from certain disaster, the Bichon finally came to a halt at the edge of the pool and began to wag and bark furiously at the humans.

"Wherc've you been, little one?"

"She spends a lot of time with Kate, in her apartment. Likes to ride up and down in the elevator with her. Oh, and she won't get in the water no matter what you do."

"Yeah, I know, mine won't go swimming either. Jumped in after me once and hasn't been back since.

On purpose, anyway." Lucie managed to get within petting distance of the dog, who was eyeing the pool, front legs tensed. She stroked her tiny head and ears while the gardener watched with interest.

"Yours, huh? Didn't figure you for a dog person."

Lucie stopped petting the dog and turned. "WHAT? You assume I don't like dogs because I objected to being squashed by the resident horsedog? That's really insulting!"

"I'm sorry, I just meant..." He stopped abruptly and decided to spin his way out of it: "Her name is Phoebe."

Lucie frowned to let him know she was still insulted, and grumbled "Why Phoebe? Odd name for a dog. Come to think of it, you people have more than your share of weird names, no names and aliases around here."

Phoebe wanted more of Lucie's attention and started to bark, sat up on her hind legs and pumped both front legs in the air. The gardener laughed and said, "We call her Phoebe because Mrs. Harris said Puff Ball was not a good name for a dog. Actually, she answers to several different names, but only when she feels like it."

Lucie rubbed Phoebe's ears and said, "I have the same problem with Murphy: instead of obeying a command, she considers her options." She looked over at him and continued, "Murph stays with my sister when I'm out of town, which is pretty often. I just can't put her – the dog, not my sister - in a kennel, not even the country-club kind."

The gardener reached over to pet Phoebe, who licked his hand. "What kind of things do you read?"

Lucie didn't see that one coming. "Why do you want to know?"

"You always so suspicious?"

Good point. Usually, she wasn't.

Lucie shrugged, "Well all right, I like murder mysteries and the occasional cerebral novel, Wine Spectator, and I read Vanity Fair cover to cover because they know stuff before anyone else does."

"Vanity Fair? Strange you should mention that." The gardener looked at her thoughtfully, but didn't explain.

"So what do you really care about, besides your daughter, cooking and dogs?"

Lucie glanced at him sharply: the subject was very important to her, and he'd better be serious with his inquiry. He seemed to be, so she answered.

"I care about giving back."

"What organizations are on your list?"

Her mouth fell open. How'd he know she had a list!? Then she gave herself a mental head slap: he knew about the list the same way he knew her other thoughts.

She took a deep breath. "Ok, here goes: mostly it's organizations that feed people and then help them establish sustainable economies so they can feed themselves. And the local food pantries. And Médecins Sans Frontières. And several environmental groups. And - oh, sorry, I tend to get carried away."

"No, really, please continue. I admire your passion."

All of a sudden Lucie felt exposed, vulnerable. She glanced down to see if her swimming suit were still in place, a physical check on mental insecurity. Then over at him. His half-naked proximity was making her twitchy, so in one swift movement, she hoisted herself out of the pool at the edge and grabbed a towel.

"Thanks for the swim, I really enjoyed it. See you tomorrow."

With a puzzled look on his face, the gardener remarked to Phoebe, "I don't *think* I said anything else to offend her, and I know you didn't..."

In her suite, Lucie showered off the chlorine and thoughts of the gardener. She told herself to remember The Rule and stay away from hired help who don't do their jobs but have strange ties to the family and who want to know too much about you. She went to sleep with that mantra and didn't wake until morning.

CHAPTER 6

Lucie woke early, and with a start: a small tongue had inserted itself into her ear and now the rest of Phoebe was wagging happily at having accomplished her goal.

She smiled at the little dog, and as she hugged her, remembered hearing scratching at her door last night, opening it, and watching the white streak shoot past her and onto the bed. Phoebe had fluffed the comforter and settled in while Lucie told her, "Yeah, well, ok, as long as you haven't invited Bruno to this slumber party."

As Lucie got dressed and applied some makeup, the image of the gardener flashed into her brain. Unbidden. She frowned, annoyed with herself for being attracted to the man: when he wasn't prying into her personal life, he was laughing at her. Unacceptable behavior, it warranted avoiding him.

She opened the door of her suite, intending to allow the little dog access to whoever fed her in the morning, but Phoebe dashed across the hall and through a partially-open door.

Alarmed, Lucie started to call her when a familiar voice laughed and said, "And where did you spend the night, you little hussy?" The Bichon probably understood him, because she barked and ran back over to Lucie, who tried to get her hands on her.

Just then the door opened wide, feet appeared, and as Lucie's gaze slowly traveled upward, over the khakis and denim shirt that he was buttoning, her mouth fell open. She stood up and started to blink rapidly. What the hell?

The gardener. In the elusive Mr. Max's suite. It actually took only a second to process the information, but it felt as though she'd been standing there for an eternity.

"Good morning." He was grinning.

"You're not a gardener." She shook her head, "Oh, man, how could I have - this is *your* home, she's *your* little dog. Noooobody told me, just assumed I knew."

She stopped suddenly and grimaced. "OhmyGod. That means Jeffrey is *your* son!"

***

The man she would now call Max or Mr. Meicklejohn or Hamish or maybe something else entirely, looked incredulous and said, "You thought I was one of the gardeners? Why?"

Then he slapped his forehead: "Oh I get it, no one ever introduced us, I'd been dragging Bruno out of the pool when you arrived, and I've looked grubby ever since, right? So you assumed – and all this time - " He began to laugh so hard he had to grasp the door jamb for support.

"That's almost as good as Bruno sitting on you!" Max howled with laughter until he noticed that Lucie was not at all amused.

She had narrowed her eyes at him and crossed her arms. "This is really embarrassing and as usual, all you can do is laugh. And mock."

Max tried to contain himself. "Sorry, no mocking intended." A chuckle escaped. "Tell you what: let's go have breakfast and talk about what's been going on, ok?"

Lucie scowled at him.

Diversion needed. He quickly closed his door and yelled "Phoebe!," who emerged from Lucie's suite with a vapor trail of toilet paper behind her. Max scooped her up and extracted bits of TP from her mouth. "You've got to stop eating paper products, especially other people's. Sorry, Ms. Richards."

Lucie sighed and unfolded her arms. "I'm used to Bichons, remember?" Before she could think about what she was doing, she held out her hand. "And call me Lucie."

He grinned, "Nice to meet you. I'm Max." He shook her hand, hers small in his large one, and Lucie felt the now-familiar zing. She pulled back quickly, but admitted to herself that she did like his firm grip. Too many men offer a limp handshake, in deference to what, the weaker sex? Rubbish.

Phoebe leaned over and licked both of them.

***

The kitchen was deserted, for which Lucie was thankful: she was still embarrassed and needed time to adjust to the paradigm shift. And add it to her mental Weird Shit list.

While Max washed some fruit, Lucie made coffee and eyed him suspiciously, wondering if he'd been playing an elaborate joke on her. Then Phoebe reminded Max to feed her by barking at him, and as he filled her doggie dish, he remarked, "You probably think I've been pranking you the last few days, and believe me, that's the last thing I'd do."

Lucie flinched. More mind reading.

They perched on stools and enjoyed crusty French rolls, sweet butter and jam, and perfectly ripe fresh fruit. Lucie was sipping her second cup of coffee when she realized that Max was staring at her chest.

"You know you have toothpaste on your shirt." Not a question.

She frowned because it was rude to mention it, then frowned again because he was right. The fact that the man was not a gardener hadn't changed anything.

Lucie squinted at him. "So what did you do for a living?"

He munched on a piece of bread and considered the question a moment too long, as far as Lucie was concerned. "I worked for the government. Had a massive heart attack a few years ago, it changed my perspective on life, and I quit the job."

"The job?" She raised one eyebrow.

"The wealth you see around here" and he waved his right arm "is, of course, inherited." He stopped, hoping the non-sequitur would divert her attention. But her eyes never wavered from his face as she continued to eat, clearly prepared to wait him out. He waggled a finger at her shirt.

"Now you've got some jam on there as well." He nodded, "Good thing you've started wearing a black chef's coat."

"The job?"

Phoebe inadvertently came to his rescue: she began to scrape the floor with her back legs, like a little bull.

"Where'd you learn that trick, Phoebes?"

Just as the dog began to make guttural noises that sounded surprisingly like telling them off for not sharing, Mrs. Harris appeared.

"Guess what? Lucie thought I was one of the gardeners."

Mrs. Harris looked puzzled. "Really? That's odd. But it does explain a few things."

"Join us?" There was an easy camaraderie that Lucie hadn't noticed before.

"Thanks, already ate." Mrs. Harris was in Perfunctory mode. "Ms. Richards - "

"Lucie."

"Very well. Lucie, the Sautiers will be here for lunch, so please feed the family and staff before that." She motioned for Max to follow her and added, "And you need to take care of something in the office."

Max picked up Phoebe and handed her to Lucie. "Would you take her out for me, please? But put a leash on her, we can't have her running off today."

"How far does she usually get?"

"To the neighbors, beyond the hedges. Then they call us – but I suspect they give her treats before they call – and then Owen goes to pick her up in the limo." He made a wry face. "She *loves* to ride in the limo."

Lucie laughed and hugged the little dog. "Ok Phoebe, I am the boss of you for a while."

Max looked pleased about that and followed Mrs. Harris.

***

She had just removed Phoebe's leash when the little dog began to bark frantically and tore off down the hallway. Alarmed, Lucie ran after her until Phoebe skidded to a halt and darted into the library.

Lucie stood in the doorway and watched in amazement: Phoebe and Bruno were racing around the room, yet somehow, miraculously, nothing was being destroyed.

"Best friends, those two, ever since you arrived. Can't imagine why. They have nothing in common, culturally."

Lucie laughed out loud as Kate's perfectly made-up face crinkled in a grin. "Good morning, chef Lucie. Could I trouble you for a Bloody Mary? You will join me, of course."

Lucie nodded, "Of course. Be right back."

Kate pointed to the corner, to the elegant, wrought-iron spiral staircase that led to the second level walkway. "You could use that and get the drinks from Max's apartment: he's got a huge bar up there."

Baffled, Lucie stared at the stretch of wall at the top of the staircase.

"There's a hidden door, you'll see the small latch beside one of the vertical panels. Leads directly into his suite. He uses it to circumvent the hallways when he wants to hang out in here."

The door, wherever it was, looked like all the other panels. Lucie squinted at the wall behind the railing, then moved side to side. Sure enough, the panels were slightly angled, but not enough to catch the eye of the casual observer. Cool.

"Um, I'll just take the overland route to the butler's pantry, if you don't mind."

Kate shrugged. "Suit yourself, but swiping Max's stuff is more fun."

Lucie returned with a pitcher of drinks, poured out two, and since Bruno and Phoebe were napping in a corner, sat down beside Kate.

"Now then, dear, you must hear the story of Max's ill-advised, multiple marriages. All four of them."

Lucie almost dropped her drink. "FOUR?"

She sighed. "That's correct, four wives in ten years. I am so glad he's past that phase. He had this habit of marrying beautiful women and then leaving for months at a time because of his hush-hush government job. Believe me, all that alimony cramps his style once in a while, although he did wise up after the second one took him for a ride and used prenups for the third and fourth."

Lucie's mind did a weird leap to *Jane Eyre* and she gazed up at the two story ceiling. Kate followed her glance and laughed. "No, there are no crazed bimbos locked in Mr. Rochester's attic. He divorced every last one."

She heard that obscure thought? Aieeeeee....

Kate screwed up her face and observed, "Probably once the lust part was over, they bored him: not one of them could have had an IQ over 80. You'd think he'd have learned, after Bambi. That's who produced Jeffrey. Then there was Isabelle and she produced my second grandchild, a spoiled princess. Then I seem to recollect someone called Tabitha, then Barbi for God's sake."

Lucie was still dumbfounded. Four. Wives. Made her own two marriages seem paltry by comparison. "So that's Spoiled Princess and Jeffrey. Any other children?"

"No, and Spoiled Princess only contacts us when she wants money. So that leaves Jeffrey the Village Idiot." Lucie choked and the old woman leaned over conspiratorially. "Confidentially, we're all hoping he's sterile; can you imagine *that* gene pool flowing into the next generation?"

Lucie choked again.

They were interrupted by Max, who had gone past the library and returned when he heard voices. "Ah, there you are, Lucie. Guess what, Gladys? Lucie thought I was a gardener. Isn't that a hoot?"

Lucie looked around for another dog or a maid.

"Gladys?"

Kate looked defensive. "Well if Hamish can be someone else, so can I. And don't touch that pitcher!" as Max reached for it.

He made a face at his mother as Lucie told her, "Good talking to you, G – er – Kate, but I need to go get ready for lunch."

Kate waved them off. "Then you two run along, don't bother about me and the dogs, we'll be just fine."

Max shook his head as he followed Lucie to the kitchen. "Sometimes I wonder about that woman."

"Well, she tells a good story."

Max suddenly looked worried, but before he could inquire about which stories she'd heard, Roland swooped into the kitchen.

"*Julia* has arrived," he announced with a shudder, "and when I informed her that she will not be needed until the business is concluded, she – " He raised his chin, lower lip quivering, and finished, "She shouted at me!" He paused, allowing them time to be appalled.

"Also, I cannot find Antonio anywhere, nor does anyone know the whereabouts of Jessica." He uttered a strange, high-pitched little noise.

Max put his arm around the butler's shoulder and steered him toward the hallway. "Not to worry, Roland, I'm sure we haven't misplaced any employees. We'll go find Mrs. Harris: she always knows where everyone is."

Lucie stared after them for a moment, shrugged and prepared lunch. When the crespeou – a huge, layered omelette cake with eggplant, zucchini, black olives, asparagus, garlic and herbs – emerged from the oven, she tossed a green salad and had John summon the family and staff.

Jeffrey arrived first and demanded Parmesan cheese as a topping; Lucie acquiesced and was surprised when each new arrival followed suit. She made a mental note to include it the next time she served the dish.

Half an hour later, the French had not yet arrived, so Lucie, who wanted to be ready for any contingency, prepared an array of appetizers that were ready to eat.

Suddenly Phoebe ran into the kitchen, barked at her and ran off; Lucie hurried to the archway of the dining room, peered into the hallway and saw the Sautier group in the immense foyer, along with a younger man who looked and sounded irate. Probably the lawyer, because he was translating Mrs. Harris' English in a staccato, impatient tone. She caught a glimpse of his face: marginally attractive with dark eyes and slicked-back dark hair, and a cruel, cold expression that suggested ruthlessness.

M. Sautier's estate manager had also accompanied the elderly couple, and Mrs. Harris had Roland take their luggage to the guest suites on the ground floor. Then she instructed John to deliver the lawyer to a guest room upstairs.

Ten minutes later, the housekeeper joined Lucie in the kitchen, indignant. "That man is absolutely despicable! He's insisting that the business meeting begin at once, says there have been enough delays already."

"Did they even have lunch?" Lucie couldn't imagine skipping a meal.

"I don't know, but he was extremely rude to that nice old couple, and he had the nerve to tell John that he got 'stuck' doing 'the old geezer's' legal work because his grandfather is M. Sautier's best friend! And it gets worse: poor M. Sautier is Gaston Laval's godfather!"

"Laval's the pissed-off lawyer?"

"He is, and arrogant as hell. Come to think of it, he reminds me of Jeffrey; they should get along well. Did you know that Jeffrey didn't even bother to greet them? Probably wants to make some sort of grand entrance."

The housekeeper ended the tirade as abruptly as she'd begun it, and was no sooner out of the kitchen when Max emerged from the butler's pantry.

"Mrs. Harris likes you," he observed.

"How do you know that?"

"It took her three years to get that kind of chatty with me."

"You were eavesdropping again."

"I - "

He was interrupted by Jessica and Antonio, who floated into the kitchen, hands all over each other. Lucie did a mental euuuw and hoped that Roland hadn't seen them like this; despite his general snottiness, she felt sorry for the man.

Lucie half-frowned. "You two need to help serve the food after the meeting, so don't get lost again."

Jessica squinted and blinked, as though she only half-understood, but Antonio bobbed his head and assured Lucie, "Got it, chef." He grabbed Jessica's hand and hurried her out of the kitchen.

Lucie rolled her eyes at Max, then slipped up the back stairs to check her email.

CHAPTER 7

As Lucie finished reading a long message from her daughter, she heard Phoebe whining and got up to play with the little dog. She had just stepped into the hallway when Max opened his door.

He looked at Lucie, pondered something for a moment, and said "You'd better come with me."

As he led her through the large living room/ kitchenette/bar area and into his bedroom, she glanced at the king sized bed; it was smoothed over and tidy, but not excessively so. So he wasn't a slob, but he wasn't a neat freak either. Lucie immediately winced, sure that he'd heard the thought, but Max was engrossed in something in the wall at the far right end of the suite.

The door. The narrow, slightly open door that didn't belong there. Max put his finger on his lips and moved her in front of him. She peered down into the library, and could not only see everyone settling in at the conference table, she could also hear them. Lucie guessed that even though it was partially open, the angled, secret door was all but invisible from below. So *this* was what Kate had been talking about.

"Pretty cool, huh?" He was whispering. "It's a listening post. My father's idea."

Max pulled her away from the door and explained, "Jeffrey brokered this acquisition all by himself, but somehow missed the part about hiring his own bilingual lawyer. Instead, he's using one of his fraternity brothers - someone called Adam Cromby – because he works cheap." Max made a face.

"So the only person with both French and English is Gaston Laval?"

"You got it. That's why we're, uh, monitoring the proceedings." He walked over to his computer desk, picked up some papers and turned to her.

"Something else, I ran a background check on Laval, and he works for a Paris-based business law firm that specializes in foreign investments in France. But he's never handled a cross-border transaction like this, so I have to wonder why his firm chose him in the first place, and then why they didn't provide some backup."

"Well, Mrs. H says he's a family friend who got coerced into the job."

Max looked unconvinced.

"So what kind of money are we talking about?"

"8,000,000 euros, asking price."

Lucie's eyes widened.

"That's for the entire estate, which includes..." He consulted his papers and continued, "Twenty-nine hectares of property, let's see, two in olive trees, four in buildings, fifteen in vin de pays vineyards, and eight in woods. The buildings include a 17th century bastide, a winemaker's house, a cottage to be restored, and a fully equipped winery with some farm equipment."

"The property has been in M. Sautier's family since the early 1800s, and he didn't want to sell out to Le

Groupe, which is probably a development company."

Lucie squinted, mental math not being her strong suit. "Let's see, what's that in dollars, about nine, no, it's almost eleven million dollars!" She blinked several times, then observed, "Still, it's a lot less than property in Napa: you'd be looking at twenty million just for the vineyards, plus another four for a winery."

"Says here most of the grapes they produce only go to a local co-op." Max glanced up. "Apparently that kept the price down, even though the estate sits in the Luberon. So they really only make a small amount of wine on site, but that didn't bother Jeffrey. I think he just wants to be able to tell people he owns a winery in France, not actually make any wine."

"He's planning on taking his 'posse' over for a visit and play big shot, is my guess. Can't wait to see the look on his face when he finds out I expect a return on the investment."

Suddenly they heard voices from below, some of them almost strident.

Lucie frowned and said, "What the heck happened to the polite preliminaries? It sounds like they've slammed into the heavy-duty part already, and that's all but unthinkable to M. Sautier's generation. It's so rude, I mean, you should see the way the French sign their business letters: 'Sincerely' just doesn't make it, they end with an entire sentence!"

Max silently placed two chairs by the door and they focused on the scene below.

The meeting progressed with a certain quick rhythm: Jeffrey and his lawyer conferred, his lawyer addressed Laval, who translated for M. Sautier, who asked questions in a soft, dignified voice. It all sounded straightforward until Jeffrey instructed his lawyer to make an opening offer of €6,000,000 and Laval turned to M. Sautier to translate.

Suddenly the French lawyer's voice assumed a new tone, an indignant one that made everyone sit up and take notice.

Lucie's life lurched in a new direction at that precise moment: *Luck*, pure and simple, plays a huge part in the course of human events, and what else could it be, having heard Phoebe whining, being invited to eavesdrop on the proceedings and overhearing the Deception?

As the lawyer spoke to the elderly Frenchman, Lucie turned to Max with an incredulous look on her face. "I thought you said Jeffrey wanted to acquire the entire parcel, winery and all."

Max nodded.

"But Laval just told Sautier that Jeffrey doesn't want the winery!" She continued to listen, intently now. "And that he wants to dig up the vineyards and build condos?"

Max stared at her. Then they peered down into the library and saw the horrified look on M. Sautier's face as Laval delivered the coup de grâce: "Il t'offre seulement trois millions cinq cent mille, et pas même en euros. Ferme."

M. Sautier looked as though he'd been struck, then his face crumpled. Not only was his family estate to be parceled off, the non-negotiable offer was an unimaginable insult.

Laval was clever enough to allow Jeffrey to hear the "million" word, but what he'd reported to M. Sautier was less than half of the original asking price. Then he'd said, 'And not even euros', which reduced the amount considerably.

Jeffrey was aware that something catastrophic had occurred, but had no idea what. His offer had obviously offended the Frenchman, but the low ball figure he proposed was SOP at the beginning of all negotiations. He was on the verge of asking his buddy Adam about arcane French business rituals when M. Sautier turned slowly, deliberately to Laval.

The elderly Frenchman gathered his dignity and quietly stated that he'd been assured of two things: that the sale of his property would be simple, in good faith, and that his estate – Mon Dieu, it had been in his family for generations - would remain intact. That assurance had been the deciding factor in selling to the young American businessman.

Lucie heard thc despair in his voice and saw a sneer on Laval's face. She was out of her chair in a second, heading for the door and buttoning up her chef's coat. Timc to suit up.

"That sonofabitch just lied through his teeth to that poor old man" was the only explanation she offered on her way out the door.

"What are you- ?" But Lucie was already taking the back stairs two at a time, concocting her story as she went. It would have to be something totally outrageous, a huge diversion. Involving food.

She burst into the library and strode to Jeffrey's side, then whispered directly into his ear: "You've got to come with me right now. Somehow rat poison got into the Parmesan cheese we used at lunch and someone's going to die!"

Jeffrey screeched "Ohmygod" and shot out of his chair so fast he knocked it over. As Lucie pulled him toward the door, he clutched his stomach, moaning and stumbling all at the same time.

The sudden, unexplained emergency rendered everyone speechless, then bewildered. Except Laval, who looked irritated and snapped, "What is that ridiculous man playing at?"

Lucie turned at the library door and told them to remain where they were, that it was nothing. As she pulled Jeffrey out of earshot, he gasped, "Who is it, who's dying? It's me, isn't it? Ahhgg, where's the ambulance?!"

Bent over, he faced the wall and slapped one hand on it for support, the other still attached to his midsection. And groaned loudly. Except for his conservative Brooks Brothers suit and garish tie – and the groaning - he resembled a flying buttress.

Lucie hissed at him, "Be quiet! The cheese wasn't poisoned and nobody's dying. I had to get you out here in a hurry so I could tell you something."

Jeffrey wailed, "I know it's me, my stomach is killing me, call 911 again, they're taking too long!""You don't need an ambulance because there Was No Poison!"

"Wait. What?" He turned to her. "Then why is someone dying?"

Lucie gritted her teeth. "Nobody's dying. Forget about dying!" She waved both hands in front of his face to erase the thought that was stuck in his brain. "Listentome! Gaston Laval just lied to M. Sautier, told him that you made a firm offer of only $3,500,000. And that you don't want the winery, you're going to build condos in the vineyards!"

Jeffrey's voice came out in a squeak: "But what's that got to do with me being poisoned?"

"Ahhhhhhhhhh! You're not LISTENING!"

Suddenly the Jeffrey fog cleared. He pointed a finger at Lucie and sputtered, "How dare you interfere - you're just a...a...cook!" He stopped abruptly, blinked several times and said, "Wait a minute. Who's Gaston Laval?"

Lucie rolled her eyes. "The – French – lawyer." Silent duh.

"But I offered six million euros. And that was just for starters."

"Yessss...." She waited.

"But he's a lawyer, so why would he do that?"

Lucie wanted to thump him on the forehead. "I don't know why! But you need to - "

Suddenly Lucie's peripheral vision caught Max and Mrs. Harris in the hallway. They were at her side in an instant, just as Jeffrey's face contorted into a snarl: "Now I get it: you're just trying to ruin my deal and make me look bad, and how the hell do you know what happened, anyway?"

Max looked disgusted. "For God's sake, Jeffrey, Mrs. Harris told you why we hired Lucie: she handles foreign clients all the time and she speaks French, and now she's trying to save your ass."

When Jeffrey opened his mouth to object, Lucie addressed Max. "We need to separate M. Sautier from Laval before he discovers we're on to him; he'll be easier to handle if he thinks he's still in control."

Max nodded.

She turned to Jeffrey. "If you're going to drop several million on this deal, you need to find out why Laval doesn't want the old man selling to you."

Jeffrey stared.

Lucie started to pace. "Let's see...how to...this has to be fast – tell you what, let's have some fun with the bastard. Mrs. Harris, have the staff set out the hors-d'oeuvres immediately, and have someone bring Bruno to the library ASAP. And to make sure those huge paws are *really* muddy. Please."

Mrs. Harris looked amused, nodded and hurried down the hall, cell phone in hand.

She turned to Jeffrey. "Go back in there and make up a long story about your stomach ache, but don't mention poison. And keep Laval busy translating until we get Bruno in there. And pretend you don't know he lied."

Lucie reached into her chef's coat pocket and handed Jeffrey a dog treat. "Get close to Laval and wave this near him, where Bruno can see it. Bruno will do the rest, and remember, Laval- Treat -Bruno. Got it?"

Jeffrey frowned and clutched his stomach, still harboring a dark suspicion that this maniac chef just might have laced his lunch with something toxic. Max had to grab his arm and give him a push, sending him staggering into the library. "Now!"

Grinning, he turned to Lucie. "What, you carry dog treats in your chef's coat?"

Lucie shrugged. "They expect it."

They eavesdropped on Jeffrey's preposterous story, punctuated by the occasional moan, until a sloppy-wet, thoroughly muddy Bruno appeared at the end of the hall, dragging Antonio behind her like a water skier. The marble floor started to resemble a child's finger painting as the man skidded toward them, wild-eyed.

Antonio panted, "We were out on the lawn and they told me you wanted mud on her paws and that was easy because she got into a pile of something the Georges dug up and I don't understand but here she is."

Lucie laughed and told him, "She's perfect, thank you so much!" She removed Bruno's lead, showed her another treat from her pocket, and tossed it into the library. She hoped Jeffrey would remember to hold the other one near Laval.

The howl from inside told her that he had; she waited for several beats and motioned for Antonio to go inside. "Tell them she got away from you and that we'll have Laval's suit cleaned while he washes up, ok?"

She turned to Max. "If you deal with him, I'll herd

everybody else into the dining room and explain what I can. You think you'll be able to get anything out of Laval?"

"Hard to tell, but if he doesn't cooperate, I'll have him recalled by his firm, immediately."

"You can do that?"

"It's my eleven million." Lucie gulped.

"And thank you, what you're doing is way above and beyond." He opened his mouth to continue, but stopped as the noise level from inside the library increased: not only was Laval shouting obscenities, but Jeffrey didn't have the sense to stop blabbering.

As Lucie observed that the Mother Ship needed to reclaim Jeffrey, Antonio emerged from the library, pulling Bruno - no small feat, because she didn't want to leave her soggy new friend. He shot them a brief, puzzled look, but was immediately jerked off balance when Bruno changed her mind and took off down the hall.

Max went to retrieve Laval and returned several seconds later, a grin on his face and a firm grip on the man's arm. When Lucie saw the bedraggled mess that Bruno had produced, she flashed back several days and understood Max's reaction to her. It *was* funny, but she'd never admit it to him.

Laval's rage spilled into the hallway. "You people cannot control your animal? This is intolerable, even for you Americans. Les Sautier and I will be leaving as soon as possible. I will make sure that...." The abuse flowed freely in French-accented English, which became more and more French the angrier he became.

As Lucie watched, Laval suddenly noticed her and glared. Un-intimidated, she stared hard at him and thought to herself, 'Uh-huh, a Player. And with eleven million dollars worth of winery property at stake, I wonder what you're up to. '

Although Laval was a head shorter than Max, he was stocky, like a street fighter, and tried repeatedly to shake off Max. Struggling to maintain his hold, Max called over his shoulder to Lucie, "Please send John to the small bedroom, off the office: we'll have Monsieur Laval wait there until we can take care of his clothes."

Then pulled him down the hall, directly through Bruno's mess.

CHAPTER 8

Lucie stepped back into the library to introduce herself to Gérard Sautier, but the instant she grasped his wrinkled hand and gazed into the brilliant, pale blue eyes, she was struck by the sensation that they already knew each other. Impossible: she was certain she'd never met the frail-on-his-way-to-being-wizened, white-haired Frenchman who stood before her.

Odder still, Sautier had tilted his head and now searched her face, clearly hoping to recognize some feature....until Jeffrey made an impatient noise, snapping Lucie back into business mode.

She quickly informed the Frenchman that there'd been a terrible mistake about the offer for his winery, but that after some refreshments, un goûter, everything would s'arrange. And that there was nothing wrong with Jeffrey. Well, not with his stomach, anyway.

Lucie told Jeffrey and Cromby, both of whom were staring at her, to remain calm, then put her arm lightly around the elderly man's shoulders.

She led him into the hallway, where they encountered Mrs. Harris, who was supervising the

Bruno cleanup. When Lucie asked her to collect the French party and escort them to the dining room, the housekeeper nodded and winked.

"Pissed-off, dark and nasty won't be joining them, he's being *detained*."

Lucie left Gérard in her capable hands and dashed into the dining room, where she found the appetizer buffet already set up: the French comfort food called rillettes, a meat spread with savory herbs, was paired with pitted black olives and cornichons. The cheesy Diablotin had been spread on thin slices of French bread, as she requested. And the small tomatoes stuffed with a macédoine of carrots, peas, asparagus, cauliflower and green beans in a thick mayonnaise looked absolutely perfect.

Lucie ran into the butler's pantry and down to wine cellar, where she quickly selected the bottles she wanted and deposited them in a carrier. She was half way out the door when her brain registered the anomaly. She turned back, placed the wire basket on a table and removed the bottles.

Uh huh, a torn, crinkled label. But recently torn, the edges were sharp. An attempt to make it look old? And a crooked label. On an expensive bottle?

She stepped over to the Major Vintages section and hurriedly examined a row of what should have been identical bottles of wine. It only took a moment to spot two sets of labels, one with a much lighter background than the other. Whoa, someone was tampering with - but playing detective would have to wait. The emergency upstairs took precedence.

Lucie grabbed the bottles, ran back up to the kitchen to put the whites in chilling sleeves and open the reds, and frowned again as she noticed several odd-looking corks. She was about to taste the wine when Jeffrey blasted through the archway, followed by

Cromby, scuttling in a half-crouch. The man's timid, geeky image was reinforced by his ill-fitting suit, large glasses, and hesitant gestures. Lucie groaned quietly. Now what?

Jeffrey scowled at her and announced, "I want you to handle the deal for us. You speak French, you can straighten things out and I won't have to hire anyone else."

"I already started to straighten things out and no, I can't handle the deal for you."

"Why not?"

"I'm not a lawyer."

Cromby moaned, "Oh no, this is terrible, isn't it Jeff?"

'Jeff' ignored the little man and pointed a finger at Lucie. "You stuck your nose in this mess, so you're obligated whether you like it or not."

Lucie remembered to speak slowly. "Your best bet is probably a Montréal-based firm that handles French-Anglo deals on a regular basis, and since it's not that far away, we might be able to get someone here quickly. I can recommend several competent people."

"That's the best you can do?" Jeffrey looked disgusted.

Lucie gritted her teeth. "Giles Montand is very good but he'll have to drop whatever he's working on, so it'll cost you. And I'll have to call in an enormous favor." Too late she remembered what the favor might involve.

Jeffrey finally relented. "Oh all right, call whoever you want, you've got me by the short hairs."

Adam nodded, "Yeah, by the short hairs."

Lucie grimaced as they heard rapid footsteps coming down the back stairs. Max nodded at them as he entered the kitchen, speaking decisively into his cell phone. "Make sure Owen is ready to transport him ASAP. Oh, and you'll like this: I've arranged for him to return to France with a little stopover in Reykjavik."

He disconnected and turned first to Jeffrey: "Laval is leaving immediately and we'll replace him. Adam, stick around. Lucie, any chance you know - "

But Lucie was already mumbling, "Phone's in my room, gotta run upstairs." She was gone by the time Julia, who'd been eavesdropping where everyone eavesdropped, stormed into the kitchen, her overlarge presence arriving in waves that didn't entirely stop undulating when she halted.

She yanked at the expensive two-piece outfit she wore, willing it to cover the bulges, but the jacket immediately began to inch its way back up and over her stomach. Julia ignored the mutiny and launched the assault.

"I cannot believe that ***I*** was not consulted about this matter; I have connections, you know, and one would think that with all the years I've been here, you'd come to me first!" Her outrage grew as she moved closer and closer to Max.

Max took a step backwards, careful not to stare at the greasy blond curls that were bobbing at him, and said, "Julia. You're going to be very busy when we close the deal and we didn't want to impose on your valuable time." He paused to see if it was working. It sort of was.

While Julia glared at him, not sure if she wanted to be placated, Lucie raced down the back stairs, cell phone in one hand, laptop under an arm and cords trailing behind her. As she entered the kitchen, she opened her mouth to ask how much she could offer Giles, to sweeten the pot, but stopped when she saw a large woman being angry at Max.

In one swift movement, Max twirled Lucie out of the kitchen, through the butler's pantry and dining room and into the hallway.

Lucie whipped her head around and said, "Wait – who - ?"

"Julia."

Lucie made a face as Max propelled her down the hall. "Whoa. Scary."

"You don't know the half of it."

"What about Laval?"

"Got nothing from him, so he's in isolation, then outa here. How'd you make out?"

"My friend Giles can be here by dinner time, wants someone to fax him the details, wants to know what I'm serving, and I just called in a favor I've been saving for a really rainy day. You owe me, big time."

"Yeah, I realize that and believe me, I'll make it up to you. And don't worry about sweetening the pot."

Ahhhgg, he did it again, dammit. Then for one moment Lucie considered that it actually saved time, his reading her mind. No no NO, mental head slap, a thought like that meant Lucie Richards was turning into one of the Resident Loonies! Plus, she realized with a shock, the poison/rampaging dog scenario was hardly the product of a normal mind.

Lucie groaned. Best worry about that later, à la Scarlett. She found herself staring at Max, who was telling her not to negotiate with Giles, just offer him double the going rate: at what point had the soppy gardener persona evaporated? Before her stood a commanding figure, wearing a really nice, expensive-looking shirt.

He had stopped talking and was watching her closely. "What?"

Lucie shook her head.

"Still rebooting?"

Damn.

"Tell me how much again?"

She left him in the hallway and ducked into the library to make another call to Montréal, then ran over to the dining room, where Mrs. Harris was just introducing everyone to the appetizers while Stella helped with the service, putting the guests at ease with her uncomplicated smiles. Lucie nodded at the French and backed out of the room.

When she was out of view, Lucie tore back into the kitchen, thinking that all she needed was slamming doors to make this a *real* farce. She tasted the first bottle of wine she'd opened, and spat it out immediately. She peered at the label, frowned, and opened the other bottles: several more were unacceptable.

What was going on here? It wasn't that the wines were corked or otherwise ruined, they were plonk. They had never, ever, been superior wines. She poured them all down the drain, not wanting to take a chance on them being served by mistake, put the good bottles on a tray and headed for the dining room.

Lucie handed the wine to Stella and returned to the library, where she left her laptop. She'd just stepped back into the hall when Max came around the corner from the office. Before she could engage the Censor Button, Lucie blurted out, "Any of your employees have a drug or gambling problem?"

"What?"

"Someone with money problems, and smart enough to figure out a way to steal your wine."

Max began to blink rapidly.

"I'm pretty sure somebody's been changing out your good wine for plonk; at dinner the other night, Mrs. Harris mentioned that some of the wine has been off lately, and just now I noticed some odd labels and corks."

"What the - ?"

"But don't worry, I dumped it."

Max looked worried anyway. "Which bottles are we talking about?"

Lucie hesitated. Maybe they shouldn't go down this road right now.

Max bent down to peer in her face. "Which bottles?"

Lucie made what she hoped was an apologetic face. "You know what, I probably shouldn't have brought this up now, we could talk about it later." She turned to escape but he caught her by the back of her chef's coat and spun her around.

"*Which ones*?"

"Ok, ok, a Sauterne, um, a Château d'Yquem."

Lucie winced.

Max winced.

This was going be painful.

"What else?"

Lucie took a deep breath: apparently there was to be no escape for the loose of mouth. "Several Cheval Blanc St. Émilions -the '82 vintage – but only one was bad."

Max groaned and closed his eyes. He could have been praying, she couldn't tell, and Lucie wondered briefly if there were a Wine God. He spoke without opening his eyes. "There's more, isn't there?"

"Um, the American Cab was one of those Napa cult vintages, a bottle of Screaming Eagle, and-" That's all the further she got.

"Ahhhgghhh, shit, shit SHIT!" He thumped the wall in exasperation. "It has to be an employee, but why would they, I mean, I pay them all incredibly well, and how the hell are they doing it anyway?"

Lucie chewed her bottom lip. "It could be as

simple as making copies of the labels and putting them on bottles of cheap wine, then changing out the real wine for the fakes. It's primitive, but with the huge inventory you have, it might have been years before anyone noticed."

"But the cellar's always locked!"

"We can't deal with that right now, Max, we have a fiasco to fix." She looked into the dining room. "Kate would be an asset for us right now, so let's ask her to join us, but Margaret doesn't need to start drinking this early, so leave her out."

Max nodded, noticing her use of "us." He also noticed that she knew a whole lot more about his household's personalities than he did.

***

He followed Lucie into the dining room, where she introduced him to the French, then deposited her laptop on the extended table. While Max topped off everyone's drinks, she conversed with the Sautiers' estate manager, Didier Roussel, a lanky man in his seventies with a grey comb-over and laughing eyes. Lucie liked him even before he told her that the 'dreadful woman' over in the corner had gotten really angry when he couldn't understand whatever language she was almost yelling at him.

Julia, whose elbows were suctioned tight against her sides, face pinched with resentment, (protective armor, game face) was pontificating at Jeffrey. Loudly. *She* also spoke French and unlike *some* people, knew how to handle these foreigners. Lucie and Didier watched in amazement as the woman seemed to expand upward and outward with self-importance, like Ursula in The Little Mermaid. As Didier's eyes widened, he turned dto Lucie and whispered, "Elle me fait peur."

She laughed and told him Julia had that effect on a lot of people; Didier was still chuckling when Madame Sautier approached them.

Because the Frenchwoman was trim in a simple black dress and her short hair was dyed a deep, rich auburn, she initially appeared younger than her husband. But when she smiled and took Lucie's hand, closer inspection revealed deep facial wrinkles and sags that put her in her eighties, as well.

She surprised Lucie by insisting that she address her as Marie-Françoise, a rare familiarity among the French. Then Lucie remembered her earlier reaction to Gérard – the feeling that they were connected on some psychic level – and figured he'd shared the experience with his wife.

Marie-Françoise thanked Lucie for her intervention and confided that her husband was extremely distraught about the behavior of their godson Gaston.

When M. Sautier joined them, Lucie explained the English part of what had occurred in the library, but with a slight spin to minimize the betrayal. Lucie apologized for any distress they felt and that she couldn't imagine why the "misunderstanding" had taken place.

But M. Sautier hung his head and said quietly that Gaston had not misunderstood, he had misrepresented. He looked up at his wife and then at Lucie. "Mais pourquoi? Je n'en comprends rien."

Lucie didn't understand the 'why' of it, either, and gently suggested that they use a lawyer she knew and trusted implicitly. She showed them the Montréal law firm's website, and after they'd perused the information in French, the Sautiers agreed to hire Giles and then notify their personal attorney of the change.

Suddenly Lucie's peripheral vision caught movement at the archway of the dining room and she swore she saw Roland fly by. In a dress! Then he did it again, in the opposite direction, like a porch chipmunk - one of those creatures who races by a human area, thinks better of it, and goes tearing back the way it came.

Lucie blinked and looked again. Kate, resplendent in a powder-blue pants outfit, appeared grandly where Roland had been, clearly pleased at being included. Phoebe came running in after her and the French, for whom dogs are right up there with food, wine and sex, lavished her with attention.

***

No one noticed when a scowling Julia oozed out of the dining room and down the hall, past the office, to the small bedroom. Its locked door seemed to quiver with the barrage of expletives being hurled from within: Gaston, who'd been forced to relinquish his clothes to an insistent John, was ranting. And had been for over an hour.

Julia tapped lightly on the door, then more forcefully, to be heard over the verbal onslaught. Gaston snarled through the barrier in French, and Julia answered in Franglais. Gaston yelled in English, "What the hell are you saying, whoever you are?"

Unperturbed, she bent down to peer through the keyhole and gasped, not realizing that her quarry would be mostly unclothed. Julia immediately pressed her eye further into the hole, watching the very small speedo-type brief turn round and round as its wearer waved his arms and continued to yell. Mesmerized, she murmured something about wanting to help...

***

Despite the language barrier, Didier was flirting shamelessly with Kate, who seemed to grow more youthful with every compliment. But M. Sautier, who suddenly looked every bit of his eighty years, politely excused himself for a rest.

Lucie left Kate and Didier to their own devices and hurried to the kitchen, where she found Mrs. Harris, Antonio and Jessica (still joined at the hip) and John, who informed them that he now preferred to be called Juan.

"We need to change out tonight's menu and somebody has to make a food run for me, ASAP." *Juan* immediately volunteered and departed as soon as Lucie handed him a list.

Lucie turned to the housekeeper: "My attorney friend who's doing us a favor is crazy about my Tournedos, so we're ditching the bifteck au poivre." Then she whispered, "Juan? But he isn't Hispanic."

"Go figure." Mrs. Harris shrugged as her cell phone rang. She listened for a moment, then handed it to Lucie. Max's voice asked softly, "Where are the Sautiers?"

"All tucked in, resting for dinner."

"Good. I'm bringing Laval out. Pass me back to Mrs. H please."

Mrs. Harris listened again and went to the house intercom to call Owen. Then she raised an eyebrow at Lucie: "Want to watch him leave?" Lucie grinned at her.

The two women moved stealthily to an alcove near the grand stairway as Max and Laval reached the front entrance, where Roland stood, looking official. Mrs. Harris whispered to Lucie, "I found him whimpering in the Salon and gave him some duties. He's really quite distraught over Jessica and Antonio, you know." Lucie looked into the older woman's face and saw compassion. Good for her, she thought. Her generation wasn't usually tolerant of alternative life styles.

The French lawyer, in a rage about being recalled to Paris, was ranting at Max when he suddenly sensed Lucie's presence. He spun around and, in an exact imitation of Jeffrey when he wanted the key to the wine cellar, snarled at her: "I do not know what you did, but I *know* it was you. Sale petite con! C'est pas fini entre nous. Je vais te..."

Caught off guard, Lucie's face flushed at the naked hate in the accusation and his use of the 'C' word. She stepped out of the shadow of the stairs and pointed at him, arm fully extended. Max had a quick vision of a sorceress about to cast a really nasty spell and fully expected a lightning bolt to shoot from her index finger.

She yelled "You miserable arrogant sonofa -" and then switched to French. "Salaud! Tu me débectes!"

Mrs. Harris tried to get Lucie to lower her arm-cum-weapon and finally managed to pull her toward the kitchen, but the death-ray glare she still held on Gaston never wavered. And Max had to literally drag the struggling man out into the driveway.

Lucie bypassed everyone in the kitchen and went outside to blow off steam, angry with herself for losing her temper. She paced until Max appeared and observed, "Piece of work, that Laval."

"Huhn."

"He threatened you, didn't he?"

"Yes, he did, but this is a job site and I shouldn't have sworn at him."

"At least you're really good at it."

Lucie made a face at him. "Do you know, that foul-mouth ratbastard called me a – a -"

"Well, whatever you yelled back at him, it sounded

really good in French." Max grinned.

Lucie flipped her eyebrows.

Max laughed and thought that it was a good thing she hadn't accosted the lawyer with her cutlery.

"He's lucky I wasn't near my knives."

Max's mouth dropped open. How'd she do that?

Lucie shot him a mental Gotcha and suddenly pointed toward the rear of the property. "You got any vegetables in your green house?"

"I do, but right now it's just tomatoes and the beginnings of squash."

"Beginnings?" She looked hopeful. "You mean, like big flowers? Do you think there might be, say, a dozen or so of them?"

"At least. Mother loves zucchini so we grow a lot of it." Then his eyes widened. "Please tell me you're going to stuff them for dinner; I love those things!"

Lucie grinned at his enthusiasm. "Just get me the flowers and you can have all the fleurs de courgette farcies you want."

As Max hurried across the lawn to his greenhouse, Lucie headed inside and thought about gardeners who were something else entirely, scary octopus accountants and fairytale-evil godsons. And wondered if the already-unbelievable day could possibly get any weirder.

CHAPTER 9

Turned out it could. Lucie had just turned into the kitchen archway when her peripheral vision registered movement. She glanced to her left and gasped: there stood Roland, dressed in full drag, looking like a demented Klinger from M*A*S*H, complete with a purse dangling from his arm. His makeup was garish and he was tugging miserably at a wig and then at his tight dress. He'd been trying to navigate the hallway in heels when he caught sight of Lucie and stopped.

She desperately wanted to pretend she didn't see him, but he was staring at her; so she grabbed his arm and steered him toward the unoccupied library, no easy feat because he was stumbling. She looked both ways to see if they'd been observed. So far, so good.

They both lurched into the room and Roland sat down in stages, unsure of the dress logistics. He started to say something, but wound up sobbing and snuffling. Lucie panicked and grabbed her cell phone to call Mrs. Harris, then reconsidered: the fewer people who saw the butler like this, the better. As she waited for Roland to get control of himself, though, she couldn't help squirming.

Roland suddenly stopped weeping, wiped his nose with his entire hand and extended it at her, pointing an accusation. Ugh, snot.

His speech jerky, the fake accent abandoned, he began, "You're – (snuffle) -just – going - (more snuffling) to make fun of me, like everyone else around here." He was clearly baiting her and Lucie ignored the remark. His eye makeup was now making dark streaks down his face and mingling with the snot, so she dug a tissue out of her pocket and warily extended it to him. And waited.

"No one understands and now he's taken up with that woman." He paused to swipe at his face with the tissue. "I want us to have a future together and – and - maybe now we can." He nodded and pointed to the dress, cupping his hands around the falsies he was wearing. Lucie stared at them. They were lopsided. Not much future there.

"Does wearing all that stuff feel right in there?" Lucie touched his chest in the vicinity of his heart, avoiding the falsies. "Do you feel more natural, more like yourself in those clothes?"

Instantly indignant, Roland pursed his lips. The British butler was back: "Of course nawt, don't be stupid!" Only it came out 'shtewpid.'

He continued to bite off his words: "This attire is intolerable. I cannot *imagine* why you females do it to yourselves, these shoes are absolutely sending waves of pain the whole way up my back, not to mention what they're doing to my feet!" Another tug at the wig restored his wretchedness and he rapidly shifted moods again, whimpering.

Lucie was getting a headache.

"But if this is what he wants..." Then Roland started to describe something physical and Lucie held up her hand. Way Too Much Information.

When she stood up, Roland challenged her in a petulant, teary voice, "You don't understand either, you're just all so judgmental."

Lucie couldn't let that one go by without comment and sat down reluctantly. She squinted at Roland, who was trying to fold his arms over his chest. The falsies were being problematic.

"This much I know, Roland, you didn't *choose* a lifestyle that brings so much criticism and grief, no one does. In school, nothing was quite right, was it? You wanted to fit in, you went through the motions but everyone had a prom date except you, everyone else found someone to start a family with, and you wanted all that, didn't you?"

Roland stared at her, unfolded his defiance, and allowed the quiet, jagged after-sobs. "How – how do you – know - that?"

Lucie shrugged and said, simply, "I have gay friends. Good friends, good people. It's not easy for them either." That was as far as she was willing to go with the conversation, so she stood up. She had no solutions, not that he wanted them from her anyhow.

"Come on, you've got to get out of this, um, outfit before Jeffrey or the French people see you. And you can't buttle in this condition, the new lawyer is due to arrive shortly." She pulled him up and marched him, wobbling on the high heels, to the door.

Lucie glanced down at his feet. "Besides, your shoes don't match the dress."

***

Giles arrived at dusk: tall, racquet-ball-fit for his sixty-eight years, silver-haired, charming, married Giles. A mover and a shaker in his day, the ability to move and shake occasionally resurrected. If properly motivated. In this case, not so properly, he'd pursued Lucie for years. But he was also the right man for the job because he would put M. Sautier at ease and the legalities would be perfect.

When Lucie reached the front entrance, Mrs. Harris and Max were already welcoming the lawyer. Giles spotted her, smiled with delight and pushed Max out of the way, ever so slightly. But the movement and its intent were not lost on Max, who frowned.

Giles planted a total of four kisses on Lucie's cheeks and hugged her. The male pheromones floated around her like a gauzy net, fragile but ready to ensnare. Even Mrs. Harris noticed the aura around Giles and seemed a little disconcerted. She was used to Max's straight-forward maleness, and the atmosphere in the entrance way was shifting to the disturbingly complex.

In his Canadian-French accented English, which most women found irresistible, he murmured, quite close to Lucie's ear, "How good it is too see you again, ma chérie. But why are we standing here when you could be accompanying me to my room? It is upstairs, non? Come, come."

As Giles took her by the elbow, Lucie felt helpless, as though a force of nature were propelling her swiftly and relentlessly up the stairs.

Max quickly grabbed the lawyer's suitcase and followed them, gritting his teeth in irritation at Giles, who kept touching Lucie. Then he heard Giles ask the location of Lucie's room and before she could answer, Max pushed in front of them and thudded the valise in Giles' room.

"Don't worry, Lucie, I'll take good care of Giles. You can get back to what you were doing."

To his surprise, Lucie looked relieved and was gone

in a second, leaving Max to wonder just what was going on between the two of them. This situation was really going to complicate things for him.

Great. Just...great.

***

The Sautiers, well rested, met Giles and decided to conclude the business of selling their winery without further delay. Clearly comfortable with the Canadian, they adjourned to the library with Jeffrey and Adam Cromby, and the sale of the estate got under way, unimpeded.

Meanwhile, Lucie was so totally focused on the meal she was preparing that she almost missed the squeak of the gate to the wine cellar. She turned her head, puzzled, then peered into the butler's pantry and saw the retreating figure of a woman. Lucie quietly followed her through the pantry, and watched as she quickly crossed the dining room and disappeared into the hallway. Lucie kicked off her clogs and ran to the archway, in time to see the figure lower what she'd been clutching to her chest: a basket of wine bottles. Then Lucie caught the woman's profile as she turned slightly. Julia! Well, well.

***

Proceedings in the library moved so quickly that there was hand shaking by 8:00pm, after which Max took Giles to the office to fax the legal documents to various destinations.

Lucie was putting the last touches on the meal when Max showed up in the kitchen, Cary Grant elegant in an expensive, well-fitted dark suit, deep blue shirt with French cuffs and classy gold cufflinks.

She stared. The laid-back gardener/dog wrangler was gone, permanently, she suspected. The man before her exuded confidence, and his handling of Laval suggested experience in taking decisive action. Perhaps Max was a Player, too?

He came over to her and *leaned,* that is he stood very close, bending proprietarily over her, and asked if she needed anything. Since the kitchen had become noticeably warmer in the last second or two, Lucie considered turning on the overhead fan, then reconsidered before he heard that thought.

She escaped to the dining room, where Mrs. Harris and Roland had successfully gathered the guests for apéritifs, and as Max sauntered by on the way to his seat, he turned his head slightly and winked at her.

Lucie gulped and turned her attention to Roland, who was now impeccably dressed and reassuringly snooty. He didn't acknowledge her presence, but she expected that: he had bared his soul to her, and was therefore vulnerable. He used what worked for him, a shield of haughtiness.

Then she checked the seating arrangements: in order, around the table, were the Sautiers, Didier, Kate, Julia, Jeffrey, Max, Giles, Adam Cromby and Margaret.

Adam, seated beside Giles, was not used to socializing with the amount of money represented at the table, and his nervousness manifested itself in a bouncing right leg, which vibrated his entire upper body. It first alarmed, then mystified Margaret, who watched him out of the corner of her eye. She asked if the reason for his affliction was that the End was coming. Cromby moaned and bounced harder.

Margaret was encouraged by the moan and babbled about the End of Days until she suddenly yelled "OH!" so loudly that several people dropped their cutlery with a clank.

An astonished look on her face, she blurted out "**I saw Jesus today!**"

The English speakers gaped at her as she continued: "There I was, having a little pick me up in the Salon - well maybe a few pick me ups - and he walked right by! And I'll just bet you didn't know he wears lipstick!"

Roland's face registered horror as she continued, "And his hair was fixed kind of funny, and come to think of it, his robe looked a bit odd with the high heels, but noooooo doubt about it, There-He-Was!" She slapped her hand down hard on the table for emphasis.

"So I waited for him to come back, I mean I had so many things to tell him, but I guess those martinis made me drowsy, anyhow when I looked around later, he was gone. And we're still here, so I suppose nothing really ended."

Giles, too dumbfounded to translate for the French, turned to Max for an explanation. Max opened his mouth but Julia got there first and snarled, "Oh put a sock in it, you old bat, you were probably delirious. What did you do, forget your meds again?"

Margaret thought about being indignant, but slugged back her apéritif instead. Kate and Didier, oblivious to the entire exchange, had fallen under the George/George Two language spell: communication didn't seem to be a problem.

***

Lucie 'had them' at the outset: fleurs de courgette farcies, served with a sparkling Argyle Brut. Giles tasted the delicate, fried zucchini blossoms stuffed with fresh sheep's milk cheese, looked deliriously happy and made ridiculously appreciative noises as he consumed one after another. When he made no move to share the dish, an annoyed Max distracted him, then whisked the platter out of his reach.

Next course, cannelloni stuffed with sole and spinach, baked in tomato and wine sauce, served with a Pinot Noir from the Russian River Valley. Then ratatouille, the fragrant French vegetable stew. Lucie was surprised when Marie-Françoise raved over it, because women from Provence rarely acknowledge anyone else's version of the dish.

Then the pièce de résistance: Tournedos Charlemagne, with Béarnaise sauce and mushrooms, served with souffléed potatoes.

Lucie had prepared the fillets of beef by roasting them gently, then slicing and reconstructing them with layers of cooked shallots and mushrooms. A Béarnaise sauce completed the exquisite dish, and Giles was ecstatic.

The accompanying wines were also spectacular, and to Max's relief, genuine. He had personally chosen several of his favorites: vintage bottles of Château Margaux and Château Palmer, and a 2003 Château Ducru-Beaucaillou from St. Julien.

A salade verte and fromages were de rigeur before the dessert - nougat ice cream with raspberry coulis - which was followed by coffee and a slow migration to the Grand Salon for after-dinner drinks. Except for a sloshed Margaret, who retired early.

Lucie followed in a few minutes, as was her custom, and chatted with the guests, graciously accepting compliments on the meal.

Max was leaning against the archway, watching her, when Jeffrey walked by. He stopped and followed Max's gaze to Lucie.

"We're going to have to do something about her: she's getting...**pushy**." The word, once he'd thought of it, shot out of his mouth and spittle landed on Max.

Max's attention didn't waver, in spite of the shower. "Look how she works the room, making everyone important. You can almost feel the positive energy." He turned to Jeffrey, who was giving him a bewildered look.

"Positive energy?"

"You could learn something from her, son." His attention returned to the room.

As Jeffrey frowned and slunk away to complain to Julia, Giles suddenly propelled Lucie toward the hall, telling her, "But you always wear the little black dress, ma petite Lucie." Then he shot Max a smug look and left them.

Lucie explained to a puzzled Max that her after-dinner schmoozing usually included a bit of a fashion show and that Giles had attended enough of her dinners to expect nothing less. And that although Lucie had politely protested, Giles was adamant.

She heaved a big sigh and shook her head as she started down the hall. "This is *not* going to end well."

Once in her suite, Lucie showered quickly and reluctantly slid into the black Armani dress. Very expensive and slightly provocative, it was cut in a deep V at the neckline, and was perfect for after-dinner conversation with the larger group of cosmopolitan professionals that Lucie had anticipated.

The right side of the dress, however, was the source of Lucie's predicament: the sleeve, see-through and trellised with black flowers and sparkly stones, led directly to the half of the bodice that was also diaphanous, and although beautiful flowers covered the essentials, it was obvious that a bare breast lurked directly underneath.

This dress, the only one she had with her, was going to cause *serious* problems.

***

Lucie tried not to make a grand entrance, but there was a collective intake of breath nonetheless. Adam Cromby's jaw dropped, followed by his coffee cup, Giles' expression turned instantly lascivious, and Max just stared.

She took a deep breath and approached M. Sautier, who was sipping his coffee. His eyes twinkled at her and, French to the core, he nodded approvingly at her attire.

Suddenly Lucie felt eyes boring into her back and turned slightly. Max had been running interference, shifting back and forth so that Giles couldn't get near her. He bent to her ear, his voice low and husky: "What are you playing at, wearing *that*?"

Lucie cut to the chase, since they both knew what he meant. "I didn't plan on Giles being here when I packed."

"But-" and then, as though they had been dancing, Giles cut in.

"Ah there you are, ma petite Lucie. It has been difficult to find you. Come, we must talk."

As he reached for her, he glared at Max.

Max glared back. A standoff. Lucie bolted for the bar, muttering, "I need a drink. A reeeaallllly big one."

Giles looked irritated, but Max turned away and grinned. Juan, the sous-chef formerly known as John, was mixing drinks and flinched when Lucie slapped her hands on the bar. "You got gin?"

His eyes widened and he nodded quickly.

"Pour me a double on the rocks, wave the tonic

over it and throw in a lime. And make it fast."

He did as he was told, dumping a lot of gin over the ice in a tall glass, but apparently not fast enough: Lucie grabbed the tonic, splashed it in the glass, leaned over the bar for a lime and jammed it into the ice. She seized the glass, turned and drained half of it. Juan raised his eyebrows.

Then she leaned back against the bar, both elbows resting on it, and let out a deep breath. This damned job was turning out to be a whole lot more than she had bargained for.

Just how much more, though, she was to discover in the next twenty-four hours.

❧ CHAPTER 10 ❧

Adam Cromby retreated into a corner: the palpable tension in the room frightened him almost more than his suspicion that he'd somehow messed up this big-money deal. If he had, Jeffrey would make his life miserable.

No one noticed as he slowly faded out of the room.

Lucie inhaled the rest of her drink and tried to think of a way to appease Giles without being seduced. Maybe more gin would help.

Half an hour passed and everyone was fairly well oiled, as Juan later described it to the staff. Giles had maneuvered Lucie onto a love seat and was leaning, pheromones working overtime. Lucie was trying for a courteous escape, not wanting to offend a friend who had graciously come to her aid on very short notice. Even though he did owe her the favor.

Giles, who had never pushed past a certain point, was now insistent. He pulled Lucie to her feet, nodding toward the hallway. Max, meanwhile, had been leaning backwards against the bar, his eyes riveted on Lucie. He'd just reached for his drink when Lucie, desperate to avoid a scene, pretended to drop something, turned slightly and shot him a look. The one he'd been waiting for.

Max immediately dug into his pocket with a grand sweeping gesture that no one missed and pretended to answer his cell phone. He had what looked like a short conversation, pocketed the phone and walked purposefully to the love seat.

He put one hand on Lucie's shoulder, moved his thumb half way up the back of her neck and, at the same time, bent close to her ear – gestures that were not lost on Giles. "Good thing I keep my cell on vibrate: your daughter just called, said your phone is turned off, and needs some advice about an inadequate caterer she got stuck with." He smiled at her and brushed her cheek lightly with his lips.

Lucie, astonished by the story Max concocted and unnerved by the intimacy, stared at him. Max pretended to remove a speck from the side of her face, his fingers lingering a few seconds too long to be confused with mere grooming. Lucie vaguely noticed an 18 Kt. gold bracelet dangling from his wrist, sparkles of light shooting from it like the myriad of tiny shocks that were zapping through her body.

"You'd better call her back, she's about to strangle some poor slob. Excuse us, Giles," he smiled, steering Lucie out of the dining room.

Max hoped she'd wait until they were in the hall to retaliate, and sure enough, Lucie motioned him down to her level. But instead of slugging him, she whispered, "That was perfect, he thinks Sophie has your cell number, that you and she are close, and that we're - "

She stopped suddenly at the implication and Max straightened up quickly. And winced.

But Lucie surprised him again when she sighed deeply and said, "Oh man, it almost got to DEFCON 2 in there. Thanks." He let out the breath he was holding.

"Is he always like this around you?"

"Pretty much. Ever since I met him at McGill. He's married, but very French when it comes to having mistresses."

"And you're not...."

"Of course I'm not." Slightly indignant. "And besides, it's way too complicated."

"Complicated how?" Max needed to know.

She turned to him. "He's got a very nice wife, kids, grandkids, the whole nine yards. Plus I'm probably the only woman his wife trusts."

"And if she didn't?"

"Wouldn't make any difference." Really indignant. "Hey, I do **not** sleep around to advance my career. What kind of person do you think I am?"

He answered the question by pushing her against the wall and, before she could object, kissing her passionately. It was all he could do to keep his hands off the flowers on her dress, so he framed her face with them instead. As he pressed his entire body against hers and used his tongue to gently separate her lips, Lucie felt herself spiraling out of control. Her arms flapped, she moaned, then pushed him away. Slowly.

She gulped as Max leaned into her again and said softly, "That was practice." His lips brushed her ear as he continued, "We need to convince Giles." Lucie was breathing heavily. Damn. As if things in the Grand Salon weren't complicated enough.

We. The word hung in the air between them. Before, it had only meant 'us against Laval.' Now, the word was imbued with body heat. Max's mouth had left no doubt that he wanted her in his bed, but as appealing as that idea was, her gut was telling her that Serious Involvement was imminent. And getting tangled up in a relationship was not what she intended for this part of her life.

Michael suddenly flashed into her brain. He and Lucie had a quid pro quo arrangement, straight up, no complications. It involved both business and bed, just what she'd needed after the last divorce.

But Michael never drove her crazy, and now cool and elegant Lucie Richards was really hot and bothered. She was staring at Max again and he had to pull her back toward the Salon.

"Come on, you have to pretend to return the call. You don't have your cell on you, do you?" He looked her up and down and realized what a dumb question that was, since there was absolutely nowhere to hide anything in that dress. Lucie's face reddened: because he could read minds, she was pretty sure he also had x-ray vision.

He handed her his phone and said, "Just stand outside here and I'll hover. You know, the male possessive thing." Lucie pretended to talk, then ended the 'conversation', nodding to include him. Max put his arm around her again and they strolled back into the Salon, laughing about a non-existent situation with a daughter he knew little about.

Juan was confused. All of a sudden, Lucie and the boss were acting like lovers! But that would mean the staff grapevine, that most impeccable source of information, was in error. And it never was. Juan grinned. This was going to be good.

He made a surreptitious call on his cell and in moments Roland appeared in the Salon, on the pretext that something just had to be delivered to the bar. Trying to look inconspicuous, he mingled with the guests, but was inexorably drawn to Giles; Roland, the impressionable sphere, was locked in a holding position and unable to break the tractor beam.

Mrs. Harris finally intervened and physically

dragged him away, whispering, "For heaven's sake, what's the matter with you?"

When she returned, she quickly scanned the room and noticed Julia. Julia, whose large body was rigid and who was staring at Max and Lucie with dead shark eyes.

Meanwhile, Max had amped up the male possessive thing, Giles had begun a serious sulk and Lucie decided she was weary of dealing with the overabundance of testosterone in the room. Time to put a wrap on the day.

She made her way over to the Sautiers, to bid them goodnight, and the Frenchman beamed: "Ah voilà, la petite Lucie et Monsieur Max." His wife nodded at both Lucie and Max, smiling benignly. Lucie half expected them to pronounce a blessing. What the hell?

She smiled back uncertainly, not sure what she had done to warrant the approval. Ok, so she had ingested an enormous amount of gin for a little person and was still clear-headed. Maybe that was it. The French admire that sort of prowess.

No matter, in a few hours Giles would depart, the French would depart and Lucie could get back to her real life in Boston, far away from the loonies. And Max. This was a most interesting interlude, but that's all it was.

When Lucie realized that M. Sautier was talking about a gift he wanted to present to her tomorrow, she was again overwhelmed by an inexplicable sense of familiarity with the elderly Frenchman.

She was about to comment when Julia shoved her way into the group, got a close look at Lucie's dress, glowered at Max and snarled, "Well we'll just see about that." She yanked at her jacket and spun around, knocking into Max as she stomped out of the room.

Everyone stared at her retreating mass.

"What just happened?"

No one answered and Mrs. Harris shot Max a deep, inscrutable look, then left the room in a hurry.

Lucie's eyes widened and she whispered to Max, "I can't believe I forgot to tell you: Julia's the one who's been stealing your wine!"

Max's jaw dropped. "Don't move, I'll be right back." He checked on Giles' whereabouts – he was deep in conversation with Kate and Didier – and ran out of the room.

When Lucie turned back to the Sautiers, Jeffrey snapped at her, "I want you to translate for me." He adopted an imperious tone with Gérard and bragged outrageously about an imagined business acumen. Lucie gagged and completely altered the text of the translation. That both parties appeared pleased at the conclusion led her to reflect that perhaps U.N. interpreters should do likewise: maybe there'd be fewer armed conflicts. Nah, there'd always be some idiot who would rat out the translators. So much for world peace.

The Sautiers wished everyone a good night and Lucie swiftly scanned the room for Max. She hated to admit it, but she was depending on him to get her out of the room and upstairs, well, safely.

Giles, who had unobtrusively moved close enough to hear her translating for Jeffrey, started to laugh. "That was quite a rendition you gave Gérard, ma chérie. Are you not worried that Jeffrey will find out what you did?"

Aha, the rat at the U.N.

"Well Giles, the only way he'd find out is if you told him, isn't it?"

Giles hovered. And leaned. "Ah, mais ma petite, there is a price for my silence." Pheromones wafted about, pervasive and compelling. Lucie braced herself.

Suddenly Max appeared out of nowhere and put his arm around her waist. He told Giles, "Excuse us for a moment" and twirled her into the dining room. "Julia has pretty much disappeared, but Mrs. Harris is still looking for her, and we both agree she's been acting really weird."

"She's acting *possessive*, Max. Over you."

"What?"

Max suddenly looked very uncomfortable.

They were interrupted by the sound of the elevator in the far corner, and a voice saying, "Not now, Phoebe." Lucie and Max watched as Phoebe was gently tossed out of the elevator and Kate and Didier rose to the upper level. A disappointed Phoebe snorted and came trotting over to them.

Max chuckled and shook his head. "Mother's a pip, isn't she?"

Lucie grinned at the disappearing elevator. "Good for you, Kate. Carpe diem."

Suddenly Giles was heading their way with a bottle of wine and two glasses. Max looked alarmed and spoke quickly: "Lucie, that lech has to believe that you'll be in my bed tonight." He paused to see what effect those words would have on Lucie, who twitched violently. "Otherwise, he'll be all over you. So we'll make a big deal about going upstairs together and when the coast is clear, you can sneak back across the hall."

Lucie looked skeptical.

"What? It'll work, trust me."

She didn't want to insult him by telling him it was the getting-out-of-his- bedroom part that she was skeptical about.

Giles sidled up to Lucie. "Ah there you are! I seem to be saying that very often this evening, ma petite Lucie. Shall we share a nightcap?"

Max answered for her: “We’d love to, but (he faked a yawn) I think we’re just going to turn in.” He turned to Lucie. “Oh and remember, Sophie wanted to talk again tonight before you- we- go to bed.”

Giles narrowed his eyes ever so slightly. He’d caught the ‘you.’

But Lucie was too tired to care, tired from the impossibly long day and tired of the game. Phoebe apparently was, too, and started to bark. Lucie reached down and scooped up the tiny fur ball.

“I agree, Phoebes.” She made a motion with her head at Max and led the way up the back stairway. When they reached Max’s rooms, he opened the door for her and she turned to Giles with a thin smile. “Bonne nuit, Giles, dors bien.”

Giles frowned and slowly trudged down the hall to his own suite. The wine glasses and bottle clanked with increasing intensity as he neared his rooms, and Max responded by making a big, noisy deal out of sequestering Lucie and Phoebe in his suite. Then he put his ear to the door.

Lucie truly was exhausted and sat down immediately on a couch, leaning back with her little buddy. Max frowned and said, “I didn’t hear his door close.”

“Damn.”

“I know.” But he didn’t sound all that upset.

Lucie stretched out on the couch and stroked Phoebe, who promptly fell asleep. She yawned and suggested, “Peek out in the hall to make sure.”

Max thought for a moment, took off his shoes and opened the door. He put them in the hall, as though he expected someone to shine them, and glanced to the left. Sure enough, there was Giles, leaning against the wall outside his suite, wine bottle on the floor and wine glass in his hand. Suspicious bastard.

Max gave him a little wave and nodded, then shut the door. He leaned against it and looked at Lucie, who was fighting to stay awake.

"I'd find a chair if I were you, this could take a while. Giles is relentless." She yawned again, then observed, "You know what, Gaston is a pirate, and not in the good sense of the word."

"What?" He frowned as he dragged a chair to the door. "What's a good pirate?"

"I said the good sense of the *word*. TV and movie pirates are basically cool, but Gaston is the rapacious kind. He's got an agenda that he was willing to risk his career for, and you need to find out what that is."

She raised an eyebrow at him. "You have connections, right?" Lucie had been thinking about Max's "government" career that no one seemed to know much about.

Max ignored the insinuation. "I'll make some inquiries. But why are we talking about pirates?"

"Because of Gaston - you need to keep up. And because pirates are everywhere, perpetrating cons, hustles, intricately-planned heists. Think about the 'Ocean's' movies, those all involve modern forms of pirates. Then there's the ultimate, beyond cool pirate, Captain Jack Sparrow."

Max looked confused. "What is it with you and pirates? Were you ever involved with one?"

"Of course not." Lucie managed a sleepy grin. "But come to think of it, I sorta got to be a pirate in the second marriage."

Max blinked.

"The sonofabitch died before the divorce papers were filed and I got everything, including a pile of money from a life insurance policy I knew nothing about. The idiot bought it for that bimbo half his age and listed my name as beneficiary because he didn't want our insurance agent to know he was diddling his secretary." She made a 'and that's what happens when men think with their dicks' face.

Max raised his eyebrows. He thought about her cutlery and involuntarily put his hand on his throat.

"Died?"

"What? **I** didn't kill him. Geez, what is it with you people around here?"

"Ok, so he died of something else entirely and you wound up, uh, fairly well off?" Max tried for a surprised look.

"Yeah, I -" Lucie suddenly squinted at Max. "Please. I'm so tired I can't see straight and I can still tell you're putting me on. You don't have to ask about my net worth because you ran a background check on me."

Max looked startled, then sheepish at being caught out. "It's just that I like to know who I'm dealing with."

Lucie changed gears abruptly and stared at him. "You got a tattoo?"

Max blinked again, then grinned: if he were ever lucky enough to spend a lot of time with this intriguing, slightly off-center woman, he would never, ever be bored.

"No, but I'm beginning to wish I did. Maybe then I'd understand this conversation."

"It's simple. I like pirates." Lucie's eyes were closing. Her last thought was that it was probably a bad idea to sleep so close to Maxxxxxxx...

Max continued to sit by the door, listening. He felt ridiculous, but if he didn't protect Lucie, Giles would have her. Giles and his damned, whatever it was that was drove all the women - and Roland – crazy.

Five minutes later, Max heard Giles' door open, then bang shut. He turned to Lucie, whispering, "It's all clear, you can –" But both females were sound asleep on the couch. He considered that the expensive dress should not be slept in, but the thought of how she'd react if he tried to undress her made him reduce his concern to a blanket for the two of them.

Max stroked Lucie's hair lightly, kissed little Phoebe on her head and as he watched them sleep, murmured, "When you do come to my bed, ma petite Lucie, it will be because you want to be there, not because you're hiding from someone."

CHAPTER 11

Most of Phoebe was asleep on Lucie when Max whispered, "Want to go outside?" The little dog immediately used Lucie as a launch pad, startling her. She yelled and fell off the couch with a thud, entangling herself in the blanket.

"Sonofabitch, I hurt my elbow!"

"My, my, aren't we cranky this morning?"

Lucie raised her head and glared at him. Max was wearing the firstday-whenBrunosatonher shitty grin and a big white bathrobe. She blinked herself awake, remembered last night's heat between them and looked around as fragments of a dream came back to her. She squinted. Was it a dream or did they - ?

Max raised one eyebrow. Uh oh. He heard that one. Best get moving.

She groaned as she fought her way out of the blanket, hoping the couture dress was intact, and pulled herself to a sitting position.

Max was still grinning as he extended the mug he was holding. "Coffee?"

Lucie frowned at him as she took it.

"Not a morning person?"

"One more question and you're going to start losing

body parts." She noted that he'd added cream to the coffee. So he was observant in addition to being annoying.

"Probably you're just hung over."

"No, I am not. Did I seem drunk to you last night?"

He conceded, "Well, no." He tilted his head. "You know, for a small person, you have an amazing capacity for booze."

"You going somewhere with all this?"

More grinning. "Good news is, you look as though you had a hard night. That'll *really* convince Giles." Lucie growled and looked around for something to throw at him. Her glance fell upon a table lamp.

Max ducked into the bathroom as he pointed out, "That was not another question."

Lucie sipped her coffee until she heard him singing in the shower - way, way too much cheeriness. She got up and quietly opened the door of the suite.

The coast was clear, so she hurried across the hall, and, minutes later, was enjoying a hot shower. When she heard a knock on the bathroom door, she shouted, loudly enough to be heard over the water, "That had better be Phoebe."

"Uh, well, no, it isn't, there's a message and Phoebes has a hard time with messages. I knocked on your bedroom door and no one answered."

He could almost hear the Duh.

Max raised his voice and spoke very slowly and distinctly. "I'll meet you in the dining room for breakfast, and don't worry, Antonio's taking care of it. He's in a really good mood this morning." Then he muttered, "Unlike some people." She turned off the water.

"Did you open the door?"

"How else was I supposed to talk to you?"

"And now you're standing in my bathroom, while I'm in the shower.

"But I can't see anything."

"You got a death wish or something?" She peered around the shower curtain in time to see the door slam shut.

***

For her last day at the château, Lucie decided on a soft azure blue outfit in another lighter-than-air cashmere blend, the V neckline providing a frame for the larimar pendant she wore. The monochromatic pants somewhat elongated her figure and the color enhanced her eyes, so she was feeling pretty good about herself when she reached for her makeup.

She was applying a mineral foundation when her peripheral vision caught movement in the shower curtain, and the thought of Max hiding in there shot through her brain. She jerked her head, caught the edge of her eye with the brush, and it flew out of her hand. With the one good eye, she saw Phoebe hop out of the bathtub.

"And what were you doing in there?" But the little dog was already scurrying off somewhere.

Lucie was still blinking as she made her way down the back staircase to the dining room, speculating about how far away Max could be and still read her mind. It turned out to be difficult, doing both at once. She missed one of the steps, uttered a few expletives, stumbled into the hallway, and limped into the dining room. She found Max sitting in front of a huge, brightly-colored platter of huevos rancheros, a pile of croissants, a pitcher of orange juice and a bowl of fruit. Phoebe sat beneath him, waiting for dropped food.

He looked up, mouth full, and peered at her. "Arouinkingame?"

"What? Why would I be wink - No I am *not* winking at you."

"En whyrybrinking?"

"I am blinking because my makeup is supposed to go Swirl Tap Buff, but it went Swirl Tap Fling instead and I poked my eye – oh never mind."

"Here, have a seat. You'll feel better if you eat something." He pulled out the chair next to him. "Want orange juice?"

Lucie nodded, and as he poured a glass for her, Antonio, smartly dressed in chefs' whites, appeared with coffee. He beamed at them as the French couple had last night. What was that about?

They ate in silence and were sipping coffee when Max suddenly moved his chair closer, almost landing a leg of it on her foot.

"Hey, watch it!"

"Smile, darlin, it's Giles." He had that amused look on his face again as he leaned over and put his arm on the back of her chair, enveloping her in the arc of his body. Possessive without touching.

As Max put his mouth near her ear and pretended to talk to her, a hint of his scent, Jean Paul Gaultier's Le Male, invaded her libido, bringing with it the memory of that kiss. Lucie barely noticed when Giles sat down beside her.

"Eh bien, Lucie, it is morning and here you are, with Monsieur Max. And yet, you wear my favorite color! What is a man to think?" He shrugged, but his eyes twinkled mischievously.

Max didn't get a chance to tell him what to think because Roland suddenly sailed into the room, Antonio and Juan following in his wake, with more food. Giles turned his attention to the platters in front of him as Kate and Didier appeared, hand in hand, then a scowling Jeffrey, then the Sautiers, smiling last night's smiles at Lucie.

When Max pointedly asked Jeffrey where Julia had gotten to, he snapped that he wasn't her keeper, so how should he know? He piled a plate high with food, and as he stood to leave, mumbled something about Owen taking her into the city earlier.

Max stared at Jeffrey for a second, assessing. His expression was shrewd and focused, a game face. Jeffrey had just reached the doorway when he turned to glare at his grandmother and Didier, causing a croissant to fly off the top of his breakfast mountain.

He snarled, "Really, Gladys, at *your* age?" And stomped out, dispersing a trail of eggs and fruit that delighted Phoebe, who had already pounced on the croissant.

Max apologized for Jeffrey's incredible lack of manners, but Kate dismissed it with a wave of her hand and announced, "We need your help, Lucie."

She extended several sheets of paper across the table and said, "We tried an online translator this morning, but it doesn't seem to know what we meant."

Lucie smiled and told her that those translations were too often literal and produced skewed results. As she checked over the correspondence of people who were sitting right next to each other, she thought how remarkable it was that they had figured out a way to try to tell each other about their childhoods, marriages, children, disappointments and a few health issues.

"Oh, and I asked Didier here if he could stay on a few days, we've been having such a lovely time, you know, and he might have agreed but I couldn't tell. Which is why you need to stay, too, and translate for us!"

Lucie spoke quietly with Didier, who smiled and nodded at Kate, who squealed with delight.

Max saw his opportunity and said loudly, "You know, Lucie that is an excellent idea, you really should stay a few extra days." Then he bent down to her ear, shot a look over at Giles and whispered, "FYI, you're wearing *my* favorite color."

Lucie wondered if the gulp were audible. She heard herself saying, "I think I'm clear until the middle of next week but I'd have to call my business manager to make sure" before she could stop herself.

She was doing a mental head slap when Giles reminded Max that he needed a ride to the airport. Gérard reminded Lucie that he had a gift for her. Mrs. Harris appeared and reminded Max that Owen had not returned from taking Julia into the City. And that he wasn't answering the phone in the limo, a cause for concern.

***

Giles needed to leave the château within the hour to make his flight, but the Sautiers were not scheduled to depart until the afternoon and had requested a packed lunch so they wouldn't have to eat the 'dreadful airplane food.'

Lucie's quick call to her business manager confirmed that she was free until the middle of next week, and she'd just slipped an apron over her outfit when Max materialized so suddenly it was as though someone had beamed him up. He startled Lucie, who smacked him. "What the – stop sneaking up on me!"

Max was clearly agitated and began to pace in front of the refrigerator. "I'm sneaking? Sorry, didn't mean to. Thing is, I have a bad feeling about Julia and I can't find Owen anywhere. He still hasn't called in and that's never happened before, so I'm going to take Giles to the airport myself."

"Anything you want me to do here?"

"Got your cell on you?"

Lucie handed him the phone, and as his thumbs flew over the keypad, he told her, "My number's under 'Max', and I'd appreciate a call if you see Julia or Owen."

He slid the phone back in her pocket and left as quickly as he'd arrived.

***

Lucie was packing up the Sautiers' lunch when her cell phone rang and Mrs. Harris informed her that Giles was ready to depart.

He smiled when Lucie met him at the front door, and when she reached up to kiss him goodbye, he wrapped her in his cloak of pheromones as he wordlessly signaled to her that things were pleasantly not finished with them. Uh huh, relentless.

She pulled back and told him pointedly to say hello to his wife for her. Giles shook his head, laughing, and quoted a French proverb about the more things change, the more they stay the same.

He was through the door when Max turned to Lucie, grinned and winked. Lucie headed back toward the kitchen and shook her head: probably Max was relentless, too.

She'd just reached the Salon when Kate popped her head out of the archway and grabbed her by the hand, pulling her into the room. "The Sautiers want to see you, my dear."

Gérard smiled and pointed at a sofa, where a shopping bag rested. He explained that they'd waited until Giles had left, their gift being of a personal nature; they liked Giles well enough, but were so very pleased that Lucie had decided to remain with Monsieur Max.

Lucie looked astonished, threw up her hands in protest and shook her head vehemently. Oh no no no, she told them, last evening and this morning were just a charade, a convenient means of avoiding an embarrassing situation with Giles!

The Sautiers looked from one to the other, puzzled. "Mais Lucie, c'est évident depuis notre arrivée!" That provoked a broad smile from Didier and a choking noise from Lucie.

They'd said '*It* was obvious since they arrived.' *IT*? What ***IT?***

"But -"

Oh yes, they said, and they were just delighted that she and Max were 'together' and what a handsome couple they made and were any children prévus?

Lucie made a strangled noise and half fell onto the sofa. Kate sat down beside her, wanting to know what was wrong, and as Lucie squeaked out an explanation, the older woman chuckled. Then she gave Lucie a penetrating look that made her blink several times.

Gérard beckoned to her, so Lucie shook it off and stood up. He took both of her hands and gazed intently into her eyes, searching her face as he had when they'd first met. Suddenly the elderly Frenchman addressed her as 'petite-fille.' Lucie gasped, reeling from the second shock in mere minutes: the elderly Frenchman had called her 'granddaughter!" Her Weird Shit list was getting longer by the second.

Lucie stood there, stunned, as Sautier pulled what looked like an old shoebox from the shopping bag and handed it to her proudly. It *was* an old shoe box.

As he clasped his hands together in front of him, he beamed at his wife and embarked on a little speech.

"Ça, c'est pour toi, Lucie. Notre cadeau contient un héritage, et nous sommes absolument certains que tu le comprendras, et le trouveras." He smiled happily and his wife nodded an approval.

Lucie was totally mystified. She removed the lid to see what sort of "legacy" the gift contained, and found old postcards. On closer inspection, they were actually very old, from World War I. The Great War. The War to End All Wars. If only.

She looked up. She was positive it wasn't a joke, but what could this possibly be about? "Je vous remercie, Gérard et Marie-Françoise, mais..."

The 'but' led the Frenchman to explain that because they had no children of their own, the gift had been intended for Gaston, who was no longer worthy of it. Gérard stopped, stared into Lucie's eyes again, and said that he was certain she understood why they felt compelled to give her what had once belonged to his father.

Lucie felt uneasy, then a little creeped-out: not only did she *not* understand his conviction that, on some level, she was family, she also could not explain her own flash of recognition the day before.

She was about to unleash an avalanche of questions when Jeffrey suddenly marched into the Salon and snarled at her.

"I've been looking for you everywhere. What are you doing about lunch?" He glared at Lucie, then noticed the shoebox. "What's that?"

"A gift from the Sautiers." No more. He wouldn't have understood anyway, since Lucie barely did.

Jeffrey made a face and then quickly erased it, remembering too late that although the Sautiers didn't speak English, they did read faces. He'd barely rearranged his expression when Julia, in full gale force, burst into the room.

Lucie groaned. Another encounter of the rude kind.

Julia shoved Jeffrey aside and demanded, "What's going on here!? In this household, business meetings are held with *me*, not that woman." She pointed at Lucie. "She is nothing but temporary help!"

When Julia placed her hands on her hips and glowered at everyone in the room, Lucie envisioned a posse of flying monkeys.

Everyone but Lucie took a step backward.

She tucked the shoebox under her arm and said, calmly, "Takc it down a notch, Julia. There's no meeting, we're just talking."

Julia shrieked at her, "*You belong in the kitchen and nothing else is any of your concern and I think you are -* "

Lucie gritted her teeth and pointed her index finger at her. "You need to work on your people skills, and FYI, I'm over forty." She raised her eyebrows. "I don't give a rat's ass what you think of me."

Julia fixed a death ray-glare on Lucie, and Kate, frowning, told her, "That's quite enough Julia, you need to leave, right now."

But Julia's gaze slid down to the shoebox and she breathed, "Well, well, well, what have we here? Something that should belong to a member of this household?"

Jeffrey sniveled, "It's what they (tilting his head sideways at the Sautiers) gave her."

Julia didn't hesitate. She had both hands on the box and would have wrenched it out of Lucie's grasp had Didier not jumped forward and seized one of her wrists, giving it a sharp twist. He must have squeezed hard, because Julia yelped and let go, turning to him in fury.

He stared right back at her as Kate clapped him on the back, whooping, "Well done, mon Didier!," and kissed him loudly on the cheek. The old man straightened his back and held his head up proudly.

Suddenly Mrs. Harris appeared out of nowhere, grabbed an enraged Julia by the elbow and shoulder and propelled her out of the room, pausing to glance at Lucie and make a phone out of her thumb and little finger.

Lucie nodded and, noting the worried expression on M. Sautier's face, assured him that she would be keeping their gift quite safe from now on.

Before she returned to the kitchen, Lucie slipped into a powder room, placed the shoebox squarely on the commode seat, flushed and called Max on her cell.

"Julia's back, behaving really badly, Mrs. Harris is with her, but I didn't see Owen yet. I don't know what she did with him. To him."

Max made a face and held the phone away from his ear, staring at it. "What's that noise?"

"Running water, so no one hears me.

"What?"

"I flushed the commode to make noise."

"Where *are* you?"

"I'm in the downstairs powder room by the kitchen."

As Max rolled his eyes, Lucie heard something buzzing.

"What's that noise?"

"Bees, lots of bees."

"What? Oh never mind, listen, the point is, Julia just did her Wicked Witch impersonation and scared the hell out of the Sautiers, and she's way too interested in what they gave me."

"What'd they give you?"

"It's a long story. Did Giles make his flight?"

"I stayed until he boarded."

Lucie laughed silently.

"I heard that."

Lucie flushed again.

Max groaned. "Please stop doing that. Probably no one can hear you in there anyway." He raised his voice over the gurgling water. "Um, hold on a minute, I have to go."

"What?"

"All that running water."

"Oh."

Lucie waited patiently for a few moments, then hung up and redialed to leave a message. 'Check on Julia's bank account, if you have the resources I think you have. She's made substantial money on your wine and you need to know if it's going anywhere.' Lucie had just picked up the box of cards when she was startled by a burst of barking.

She opened the powder room door and looked down; tiny Phoebe immediately pushed past her and lunged for the toilet paper, but Lucie had anticipated the move. Shoebox tucked under one arm, she adroitly picked up the little dog with the other, promising her a non-paper treat as she headed for the kitchen.

In the hallway, she encountered Didier and Kate, who half-whispered to her, "Didier here has been trying to tell me about your, um -" She glanced down with a dubious cxpression – "*gift,* and I can't make out what he's saying. I don't want to hurt his feelings, but, oh my, it's an odd thing to give a person, isn't it!"

Lucie smiled, released Phoebe and related the little she knew about it. She let them poke at the postcards, which only resulted in baffling Kate further. Didier, however, nodded energetically, assuring Lucie that the legacy was, indeed, a thing of great value. Family stories about it had circulated for decades.

Kate shrugged and remarked that the Sautiers must think very highly of Lucie, despite the appearance of the 'gift.'

***

Suddenly an idea flashed into Lucie's brain and she called Mrs. Harris. "You still have Julia with you?"

The housekeeper sounded angry. "No, that lunatic got away from me."

"Hunh. Mrs. Harris, you got any idea why she has a permanent bug up her ass?"

"There's something you should know about Julia, if you haven't already guessed." Mrs. Harris spoke for another minute, then disconnected.

Lucie mulled over the information as she pulled leftover fillet and souffléed potatoes out of the frig, heated them gently so as not to overcook the medium-rare steak, and grabbed a bottle of water.

She found Owen in the driveway just outside the large garage. It had drizzled earlier, and she figured that if he were on the premises, he'd be washing the limo. Sure enough, he was rubbing the vehicle with a chamois cloth, occasionally stopping to wave his arms around and raise his voice to no one, then back to the familiar task that would calm him down. It didn't take a genius to see that he was agitated.

Lucie waited until he stepped back from the car to check on his progress, then ahemed and said, "Thought you might be hungry."

Owen jerked his head toward her, panic on his face.

Lucie calmly sat on the stone wall that bordered

the driveway and put the plate on it, motioning him over.

He must have been ravenous, because the food disappeared quickly. Then, in what had to have been a rare moment of camaraderie, Owen sat down beside her.

"Thanks ma'am. I was real hungry. She wouldn't let me stop for food."

Lucie smiled and waited.

"She wouldn't let me call in, either. Told her there'd be trouble over that and you know what she said to me?" He turned to Lucie, an incredulous look on his face. He mimicked Julia's high, thin voice: "'Do you know how much trouble I can bring to your door?' Ma'am, I don't even have a door - I don't live here!"

Lucie stifled a laugh and tried to look sympathetic. It worked.

"Where did she make you take her?"

He screwed up his face in concentration.

"Well, she had this big tote bag thing and I could tell it was real heavy. She took it to one of those big apartment buildings with a guard out front and when she came back, she didn't have it. Then we went to her bank but she wasn't in there long. That's when she wouldn't let me eat. " He frowned.

Owen got up to finish polishing the car, then suddenly turned. "I almost forgot - she got back in the car and made a big deal about how she had to make a private phone call and that I should mind my own business and then she put up the shield to the back seats. But I was real mad about no breakfast and no lunch, so I left the intercom on and she didn't even notice." He rubbed the back of his neck with the effort at remembering.

"She looked at a piece of paper and punched a lot of numbers into her cell phone and talked for a while.

I heard her say 'winery', and something like 'We'll file,' and then 'declared.' And..." Owen squinted in concentration. "I think she said 'senile' and I heard, 'that damned chef.' OH!" He looked up, eyes wide. "Ma'am, I'm sorry, but that's what she said."

"That's ok, Owen." Lucie mentally filed away another shot she owed Julia.

"I can't remember much after that, but I think she said something about making another call tonight."

Owen scratched his head, totally perplexed.

"That's very good, Owen. Mr. Max and Mrs. Harris won't be at all happy with Julia."

Owen smiled shyly, clearly relieved. "No, ma'am, they will not." He picked up the chamois and started to hum.

Lucie picked up the empty plate and stood, pondering Julia's bizarre behavior: her over-the-top reaction to Lucie's imaginary romance with Max, her rage-driven agenda that included wine theft on a grand scale, and now, something sinister involving Gérard.

She returned to the kitchen to find Antonio making a quick lunch for the staff. When she asked if Max had returned, he shook his head.

Lucie frowned and called Max's cell. No answer. Odd.

Why couldn't he materialize when she needed him?

CHAPTER 12

The Sautiers were already packed and waiting for Owen to transport them when Lucie delivered the lunch she'd prepared for their journey. She hugged them goodbye, reluctantly: the deep connection she felt with the French couple made parting difficult.

Owen appeared on schedule, resplendent in his chauffeur's uniform, hat tucked ceremoniously under his arm. As he carried the luggage to the limo, he told Lucie that Julia had left in a hurry, taking one of the cars reserved for the permanent staff. Without asking. A silent, 'See, she's at it again' message passed between them.

When she returned to the kitchen, she ran smack into Antonio, who babbled, "¡Mira chef, who could have done this terrible thing, Madre de Dios! I only left for a moment!"

Lucie gazed in horror: someone had the cojones to dump all her knives into the garbage can, and leave the lid off to make the desecration visible!

She bellowed, 'SONOFABITCH' in a decibel that sent Antonio scurrying to the displaced cutlery. "Don't touch them!" flattened him against the wall, where he remained: Lucie, anger and her knives were a dangerous combination.

Glowering, she took out her phone, called Mrs. Harris and asked her to check her suite for damage. While she waited for a reply, she extracted, then lovingly and carefully cleaned each knife, removing the contamination they'd suffered as quickly as possible.

When she finished, she took several deep breaths, turned to Antonio, and explained, "It had to be Julia. Owen said she's gone, left in a hurry."

"But why?"

Lucie went over to the double oven and opened the bottom one, extracted the box of postcards and showed Antonio. "Because she couldn't find this."

He raised one eyebrow skeptically.

"Yeah, I know. But the Sautiers seem to think it's valuable, and I guess Julia does, too."

Moments later, Mrs. Harris called. "Sorry, Lucie, she got to your suite; my guess is she couldn't find the gift there, so she went after your knives out of spite. You have your laptop with you? It's not here."

"It's been in the library since the meeting. Wait a minute – *my dress*!" Panicked, Lucie had shrieked. The Armani was her absolute favorite, had cost a fortune, and besides, she'd already lost a pair of Jimmy Choos on this job.

"Not to worry, this morning I sent it down to the laundry to have it freshened, so it's safe and now we're tidying things here."

She let out the breath she was holding. "Thanks, Mrs. H, I owe you."

***

Lucie retrieved her laptop and hid it in the bottom oven with the postcards, then went to look for Max.

She found Kate and Didier having martinis in the dining room, politely turned down their offer of a drink and told them, in vivid detail, about the desecration of her knives and what she'd like to do to Julia.

Kate nodded and was in the middle of an extended TskTsk when she caught movement out of the corner of her eye. Suddenly Max burst into the room, startling everyone. Kate yelped in astonishment and grumbled to Didier and Lucie, "Somebody should put a bell on that boy."

"Hello mother, Didier." Max swooped by Lucie, grabbed her by the elbow and whisked her into the butler's pantry. He opened the wrought iron gate that led to the wine cellar, and, with Lucie in tow, bounded down the steps. Lucie missed the last one, stubbed a toe and fell hard against Max's back. He unlocked the door without disentangling himself from her, and they stumbled into the anteroom.

"Owwwwww." Lucie hopped over to lean against a table. "What – is – wrong with you!? And why couldn't we just use the powder room? No one can hear in there."

Max interrupted tersely, "Because I'm thirsty." He headed for the bottles as Lucie hobbled back up the stairs.

He called after her, "Nonono, we're hiding down here!"

Then he heard, "Stop wiggling."

Lucie returned, Phoebe under her arm.

"We didn't really need -"

"You can't hide with the Town Crier outside your door." She plopped Phoebe on the floor and the little dog took off to explore.

Max shook his head and placed a bottle of Pinot Noir and two glasses on the tasting table. Lucie watched his hands operate the waiter's corkscrew with practiced ease, and as he pulled the cork from the bottle with a minor pop and reached for the glasses, she thought about how sexy it is when a man – other than your waiter – pours wine for you.

They sipped the Pinot for a moment, then Lucie said, “So what did you -” but Max held up a hand to stop her. He drained the glass of wine and sighed deeply. “Sometimes I hide down here for hours. With some men it’s the bathroom, but I’ve got this.” He waved his left arm around the room. “With a house full of crazies, you gotta have a sanctuary.”

His thoughts wandered off and Lucie stared, willing him to talk. Then couldn’t sit anymore.

“Tell you what. My toe stopped throbbing, so I’ll go get you some food and the thing the Sautiers gave me, ok?”

Max nodded absently. “That would be nice, I missed lunch.” He looked really tired.

When Lucie returned with rillettes, crackers, warmed slices of crespeou and a small salad, though, he revived.

Phoebe smelled the food and came running, barking all the way.

Max shared, and between mouthfuls, told her that after he’d delivered Giles to the nearby private airport, he’d gone into the City to check on Julia and Laval.

“Guess what. Laval wasn’t even authorized to act on behalf of his firm. Turns out he’s on probation for incurring enormous gambling debts with the French Mafia, a fact he neglected to share with his godfather. The Sûreté even got wind of it - of course they’d want to know about a compromised lawyer.”

So Max’s connections reached to the French National Police Force.

“But why thwart the winery sale?”

“I think he planned to hurry the Sautiers back to

France, then offer to buy the winery himself, for next to nothing. Tell them it isn't worth as much as they thought, but that he'd take it off their hands as a favor. Then, because the location makes that property valuable, he'd either turn it over to the Mob or sell it at a huge profit and cover his debts."

They both shook their heads at the young man's loss of humanity.

Max's food was gone and he poured another glass of wine, relaxed now. "I'm having my people check on the Mafia connection: I don't want Jeffrey involved in anything they're interested in. He's in over his head as it is."

"By the way, Julia has insinuated herself into this scenario."

"How?"

"Owen told me –"

Max looked astounded and interrupted, "Owen *talked* to you? Actually talked?"

"I fed him. Can we get on with this?" Max nodded, then shook his head and put up a hand.

"Wait a minute, the man has yet to talk to me, and I pay him!"

Lucie tilted her head to one side and raised an eyebrow.

"Sorry."

"Owen told me that Julia kept him in the City today to deliver what was probably more wine – I can get you the address – and then had him take her to the bank. Then she made a long phone call, I'm thinking to Laval, and it had to do with the Sautiers. Something about having Gérard declared incompetent. Oh and remind me to slap her when she shows up again, ok?"

Max blinked at the non-sequitur.

"Here's what the Sautiers gave me." She shoved

the gift in his direction.

Max frowned. "It's a shoe box."

"Not the box, the contents."

He flipped the lid. "They gave you postcards?" Max pulled out several of them and noted the age. "Hmm, really old postcards." He looked up. "As a gift. I don't get it."

"I don't either, really. We have this, uh, psychic bond thing going and, um, it's hard to explain." Lucie waved one arm around in the attempt.

Max squinted.

"As nearly as I can tell, this is some sort of family legacy that Gaston the godson was supposed to inherit because the Sautiers have no children, but of course he doesn't deserve it now. So, and I know this sounds crazy, they gave it to me because they consider me family." Lucie scrunched up her face. It *did* sound crazy.

Max topped off his glass of wine, looked at hers and said, "You need to catch up."

"And Julia tried to get her grubby hands on it right after the Sautiers gave it to me."

"What does Julia want with it?"

"Who knows, but according to her, it should belong to a member of this household. Then she ransacked my suite to find it." She narrowed her eyes and her voice became sepulchral. ***"And she messed with my knives."*** She was gratified when Max looked appropriately shocked and nodded her head, "I know, I know, I couldn't believe it either."

"So why are these old postcards valuable? Do we look for a rare stamp like in that movie, damn, what's the name of it..."

"I don't know, but -"

"Charade!" Max's arms flew up and he almost knocked over his wine glass. Lucie threw her hands up to ward off whatever was incoming, then reached over and smacked him.

"Don't do that!"

"But I thought of the movie." He looked pleased with himself.

Lucie rolled her eyes. "So what did you find out about Julia today?"

"Suspiciously large amounts of money have, at irregular intervals, been turning up in her bank account for about two years now." Max stopped abruptly and muttered to himself, 'Come to think of it, right around the time she put on fifty pounds.'

Lucie frowned. "What? Oh never mind, how much money altogether?"

"Half a million."

Lucie choked on the wine she'd just drunk.

He glanced sadly around at the rows of bottles. "I'm sure a lot of the best vintages are gone, and – wait a minute." He took out his cell phone, paged through his contacts and was soon talking to a locksmith who apparently made house calls on short notice. He turned back to Lucie.

"So far none of her account has been transferred anywhere, but I have, um, a watch on it."

"Isn't that illegal?"

Max made a wry face at her.

She drank her wine and reached for the bottle, which Max intercepted and poured for her. Lucie gave him an almost imperceptible nod. Max noticed.

Lucie looked thoughtful. "So for two years Julia steals your wine, then all of a sudden makes a move with Laval. Max, I think your little exhibition for Giles pushed her over the edge."

"What?"

"She acted jealous last night, and made very territorial remarks today: only reason Julia would be jealous of a pretend relationship is if she thought you belong to her. Mrs. Harris thinks so, too."

Max looked sick.

"Look, it's none of my business, but rejection can warp a person, and -"

Max stood up abruptly and said, "If Julia and Laval intend to have Sautier declared incompetent, we have to contact him ASAP so he can make a pre-emptive strike. I just hope his lawyer is sharp." He rubbed his shoulder and whistled for Phoebe.

"Joint pain?"

"Something like that."

Lucie picked up the food tray and put the shoebox on it, then started up the stairs; Max grabbed several bottles of very good red wine before he followed her. That Lucie liked to lead was firmly imbedded in his mind.

They reached the kitchen before Max spoke again. "Lucie, don't even think about making a late dinner. There's a ton of food in the frig, so I'll have Mrs. Harris tell everyone who's still on site to help themselves."

"I don't mind."

"We need to have a serious look at those postcards, as soon as possible. I have a feeling Sautier wasn't kidding about them being important."

"Well, ok then."

"And how about typing up something I can fax to Gérard's lawyer, in case he doesn't speak English."

"Sure." As Lucie went to the oven for her laptop, Max said, "Wait a minute, I said I don't want you to cook."

Lucie grinned at him as she removed her computer, then picked up the box of cards.

Max laughed, shook his head and headed for the back stairs. "I gotta grab a quick nap. You might want to, too: it's going to be a late night. Keep your cell on, I'll call when I wake up, ok?"

Lucie nodded and unlocked the door to her suite. She started on the letter for the French lawyer immediately: no point in napping, she might miss something.

***

When her cell phone rang several hours later, Lucie was already dressed in faded denim jeans and a light, black tunic sweater. She grabbed the box of postcards, opened her door and took one step into the hallway.

Whoa, what the hell? Lucie was assaulted by total darkness and an oppressive, sinister silence that hung in the air, heavy like a wet woolen coat. The hair on the back of her neck stood up as she realized that the beautiful wall sconces that lit the hallway were dark, and someone had drawn immense curtains across the huge windows that normally let in so much light across the back of the hallway.

Lucie suddenly realized that she was backlit and turned to flick off the light in her room. At that same instant, something zinged past her head. She quickly dropped to a crouch so that whoever had shot at her would find nothing but thin air where she'd stood a second ago. And started deep-breathing to quell the fear.

She ducked-walked backwards into her room, rose and slammed the door, locking it swiftly. She turned on the light, grabbed her bought-at-an-outlet-incredibly-soft-leather Louis-Vuitton backpack that served as both purse and flight bag, and rapidly stuffed it with the box of postcards and her jewelry wrap. She slung it over her shoulder, grabbed the black couture dress that had reappeared, seized the knife she was keeping on the nightstand, and picked up her laptop attaché. Dammit, getting shot at was definitely not part of the deal!

Lucie turned off the light, crouched again and quietly unlocked her door, listening carefully for any noise from the other side. When she heard Max open his door, she flung hers wide and ran across the hall and into his suite, yelling "You are such a bitch, Julia! Lock your door, Max."

He had opened his mouth to greet her, but she was already in his living area, throwing her armful on a couch.

He quickly followed her into his suite, an astonished look on his face.

"You got a weapon?"

"Why do you need a weapon?"

"The hall lights are dead, and somebody covered the windows at the back. And – oh yeah – SOMEBODY SHOT AT ME! So do you have anything better than this?" She waved the knife at him. "I'll need a flashlight, too."

Max blinked several times and pulled out his cell phone. He pressed one key and said, with no explanation, "We need to secure the building. Outside my suite in two."

He grabbed a black jacket that was slung over the back of a chair, opened a closet and took a Glock from the top shelf.

Lucie's eyes were glued to the gun. "Wow, you have a Glock. Thanks." And reached for it.

"You've got to be kidding: you're a self-avowed lousy shot."

Lucie stared at him defiantly. "So I'll use it to scare her, then get close and shoot her in the foot."

He moved quickly to the door and turned. "Just guard the postcards, ok? Mrs. Harris and I will check things out, and I want to make sure my mother is all right." The Glock went into his waistband.

"You and Mrs. Harris? Then I'm in, too."

"No, you're not."

"But -"

"No buts, stay here."

"Bummer. So I have to just sit here and wait. Boriiiinnnnggg." Lucie grabbed her knife and the shoebox, then moved to the corner between the hallway door and the French doors that opened onto the balcony. She frowned, sat on the floor and said, "What about the flashlight?"

Max took a maglite from a kitchen drawer and handed it down to her. Lucie looked up at him, twirled the large knife into the air and caught the handle.

"Turn out the lights when you leave."

Max shook his head and grinned as he locked the dead bolt on his door.

Lucie, frowning in the darkness, muttered "Mrs. Harris, huh? Now I wonder what *that's* about?"

CHAPTER 13

Max muttered something about not wanting his ankles sliced up and yelled to the door, "It's me, Lucie, you can put your knife down." Lucie got up slowly, her legs stiff from sitting on the floor, as Max unlocked the door, flipped on the lights and led a dog parade into the room: Phoebe and Bruno, looking smug, trotted along right behind him.

He pulled off his jacket as he headed for the kitchen, put his weapon on the counter and opened the refrigerator door.

Lucie, hands on her hips, made a face. "That's just great. I have to stay here in the dark, but you let those two -"

"There wasn't any 'letting' involved. Mother yelled at me for disturbing Didier and her and said I had to take the dogs with me to make up for it."

"You and the dogs see anything?"

Max stuck his head in the refrigerator, so his voice was muffled. "Just what we expected: someone searched the office and the library, probably Julia, since the security system wasn't breached and she still has the code. Didn't think to change it, guess I'm slipping. Anyhow, Mrs. Harris is taking care of that now. You hungry?"

"Yeah, I could eat a little."

Max pulled out a container of cold chicken, some cheeses that hadn't come from the kitchen downstairs, a platter of cut fruit, and, from the top of the frig, a baguette. Totally at ease in his kitchen, he opened a bottle of wine, sliced the bread, and plated the food almost artistically.

Lucie found herself noticing his dark blue shirt, sleeves rolled up and open at the neck by two buttons. And faded, comfortable jeans like hers, expensive to begin with, then worn and treasured because they knew the body they adorned.

Max put everything on a tray, turned and almost tripped over the dogs. "Move it, you two" was largely ignored. As he pushed them aside, he told Lucie, "So anyway, the car Julia took earlier was spotted on the grounds a little while ago and now it's gone. Again." He made a face. "That woman just never stops being a pain in the ass, but since we don't have proof she's the shooter, I'll give her 'til morning to come back. She doesn't, I'll have a little talk with the police about our stolen vehicle."

He deposited the tray on a coffee table, then reached into his pocket and handed her a bullet. "Dug this out of the wall at the end of the hall." He gazed into her eyes and Lucie saw him struggle to keep emotion out of his voice. "I'm sorry this happened in my home. Clearly, I underestimated Julia."

Lucie stared at the bullet and a shiver ran down her back: being brave was easy before she saw that piece of lead. Max noticed the reaction and distracted her with the food and small talk about the dogs, who were transfixed by all those goodies at nose level.

Between mouthfuls, Max observed, "I get it that Julia's nuts and she thinks the shoebox should be hers, so she keeps trying to steal it. But why take it to a whole other level by shooting at you? Only thing that makes sense is that Gaston told her something compelling about those postcards, something we don't know." He nonchalantly looked over at Lucie. "Do we?"

Lucie's mouth fell open. "You think I'm holding out on you? If all I wanted was to keep some French family heirloom for myself, I'd be long gone." Lucie stopped abruptly. She hadn't meant to say 'if all I wanted.'

She pushed herself into the corner of the couch so she could face him, and crossed her arms. The dogs, sensing an impending storm, rethought the preemptive strike they were considering and slunk off to the kitchen area.

"You don't trust me!"

Max was still eating and glanced at her sideways. "I trust you, it's just that maybe the Sautiers told you something major, but it didn't seem like it at the time."

Lucie narrowed her eyes. "Oh no you don't, you cannot spin not trusting me." Max put down his fork and turned to her.

"Lucie, their use of violence means we have to be very, very careful from now on." He stared at her, intently. "I want to be absolutely certain that I'm not missing something that will put you in harm's way again."

He leaned back into the sofa and waited for her response.

A shrewd glint appeared in Lucie's eyes and she unfolded her arms so she could gesture with them. "You know what I think? I think the only person you really trust is Mrs. Harris and I'll bet both of you were involved in a clandestine profession, and I think you've lived outside the country for extended periods of time."

That took Max by surprise and he opened his mouth to comment, but Lucie was on a roll. That she was interested enough in his life to have speculated extensively both flattered and worried him.

"Ok, taken independently, the following observations mean nothing. When viewed as a whole, however -" She raised both eyebrows and lowered her head slightly, for effect. "Let's start with the little stuff." She ticked off the ideas with her hand, starting with her thumb: "You eat with your fork in your left hand, continental style and you are not left-handed."

Lucie continued, "You wear nothing but 18K gold, certainly available but not so common in this country, a taste acquired in Italy, I'd say. And the suits I've seen you wear are European-cut, and the Armani suits that Mrs. Harris wears are not sold in this hemisphere. I wear Armani and I've never seen that design here, not even in Montréal."

"And you have 'People' who skirt the law to do things for you and you have connections in the Sûreté. And your own mother has no idea what you did for a living!" She opened her eyes wide: "You don't even trust *your own mother*!"

When he failed to respond, Lucie continued, "Oh yeah, and this really amuses me by the way: you are linguistically bereft, so, what, you probably had to drag around an interpreter?"

She nodded, pleased with herself. "How'm I doin so far?"

Max looked at her levelly. She clearly wasn't going to let go unless he gave her something. But how much? The decision involved the demon from his past, knowledge of which meant peril to one's life. But so did the bullet in Lucie's pocket.

Max stood up and shifted to an armchair that put her in his direct line of sight.

"Mrs. Harris speaks Arabic and Farsi and some Italian and a Chinese dialect."

"What!"

He leaned forward, hands clasped, elbows on the armrests. "You've guessed correctly, Mrs. Harris and I did have an irregular profession: none of our activities were ever on paper, not known except in one corridor in the Pentagon. The job involved intelligence gathering and some fixing, and over the years we met a lot of people with a lot of influence."

Lucie's eyes widened.

Max almost smiled. "You're getting a visual of spies and secret missions, aren't you?"

"Well -"

"Not nearly that exciting." He paused and looked away for a moment, then back at Lucie. "Anyhow, one day Mrs. Harris and I took a good, hard look at what we were doing and got disgusted. We decided that even if those in power had lost their moral center, taking orders from them shouldn't involve compromising ours."

"Problem is, you don't just 'resign' from that kind of work. So we started to *fix* things our own way. Nothing more illegal than what the current bozos in the White House have done since they started with those two rigged elections, and nothing we're really ashamed of. Somewhere along the way we started to make serious money: not in arms or drug trafficking or anything like that, it involved a lot of, uh, information changing hands. Actually MISinformation."

Max was beginning to warm to the subject and managed a full-on grin at the memory. "If you're good at it, you can create a lot of untraceable havoc with greedy people, especially those closest to the Real Power in government. They aren't in a position to out anyone, because it might draw unwanted attention to their own activities. Those are the most dangerous targets, but also the most fun to fuck with."

He looked away again and the grin faded. "Then I had a massive heart attack. Let me tell you, that really changes your priorities. Since Mrs. Harris was getting tired of the white-collar-scum game anyway, she decided to help me devise an incredibly clever, mutually beneficial exit strategy, and that's how we wound up back here, together." His attention returned to Lucie.

Lucie looked puzzled. "But why in the world would she want to be your housekeeper?"

"She got bored doing nothing, and this way, no one ever questions her presence here. Besides, she says it amuses her."

"Oh." Lucie raised her eyebrows and was silent for a moment. "So if resigning wasn't an option, how did the two of you get out?'

"We created a situation in which it was in their best interest to let us go."

Lucie waited. Max took another deep breath and unleashed the demon.

"Turned out Mrs. Harris had been accumulating detailed documentation of corruption, treachery, and even treason. What she's got implicates powerful, highly-placed people and companies."

"And you blackmailed the bastards?"

"More like made them aware of our 'leverage.' She has hard copies of incriminating memos, illegal government contracts, bills of lading for items never delivered to war zones, and the list goes on. My personal favorite is some irrefutable evidence on video." He paused for effect. "Ever wonder what happened to the missing $9 billion in Iraq?"

Lucie gasped and moved closer to the edge of her seat.

"I had no idea she'd been collecting such explosive evidence all those years: she was extremely careful to keep its existence a secret. Hell, even **I** don't know where she has it stashed." He made a wry face.

Lucie asked, "But how'd you manage to use your leverage without getting killed?" Then thought, 'I don't even believe I'm having this conversation.'

"Two things happened simultaneously: we leaked just one of the items, with evidence, to two publications whose editors can't be bought or intimidated. One in Europe, and – you'll like this – Vanity Fair, for immediate publication. As the shit hit the fan, we gave the Powers That Be a partial list of the rest of what we had and told them we wanted out. And that if anything were to happen to us or our families, the entire package would be public knowledge within hours."

"And your backup?"

"An astute question. A billionaire friend who can't be turned and a sealed envelope with the location of the goods. If we don't check in with her on a regular basis, she'll collect the package and turn it over to Graydon Carter first, then the European editor."

"So you were out."

"Uh huh, retired, pensions intact. And no one has bothered us. Yet. We keep our ears to the ground, though, and there's an arsenal hidden in the house. Just in case."

Lucie reached for the bottle of wine, her hand shaking slightly, but Max got there first and filled her glass.

"I liked it better when I thought you were a gardener." She drew her legs under her and gulped the wine.

Meanwhile, Max sat back in his chair and watched Lucie, already regretting the burden he just placed on her; he should have spun the story, side-stepped. But the Sautiers had also burdened her, unwittingly, with their gift and its inherent danger. Lucie probably had a nice, safe life before coming to the château.

She chewed on her bottom lip, put the glass on the table and looked squarely at Max.

"So what's Mrs. Harris' first name?"

***

Max blinked several times in astonishment, then threw his head back and laughed. "I have no idea! She signs everything E. Harris, and won't tell me what the E is for, so I call her Emma. As in Peel."

Lucie raised an eyebrow at him and let a grin spread slowly over her face. She shook off the specter of Max's past, put her feet on the floor and said, "So. Let's find out what the deal is with these cards."

"Excellent idea." Max was relieved: she was handling this so much better than he'd expected. "Ok, you said the Sautiers originally intended the box for Laval, right?"

"Uh-huh, it's really important to them. They said it contains a family legacy, and I think they brought it here so they could make a big presentation after Gaston helped them sell the winery."

Max looked thoughtful. "So after Julia sees you with the cards, she calls Laval again, mentions she's pissed off because *you* got the gift, and he tells her to get her hands on it any way she can."

"So of course she shoots at me." Lucie made a face and pulled a scrap of paper from her pocket. "I read some of the postcards while you rested, and it looks like the cards are a record of an American soldier's travels in France, starting near the end of World War I and continuing to around 1927. Most of the cards are in English and addressed to an Augustin Sautier, presumably Gérard's father, also a soldier."

Max nodded. "Saw the name on our copy of the deed to the winery."

"Apparently they became friends before the war, when James - that's the American – spent a few months traveling around France, because he refers to the 'fun we had at your winery.' He says he hopes Augustin's convalescence is going well, so Gérard's father was probably wounded. Says he's sorry to have forgotten most of the French he learned, but has asked a mutual friend called Marie Bottecher to translate the English for Augustin. Then the later cards, from after the war, are between Marie and James, and that's all the further I got."

"So, three players: Augustin, James and Marie."

"Yes. And look at this." As she reached for the postcards, Bruno and Phoebe, who had ambled back to the table and noticed a shift in the humans' attention, decided on a frontal assault on the food.

Bruno took point and lunged across the table, accidentally catching the end of the box with one giant paw and flipping it into the air. Lucie yelled and jumped out of the way, it rained postcards, and both dogs grabbed the remnants of the picnic and ran for it.

Lucie and Max stared at the dogs, now happily chomping their ill gotten booty. Max was incredulous. "Since when have you two been in cahoots?" Bruno and Phoebe raised their heads for a millisecond and looked at each other. Lucie could swear she saw a doggie grin.

She sighed, "Well, I hope the legacy thing wasn't based on the order the cards used to be in."

They gathered up what looked like a new layer of carpet and noticed a tiny tintype, only 2 ¾ inches long, among the cards.

Lucie picked it up carefully and studied it. "Wow, I think we're looking at Lt. James Milnar."

They stared at it for a moment, then Lucie put the picture in a secure pocket in her backpack-cum-purse.

"So, we arrange the cards according to the year they were sent?"

Max nodded, and they worked silently until Lucie stood up and stretched her back. Max opened his French doors, stepped out on the balcony and immediately motioned for Lucie to join him. Laughing, he whispered, "You aren't going to believe this."

It had been October for several days, but neither Lucie nor the weather had registered that change: the sky was clear, with crisp air not yet soured by the autumn smell of decaying leaves.

The sound of a couple making love drifted up to them with giggles, breathy noises and grunts. When it became obvious that someone was working up to a shriek, Lucie grabbed Max's sleeve and pulled him back into the room. Being careful not to actually touch him.

"C'mon, I'm starting to feel like a voyeur, um, I mean an écouteur."

"A what?"

"Someone who's listening."

"That's not a word."

"Yes it is, it's French. Like voyeur is French."

Max remained unconvinced.

"So anyway, who's too cheap to get a motel room?"

"Gotta be Jessica and Antonio: they've been all over each other since, yesterday, I think."

Lucie smiled inwardly: Max was starting to pay attention to the lives of his employees.

Neither of them was aware that there was someone else paying attention at that moment.

And Jeffrey was seething.

***

A cursory examination of the cards revealed neither rare stamps nor cryptic messages. The night had long since stretched into the next day and Lucie's energy reserves were depleted, but she was too intrigued by the puzzle to give up.

Max got up, rubbed his neck and wandered into his bedroom. Lucie caught the glance at his bed and sent him the thought, 'Timing's not right, Max.' Then said out loud, "We need a big table and access to office supplies. What do you say we move all this down to the library?"

Staying in the immediate proximity of his bed had been Max's plan, but he acquiesced. He wanted it to be her choice.

They put the cards back in the box, Max retrieved his Glock, Lucie hoisted her backpack and laptop attaché, grabbed the knife, then glanced at Max. They burst out laughing at the same instant.

"Yeah, I know, looks like we're on maneuvers. So can we use the secret door?"

"Sure, but Bruno will want to come along so be careful she doesn't trip you." He glanced at the dogs. Bruno burped. Max made a face and said, "We should probably take them out, too, all things considered."

He searched the wall for the tiny latch, flipped it and the slim door swung open, silently. Then he touched a small button on the wall and the library below was bathed in light. They peered into the silent chasm, but nothing ran for the shadows.

Bruno knocked into Max, almost upending him, then Phoebe began to bark, impatient with the large, lumbering object blocking her way down.

"Watch where you're going, you big lummox" was, as usual, largely ignored.

Max let Lucie precede him, and asked, "Mind if I bring Mrs. Harris in on this? She has a wonderfully analytical mind and I know she's wired and probably still looking for intruders."

Lucie opened her mouth to reply, but Max interrupted, "Unless you - I mean, the cards belong to you, as does anything we – you – find, so..."

She held up her hand to stop him. "I think she'd be a valuable, uh, asset? Is that the word you two would use?" She was teasing, but Max was already on his cell.

When Lucie reached the bottom of the steps, he said quietly to his former partner, "I told her about us. Yes, everything. Because I trust her and I thought she should know."

***

Mrs. Harris appeared ten minutes later, carrying a laptop and dressed in a black outfit that looked spookily like a SWAT uniform. Lucie's mouth fell open and the older woman grinned. "Old habits die hard." And to Max, "So, we're in business again? Good. Been too long and we're getting rusty."

Lucie looked at Max, incredulous. "I thought you said you two were NOT -"

Max shrugged. Lucie blinked. Another entry on the Weird Shit list.

"Ok, so bring Mrs. Harris up to speed while I let the dogs out."

Max glanced over at her. "Want me to go with you?"

Lucie grabbed her knife, whistled for the dogs and raised an eyebrow.

"I'll take that as a no."

On her way out, she glanced back at the conspirators: heads together, they bent excitedly over the piles of cards, like little kids with a new toy.

When Lucie returned, she found Max and Mrs. Harris deep in conversation, so involved that neither of them noticed her presence. Lucie felt a momentary pang of jealousy at being the outsider, but the feeling evaporated as she asked, "So, what have you got?"

Mrs. Harris looked up. "There are 162 cards altogether and we've sorted each year as to day and month; while you read for content, I'm going to pursue a line of inquiry on the web, and I need your help, Max."

Lucie settled herself with a notepad and began with the 1918 pile of postcards.

***

Lucie had completely lost track of time, but her notes were complete, and although her eyes were drooping, she wanted to share the information.

"Listen up, you two, it's story time."

Max and Mrs. Harris looked up from her computer.

"One Lt. James Milnar, an American soldier, arrives in France near the end of the War, reconnects with Gérard's father, Augustin, has at least one more tour of duty in Europe, sends his friend packages to cheer him up, is stationed near the German border, he's probably in charge of supply since he mentions the quartermaster's office where he works, is well versed in French history and architecture – many of the cards were of cathedrals, which seem to fascinate him – then he travels around France and tells Augustin all about it - "

Max yelled "Breathe, Lucie!" and Lucie did, unaware that she hadn't.

"Anything seem odd, jump out at you?"

Lucie sighed. "Nooo."

"Guess it was too much to hope for, a slightly oblique reference to something extremely valuable."

Mrs. Harris motioned her to the other side of the table. "I ran a search on the three people we're dealing with, but I could only find Augustin. I need you to translate this information."

When Lucie saw the screen, she screeched, "OhMyGod, that's a restricted French government site! What were you thinking, they'll trace this breach back to us and we're gonna be in so much trouble!" She narrowed her eyes at both of them.

Max and Mrs. Harris exchanged glances and Max whispered, "She hasn't had much sleep and she gets grumpy."

"Not. Funny." Lucie bent down and peered at the screen. "Augustin Sautier, born 1889, granted a delay in being called up in August of 1914 – let's see, he'd be twenty-five years old – because he and his family were winegrowers." She raised her eyes to them. "You know, because the harvest would be ready in just a few months. Common practice, I read somewhere that happened in 1939, too. Plus the vineyards might turn into battle fields, they didn't know how far into France the Germans would advance."

"What else?" Max tapped the computer screen.

"Hmm, he eventually served in the trenches and was badly wounded, had to have a leg amputated, subsequently collected a sort of, (Lucie squinted in concentration) looks like a lifelong veteran's disability because of being permanently crippled and exposed to 'ypérite'?" Lucie looked puzzled, then grabbed her laptop.

"We really don't need -"

"Yes we do, it'll drive me nuts if I don't know what that word means."

Max sighed and waited.

A few taps later: "He was gassed. I read about how the men in the trenches would see the gas rolling over No Man's Land toward them and scramble for gas masks, and this one is mustard gas, produces nasty blisters wherever there's contact, causes vomiting, burns the eyes, and sears the lungs."

"Lucie!"

"I bet he developed cancer later on; my own grandfather died of leukemia as a result of being gassed during the war." She stopped to look at them. "What?"

Mrs. Harris pointed at the computer.

"Anyway. Was exempted from service in WWII because of it, let's see, he'd be fifty then."

Lucie bit her bottom lip again. "What about Gérard? Maybe there's something in his past."

Mrs. Harris nodded and typed rapidly. "Have a look."

Lucie studied the screen. "Gérard Sautier, born 1923, that makes him eighty-four now, called up for military service at the beginning of the war, surrendered with the rest of the French army, scheduled to be deported to Germany to work in the munitions factories, escaped and joined the Résistance."

She looked up and sighed. "Interesting, but it leads nowhere."

Max said quietly, "Any good investigation requires time, Lucie. Think about it: a Frenchman kept those postcards his whole life, even though he couldn't understand a word on them, then passed them on to his son, with a cryptic allusion to a legacy. So what if the clues are more subtle than we anticipated? We'll find them."

"Aghhh, I can't think anymore." Lucie shuffled off in the direction of a huge couch across the room.

"Uh, Lucie, do you have the fax for Gérard's lawyer handy?"

"Laptop, desktop, title is Fax for Gérard's Lawyer. No password, help yourself."

"You want to call Gérard now? He's probably -"

"I'll just go rest a few minutes..." was the last thing Lucie remembered saying, to no one in particular.

CHAPTER 14

Lucie woke up in a panic: she couldn't move her legs, and because Max's arm was flung across her head, couldn't see why not. She pushed the arm away, the motion caught the attention of the leg weights, Phoebe scampered the length of her body and started to lick her face and Bruno fell off the couch with a loud thud. Lucie groaned, wriggled to avoid the tongue that had now found her ear and suddenly yelled.

"Hey! What's poking me in the back?"

"MyockIthnk"

"Your WHAT?"

Max struggled into wakefulness. "My glock. Sorry, forgot to park it last night."

"Why are you behind me on this couch?"

"Emma went to bed and -"

"Who?"

"*Mrs. Harris,* remember? Since we're all working together, I think it'd be simpler if we call her by her, um, first name. Anyway, I was too tired to go anywhere and there was plenty of room. At least until these two decided to invade. And you said I could."

"I what?"

"I very clearly asked if you would share the couch and you said yes."

Yeah, right. Lucie made a face he couldn't see and rolled off the couch.

Max pointed to the staircase to his suite. "C'mon, I'll make us coffee." When Lucie hesitated, Max made a wry face. "Just coffee."

***

Lucie was sitting cross-legged on her bed and had just finished a lengthy email message to her daughter when Max knocked. She appreciated the courtesy and yelled, "It's open!"

As he ambled into the room, Phoebe and her new best friend pushed past him to the French doors and barked until he let them out.

Max observed, "Those two are making a habit of boorish behavior," and threw a key and a laminated card on the bed. "New wine cellar key and security code for the front door, in case you lock yourself out."

Lucie picked up the cellar key. "That was fast."

"Locksmith owes me a few favors."

She tried to hand it back. "I really don't need this anymore, Max."

"I know, but I kind of like it that you have a key to my prize possessions. And by the way, you're a guest now, not an employee, so I had Anth- er – Antonio make lunch."

Lucie started to get up, then noticed a text on her phone. She accessed it, smiled and said, "Nice!" To Max she said, "My daughter suggests that if the messages on the cards hold no clues, perhaps the cards *themselves* are the clues: postcards are, after all, about locations. Maybe if we attach them to a huge map of France, we'll see a pattern." She smiled again and remarked, "Reminds me of one of her school projects" as she texted her back, 'Good idea, Soph, and thanks.'

"You have anything we could pin all those cards on?"

Max looked thoughtful. "I seem to remember a large projection screen from my father's home movie days, will that do?"

Lucie nodded and started to gather her valuables, but Max took them from her and motioned for her to follow him.

"We'll put your important stuff in the priest hole in my suite."

Lucie was right on his heels. "You have a priest hole? Seriously? A priest hole!"

Max locked his door behind them and went over to his kitchenette.

Lucie looked skeptical. "You aren't putting me on, are you? Because hiding places are right up there with pirates."

Max released a switch under the edge of the countertop to the left of the sink and flipped the entire portion up, then bent to shove aside some dish detergent.

Lucie squatted beside him as he pushed a small button on the inside cabinet wall; the bottom of the cabinet retracted into nothingness.

They both stared at lighted, narrow steps leading downward.

"Whoa."

Max explained, "My father had it built the same time as the listening post. Told everybody there was structural damage in the building stone when the place was half constructed, threw everybody off the site and had a special crew alter the walls of the rooms below to accommodate this space." He glanced sideways and grinned at her.

"Want to see it?" Knowing the answer.

They slowly descended into a small, L-shaped room with an air shaft, a table and chair, and shelves covered with neatly stacked weapons of various shapes and sizes: Max's 'arsenal.'

"Kinda big for a priest hole. Don't suppose you ever actually hid down here?"

Max looked sheepish. "One of my divorces got ugly when the ex somehow forgot about the pre-nup and got her hands on a gun. Emma convinced her that I had left for parts unknown, which wasn't really a lie because nobody besides Em – and now you – knows about this."

Suddenly Lucie was acutely aware of Max's proximity, of his Le Male body wash, of the silky black shirt that hung out over his jeans.

"This is really cool, thanks." She scurried up the stairs.

Max followed her and said, nonchalantly, "Feel free to use it anytime." And smiled to himself: not only had he *not* annoyed her, she was actually impressed!

***

The aroma of frying applewood bacon had lured everyone to the kitchen, where the staff were already enjoying wonderful, gooey grilled sandwiches made with several kinds of cheese, the bacon and a slab of mild dill pickle, as well as Juan's salad of chopped tomatoes with balsamic vinegar, basil and garlic salt.

Before Lucie took her lunch into the dining room to

join Emma, Max, his mother and Didier, she noticed that Roland and Juan were conversing quietly. Juan shy, Roland cautious. Interesting.

As Lucie sat down, Kate turned to her and asked, "Are you all right, my dear? What a terrible thing to happen, right here in our home!"

Between mouthfuls, Lucie assured her, "I'm fine, now we just have to find Julia and beat her senseless."

Kate laughed, "That's an excellent idea!"

Max wore a grim expression: "She returned the staff car, but nobody's seen her."

***

Lucie couldn't wait to get back to the postcards and apparently neither could Emma, who had assumed a whole new persona. Which made the staff nervous, judging by the raised eyebrows, twitching and whispering that occurred when she passed them: in addition to the black SWAT attire, her gray hair was now severely pulled from her face and secured with a helmet of bobby pins.

Max had almost closed the now-constantly-locked library door when Roland jammed a tray into the opening.

"Er, Antonio asked me to deliver this."

Max looked down at the tray, which contained bottles of water, crackers, cheeses and grapes, and then at Roland, who was craning his neck and trying to squeeze past Max to see into the room.

"Roland, we just ate," Max pointed out.

"Well yes of course but we thought you might want to nosh – unh- ouf - a tad later." Roland had managed to insinuate half his body into the room by squirming against Max and the door, an action that sent the food sliding back and forth on the tray, and prompted Emma to poke Lucie's arm.

"Would you just look at that ridiculous man!" She snorted and turned back to the cards.

Lucie couldn't help laughing and hurried over to the door, ducked under Max's arms and took the tray from Roland before he could protest.

"Tell Antonio thanks, and we won't need anything further this afternoon, ok?"

Max gently backed the butler out of the room, locked the door and showed Lucie the huge white screen he'd found. He extended it to its full height and asked, "This big enough?"

"If we don't put all one hundred sixty-two cards on it, yes. Ok if we ruin it?"

"Suit yourself."

"Then hand me that marker and the laptop, will you?"

Lucie studied the image of France on Emma's computer and placed it beside the projection screen. She sketched an outline, then stood back, tilted her head and proclaimed it ready.

"So. We eliminate any cards of the 'wish you were here' variety, but all three of us will examine each card, ok? Make sure we don't miss anything. The ones that make it to the screen-worthy pile get logged in with a date and number, One being the earliest. Your job, Max."

Max grabbed a legal pad and quickly made columns for locations and dates; then he reached for the 1918 pile and pointed at the card on top.

"Look, there's a bombed-out building on this card." He looked uneasy. "Makes me feel like I'm ogling a car accident, you know, morbid fascination with wreckage. " He shook his head.

"Postcards should have palm trees and beaches, not devastation."

Max flipped another card over, and as he read it, his voice softened. "James says he saw the trenches for the first time and can only imagine his friend's nightmares of the shelling and the gas."

He continued, "Here's one of a village in Lorraine and James says he passed it on the way to Verdun. And that it's all in ruins now." He suddenly looked up. "This hits you in the gut like the 9/11 images, I –"

They were suddenly interrupted by a thunderous assault on the library door. "You people need to open up, RIGHT NOW!"

Max looked disgusted as put his cards back on the pile and went to unlock the door. He'd just opened it when Jeffrey slammed it into his father's face and burst into the room, waving a bunch of papers at the women.

He shrieked, "What is the meaning of this?" as he threw the papers sideways, like a frisbee, onto the table, sending several piles of postcards flying.

Lucie frowned. “He’s as bad as the dogs.”

Emma frowned. “Worse.”

Max, gingerly checking his nose for damage, strode to the table and grabbed the papers. He was furious, but the only evidence was his clenched jaw and his right hand, which was now flexing. Lucie really hoped he was going to punch Jeffrey. Or, even better, drop him with one of those thumb-to-the-nerve-on-the-inside-shoulder things.

Max’s voice was ominous. “What the *hell* is your problem?”

“Well, (Jeffrey cleared his throat) I’ve been investigating my new business opportunity. It’s a big responsibility, you know, owning a winery, and KyleeSuanne thinks we should turn it into a Bed and Breakfast.”

“Is that one person?”

“Who”

“KyleeSuanne.”

Jeffrey made a face. “*She* is the chef at the Steak House. We’re leaving in two days to inspect the property and you have no idea how hard it is for KyleeSuanne to get off work, but she’s doing it for me. Anyway, there I was, arranging everything and that (he pointed at the papers) came through and I DEMAND AN EXPLANATION!”

Max motioned for the women to come look at the fax with him. He glanced at the cover sheet, frowned and handed the rest to Lucie.

“Jeffrey, these are addressed to Lucie.”

“I saw that, but since she’s holed up in here with you two -” Something in Jeffrey’s pocket made a noise and he jumped. He whipped out his cell phone and said, “It’s KyleeSuanne and I have to take this.” Max grabbed his wrist, the phone clattered to the floor, and Max leaned into his face.

"*These are addressed to Lucie.*"

Jeffrey missed the storm warning and babbled on, twisting his arm to get Max to release him.

"The fax is about my winery and that's none of her business." He took a breath for the second part of the rant, but stopped abruptly when he saw the look on Max's face.

Exactly two seconds passed before the air got sucked out of the room, as though a tornado were imminent. Terrified, Jeffrey quickly dropped to the floor to retrieve his phone and ran for the exit, turning at the last moment to see if Max had come after him. He smacked into the door, hopped three steps backward, and finally stumbled into the hallway.

Max rubbed his nose and, heading for the door, growled, "That boy has no respect for anything!"

"Let it go, Max." Emma turned to Lucie and spoke quietly: "You have to understand that people like us don't get to have normal family lives. So after he quit the job, Max tried to make up for never being around for Jeffrey when he was growing up. Hasn't made any difference, though; Jeffrey is, well, a bad seed. I think he actually enjoys being a horrible human being and I'm afraid one of these days, Max will snap. He can kill with his bare hands, you know."

Lucie raised her eyebrows. "Really. His story has you two being refined deal makers, not field operatives." She sat down to read her fax and glanced up for the older woman's reaction. Emma merely flashed a ghost of a grin and turned back to Max.

"You want ice for your nose?"

"Nah, it isn't swelling; Lucie, what's in the fax?"

Lucie stared at the pages she'd been reading. "You

aren't going to believe this! It's a notarized summary of Gérard's will, from his lawyer, it's in very clear English and it says that the Sautiers have left me all their worldly goods except the winery! And that the entire will is going to be delivered here, in your name, Max, via certified mail. And it's dated *yesterday*!" She looked up, totally bewildered.

She passed the pages to Emma, who, Lucie discovered, could speed read. "Looks like Sautier instructed his attorney to draw this up at the same time he was telling him that Giles would handle the winery sale." She snorted, "Nothing senile about that old man!"

"But that was before he even gave me the postcards. He – I -"

Max peered at the pages over Emma's shoulder and said softly, "Lucie, what's going on with you and the Sautiers?"

Lucie winced. "Don't suppose either of you believe in reincarnation, former lives?"

Max and Emma shot each other an enigmatic look that encouraged Lucie to continue, "I'm pretty sure Gérard is convinced that I was his granddaughter, in another life."

She waited to hear them laugh. They didn't. "The really weird thing is, my gut is telling me that I know him from somewhere." Still no laughter.

Instead, Emma nodded and returned the documents to Lucie. "So you now have a legal right to the postcards." She looked over at Max. "He must have signed this the minute he was back in France. This is heavy, Max, for him to go to all that trouble so quickly. We have to proceed very, very carefully here."

Suddenly Lucie shook her head violently, made an "Ahhhggg" noise and stood up. "I've got a Legacy that involves a sniper, I'm the sole beneficiary of a stranger's will and when Gaston hears about it, he'll throw a fit and what if he's a good shot and, oh yeah, he's - " she pointed at Max "- got hands that are registered somewhere and do I really need *that* kind of trouble?"

Max looked at Emma, puzzled. "What'd she say about my hands?"

"Nevermind."

Emma tried for a soothing voice: "It's ok, Lucie, Max and I are going to help you, we're good at this kind of thing." Lucie half-frowned and half-smiled at her, then rolled her eyes and groaned, "Oh what the hell. But I need a drink before I can even think about looking at those cards again."

"Fine with me, we'll sit on my balcony until you feel better about this, ok?"

"Yeah, but wait a minute." Lucie suddenly hurried to the computer and logged onto the Internet. "Marie-Françoise gave me her email address, said to contact her anytime, and right now I need an explanation."

Several minutes later, Lucie hit 'send,' Max grabbed Roland's snack tray and they both followed Emma up the spiral stairs.

When she effortlessly unlatched the secret door at the top, Max whispered to Lucie, an exasperated look on his face: "Did you see that? I never told her how to do that. That woman knows everything and she *still* won't share stuff with me."

"Let it go, Max."

Max snorted.

***

The air was surprisingly balmy on Max's balcony,

and they enjoyed an excellent wine, each other's company and Roland's snacks until woo-hooing from the lawn below disrupted the lull.

The two Georges were rounding the side of the house, Phoebe and Bruno in tow. The George who spoke English yelled up at them, "Owen just dropped these two off and he said -" He was interrupted by George Too, who started to speak Japanese.

He looked down at the smaller man and said patiently, "Not *now*, George." George Too looked hurt.

George readdressed the balcony. "Owen said to tell you that Phoebe here took Bruno next door and he had to go get them. He said – wait, I wrote it down." George extracted a picce of paper from his pocket. "The neighbors want to know what sort of (he squinted at his note) 'beast' Bruno is." He looked up at them and grinned. "Heh heh, guess they don't know an extra large dog when they see one." He consulted the paper one last time. "And Owen says Bruno can't ride in the limo anymore." He looked up. "Said you probably don't want to know about that part."

He put the paper back in his pocket and looked down at his companion. "Guess that's about it, George." George Too nodded, having somehow understood, and the two took off down the lawn, followed by the dogs.

Emma shook her head at them and murmured, "Loonies. I am surrounded by loonies." Then she stood and announced, "Enough fun, we need to get back to our project. And I'm going to have Roland order Chinese for tonight."

***

Several hours later, the 'screen-worthy' cards were

attached to the map and Max's log was complete.

1. St. Nazaire, April 13, 1918
2. Quimper, Sept. 28, 1918
3. Rennes, Sept. 30, 1918
4. Le Mans, Oct. 1, 1918
5. Tours, Oct. 2, 1918
6. Château- du–Loir, Nov. 11, 1918
7. Châteaudun, Nov. 1918
8. Épinal, Mar./Apr. 1919
9. Commercy, 1919
10. Nancy, April 14, 1919
11. Toul, 1919
12. Lyon, May 6, 1919
13. Marseille, May 9, 1919
14. Nice, May 12, 1919
15. Angers, June 1927

They stepped back and waited for inspiration, hoping to see a pattern that would lead them to the Legacy.

CHAPTER 15

Nothing. They continued to stare until Max announced, "Second elimination round, ladies." He unpinned the St. Nazaire card. "Ok, we only included this card as a starting point because James landed here on April 13, 1918, as part of the American Expeditionary Force. But there's nothing else on it, so it goes." The women nodded.

Max squinted at the second card and said, "This is

dated Sept. 28, 1918, from Quimper. Hey look, I think it has an X on a window!" He squinted again and Emma dug around in a nearby drawer, then handed him an enormous magnifier.

"Saw your *mother* with this the other day."

Max made a face at her as she unpinned and carefully examined both the front and the back of the card. "It just talks about the café he ate in."

She removed the next card and said, "He went to Rennes on Sept. 30th and – surprise, surprise - he's eating again. Wait a minute!" Emma lunged at the screen, unpinned several postcards and flipped them over. She nodded to herself, grinned and turned to Max and Lucie.

"Clever. They kept it simple, just enough to attract attention, but only if you're looking for something."

Lucie gazed at the postcard and said she didn't see anything. Emma asked Max what he saw.

"You mean the OXO in the sign on the building, don't you?"

"I do indeed. Now look at the next card, you'll see the pattern."

Lucie took it, wanting to discover something, too. "But there's no X or O on the church."

"Look at the back, carefully."

"I see it! Underlined Os and he corrected his grammar with a whole bunch of Xs. And look,

CARTE POSTALE

Tous les Pays étrangers n'acceptent pas la Correspondance au recto. — Se renseigner à la Poste.

CORRESPONDANCE | ADRESSE

more eating: we have the code!"

Lucie looked up and grinned. "This is *fun!*"

Max pointed out, "This looks like the same handwriting, but someone called Earle signed it."

Lucie explained, "Middle name, there's JEM on quite a few of them. So anyway, we need all the cards with X or O on them, and references to eating, right?" Emma nodded.

Max took a turn with a card from Le Mans.

"October 1, 1918, and this one's got writing on both sides, plus an X. And a reference to having dinner on the front. It's in."

"Ok, there's a lot of the next place, Tours, but no code, they're out."

Lucie removed card number six from the screen, flipped it over and said, reverently, "Hard to believe I'm

holding something that was written on Armistice Day: look at this, it's amazing, the war ended just before James wrote this."

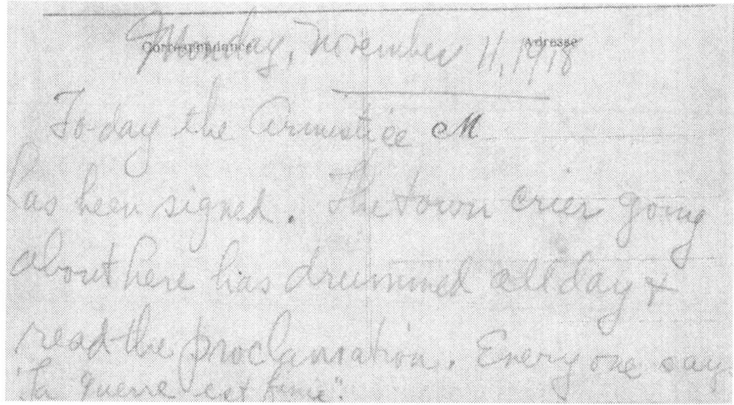

Correspondance   Adresse

Monday, November 11, 1918

To-day the Armistice has been signed. The town crier going about here has drummed all day & read the proclamation. Every one says 'La guerre est finie'.

"He says that the town crier drummed all day and read the proclamation, 'La guerre est finie.'"

She hesitated a moment, then said, "Probably shouldn't tell you this, but I get a funny feeling when I hold some of the cards."

She waited for Max to snicker.

Instead, he looked very serious. "I think you should go with your instincts." Emma nodded in agreement, examined the last card from 1918 and said, "From Châteaudun, November of 1918 and he's indicating where he had dinner with an XO. Keeper." She carefully re-pinned the 1918 clue cards to the map.

Max observed, "The next messages to Augustin are in March and April of 1919, from Épinal. Hmm, lots of writing and Xs. Seems James was stationed there. On this one he says that he ate in the café just past the carriage in the picture. Keepers."

Lucie removed the next card and stared at it. "Well, well, I didn't notice that before."

Max looked at it with the magnifier. “What? No XOs, no food.”

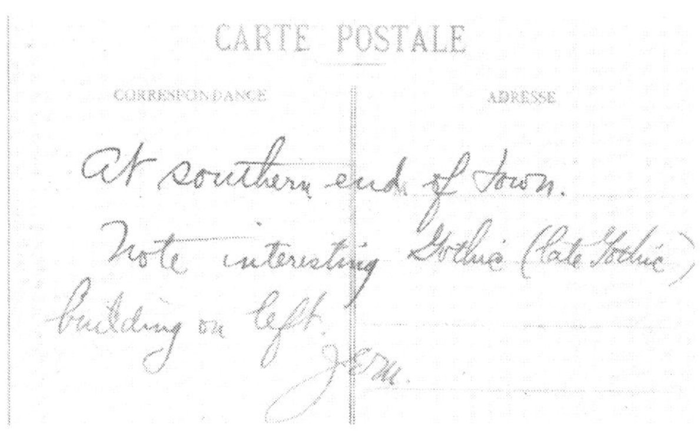
CARTE POSTALE

CORRESPONDANCE | ADRESSE

At southern end of town.
Note interesting Gothic (Late Gothic)
building on left.
J.E.M.

“It’s a marker: he’s telling us we’re on the right track. Look at the street name, then read the back again.”

Max slapped his forehead. “Avenue des Templiers – Templars. Treasure seekers. Or Treasure Protectors. And just in case we missed that, on the back there’s the suggestion to ‘note’ something.”

Someone’s stomach growled. Lucie winced. “Sorry.”

Emma called Roland and then grinned at them: “Roland says that ‘dinnah has arrived’ and could he please delivah it.”

Moments later, Roland was admitted to the inner sanctum, pushing an enormous food trolley. “How many people were you expecting to feed, Roland?”

“I just wanted to make sure that you were well nourished for your, er, endeavor.” He cast a surreptitious glance around the room, then ventured, “You know, I could be of help to you.”

Max put his arm around the butler’s shoulder and escorted him to the door. Roland’s body was pointed out of the room, but his head was turned toward

Lucie and Emma. He implored, “I could tidy up or -”

“Not necessary, but thanks for offering.” Max shoved the last bit of Roland out the door.

Between mouthfuls of every Chinese dish imaginable, they unpinned and studied more of the cards. Emma began a ruthless purge:

“Commercy, another place where James was stationed, we’ve got Xs and an O on the front; on the back he tells Augustin it’s lucky the Germans didn’t make it to Provence, that he saw vineyards blown up, sliced up by the trenches, and poisoned by chemical shells that leaked into the soil. But no eating. Reject. Next, Nancy, date is April 14, 1919, this one’s got an X on it, says it’s the Red Cross Hotel, but nothing else. It goes. Here’s one from Toul, a monument to the 1870 war with Germany. Nothing on it.”

Lucie suddenly dropped her chopsticks and nearly choked on a piece of sesame beef. She shot out of her chair, eyes wide.

“I can’t believe I missed it, he couldn’t have, there’s that damned ‘e’ on the end!” She stared at them, a look of amazement on her face. “Of *course* he’s lying – but why?”

Max opened his mouth, but Emma squeezed his arm to stop him.

“Look, our James was classically educated, I’m sure of it: his attention to the geography of the regions, his knowledge of French history and architecture. Learning French would have been an integral part of his education, plus he lived in France before the war, then he was stationed in France – *no way he completely forgot the language, as he claimed on that one postcard!*”

A wry expression on his face, Max pointed out, “He could have, not all of us are linguists, you know.”

Emma squinted at Lucie. “What were you saying

about an 'e'?"

Lucie grabbed the Armistice Day card. "Look, he wrote, 'La guerre est finie.' The war is over. It's what he was hearing in the streets, so obviously he remembered enough French to record it: but he spelled 'finie' with an E!"

Max began, "I don't - " but Emma clamped his arm in a vise-like grip.

"James put the silent E on the end of the adjective, to make it agree with the noun. Flawless grammar."

She raised one eyebrow at them. "So. We need a reason for him to be writing to Augustin in English, when by all accounts he could write perfect French."

This time Max was silent.

Lucie folded her arms over her chest. "Know what I think? I think the Army stationed this highly educated, bilingual officer right on the fortified lines near Germany, where he had a great cover as a supply officer and where he had access to all kinds of materiel."

She met Emma's shrewd stare. "He was one of you, *wasn't he?*"

Max gazed intently at her. "It only works if the person who translated the cards for Augustin was in Intelligence, too." He turned to Emma. "What do you think Em, was James passing intel to Marie Bottecher?"

Emma started to pace. "How about this: James sends postcards and packages to his good friend Augustin, nothing out of the ordinary there. Augustin had been gassed, badly wounded, had his leg amputated; the correspondence would have provided entertainment during his long convalescence. Only they're written in English to make sure Marie's involved and to discourage anyone else's interest in what James was sending."

"So they kept Augustin out of it?"

"During the war, anyway."

"You think these cards contain military information?" Lucie's eyes widened.

"No, no, they were a cover: the intel is long gone, destroyed once she extracted it and passed it on."

Lucie was fascinated. "Wow. So Augustin kept the cards his friend sent him, then somebody very clever decided to use them as clues to something altogether different."

"Let's verify their involvement in -"

"Right. Max, I need to use the secure line in the office." Emma was gone in an instant.

Lucie sat down at Emma's computer. "Let's see if Marie-Françoise got back to me."

Max leaned over Lucie's shoulder as she accessed her email, then sat back and looked disappointed. "Marie-Françoise says that when we come to search for the legacy, we're to visit and we can discuss the will then; but that they have no intention of changing their minds. And that the postcards are a mystery to her, too." Lucie blew out a sigh. "Drat."

Max pulled her over to the large screen, and they had just eliminated the 1919 postcard from Lyon when Emma burst into the library. "You were right, Lucie. Our Lt. James Milnar was in the Military Intelligence Division. And this one's for you, Max. Guess what he did during WWII?"

"OSS."

"Bingo."

Lucie frowned. "Oh man, I hate to sound callous, but I really hope this legacy has nothing to do with a bunch of outdated secret documents. I was anticipating a family heirloom, something old and cool."

Max made a face at her.

Emma ignored them and went on. "There's a void where Marie Bottecher is concerned, though. I'll have to dig a bit deeper for that, I'm afraid, if we want confirmation that she was an agent, too."

Lucie suddenly looked thoughtful. "I think there's more to this than just intelligence gathering: Marie wrote to James from Bussang in 1919 and the rest of the cards to Augustin extend to the late 1920s. The friendships, or whatever, lasted well beyond the war – so now I'm wondering if all three of them were part of the legacy thing." She raised her eyebrows. "That would make it way bigger than a family heirloom."

Emma moved to the screen. "Let's finish the cards, I'm getting tired." She removed the next card and said, "He's on the coast, in Marseille, on May 9, 1919, says he had bouillabaisse at a charming restaurant, but no X or O. It goes. Then he goes to Nice on the 12th, but no code, and we skip to 1927."

"What happened to the ones from the early 1920s?" Lucie looked at the table.

Max rubbed his eyes. "Hard to tell, after 162 cards, I close my eyes and see Xs on the inside of my eyelids. I'm thinking you pitched them, must not have had anything interesting on them." Max looked around briefly and shrugged.

"Ok, so he's on leave in June of 1927, goes to see the Loire Valley castles, but the Angers card has no code. And that's the last one."

They stepped back once more, frowning. "Anybody see anything?"

Lucie complained, "All we've got is chronologically arranged clue-cards. What are we supposed to do, go looking for the legacy in the city with the latest date? That can't be all there is to it. Plus we'd have no idea what to look for. We're missing something."

"What's that noise?"

Lucie got up and walked to the main door. "Somebody's scraping their toenails so we notice that they're out there and not in here, where they want to be." She paused before opening it, and heard Roland's voice, petulant as usual.

"Get away from there, you two. If I'm not allowed in, neither are you! Now shoo!" The scratching stopped, but Lucie didn't hear the click of toenails walking away. "Very well, be that way" was accompanied by the sound of a loud humph and a human retreat.

Lucie opened the door cautiously, her foot behind it: she didn't want to suffer the same indignity that Max had. Surc enough, Bruno leaned hard against the door and Lucie had to ease the dogs in. They bounded happily to the table, Max put up a restraining arm and Bruno shoved her snout in his crotch. Max grimaced and pushed her away.

Lucie went back to the screen and began, "We have three first-class minds working here and we ought to be able to -" but was interrupted by scuffling noises. Phoebe and Bruno were tussling over something under the table and didn't stop until Max yelled 'treat!' They dropped their prizes and ran to Lucie, their usual source of goodies. Max grabbed the postcards before they changed their minds and wiped off the dog slobber.

"Look at this, the dogs got their paws on some cards that haven't been logged."

"How?"

Max frowned. "I have no idea, unless, maybe they flew off the table when Jeffrey tossed the papers on it."

Phoebe and Bruno, tired of waiting for the promised treats, started a loud protest. Lucie glanced around the room for something to appease them and found some fortune cookies from dinner. Before she could remove the paper fortunes, the dogs grabbed their prizes and ran off with them, tossing them in the air like toys.

Lucie laughed and shook her head, then asked to see the cards. She examined one and felt the hair stand up on her neck.

CHAPTER 16

Emma moved quickly to her side and asked, "What is it, Lucie - vibes?"

"Something has happened; this card's got a totally different feel to it, and not just because it's in French and from Marie to Augustin." She looked up.

"I think it's a message about the legacy itself!"

"Then all three of them *were* involved. What does it say?"

"It's dated October of 1919, there was a flood in Épinal, and their friend James' favorite restaurant was some-what damaged but that the office of the military police is ok."

"So we've got 1919, no mention of where

James is and Augustin probably still can't travel because of his injuries. So, Marie is keeping an eye on Épinal for them." Max poked at eastern France on the screen. "Here."

Emma took the card and studied it for several minutes. "I think Marie is telling Augustin that the flood has damaged the legacy, because she refers to food - but that James took care of it, the military being ok." She glanced at them for affirmation and they nodded.

Lucie picked up the second card. "We're back to clue cards with this one: James is in Épinal again in 1924, we've got an X to mark his room, he eats downstairs, and – no way!"

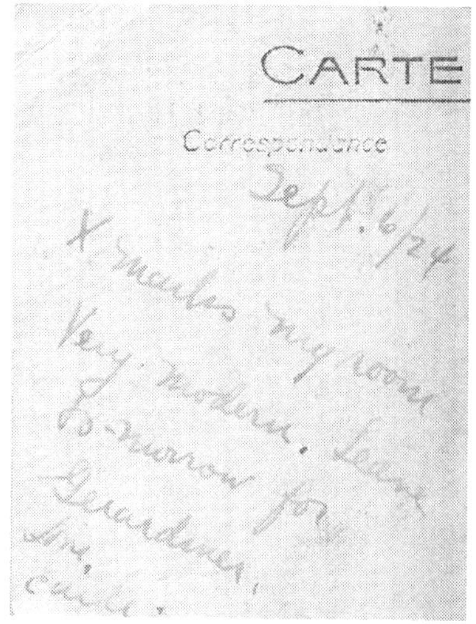

Her eyes widened. "The first mention of a destination: Earle is leaving tomorrow for Gérardmer."

She swallowed hard and stared at the writing. "It can't be."

She grabbed the last card and yelled, “BUT IT IS! OhmyGod, we found it, look, it has to be: Gérardmer. **GÉRARD. MER.**”

This is the One, I know it is. It’s dated November of 1924, has an X on the back and he says he ate nearby.” She sat down hard and her hand shook as she held the card.

Emma typed furiously on her keyboard, and said, without looking up, “It’s a little bit south and pretty much due east of Épinal, and it’s directly north of Bussang.” She grabbed the card and added to the map. Number sixteen. Then she took Lucie’s marker and drew a line, west to east, starting with the earliest dated card.

“Two, three, four, seven, eight - and sixteen. A straight shot, right across France.” Shc stood back and gazed, deep in thought.

Max bent down to Lucie. “You’re sure, aren’t you.” Not a question.

Lucie nodded gravely and looked at the card. “I know, it seems too obvious, the key card bearing

Augustin's son's name. But this is it."

Emma turned to them: "So if your assumption about the Épinal card is correct, at some point they moved the legacy to a town with Gérard's name. He'd been born in 1923, it's plausible."

Lucie stared at the card. "But it's just a picture of a lake and mountains. What kind of dumbass clue is that? I just hope they didn't dump the treasure in the lake, like that gold the Germans supposedly hid in, I think it was Switzerland, during WWII. And this card is from 1924: the landscape has to have changed dramatically. This treasure could be anywhere!"

"Treasure, huh? You sure it's a treasure?"

"Gérard was emphatic about its value, and let's not forget Gaston's intense interest – I'm thinking jewels, art, or gold. We're way past a simple family heirloom."

Emma went back to her computer. "Says here Gérardmer is now a tourist destination: in the winter, it's a ski resort, in the summer, there's boating and fishing on the lake. Looks prosperous."

Max shook his head. "But I still don't see why he – they – hid something valuable so close to the German border. Doesn't make sense. Would've been a lot safer on Sautier's property."

"But I'm *positive.*"

Lucie gazed around the room without looking at anything, tuning them out while she gathered her thoughts. Suddenly focused, she turned to them.

"Ever since M. Sautier gave me the cards, I've been thinking about my grandfather and the Great War and about a book I just read called *The Guns of August.*" She went over to the discarded postcards, sifted through them and chose one.

"Max, remember the effect that this picture of the devastation had on you?"

He nodded.

"They called it a World War, but it didn't have a number back then because they had to believe that carnage of that magnitude would never happen again. How else could they endure the pain and the loss of hundreds of thousands of lives to - let me think, the author was so eloquent – *'gain ten yards and exchange one wet-bottomed trench for another.'* " Lucie's eyes blazed with intensity.

"I get the sense that creating the Legacy was an act of defiance, and they needed to carry it out right under the Germans' noses. Daring, arrogant maybe, but it got Augustin and his friends through the horror. And lurking just under those Teutonic schnozzes was the perfect hiding place, a town named for a son he never thought he'd live to create: Gérardmer!"

Her audience nodded. It finally made sense.

"And you know what else? I think those three knew it wasn't over with les Boches, that there would be Germans on French soil again, coveting, stealing, destroying. So this wasn't just a hidden treasure thing, it was also something to sustain them through the *next* disaster of epic proportions."

Max stared at her for a moment. "So, Lucie, you got a hat trick: first Gaston's deception, then James' lie about not speaking French, now Gérardmer. Congratulations. M. Sautier's faith in you is entirely justified."

He rose and returned with a bottle of wine and three glasses. He poured the wine reverently and handed them each a glass.

"Here's to Augustin."

"To Augustin." They raised their glasses and drank solemnly.

Lucie chewed her bottom lip. "It's been years since I took a vacation..." Suddenly she thumped down her wineglass, startling Max and Emma. She rose quickly and, heading for the spiral staircase, announced, "We need to go to France!"

"What, right this minute?"

"Nooo, of course not. First I have to see if Sophie is free: I figure if we're going to be in Europe, I might as well enjoy some time with my daughter before we go looking for treasure." She stopped, one foot on the bottom step. "So are you two in or what?"

"Of course we're in." Emma smiled, but the smile faded as she added, "I need to rest now, so goodnight, you two." She turned and gave Max a sly look as she left, and Max pretended not to notice.

"Shouldn't you go with her?"

Max grinned. "She's armed to the teeth, Lucie. God help Julia if she tries something, even if Em is tired." He noted that Bruno was fast asleep on the couch, so he grabbed Phoebe and followed Lucie up the staircase.

Half way up, she stopped and squinted at Max. "Um, would you mind if I, that is, it's not that I'm afraid to sleep in my room, it's just that - "

"No problem, you can have my bed."

Lucie gulped, inaudibly she hoped, and said, "That's ok, I'll take the couch and I don't want to sleep in my clothes, ahhh, I mean I want my sleepwear." Damn. Why was this so hard?

"Are you finished? Because if you are, unlatch the door and stop worrying."

***

Max waited while Lucie got ready for bed, relieved that she was going to let him protect her.

"You're taking the bed, there are fresh sheets on it and I hope you don't mind company." Lucie peered at him from the bathroom.

"I'm pretty sure Phoebe will want to sleep with you."

Max laughed silently.

Lucie thought about revenge.

CHAPTER 17

Sleeping in Max's bed was like floating on air, and it seemed that Lucie's head had barely hit the pillow when Phoebe began to lick her face. As she petted the little dog, Max emerged from the bathroom, fully dressed, and smiled at her.

"Want coffee?"

"Definitely.'

He poured it for her and motioned at the door. "C'mon, I'll check your suite and wait while you get ready."

"You don't need to - "

"Yes, I do."

***

Emma looked surprised, then faintly disappointed at finding Max and Lucie calmly having breakfast in the kitchen: she'd imagined they'd be all over each other. She shrugged, helped herself to some fruit and raised an eyebrow at Max.

"What?" Max squinted at her.

Lucie regarded them both suspiciously, then asked, "You two have any time restraints about this trip to France?"

They answered in unison, "None."

"Good. One, we visit the Sautiers and show them what we have, see if they remember anything useful. Two, since Marie lived just south of Gérardmer, we might be able to access their local records for background on her. Three, I guess it's too much to hope for that James stayed in France and there's still a trace of him." She looked up expectantly.

"Excellent plan, just tell us when to show up."

"You got it." Lucie stood and said, "Max, I need to get my stuff from the, um, hiding place." She tapped the side of her nose in a con artist's signal, and Max laughed out loud.

Emma rolled her eyes and headed for the hall. "C'mon you two, we need to store the postcards somewhere safe, so as long as you're going to access the PH, let's go collect them now."

They unlocked the library and carefully removed the clue cards from the screen, secured them in a plastic bag, then put the cards that hadn't been used in another bag. And just in case, used the spiral staircase to get to Max's suite.

It didn't take long for Lucie to check with her business manager, Sophie and the Sautiers. Without looking away from her computer screen, she asked Max and Emma, "Can you both be in France in two weeks? Because that's what'll work for me: I found someone to cover my business obligations, Sophie can get the time off and the Sautiers said whenever we get there is good for them."

Someone answered, "Perfect," so Lucie made the travel arrangements.

She had just snapped her computer closed when Max got up and handed her a key. "For my suite, feel free to use it anytime."

"But I'm leaving tomorrow, remember?"

Remember? It was all Max could think about. Well, almost all. His phone interrupted that particular thought. He listened, replied "Right now?" and then "Ok, we'll be right down."

"Mother wants us to join her in the Salon and won't tell me what it's about." He raised his eyebrows and shrugged.

***

Didier had already poured flutes of champagne by the time they walked into the large room, and handed one to each of them, beaming. Kate rushed to her son and squeaked, "We're getting married and I'm so happy!"

Max looked astonished and said, "Wow, that was fast, um, are you sure, mother?"

Kate raised her flute to Didier and said, emphatically, "Carpe diem, son, carpe diem."

"Then I'm happy, too. Here, let me pour that for you." He took the bottle from Didier and refilled his mother's glass, then turned to Margaret, who was waving her flute around wildly. As Max weaved and bobbed in an attempt to refill Margaret's drink, she babbled to no one in particular, "Isn't it just a good thing I saw Jesus, just when Kate and Didier got together and now I'll be famous when I'm on that talk show. And I get to stay with my second cousin once removed in the City because they want me on the show all week!"

"Ouf – stand still, Margaret."

Lucie hugged Kate, then Didier, and asked, "Have you set a date?"

"Within the month, I hope. At our ages, putting things off isn't such a good idea. But we wanted to check your schedule first, you're the Person of Honor."

Lucie was dumbfounded. "But don't you want - "

Kate regarded her levelly. "If it weren't for you, I wouldn't be marrying my sweetheart at this stage of my life, so, yes, I want you to stand for me."

When Max raised his glass and wished Kate and Didier much happiness, his mother sipped her champagne and continued, "We'd like to have the ceremony in Didier's hometown."

"That works for us, mother, just so happens the three of us will be in France in two weeks." He grinned and added, "Can you wait that long?"

Kate giggled. "Don't be silly, son, of course we can." She turned to her fiancé and tapped her wrist watch, then turned back to Max. "Owen is taking us into the City in a few minutes, and we'll call later to let you know when we're coming back."

Max kissed his mother, shook Didier's hand and tilted his head at Lucie and Emma. "C'mon, we've earned a nice lunch in the village."

As they headed toward the back staircase, Lucie asked, "What village?"

"A little hideaway, for people who want something cool without going into the City. And Emma, would you *please* wear something besides SWAT black? I don't want to alarm the wait staff."

"Humph. Whatever."

Max looked puzzled. "When did you start saying Whatever?"

Emma flipped her eyebrows at him.

***

Lucie knocked on Max's door and hoped he didn't hear her sharp intake of breath when he appeared in dark-shirt-and-jacket casual chic. Then she noticed the Vacheron watch on his wrist: obviously gold, elegant, sleek and sexy against his fading tan. “Extraordinary timepiece.”

He held out his arm. “Emma gave it to me right after we, uh, retired. Even had it inscribed.” He rotated his wrist so Lucie could see all of it. “Honestly, I like my steel Tag Heuer better – pinkish gold really isn’t my thing - but Em spent a fortune on this one. Says I should wear it more often.”

He whistled for Phoebe and moments later, they met Emma at the bottom of the back steps. A vision in navy Armani, sans bobby pin helmet, she commented, “My my haven’t the two of you just totally amped up your appearance? Nice watch, Max.”

Max turned to Lucie with an exasperated expression. “What *is* it with her and the slang?”

***

They took Max’s sleek, black Porsche and parked a block away from the pedestrian-only location of the café. The area felt European, with food smells wafting everywhere, and as a bonus, air that was still warm enough for the sidewalks to be sprinkled with tables, chairs and lots of people.

Max’s café could have been transplanted from France: a storefront that was all wood and glass, an easel that proudly displayed the menu, potted bushes among the outside tables, trees growing intentionally out of the sidewalk, and a large yellow dog sleeping under its owner’s chair.

As they approached, Phoebe began to pull on her lead, anxious to greet her friend: a waiter dressed in a black vest, a black bowtie, a white long sleeved shirt, a long white apron, and a slight air of disdain.

He ignored the humans as he bent down to scratch

her ears and seated them at what was apparently Max's permanent outdoor table. But he disappeared before they could order their drinks, and when he returned, bore a small dish with fragrant, tiny cubes of meat. He waited while Phoebe jumped onto her chair and wagged at him, served her and finally turned to Max.

***

They'd lingered over an excellent salade niçoise and an array of crêpes - Lucie resolved to add the caramelized onion, fresh mushrooms and goat cheese crêpe to her own repertoire - for an hour and a half when Emma asked about Max's background check on Didier.

"He's a widower and solvent, no history of anything that would preclude their marriage."

Lucie nodded as though it were the most natural thing in the world to be discussing.

Emma stood up and commented, "Good. And now I'm off to D.C. for information I couldn't find in any of my databases. My cab's waiting at the end of the street."

Max looked concerned, but kept his voice level. "You'll be on *their* turf. You want...company?"

Emma shook her head. "I'll call you when I've got what I need."

"All right. How about we take mother's Gulfstream to France; we can drop the engaged couple off at the winery, check up on Jeffrey and then meet Lucie in Paris."

"That works."

"Uh, Em, this is just about the Legacy, right?"

"Absolutely." She was gone before anyone could inquire further.

Max turned to Lucie. "Know that look on someone's face when you know *absolutely* she's telling the truth?"

Lucie tilted her head at him.

"Me neither."

***

The day was still balmy, so Max and Lucie strolled to a small open-air market, where Max bought several kinds of greens, tomatoes, Roquefort cheese, and some blueberry pastries.

"The Sautier will is supposed to arrive at my place in a few days, so do you want me to send it to you?"

"Would you make a copy and bring it to France with you? Keep the original in the priest's hole, that way I won't have to get into my safe deposit box before the trip."

"Of course." Max smiled to himself: she trusted him.

The smile faded when he answered his cell phone. "Uh-huh, ok, I see. I can be there in half an hour." He sighed. "Mrs. Harris is NOT a gorgon. No, I have plans for this evening. It's not like signing a check is going to take all night...that is not sarcasm... ok, it IS sarcasm, I have to go." He disconnected.

"We have to get back. Dylan is putting in an appearance."

Lucie squinted: in an earlier version of herself, she might have experienced a jealous twinge and confronted Max with a 'Who is She' conversation. Now, however, she merely commented, "Your daughter?"

Max sighed again. "Unfortunately."

"Unfortunately she's your daughter, or unfortunately she's showing up?"

"Both."

***

Twenty minutes later, they were standing in front of the château. Lucie took the bags of food as Max entered the security code on the keypad by the door, put his hand on the doorknob and pushed it slightly; Phoebe squeezed past him, into the house, but Max stopped suddenly and Lucie bumped into him.

"Ow. What's the matter?"

"She's in there already, I know she is."

"How do you know that?"

"I feel impending doom, just like when her mother used to show up to complain about the divorce."

"Which wife was that?"

"Isabelle."

"Forgotten pre-nup, gun fetish?"

"Uh-huh."

"Max, you have to go in."

Max sighed and pushed the door inward. Lucie immediately had the impression of being on a movie soundstage: the three of them had positioned themselves on the marble staircase to the right, Dylan flanked by Juan and Roland. Lucie half expected them to fling their arms wide, break into song and dance down to them.

Instead, the obviously furious young woman started toward Max and the two men immediately grabbed her arms. She tried to shake them off, failed and shot Max a look that would have turned a lesser man to stone.

"About time, *Daddy.*" She spat the word at him. "Tell these two queens to take their fucking hands off me."

***

Lucie gaped, Max growled. At least it sounded like growling. "Your daughter look like that?"

"Um, no."

"Didn't think so."

Dylan had Trouble written all over her, and would have been lovely – she looked like Max – if her face hadn't been pierced with metal acne.

Max was saying, "Watch your mouth, you're in my house now."

Roland rushed forward, stopped and turned to Juan. "Don't let go of her until I tell them what she did, ok?" He ran down the rest of the steps, giddy with importance.

Juan, who had curled his lip at Dylan's 'queen' remark, was – wait a minute, Juan was RIPPED! He was wearing a paper-thin tee shirt that displayed impressive abs and biceps that Lucie had somehow missed, and his firm grip on Dylan's arm meant she wasn't going anywhere.

Roland stopped right in front of Max and blurted out, "We had to let her in, of course, the security code was new, and we only left her alone for a moment and *there she was*, trying to get into your suite to do God knows what and that's why we, um, detained her here until you returned!"

"Thank you, Roland, you and Juan have done very well. You can both go back to whatever it was you were doing."

Juan let go of Dylan, but kept a wary eye on her as he descended the stairs and turned into the hallway. Roland shot her a withering 'Told you so' look and trotted after Juan. Interesting dynamics. Plus, Roland hadn't even tried for the fake accent.

Dylan brushed off her sleeves as though the men had contaminated her and stomped down the stairs. She planted herself in front of Max and pointed her finger at him.

Max put his hands on his hips. "Really?"

She lowered her finger, crossed her arms, tossed her dark hair and leaned back on one foot. Total arrogance.

"Heard you bought Jeffrey a winery. I want in."

Max raised his eyebrows. Nothing like getting right to the point.

"So when did you talk to Julia?" He could come to the point, too.

Dylan stood up straight. "How'd you - ? Yesterday."

"She also told you to look for something, so you thought you'd just break into my apartment.

"I did *not*!" Dylan tried to sound indignant.

"Please." Max waved his arms around. "Seriously, Dylan, wreck your car again? Another DUI? How much this time?"

"I told you, I want in on the winery thing."

Max gritted his teeth. "Tell you what. We'll go find Jeffrey and you can discuss it with him. And just for the record, I did not *give* him a winery, I expect a return on the investment."

"Whatever." Suddenly she noticed Lucie. "Who's this?"

Lucie reflected that while Dylan and Jeffrey looked nothing alike, they did have the rudeness gene in common.

A wry expression on her face, Lucie pushed past the girl and answered, "Someone who's tired of this conversation."

Dylan watched as she headed down the hall with the bags of groceries, frowned and observed, "Your help has a bad attitude."

Max heard a faint 'Whatever,' and sighed.

***

Lucie had used the key Max had given her, changed to her most comfortable jeans, and was sitting on his bed with her computer and Phoebe when he returned and headed for his kitchen. She looked up and asked, “So are you really going to give Dylan part interest in the winery?”

“Hell no, I was hoping she and Jeffrey would kill each other over it and then I wouldn’t have to deal with either one of them. They left half an hour ago to discuss what I’m sure is not in my best interest, since they don’t want to be overheard.” He stopped abruptly. “You hungry?”

“Yeah, I could eat something.”

“Good. I’m making dinner.”

Lucie raised both eyebrows.

“I have two prime Black Angus rib eyes, the makings of a very nice salad, and two bottles of - ” he paused for effect – “DRC Romanée-Conti ’85, already open and breathing. At least I hope that’s what they are, otherwise I’m out almost $32,000. I know the steaks merit a Bordeaux, but I’ve been waiting to try the DRC.”

Lucie gasped, “Oh no no no, that’s way too much!”

“Since when are you afraid of expensive wine?”

“Hey, I’m well-off, not obscenely wealthy like you, and wine that costs that much makes me nervous.”

Max, who was now rummaging in his frig, turned to her. “Don’t be. It might turn out to be Julia’s, ah, plonk.”

Lucie got up and followed him. “Well, ok then. Sure you don’t want help?”

“Absolutely not. I’m going to let these steaks come to room temperature and pour you a glass of wine. *You* are going to sit down and watch someone else prepare your food. You more than deserve it, and don’t worry, I kept it simple.” Max wiped out two already sparkling Pinot Noir glasses and reverently poured them each a glass. They inhaled the aroma, swirled and tasted. Eyes wide, both started talking at once.

"This isn't wine, it's ambrosia!"

"Thank God Julia didn't get to it!"

"I've never tasted *anything* like this!" She stopped abruptly, suddenly aware that Max was gazing at her intently.

He smiled and raised the glass to her. "You, Madame Chef, are the perfect person for sharing this moment."

Lucie was smiling, too, as she clinked her glass against his. They finished off the first glass and Max poured them both another.

Max was in no hurry as he prepared the salad with the ingredients he'd bought at the open-air market. Lucie, now contentedly sitting with Phoebe in her lap and sipping the wine, watched his hands work the food, the gold bracelet dangling from his wrist with the movement. She was amazed at the confidence he displayed; most men were intimidated by her profession and would never have dared cook for her.

And he was still wearing the sexy black shirt.

Max caught her look. "What?"

"Nothing, just watching you."

Max grinned inwardly as he whisked a vinaigrette dressing, which he gently massaged into the lettuces. He added the tomatoes he'd just cut, and held a pepper grinder over his creation.

"You like lots of pepper, right?"

There was no point debating his knowledge of her preferences, so Lucie just nodded. He added sea salt and crowned the salad with lots of small chunks of bleu cheese. Setting that aside, he turned to Lucie.

"Want to take our wine out to the terrace for a little while?"

She held her glass out for Max to refill, then nudged Phoebe off her lap, motioning for the little dog to follow them. But Phoebe decided to stay and guard the beef on the counter.

As Lucie settled into one of Max's comfortable chairs, he turned on an electric heater by the patio table and explained, "No bugs this time of year, and this makes it really nice out here."

They enjoyed their wine and listened to the night sounds around them until Max rose and beckoned her back inside. He heated a cast iron grill pan, drizzled a bit of olive oil into it and looked over at Lucie. "Medium rare, right?"

Lucie nodded and watched him sear the steaks on each side, season them, then quickly put them on a plate, which he covered loosely with aluminum foil.

While the steaks 'rested,' he got two trays from a cupboard, added the food, wine, plates and cutlery, and they transported dinner to the terrace. This time Phoebe followed.

The beef was, of course, superb. Lucie closed her eyes with the first bite, and moaned as she chewed. Max looked pleased.

They shared bits of steak with Phoebe and were enjoying the second bottle of wine with Max's favorite artisanal chocolate when he slapped his forehead and said, "I nearly forgot to tell you about Didier. Gérard's lawyer faxed me a codicil to the will: when the dust settles from the winery sale, Gérard is giving Didier $500,000 and a small residence."

Lucie smiled. "That's great!" She took another bite of chocolate and said, "Mmmm, Max, this is fantastic. I want the name of your chocolatier."

"And just so you know, my own money isn't tied to mother's."

"And that matters to me why?"

"They're going to live six months in each country."

"That's a non-sequitur. I asked you why you think I care about your money."

"Most women want that kind of information."

"I'm not - "

"Most women. Believe me, I'm well aware of that. But I wanted you to know anyhow."

Lucie half frowned at him and Max quickly poured her another glass. He still annoyed her, but it seemed to matter less and less.

She sipped her wine contentedly, enjoying the warm-all-over feeling it always produced, and it occurred to her that this was one hell of a seduction scene.

Max put his glass down and leaned into her ear, his voice deep and husky.

"And is it working?"

CHAPTER 18

Before Max knew what was happening, Lucie was on her feet; she seized the front of his shirt and pulled his face to hers, kissing him passionately and dragging him toward his bedroom. Phoebe started to bark, and Max almost tripped over her. He had definitely *not* anticipated Lucie making the first move.

Once inside, Max locked the French doors, not an easy feat because Lucie hadn't relinquished her grip. Clothes became projectiles and they were on the bed in what seemed like seconds. Max kissed the breast that drove him crazy the night she wore the black dress, then started to move his mouth over her neck.

He drew back to gaze at her and Lucie involuntarily moaned when she saw the raw desire in his eyes. As she lifted her head to kiss him, her eyes shifted to his shoulder, to the tiny pirate: a wicked, wicked pirate tattoo, complete with a magnificent hat and eye patch!

Lucie whooped, "So *that* was the buzzing noise on the phone!" She flicked her tongue on it, flopped back down and swiftly pulled him into her.

Minutes later, Lucie shrieked as the first orgasm slammed into her like a tidal wave.

Max, who was breathing heavily, managed, "You're a screamer." More panting. "Good to know."

"Sorry, didn't mean to be loud."

"No no, I meant I'll always know when I'm doing something right."

Lucie reached down and caressed him, never taking her eyes off his face, then slid him back inside her. He came in moments, and they flopped on each side of the bed, gasping.

"That - was – great!"

Lucie looked over at him. "Raise the bar, Max. That qualifies as Up to No Good. We'll hit *great* a little later."

***

They took their time after that, pleasuring each other slowly. Their mouths found the spots that drove them wild, and Max held Lucie off until her next orgasm washed up over her slowly and intensely, as he intended. The guttural noise she made was primal and seemed to last forever, utterly gratifying to Max.

This time she flopped over and announced, "I'm hungry."

He laughed, rolled off the bed, pulled on his silk sleep pants and headed for the kitchen. "Uh huh, the other half of your steak." He quickly heated the pan, then lightly seared the meat and returned to the bedroom.

"Thing is, I noticed you don't eat a lot at one time. Now, about your drinking habits - "

Lucie threw a pillow at him, then shared her steak and fell asleep in his arms. Max looked down at her and knew beyond the shadow of a doubt that he needed her in his life. Problem was, he was fairly certain she didn't need *him* in hers.

***

They slept until Phoebe indicated that she needed to go outside. Max stumbled to the French doors and told the little dog to come right back, there would be a treat for her. He ambled back to the bedroom to wait, but stopped at the archway and stared at Lucie: her breasts were exposed above the sheet and she made no attempt to cover them.

His scrutiny apparently amused her and she smiled at him, then threw off the remaining covers. Max almost forgot about his dog.

"We should get married." Damn! He hadn't meant to spring it on her like this.

Lucie was incredulous. "You want to get *married*?"

"Un-huh."

"Why? Because of - " and she gestured at the rumpled sheets. "You cannot base a relationship on sex!"

"What about great sex?"

"Not even great sex."

"Why not?"

"I can see how you wound up with four wives."

Max thought about that as he went to let Phoebe in.

As he crawled back into bed, Lucie told him, "Plus I wouldn't want to be related to Jeffrey."

"Mmm, see your point. That *is* a deal breaker."

***

Sounds in the kitchen woke Lucie, who, as she stretched, noticed Max's lingering scent on her body and was immediately aroused, the electric tingle shooting in all directions. Breakfast first, though, she was hungry.

Phoebe jumped off the large bed, wide awake with the aroma of slightly heated blueberry pastries, and Lucie pulled Max's tee shirt over her head as she followed the dog. She smiled a good morning at Max and took the mug of steaming coffee he offered her.

He had opened the curtains on the French doors, so they ate their breakfast on his couch and watched the morning. Then Max moved behind her and caressed her neck and shoulder, leaning to kiss her earlobe. "You have any idea how hard it's been for me to keep my hands off you all weck?"

She touched the side of his face and smiled at him again.

Phoebe started to bark, frustrated by the lack of attention, so Max fed her, then let her outside. A mischievous look in her eyes, Lucie slowly licked the remains of blueberry from her fingers and asked, "So, you treat all your help like this?"

Max retaliated, "So, we raise the bar last night or not?"

"Jury isn't in on that one - " She didn't get to finish the sentence because Max reached for her as she made a dash for his bed.

"You little hussy, that was LoseYourMind sex and you know it!"

***

"I have a plane to catch before dinner, so I'm gonna go shower and pack."

Max, whose face was in a pillow, said what sounded like, "Iwahudasay."

Lucie poked at him. "Speak English."

He lifted his head and said, "I want you to stay, on your terms, And I do understand about not wanting to get married. So what's it gonna take?"

Lucie heard a serious tone in his voice and did not want to go there.

"Hmm, well, I know you're not offering me money, so what else did you have in mind?"

He made a grab for her and she kissed him without getting caught, throwing the sheets over him as she headed for the bathroom. The voice from under the covers stopped her at the door, however.

"You're like a light in my life, Lucie." He threw the covers off his upper body and continued, "That's what your name means in Latin, I looked it up. I'm sure we were meant to be together."

Lucie made a face at him. "Ok, c'mon, let's be together in the shower; that'll make you feel better about, um, things."

CHAPTER 19

The showcr took longer than expected, especially after Lucie teased Max about his staying power. "I thought those little blue pills only lasted four hours" produced a "Hey, I don't take - and an activity that could have drowned those less determined.

Max remained in the bathroom, having noticed an exfoliating product in Lucie's cosmetic bag and deciding that his face needed attention. As he stood in front of the mirror, humming happily, Lucie threw on a tee shirt, her sleep pants and slip-on shoes.

She ran down to the kitchen and left a note for Antonio, who had offered to pack up her knives, spices and cookware, and as she hurried back up the stairs, she unconsciously hummed Max's tune.

Someone else was moving about the château, and had entered Max's suite via the door that Lucie had forgotten to lock. Dressed entirely in black, he moved purposefully to the bathroom door and barricaded it, imprisoning Max. Then he lay in wait by the hallway entrance.

Lucie had barely pushed the door open when it was wrenched out of her hand, causing her to stumble into the room. She screamed as Jeffrey seized her by the hair, flung her face first against the wall and quickly bound her wrists with a necktie.

He spun her around and, his hot breath on her face, grabbed her throat and began to squeeze, slowly restricting the air flow.

Lucie vaguely heard Max pound on the bathroom door and yell, "*Let me out of here*!" His incapacitation seemed to empower Jeffrey, who used his free hand to tear at her pants – difficult, though, because he'd pressed himself tightly against her.

"This what you want, bitch?"

Lucie struggled, trying for any kind of leverage before she passed out.

"Screwing an old man, when you could have had me. And you just had to mess with my deal and make me look bad, didn't you?"

He paused long enough to let her see the naked hate in his eyes. "And Jessica just had to take up with that spic, which never would have happened if you hadn't interfered."

Lucie was getting lightheaded, her throat almost totally constricted by his meaty hand. "You - don't - want - to do this" was all she could manage to rasp.

Jeffrey mocked her: "Not so brave without your knives, are you?"

Suddenly he noticed the blood on his hand: his fraternity ring, a massive, meant-to-impress multi-pronged piece, had torn open a nasty gash under Lucie's chin. Jeffrey's eyes widened as he panicked, thinking that it was his own blood. *Leverage!*

Lucie quickly made the craziest face she could manage.

"What the?"

Momentarily caught off guard, Jeffrey relaxed his hold on her and inadvertently stepped backward; Lucie gasped a lungful of air and head-butted him hard, right on his nose, producing a satisfying, cracking sound.

Then she stomped as hard as she could on his foot, and he yowled, simultaneously hopping and clutching his bleeding nose.

As Jeffrey squealed "Look what you did to me!" Lucie wriggled out of the necktie handcuffs and, in full warrior mode, opened one of the French doors and propelled him through it to the balcony beyond.

He tripped and fell, and before he could recover, she kicked him viciously in the groin. Twice. Jeffrey screamed and Lucie jumped on him, her knee in his gut. She grabbed his hair and thwacked his head on the cement as he shrieked, "Stop it, you crazy bitch!"

"Shut your face or I swear I'll throw you off this balcony!"

A lifetime of misogyny overrode good sense and Jeffrey bellowed, "Get off me, ***you filthy slut***!"

Lucie leaned close to him, and in a voice suddenly devoid of emotion, said succinctly, "You really shouldn't have said that." She curled her fingers, drew back her arm and tilted the heel of her right hand, ready to shove his crooked, bleeding nose into his brains.

Jeffrey finally understood the gravity of the situation. Terrified, he retched on himself and gurgled, "Oh God, somebody hellllp meeeee!"

Just as Lucie tensed her arm for full impact, Max's voice suddenly boomed, "Don't do it, he's not worth it!" and then a combination of clanking, barking and yelling rose from the bottom of the balcony steps.

Lucie's eyes followed Max's voice: he was wedged in his bathroom window, stuck at the shoulders, waving his arms around like a whirligig.

And still yelling. "You'll kill him!"

"That's kinda the point," she yelled back at him.

But she slowly unclenched her fingers as the dogs burst onto the balcony, followed by vigilantes Roland and Juan, who were dressed in camouflage and brandishing an assortment of garden tools.

As the men pointed their weapons at Jeffrey, Lucie slowly rose, took several deep breaths and arched one of her eyebrows.

"Those things loaded?" Bruno and Phoebe barked an affirmative and started racing frantically around Jeffrey.

Max stopped struggling and stared in amazement. "What the hell?"

Just then Jeffrey made an attempt to get up, and Lucie kicked him hard in the groin. Again. He curled into a fetal position and began a low, incessant wail.

She looked down at him contemptuously. "Well, if I'm not allowed to kill your sorry ass, at least I made sure the gene pool doesn't make it to the next generation."

Suddenly Bruno stopped circling and hovered over Jeffrey, ears flattened. She emitted a low growl, lunged at him and chomped the only appendage he wasn't protecting. He yowled and grabbed his ear. Uh-huh, payback for Jeffrey's 'training' techniques.

Roland patted Bruno on the head, "Well done, you are a very good doggie!" He turned to Lucie and explained, "Since Mrs. Harris is away, we thought we'd patrol the area today - and - wouldn't you know? - we *both* had camo outfits and then it sounded like World War Three up here and, well, Here. We. Are!"

Max had had enough. "SOMEBODY GET ME OUT OF HERE!" Bruno's attention immediately shifted to Max; she abandoned Jeffrey and joyously padded over to him, put her huge paws on either side of the bathroom window and slurped his newly-exfoliated face. Max howled and tried to push her away.

When Bruno's tongue found his open mouth, Max gagged.

"Maybe you'd better go help him."

"You ok with - "

"This hot mess?" Lucie grabbed a shovel and pointed it at Jeffrey's vomit-covered face. "Definitely."

***

Roland and Juan decided that extracting Max from the bathroom side of his dilemma would be better than trying to pry Bruno away and pull him out the balcony side, so they lubricated his shoulders with shower gel and yanked at him. He plopped on the floor and they looked at him as he ran for the door. "He's larger than I expected," Roland observed, and Juan nodded.

Max, wearing only pajama bottoms, ran out to Lucie. She dropped the shovel as he engulfed her in his arms, clutching her head tightly to his chest as she started to shake. A whimper escaped as Roland and Juan reappeared to stand guard over a moaning Jeffrey.

"Are you all right? I saw blood all over the carpet!" He held her at arms' length to assess the damage himself and saw the gash under her chin and the torn pajama pants. His face contorted with rage, he choked out, "I'll kill the sonofabitch myself if he - ?"

She pulled herself together and said "No, he didn't get the chance to and that's his blood in there: I broke his nose." She stopped, suddenly indignant about something besides the attempted rape.

Turning slowly to Jeffrey, Lucie shoved the vigilantes aside and glowered at him. Curling the fingers on her right hand again, she leaned down and hissed, "I swear to God, if I could prove you had anything to do with that nutcase Julia shooting at me -"

Jeffrey squealed, "All she wanted to know was where you two were keeping that box!" Lucie growled, pulled her right arm back and slammed her fist into his face. Jeffrey's eyes rolled up in his head just before he passed out.

As Max stared at the inert form with disgust, he came to the conclusion that even *exemplary* parenting would not have changed the fact that Jeffrey was a malicious, rotten person.

Meanwhile, Lucie wiped her hand on Jeffrey's shirt, stood and squinted at him. Suddenly she decided she wanted to throw him off the balcony after all, so she grabbed him by one foot and started to tug.

"Lucie, you can't throw an unconscious man off a balcony."

"Watch me."

"He's out cold and dead weight. You'll hurt yourself."

"Actually, I was planning on rolling him down the steps." She pulled him several feet toward the stairs and shook her head when Roland and Juan offered to help.

"Lucie."

She glared at Max. "You trying to protect him?"

"Hell no, it's just that he'll wake up at the bottom of the balcony and won't know how he got there. Half the fun would be missing."

When Lucie stopped to consider that, Max grabbed her around the waist, hoisted her with one arm and quickly headed for the door. He called back over his shoulder to Roland and Juan, "I need you to pack up Jeffrey's clothes – just his clothes, nothing else, then tell Owen to bring the limo around, load everything into it and set the GPS for New Jersey. I'll get Jeffrey cleaned up and in traveling condition."

Max hurried inside, and when he was sure Lucie

wouldn't run back out on the balcony, tilted her chin up to examine the wound. "Hmm, good news, you won't need stitches, bad news, it'll sting when I clean it. C'mon, we need to take care of this."

Lucie frowned and observed, I'm going to have to shower for an entire week to get his kooties off me."

***

Max was stretched out on one of the loungers on his balcony, keeping a close eye on Lucie, who was savagely pruning in the yard below. Cell phone to his ear, he explained to Emma, "Heart's ok, but I did pop a few of those – what? No, she's done being upset, now she's extremely pissed off so she's whacking away at the bushes near the edge of the property. Yeah, it's apparently how she copes. Anyhow, she assured me she has to get it out of her system or Jeffrey won't live to see tomorrow. And I believe her."

"What? No, *I'd* have killed him if he had. All she needed was some butterfly closures for the throat wound and I gave her some antibiotics just in case, you never know where Jeffrey's ring has been. Oh, and Roland and Juan are telling everyone they rescued Lucie and she's backing them up."

His voice hardened as he continued, "Anyhow, I snapped his nose back in place, packed it with gauze and gave him a load of vicodin for the rest of his problems. He's out of here as soon as his stuff is loaded in the limo."

As Emma replied, Max got up and began to pace, oblivious to the sounds of birds, insects and irate women chopping at foliage. "Yeah, I *know* it's a big step, but I gave it my best shot, Em; he's had every rich-kid advantage, he blew that and he just attacked Lucie. Jeffrey's a miserable excuse for a human being and I'm done with him. Already called our lawyer. He's out of my will, I'm taking over the winery and as of today, his sorry ass is his mother's problem."

"Yeah, ok, I have to go, too." Max couldn't keep the sadness out of his voice as he continued, "I have to get her to the airport. Yes, I am aware that she's an extraordinary person. Yes, of course I asked her to marry me. Of course not....Stop laughing."

Max made a face at the phone and disconnected as Lucie trudged up the balcony steps, twigs stuck in her hair and dragging the pruning shears. He grinned at her and, once inside the house, locked his French doors behind them.

A sudden noise just outside made them both jump: Roland and Juan, still in camo, tromped past the glass door, nodding and saluting. They carried the shovels like rifles and shouted to Max, "We'll patrol the grounds until Lucie is safely away."

Max shook his head slowly. "I don't think Roland wants to be a butler anymore."

***

As Lucie gathered her belongings, she glanced at the unmade bed. Last night, magical though it had been, now seemed a distant memory. In perspective, she realized that the passion Max aroused in her was due, in part, to a growing emotional involvement with him. And that had *not* been her intention.

Suddenly Lucie felt Max's gaze and turned cautiously. He was leaning against the wall, arms crossed, full-on bedroom eyes and the sexiest grin she'd ever seen. That image would stay with her, and he knew it.

"So, you gonna call me a cab for the airport?" Logistics were always a mood-killer.

"No, I'm driving you there myself. Don't want anything else to happen to you on my watch." His grin didn't waver as he unfolded himself and went to the priest hole to get the postcards.

Moments later, as he handed her the cards, Max looked deeply into Lucie's eyes and asked quietly, "You sure you're ok?"

Lucie considered the question, then said thoughtfully, "Yeah, I think am. I mean, how many women actually get to beat the crap out of their assailants? It's unbelievably empowering." She raised her eyebrows at him and nodded.

Max continued, in what he hoped was a nonchalant tone, "Uh, Lucie, not that I'd blame you, but have you changed your mind about wanting to go to France with Emma and me?"

"Of course not. My wanting to kill Jeffrey is a separate issue altogether, and France is gorgeous this time of year and we can't let Gérard down."

Max breathed a sigh of relief as Lucie turned her attention to the postcards. "I'm going to scan these and email you copies when I get home, just in case. Print them and secure them with Gérard's will when it arrives, ok?" More logistics, something she could control. Unlike her emotions.

"Sure." He sauntered over to her suitcase and located a pair of panties. He took them to his desk and wrote his email address on the crotch, then handed them to her.

"Hey, those were expensive!"

"It's permanent ink, it's not going anywhere it shouldn't."

So much for control.

Then Max remembered something and took his cell phone from his pocket. "Excuse me a minute - unfinished business." He walked over to the doors, but spoke loudly enough for Lucie to hear.

"Audrey? Max. Just wanted to let you know that Jeffrey's on his way to your place and he'll be staying with you indefinitely."

Lucie heard the squawking from the other side of the room.

"Yeah, well, his life expectancy here isn't promising, so a change of residence is in his best interest."

Max held the phone away from his ear, chuckled, and disconnected.

"Who's Audrey?"

"Jeffrey's mother."

"I thought her name was Bambi."

"What?"

"And you said that Isabelle is - "

"Dylan's mother. Right."

"What about Tabitha and Barbi?"

"Who?"

"Your mother said - "

Max laughed. "Oh, right, my mother: Kate invents new names for the ex-wives a least once a year."

"So, you'll call me if Emma finds something on Marie Bottechar, yes?" Lucie was in the Zone again, focusing on the quest - not the bed they shared.

Max, on the other hand, was already anticipating time alone with Lucie in France.

***

Jeffrey's departure had been swift, and no one waved goodbye, at least not with all their fingers. But he'd been too high on the pain killer to notice, and didn't even protest when he learned he'd be residing in New Jersey for the foreseeable future. Or wonder why his dog hadn't accompanied him: Juan and Roland couldn't bear to send Bruno to live with 'That Despicable Man,' so they adopted her.

In marked contrast, the staff was now standing at attention in the driveway (lined up like at the manor houses in British movies) to say goodbye to Lucie. Max was astounded. They hadn't cared enough to organize themselves since - well, ever. As she shook hands, they all pleaded with Lucie to return as soon as possible.

Antonio winked at her and said, "¡Vuelve pronto, chef! This week has been fantastica. Nothing interesting ever happened before you showed up!"

An officious-looking Roland reported that Owen, currently on the relocation mission with That Despicable Man, sent his regards.

Lucie, the goodbye-hater, smiled and promised a quick return. Once out of the gates, Max put his phone on speaker and called Kate and Didier. Kate immediately asked if Lucie had recovered from the attack, and gave her an 'atta girl' for thrashing Jeffrey.

Then Kate asked Lucie why Didier held up ten fingers when they tried to set a date for the wedding. Lucie explained to her that Banns had to be posted at the town hall where they'd be married, at least ten days prior to the marriage.

Kate didn't much like the sound of a wedding in a town hall, especially a foreign one.

"Well, because of the French Revolution, you have to be married by a French civil authority in a town hall before you can get married in a religious ceremony, because in 1792, the clergy was generally despised." When Lucie took a breath to continue, Max waved her off and shook his head. TMI.

"Anyhow, where's it gonna be?"

"At the Sautier winery, if Jeffrey doesn't throw a fit. Oh – will that be a problem?"

Max answered, "Not in the least, mother. I now own it, or at least I will when the lawyers finish the transfer. The Village Idiot has been disinherited, and is currently looking for a new Village. To be the Idiot, um, of."

"Whatever, son," made Max stare at the phone in disbelief. He turned to Lucie: "What is it with the older women in my life?"

To Kate: "Gladys, your use of the vernacular is nothing short of - "

"Who are you calling older, son? Be quiet now, I want to talk to Lucie again." Max made a face.

"Lucie dear, Didier and I are taking the Gulfstream to France with Max and Mrs. Harris. We'll go directly to Didier's apartment in Provence, do the Banns thing and wait for all of you to find what it is you're looking for. And Lucie?"

"Yes?"

"You *do* know what you're looking for, don't you?"

Lucie frowned at the phone, not sure of what she meant.

"Follow your heart, dear. Life is short." Enigmatic, if she were talking about the treasure. Otherwise...

Max intervened. "So are you and Didier coming home tonight? I'll have Antonio prepare something."

"No, son, Didier and I are going to practice living in sin in this hotel for a while and we'll let you know when we get tired of room service."

Max intoned, "Goodbye, mother."

CHAPTER 20

Max had insisted that they sit against a wall in the airport and while he looked relaxed, Lucie noticed him scanning the area every few seconds. She squinted at him and observed, "Tell me again why you're sitting here with me? I can get on a plane by myself."

"Sure you can, but it'll make me feel better if I actually see you leave without being shot at or attacked. Humor me?"

Lucie sighed. "You aren't going to behave like this in France, are you?"

"I hope I don't have a reason to."

Fair enough.

"So why didn't you and Emma just go into hiding, you know, change your identities, and then you wouldn't have to worry about those People?"

Max lowered his voice and continued to scan. "Because they'd never give up trying to find us, and might get pissed off because of the extra effort. The present arrangement ensures a status quo, no one makes any sudden moves: sort of like your trenches."

As Lucie thought about that, Max changed the subject: "So, about getting married."

"And get stuck with that tangled-up mess of a name that's attached to you?" Lucie gave him a sideways glance. "Let's see, Hamish Ethelbert-Meicklejohn. And we won't even mention the middle name because it makes my tongue twitchy."

"My name is Max."

"Yeah, right."

"Well, you could keep your own name."

"And let's not forget that your mother says you've always had terrible taste in women." She turned to him and raised an eyebrow. "A marriage proposal does *not* reflect well on me."

"That was a lifetime ago."

"And we've never watched TV or a movie together. And we've only had one real date."

"But I-"

"And then there's the whole 'I love you' issue we haven't gotten to."

"Speak for yourself."

"Max, give it a rest."

Max sighed. Time to capitulate. For now.

Actually, Lucie had been thinking just how easy it would be to drift into a relationship with Max: he was handsome, smart, sexy, amusing, and only occasionally annoying.

But ever since the breakup of her second marriage, she'd lived by a hard and fast rule: No Drifting. All decisions that affected her life had to be well-considered and logical.

Plus, a serious relationship with Max would involve the specter of his past. Lucie's eyes darted uneasily at the man sitting next to her. Max would probably never be able to stop looking over his shoulder...

CHAPTER 21

Lucie

Tucked into her 'it's-got-every-convenience' cocoon in Business Class on British Airways, Lucie finished the appetizer she'd ordered - gruyère cheese and red onion timbale with red pepper coulis - took a sip of an excellent wine and rewound the past week in her mind.

Lucie had needed a stretch of normality and found it at home, lavishing attention on Murphy and tending to domestic chores. She met with her business manager, who assured her that, given the small fortune she'd just earned, she and her crew could take the next few weeks off, no worries.

Giles had called, wanting to know why the winery documents were back on his desk. That he hadn't called Max directly was a transparent ploy, but she patiently explained that Jeffrey had proven himself unworthy of the Sautier winery and that he'd been disinherited. And that he'd been exiled to New Jersey. And that Max had repossessed the French property.

"Well, ma petite Lucie, all of that was surely a joke on Max, no?"

"You could say that" was all she'd allow.

"So what are you doing now? You should come to Montréal, it is très belle this time of year." She held the phone away from her ear. Damned pheromones.

"So is Paris, and that's where I'm going, Giles."

"Do you need company?"

"I'm meeting Sophie."

Giles waited.

"I'll be seeing M. and Mme Sautier, I'll give them your best, Giles. And now I must go pack. À la prochaine, mon ami."

Lucie waved at the air around the phone, but told herself that was just silly, pheromones can't be transmitted like that. When it rang again, it startled her.

Michael's "Hiya Lucie" was the antithesis of Giles' suave conversational style.

"So how'd it go at the château? Some place, huh? I hope the kid didn't cause you too much grief, but when Mrs. Harris called me -"

"How do you know her, Michael?"

"Friend of a friend of a friend of my mother, you know how that goes."

Rats. Lucie was hoping he'd know her first name.

"- and insisted on that huge advance for your services, well, pretty good gig, huh?"

"Sure, if you don't consider the part where I got shot at and attacked. And by the way, the 'kid' speaks in a much higher register now. But I did meet people who gave me clues to a treasure in France, so, yeah, it *was* a pretty good gig."

She heard Michael suck in his breath.

"Long story, Michael, and I gotta go pack. See you when I get back." Maybe.

Lucie actually dropped the phone when it rang for the third time.

"Uh, hello?"

"It's good to hear your voice" was a welcome middle ground between Giles and Michael. Lucie smiled.

"Good to hear yours, too." Suddenly the image of Max leaning against the wall in his bedroom, arms crossed and sexy grin on his face, flashed through her brain like a Times Square LED sign. Followed by the familiar zing of sexual energy. Max, without knowing it, was handing Giles' pheromones a throwdown.

"How are you, Lucie? How's the wound?"

"Healing fast, and it doesn't look like it's going to scar: whatever you used on it worked really well. So, you keeping busy?"

"Sort of, I mean, well, it's really quiet around here now." His dejected tone made Lucie think he was scuffling his feet and looking down at them.

"Why don't you and Emma sort out your wine cellar and see what's been tampered with?"

"She's not back yet, and she yells at me if I disturb her before she's done with, uh, whatever it is she's doing."

"Then get Kate and Didier to help you."

Max brightened. "Good idea, I'll ask them." His voice suddenly took on an urgent tone. "But the main reason I called is the conversation I had yesterday with attorney Renaud - that's Gérard's lawyer. He said Gaston showed up in his office in Lourmarin and informed him he was going to have Gérard declared mentally incompetent. Renaud told Gaston that was not going to happen, that he's no longer executor of the Sautier will, and that there's a new one in place. Gaston got violent and had to be forcibly ejected."

Lucie's smile faded as Max continued. "Thing is, by now Gaston probably knows you're the sole beneficiary."

"How?"

"I figure Gaston called Julia, Julia contacted

Jeffrey and he told her about that fax he had no business reading."

A shiver shot down Lucie's back. "So, Gaston lost his inheritance and probably his job, and he still owes big time gambling money to some very scary people."

Max's voice was quiet, and he kept it level. "You got it, he's desperate, and when you add Julia to the scenario – uh, Lucie, how about I have some people keep an eye on you for a while? They'd be discreet, you wouldn't even know they're there."

"No thanks, but point taken, I'll be careful. I'm actually more worried about Gérard and Marie-Françoise. You don't think he'd hurt them, do you?"

"Probably not, but if it makes you feel any better, I'll arrange for protective surveillance. Maybe *they'll* see the sense in it."

Lucie stuck her tongue out at the phone.

"Stop that. I have your best interest at heart and you know it."

"All right, make the call. I'll contact Gérard and let him know about our concerns."

What Max didn't tell her was that a surveillance team was already in place and had reported Gaston prowling around the Sautiers' townhouse.

"What?"

"I didn't say anything, Lucie, it must be, uh, background noise." Damn. She was getting good at this.

Luckily, Lucie distracted herself almost immediately. "So, uh, Max, is there any way Julia could know I'm leaving for France in a few days?" She had no intention of putting Sophie in harm's way.

"Absolutely not, so just relax and enjoy your time with your daughter."

Lucie wasn't convinced and knew she'd be constantly looking over her shoulder; then it hit her, the reality of Max's life. Never-ending, bone-wearying vigilance. She sighed as sadness for him washed over her.

"You still there?"

"Um."

"Want to hear what the Resident Loonies have been up to?"

Lucie held the phone out and stared at it. "How'd you know that's what I call them?"

"Please."

Lucie sighed, hoping she'd never have to keep a huge secret from Max.

"I'll take that as a yes. Ok, first, the new couple. Roland told Juan that some sort of parental responsibility was necessary to hold a relationship together, and I guess that's why they adopted the Beast; so now they're shopping for a matching camouflage outfit for Bruno, only nothing's big enough."

"Jeffrey calls on a daily basis and whines to anyone who'll listen, and – you'll like this – the Idiot tried to hire Adam Cromby to get the winery back. So Cromby called me, said he wouldn't be representing Jeffrey again in this lifetime, not for any reason, and wanted to know what was wrong with Jeffrey's voice. I guess Adam finally grew a pair, just when Jeffrey lost his." Max howled with laughter at that, and Lucie smiled at her phone.

"Anything from Dylan on the winery issue?"

"Matter of fact, that's next: Dylan called right after you left and I naturally assumed she knew about Jeffrey being disinherited, figured she was trying to move in on the winery deal. But she seemed shocked when I told her, then she said, 'I'm really glad your chef beat the shit out of Jeffrey.' Sounded just like Kate."

Max chuckled and continued, "And she wanted to talk about winemaking. Has been doing a lot of research, actually sounds interested in something besides clubs, booze and men. Thing is, Dylan asked, not demanded, if I'd consider letting her run the winery. What do you think?"

"If you believe she's serious, I'd say give her a chance. Uh, Max, I have a million things to do before - ouch, my ear."

"Maybe you should see a doctor, you don't want to fly with an ear problem."

"No, it's, um, actually, Iburnedit." Lucie blurted the last part.

"Sorry?" She could hear the smile.

Lucie gritted her teeth. "I burned the top of my ear with a curling iron, all right? Max, I have to go." She could hear him trying to stifle the laughter. The man still annoyed her.

"Ok, end of newscast: everyone here sends regards, especially Kate and Didier, and everyone misses you. Especially me."

This new, chatty Max would take some getting used to.

***

The day before Lucie left for France, Kate surprised her with a call. "Lucie dear, thank you so much for telling my son to include Didier in sorting out his wine, my Intended was a great help and he was simply appalled that, after all those years with the family, Julia would steal from us! I - wait a minute - oh my goodness, Lucie, turn on your TV! You'll never guess who's on channel five's Talk Show: looks like we know a celebrity!"

Lucie located the show and stared at the screen in

disbelief: Margaret was jabbering and wildly waving her arms around, describing her encounter with 'Jesus.' And giving her own warped explanation of his odd appearance. And rapturing about an anticipated second sighting.

When the host declared that the station's phone lines were being flooded with calls, Lucie shook her head. Go figure.

***

As Lucie sipped her wine and looked out the airplane window, she considered the comment her best friend had made during their lunch together: "Max does *not* sound like the kind of man who waits very long to get what he wants."

Max. A man flawed by an outlaw profession, a man with an abysmal track record in relationships, (never mind that her own was nothing to brag about), a man who... right. A man about whom she obviously couldn't stop thinking.

She sighed as the flight attendant served the main course: fresh pasta with mushroom and thyme cream sauce, accompanied by grilled fillet of beef marinated in red wine, prepared medium rare. Perfect. She cleansed her palate with a simple green salad, and since dessert wasn't supposed to arrive for another twenty minutes, took out her laptop and inserted the flash drive where she'd stored the images of her postcards.

Lucie stared at them and worried: maybe Gérardmer *was* too obvious, maybe the clue-giver had been more subtle than she imagined. Or, whole other scenario, the last date on the cards was 1927: the treasure could have been destroyed during the second World War. Lucie groaned and then groaned again. A passing flight attendant, dismayed at Business Class groaning, asked if there were anything wrong.

Lucie gave her an embarrassed half-smile and pretended to be engrossed in finding her schedule on the computer.

Dessert arrived, followed by coffee, then Lucie reclined her seat to the sleeping position. The small movie screen that was hers alone beckoned, but her mind was too occupied with spending time with her daughter, seeking a treasure, Max...

***

Lucie woke up with the uneasy feeling you get when your subconscious has produced images so powerful that, for a few seconds, reality is the dream you still inhabit. Her mind scrambled madly, trying to reboot and find solid ground. Then the smell of freshly brewing coffee restored the here and now, and as Lucie stretched and stumbled to the restroom, she shook off the remaining tendrils of the dream, resolving to make sense of it later.

Croissants, coffee and seasonal fruit were all she'd requested for breakfast, and they were waiting at her seat when she returned. An hour later, she stood on French soil, praying that the Baggage Gods would be kind to her: Paris' Charles de Gaulle airport contained a black hole that specialized in making luggage disappear forever, therefore requiring the airport staff to become adept in keeping that fact from the passengers for as long as possible.

As in, 'My bags have not appeared in the Baggage Claim area. Where are they?' 'Your bags are in transit.' 'But how do you know that?' 'If they were not in transit, they would be here.' With a Gallic shrug. And so on.

She tiptoed to the designated conveyer belt and peeped around several people, mentally suiting up to challenge the powers that surround the rotating belly of the beast. Suddenly, Voilà! Her bright red suitcase shot out of the monster's mouth and as several travelers eyed it hopefully, she announced proudly, "Ça, c'est la mienne!" And snatched it before it had a chance to vanish into the 'In Transit' void.

Half an hour later, Lucie was comfortably settled on the train that connected the airport to the city, smiling to herself as she looked out the window.

She'd only been in her seat for five minutes when something flashed through her brain, causing her to scramble for her cell phone. She found Max's number, pushed 'send' and remembered too late that it was only 3:00 am in New York. He answered on the third ring and mumbled, "Lucie?"

"Uh, yeah, it's me, Max." She scrunched up her face, causing the man in the seat across from her to start watching her suspiciously. He fidgeted for a few minutes then slunk off to another seat. At the other end of the train car.

"Hmmmm." Trying to wake up. "You're safely in France, right?"

"Yes, and I'm sorry I woke you."

His voice was warm, comforting, and she could hear him moving about in his bed. Max's bed. "Don't be. Remember, I asked you to let me know when you arrived. Could you hold on a minute?"

He put the phone down and she heard him talk to someone.

Lucie's face flushed with anger, which made her even angrier, because she didn't want to be angry.

"Phoebe, stop that. What's with digging at my pillow?"

Lucie heard the little dog snort and realized that

she'd been holding her breath.

"Rearranging your bed, huh?" Lucie smiled hugely. She could think about the anger issue later.

"Yeah, and she's good at it."

Lucie laughed. "Max, I need Emma to get some information for me. I assume she's still in D.C., digging around in places we don't want to know about?"

"Probably, I'm afraid to call her. Hey, maybe if I tell her it's for you, a vital piece of information for the treasure; it is, isn't it?"

"Yeah, but it's a shot in the dark."

"What do you need?" She heard him opening a drawer for paper.

"The other day I was reading about how the Krupp family produced most of the artillery for the Imperial German Army, and the part about the huge railway mounted guns, the Big Berthas, is really interesting."

"Lucie. It's three in the morning. I wouldn't mind if you called to be romantic, but really, Big Bertha?"

"Sorry."

"Let's go straight to the part about the information you need."

"So Germany loses the war and is required to disarm. Except that the Krupps, in direct violation of the Treaty of Versailles, -"

Max sighed and flopped back on his newly-fluffed pillow.

"- begin secret arms manufacturing during the Weimar Republic. And then of course go on to totally rearm Nazi Germany: submarines, tanks, and artillery."

Max groaned loud enough to alarm Phoebe, who barked.

"What's going on there?"

"Lucie, I swear to God you can have any World War One book you want from my library, even the first editions, if you'll ***get to the point***! And make it fast, Phoebes just decided she has to go outside."

"You don't have to yell." She frowned at the phone.

"LUCIE!"

Lucie spoke rapidly, "Ok, ok, so I found an obscure reference to the Krupp family's bottomless coffers, and to a gold shipment that might have gone missing toward the end of the war. Near France's Eastern Front. Near where James was a supply officer, had access to transportation."

Max had stopped groaning.

"Are you still there?"

"Ok, now *that's* interesting." He was obviously taking notes.

Just as Lucie made another face at the phone, the recently relocated traveler turned in his seat and glanced at her. His eyes widened, he gathered his bags and pushed the button to open the exit to the next car, stopping to gesticulate at the conductor who happened by. And looked alarmed.

Lucie started to fan herself, opened the top five buttons of the blouse she was wearing, snaked her hand down to her breast, writhed a bit and moaned.

"Where the hell are you and what are you doing?" Max's turn to be angry.

Lucie whispered into the phone, "I'm gonna get thrown off this stupid train if I don't pretend I'm having really good phone sex with you."

Max held the phone away from his ear and stared at it. No way was he going to ask her to explain that one. Better to just enjoy the next few minutes.

***

Lucie and Sophie were chatting and laughing to each other, unlike the other Métro riders, who silently read books or stared off into the black of the tunnels. The Code of the Subway Rider: don't make eye contact.

Their destination was one of their Every Time We're In Paris Together traditions: the St-Ouen de Clignancourt Marché aux Puces, the world's largest Flea Market. They rode to the northern tip of Paris and disembarked at the veritable city of distinct villages with street names, and market stalls disguised as tiny abodes, complete with numbered addresses and sidewalks.

As the two women headed for the Vernaison market to search for the Provençal cookware that Lucie wanted, they checked out the tiny stalls that lined the entrance avenue and bought this year's color of pashminas. Then on to other markets for art and antiques that were destined for Sophie's high-end clients.

Hours later, as she leaned against a store front, Lucie watched her daughter barter with a vendor, then walk away triumphant.

"Didn't know you were any good at haggling, daughter.

"I prefer the term 'softening the price.'"

"Whatever. I'm about done: my feet are killing me and the merchants are getting snotty." She frowned at the man who had just requested that she not block his window display with her body.

"You're getting grumpy, mom."

"I need a drink."

"Yes, you do. Come on." Sophie grabbed her mother's arm and they serpentined through the maze of shops and stalls, finally arriving at Le Soleil, their favorite café in the area. Compressed around a tiny outdoor table, they ordered chicken sautéed in a light cream sauce and fresh Norman cod with tiny mussels cooked in a rich broth. The food, plus a bottle of

Vouvray that the waiter had recommended, went a long way to improve Lucie's disposition.

"You know this trip is a write-off for me." Between mouthfuls.

"I didn't buy enough cookware to qualify. Hmm, I wonder if consuming a ton of French food would be considered a job-related expense."

"Yeah, right. So...Max."

Lucie sidestepped the issue. "I had the house dream on the plane, Sophie, first time since the divorce. All those rundown rooms I can't get to, and that spooky-weird kitchen, the old cruddy one that lurks in the dark behind the new one."

Sophie raised an eyebrow. "Dream Interpretation 101, mom: you always have that dream when you're stressed."

Lucie frowned. "I look stressed?"

Sophie laughed. "Duuuhhh! Let's see, you got shot at, then that little prick mauled you, and now you're going on this really cool, but dangerous, treasure hunt with a man who has you all – " She turned to her mother with a sly grin, "What did they call it in all those BritComs we watched when I was a kid? Oh yeah. Flummoxed. Plus you keep looking over your shoulder, which, I gotta tell you, is starting to creep me out."

"Geez, Soph."

Sophie shook her head and tsked. "I cannot understand why you don't want to talk about your relationship with Max, it's very unlike you."

"There *is no* relationship."

"Whatever."

Lucie stared at Sophie. "Finish your food, daughter, we need to talk about the guy you want to bring along for Thanksgiving."

Sophie's turn to stare. "Wait. What? How'd you know!"

Lucie grinned. Smugly. No need to tell Sophie about her newly acquired ability just yet.

CHAPTER 22

Max

Max stood on his balcony, staring at nothing. An unsettling emptiness, definitely more complicated than simply missing Lucie, had accompanied him home from the airport.

Then he'd forgotten the new security code for the front door and had to ring to enter his own home. (He hated that doorbell: one of his wives had insisted that the chimes play It's a Small World After All and no one had ever bothered to switch the tune.)

Roland and Juan had admitted him with a deluge of questions about Lucie's welfare, until Max growled, "She's fine, now get the damned door bell changed!"

Raised eyebrows had followed him up the stairs, along with "Well isn't Someone in a snit this evening!"

So there he was, alone on his balcony, thinking that introspection was probably called for.

"Well. It's abundantly clear that I want – need - Lucie Richards in my life." Good place to begin. Wanting and acquiring a woman, nothing new there.

Ah, but not just *any* woman, this one had burst into his life a week ago and he'd shared more than his bed with her, willingly confiding his darkest secret.

What else? Max thought about his past: he'd survived an isolated, dangerous profession, a massive heart attack and four disastrous marriages. He'd made it into his fifties, but he supposed that a psychologist would ask if his life had purpose.

Max groaned, sensing that a turning point was imminent. He hoped it wouldn't give him a headache when it arrived.

He pondered the Life Purpose issue for a while, but couldn't think of anything other than surviving, with Emma. Ok, revelation number two: he wasn't adding much to the general scheme of things, cosmic-wise.

Max nodded and stood up, pleased with himself: he'd come to several life-changing conclusions without funding a shrink's retirement home. He needed to 1: figure out a way to win Lucie permanently, which just might facilitate number 2: find a Purpose. Heavy stuff. But on the other hand, it hadn't given him a headache.

He smiled as he returned to his suite: he now had an agenda, which dispelled the uncertainty. For now. He opened a bottle of Pinot Noir. Good company at last.

***

The next evening, Max found himself out on the balcony again. Emma was still unavailable, and Lucie, well, nothing was fun without Lucie, and the day had stretched on interminably.

Suddenly the French doors swung open with a bang and Phoebe raced out of his suite, almost tripping his mother, who stopped abruptly and almost upended Didier, who was right behind her.

"So this is where you've been hiding! Son, you have *got* to stop moping."

"I'm not moping."

"Yes, you are." Kate shoved a sheaf of papers at him. "Fax from Lucie, it's all those postcards, and the top sheet says something about not being able to email them because your address got lost in the wash."

Max smiled at that as Kate poked at Didier, who handed him the large brown envelope he'd been holding.

"It's from France, I'm assuming it's the Sautier will you told me about."

Max opened it and nodded. "Got to make a copy of this for Lucie, she told me to keep the original." Then he sighed.

"Son, you need to shake off this dismal-swamp funk you've gotten yourself into, so we'll expect you downstairs to have dinner with us in an hour."

"All right, mother, but I need to deal with the paperwork first."

"Come on, Didier, we can always come back and drag him if we have to." Didier seemed to understand, and Max reflected that his English was improving exponentially.

CHAPTER 23

Paris

Sophie returned to her job and life stateside, leaving Lucie to prowl the city's markets for unusual spices and haunt her favorite restaurants for recipes to steal. The day before Max and company were to arrive, Lucie arranged to have lunch near her hotel, with the son of a family friend.

She'd just chosen a table on the heated terrace when a young Frenchman strolled over, exuding the raw sexuality of a healthy twenty-something. But he'd arrived with long, wet hair that signaled, 'this event wasn't important enough to shower early' and which had to be dramatically and continually dragged out of his eyes - while he checked out the talent that passed by.

Because Lucie valued the friendship with his parents, however, she smiled politely, kept up with his French and endured the endless monologue about his favorite subject: himself.

Somewhere between the first course of half-dozen oysters and main course of blanquette de veau, Julien smiled to himself in youthful arrogance: if his luck held, his mother's very attractive friend would turn out to be a Grateful Older Woman.

After they'd worked their way through the main course, Julien loudly informed her that they should order their dessert to take out, an accompaniment to the *real dessert* at his flat. The lazy-eyed look he bestowed upon Lucie was supposed to seal the deal, and since there was a hot girl at the next table, he amped up his performance with the dramatic head toss, running his hand slowly through his hair. The girl did notice, and the man with her looked as though he wanted to mop up the floor with Julien.

Lucie sighed. Jeffrey, Julien what was it with men whose names start with J? The dwindling patience she'd been nurturing evaporated, so she signaled for the check as she told him she wasn't interested in dessert. At all.

Julien's eyes widened in astonishment. "Mais?" She was rejecting his most generous offer of afternoon sex!? He raised his hands, fingers spread, to accentuate his total disbelief. "Quoi?! Mais, c'était prévu que – enfin, merde!" He rose angrily, pausing briefly for the never-to-be-ignored ritual of the French, the exit kisses, tossed his head and leered at the hottie on his way out of the dining area.

Once in the street, he paused to extract a lip balm from his pocket; but instead of rubbing the tiny stick over his lips, he held it still and moved his head back and forth like an oscillating fan. Lucie shook her head and chuckled.

When Julien told a passerby, loudly, that the blond American over there was *surely* a lesbian, she laughed out loud.

Lucie's elderly waiter had been watching Julien with dismay, and as he approached her table, his deference to her was evident. It vanished, however, when Lucie mischievously grinned at him, raised one eyebrow and ordered coffee with an array of desserts.

***

Max had the Gulfstream drop him in Paris a day early, anxious to be with Lucie, anxious to get on with his life. He'd found Lucie's hotel and was wandering in the neighborhood when he spotted her with Julien. His heart sank as he sat down at an adjacent café, telling himself to act his age. He'd been wondering about Lucie and younger men: couldn't really blame her, but he'd fervently hoped...

He ordered a vin blanc and pretended to people-watch, noting that Lucie and the testosterone-laden French kid had not touched since he arrived. Well, good news there.

Suddenly the young man rose and bent down to kiss Lucie. She leaned away from him, however, after the second cheek-kiss, and Max drank a silent toast: they were definitely *not* intimate. He left some Euros by his glass and got up quickly.

As Max wove his way through the maze of tiny tables on the sidewalk, the girl next to Lucie shot him an appraising glance, which didn't go unnoticed by her long-suffering date: Max was tall and imposing in a well-cut black blazer, black silk shirt and expensive jeans.

His eyes riveted on Lucie, he arrived at her table with just the right amount of confidence, only some of which he felt. You never knew, with Lucie. The elderly waiter had brought a long, curved porcelain plank of mini-desserts, and was in the process of explaining each when Max pulled out the chair next to Lucie and asked, simply, "May I?"

Lucie gaped at him and blinked several times. Then she smiled and said, "Of course, Max, sit down."

Max sat, leaned in close and, placing his hand on her face the way he had the night she wore The Black Dress, kissed her passionately. When he drew back, he braced himself for total annihilation.

But Lucie just stared at him for a second, then raised her eyebrows and said, in a sultry Mae West voice, "Well! Good to see you, too, Max."

Max believed that he could have another heart attack right then and there, and die a happy man.

Hottie's date sighed: *finally* the drama at the next table would be self-contained and of no further aggravation to him.

The elderly waiter thought of his wife, Mathilde, and wondered if he could leave work early.

CHAPTER 24

Max smiled broadly. "You look terrific." Lucie smiled, too: she was wearing one of her chic Paris black outfits, accented by a colorful scarf. "Phoebe has your suite staked out, in case you show up unexpectedly."

"I miss her, too."

"Mind if I have lunch while you demolish that?" He pointed at the plank of pastries. "I'm really hungry all of a sudden, and I'd kill for steak-frites."

Lucie spoke softly to the hovering waiter, then turned to Max and raised her eyebrows: "You have no idea what a relief it is to talk to an adult!"

Max decided not to ask: whatever had transpired with the young man resulted in his leaving abruptly. And alone. Life was good.

A bottle of wine appeared and as Max poured, Lucie asked "So, Emma find out anything interesting in DC?"

"Yes, she did, but you've got to hear this first: Mother, Didier and I went to pick her up at a private airfield and she shows up in a wheelchair, looking twenty pounds heavier, with curly silver hair, a ratty purple jogging suit and Velcro sneakers. We're trying to figure out why a nursing home refugee is trying to board the Gulfstream when she pokes her cane at me and yells, 'Move it or lose it, sonny'."

Lucie started to laugh as the image came to her mind.

"Wait, it gets better. The guy pushing her wheelchair looks really bummed, so I tell him, 'Leave the old bag, she belongs to us.' He says, 'Good luck with that' and before I could give him a tip, Emma tries to whack him with her cane and he runs for it."

Lucie laughed so hard that she was wiping the tears away when the waiter brought Max's simple lunch of steak with peppercorn sauce and a huge pile of crispy fries. "So, why the disguise?"

Max explained, between mouthfuls. "Long story: Em wanted a hard copy of Lt. Milnar's military file, thought Marie Bottecher's info might be attached, but couldn't get access: classified information. So she talked her way into a restricted area, had to use a doctored version of her government ID, and that alerted *Them* to her presence in the city. And necessitated a covert exit a few hours later."

"She ok?"

"Oh yeah, not her first rodeo." He paused to stuff frites into his mouth. "These are amazing."

"Focus, Max. Marie?"

"Ok, so Emma finally located the Lieutenant's file and bingo, there was Marie. Turns out she was born in the same town as Augustin, and we were right, she did work with James in Intelligence during World War I. No mention of anything after that."

Max poured them both more wine. "Weird thing, though, not only is his file still classified, there are no entries to it after World War II: he's not listed as missing, dead, or discharged. He just - vanished."

Lucie looked thoughtful, leaned back in her chair

and crossed her arms. “So, dead end for James. Was Emma able to get into any foreign databases, like the one where she found background on Augustin?”

“Matter of fact, she did hack into another French military site, but only male soldiers from World War I were listed. So she tried a non-military search and found a link to old French census records.”

Max eyed Lucie’s desserts, jabbed a tiny profiterole and ate it in one bite before continuing. “She searched the eastern towns mentioned on the post cards and came up with Marie and a female child, Albertine, living together in a household in 1928, in - ”

“Épinal.”

Max’s eyebrows shot up. “Exactly! How did you know? ”

Lucie said, airily, “It was on one of her postcards: ‘Write always to Épinal.’ Remember? Here, have another pastry and tell me the rest.”

“Ok, Marie disappeared from Épinal after that. Emma was going to try a different search, but the system shut down and she had to leave in a hurry.”

“No mention of a husband, huh?”

“No.”

“Well, the Great Depression hit France around 1931, so let’s assume Marie was a single mother and had to move around; I can’t imagine that the spy business paid very well. Soooo, we need to find Albertine’s descendants, hopefully they’ll have stories about the legacy like the Sautier family does.”

Further discussion was precluded when Max’s phone rang.

***

They strolled to Lucie’s hotel while Max talked with Emma. “Well, sure, if that’s what you really want to do." He disconnected, a bewildered look on his face. "She wants to go to the top of the Eiffel Tower."

"Really?"

"Says she's never been, that it's about time. Very, very unlike her." He looked down at Lucie. "And another strange thing, she's apparently made friends with Gérard's lawyer, and she's - wait a minute, would you look at that wine, the bottle on the left!" Max stopped abruptly in front of a wine store.

"That's actually a very good price. We should get a case, for nightcaps, for the train ride south." He was in the store in a flash, and it took only a few minutes to complete the transaction. He emerged, looking pleased, and told Lucie that the store would deliver to the hotel.

"Anyway, my point was that normally, Em just intimidates people to get what she wants, but she actually asked the lawyer, *Jean-Luc* (he enunciated the name as he pushed open the door at the entrance of the hotel) to access the town's records for us."

"Plus Didier is going to check with the locals, see if any of the old-timers kept track of Marie's people." He stopped just inside the door. "Wait a minute, I just thought of something: Didier should call the parish priest, too. There might be church records."

While Max speed-dialed Emma's number, Lucie asked for her key at Réception, then requested a room for Max; the man looked past her to the door, and said, "Ah the gentleman who said to put his suitcases in your room for safekeeping." Then he shrugged and Lucie thought, look out, here it comes. Sure enough, the word 'Mais' began his next sentence. 'But'. A speed bump in some languages, a major roadblock in French.

She turned to Max, who'd finished his call. He was standing right behind her, so of course she bumped into him, which annoyed her. Then he did the leaning thing, and his proximity reminded Lucie that the man knew every inch of her body, causing an immediate rise in her body temperature.

He looked at her intently, put his hand under her chin and tilted it. "Mmm, the wound has healed nicely, now let's look at that ear you singed." Lucie pushed his hand away and spun around at the receptionist, who was grinning a shitty, French grin. Dammit.

She glared at him as he recited his No Vacancy litany. Absolutely no rooms available. There were before, but now, non. There you have it, C'est normal, this time of year.

"But it's off-season."

"Can't be helped." The French palms were now upright, in front of his chest, a physical barrier to further discussion.

Lucie turned her head slowly to Max and growled in a low voice, "We need to talk." She crooked her index finger at him to a spot around the corner. Then she grabbed his shirt and pulled him out of earshot of the desk clerk, who had stretched over the counter to eavesdrop. The man who had bribed him and the reluctant woman were obviously intimate, so he couldn't understand the fuss about sharing the room. Americans, go figure.

The reluctant woman's fist was still involved with Max's shirt as she glowered at him and hissed, "Max. I need my own space. I'm not a dewy twenty something, I exercise in the morning and I don't like being watched and I hate it when somebody moves my toothbrush!"

"What's your point? We've slept together before."

"You call that sleeping?" Max opened his mouth to reply. "Don't even go there; besides, that was a sleepover. This - (she let go of his shirt and waved her arm around) - would be cohabiting." Lucie had planned on 'visits' to and from Max's room in Paris, not cohabiting.

Max looked way too pleased about that and smoothed out the front of his shirt.

Lucie snarled, pushed him out of the way and stormed the front desk, causing the clerk to jump back in alarm. She told him Monsieur would be staying with her and stomped off to the elevator, Max right behind her. Lucky for him, Lucie did not see the wink he gave the clerk.

They crammed into the tiny elevator, waving off several small Asian girls who may have put the device over its weight limit, and rode in silence to the top floor. Lucie unlocked the door with the key attached to a giant pendant – the boutique hotel had not as yet succumbed to key cards– and stepped into a bright, airy room with tall ceilings that gave the impression of a much larger space.

Comfortably furnished, the room featured a king-sized bed and sitting area, but Max was entranced by the balcony just beyond the large glass door. There was just enough room for two chairs, a round table and a pot with something large and green growing in it. Max stepped into both the sun of late afternoon and the skyline of Paris.

Suddenly he thought about standing on his own balcony a few days earlier: there, a man with a void in his life. Here, a man with direction. He'd made his decision half way across the Atlantic, and with it, a call to his attorney in New York. Max reflected that he hadn't just crossed an ocean between the balconies, he'd pole-vaulted into a whole new phase of his life.

He leaned over and rested his arms on the ornate wrought-iron railing.

Lucie joined him and remarked, “I booked this hotel because I love looking out over the rooftops in this area of Paris: no monuments, just cool old buildings. Look over there, there’s a small village on the top of that one.”

Max stared at a rooftop whose one corner, embellished with tiny apartments, was a two-tiered affair with a spiral staircase leading to the second level. And the inhabitants had created, in the remaining space of their aeire, a miniature park with entire trees, shrubs, flowers, tables and chairs.

“Spectacular.” Max admired the view until Lucie, still irritated with the arrangements, dragged him back into the room.

“You might as well unpack your stuff. And you need to know, I’m feeling claustrophobic. You promise to sleep on the couch?”

“Yes, absolutely, if you want me to.”

Lucie narrowed her eyes at Max. “That is a *lousy* answer.”

***

Max hummed as he stowed his toiletries in the bathroom, and Lucie fumed until she remembered that the Louvre was open until 10pm that day.

“Are you a museum person?”

Max stuck his head around the corner, but before he could respond, Lucie grumbled, “See? You want to cohabit and I don’t even know if you like museums! This is hopeless.”

“Wait a minute, I *do* like museums, but no one will ever go with me because I spend too long looking at things.” The So There was silent. “But I don’t like weird stuff, like wax museums.”

“I was thinking of the Louvre.”

Max's face lit up. "Could we use the pyramid entrance? I think the spiral staircase is cool, and - " Chatty Max was back. Lucie rolled her eyes.

***

Max passed the Museum Test with flying colors and showed appropriate enthusiasm for all of Lucie's favorite pieces, especially the Winged Victory: as they admired it from one floor below, Max had remarked that, from that angle, he always got the sensation that the statue was going to swoop down the staircase. Lucie was impressed.

Then they wandered outside, down one of the many stone stairways to a quai, a riverfront walkway on the Seine. The benches were busy with lovers in various forms of embrace, and Lucie took Max's arm unconsciously. They walked along in silence, enjoying the beauty of nighttime Paris until Lucie suddenly declared that she was hungry.

"You have a restaurant in mind?"

Lucie said she'd actually like something light, didn't matter where, so they took the métro to their hotel area, then strolled down the still-busy street until Lucie stopped and said, "Oh look, a restaurant called le Viking." She peered inside and announced, "This is acceptable, Max, all locals in there. Come on."

They were greeted by the proprietress, a woman of a certain age who didn't mind at all that they were American, especially when Lucie greeted her warmly in French. The waiter approved of the late-night omelettes they ordered, the simple salads, and the glasses of Muscadet.

They walked the short distance to the hotel, where the night receptionist informed them that he had personally overseen the delivery of the case of wine to their room. Max tipped him and they took the elevator to their floor.

Lucie threw her purse on the couch and headed for the bathroom. "I get the first shower, since you're a squatter."

"Fine with me, I'm going to open one of these bottles and go out on the balcony." Good move, he thought. Give her lots of space.

"Corkscrew's in my purse."

"Thanks anyway, I have my own."

Max couldn't see the smile.

***

Lucie, enveloped in a thick bathrobe, opened the doors to the balcony.

"Want a nightcap?" When she nodded, he poured for her and raised his glass: "Here's to a terrific day."

Lucie clinked her glass against his, with her own toast: "Here's to a day that turned out a whole lot better than I thought it would." She tasted the wine, settled back in her chair and nodded: "This is really good, Max." Then the night air penetrated her robe and she shivered. Max turned, stretched out his arm and pulled her into his warmth. They sat like that, suspended above the city, watching the lights of Paris, sometimes talking, but not needing to.

Finally Lucie got up, stating that her posterior had fallen asleep on the metal chair. Max laughed and opened the door for her. As she headed for her bed, Lucie noticed that the couch had acquired bed linens.

"Quick shower, then I'll turn out the lights." And he was gone.

Lucie must have fallen asleep, because it seemed like only seconds since Max had said something about a shower, and there he was, leaning over her bed, grinning. Lucie yelled and swatted him. "Don't do that, you scared me."

"You were snoring."

"Was not." She was trying to think of a better retort when Max gave her a chaste kiss on the forehead, turned out the light and headed for the couch.

"Goodnight, Lucie."

"Um, goodnight." Lucie frowned: the scent of his body wash lingered in the space he'd just occupied.

"Um, Max?"

Max groaned. "This isn't going to turn into one of your late night discussions about German armaments, is it?"

Her resolve to discourage co-habiting was dwindling rapidly. She told herself, 'Fight it, girl, if you let him sleep with you tonight, he'll be in your bed for the whole trip.'

"Lucie?"

"I can't sleep with you over there."

Max grinned in the darkened room. "Well, I'd rather not go out on the balcony or sleep in the hall. I guess I could find another hotel, but it's late and I'm tired. Couldn't you just pretend I'm not here?"

"Already tried that." The words came out in a rush: "I don't want you to sleep on the couch."

"You already said that."

"No, I said I couldn't sleep with you *over there.* It's not the same at all."

"Ok, this conversation is now officially right up there with the one about Big Bertha."

"Humph."

"Lucie, what **do** you want me to do?"

"Come to bed."

CHAPTER 25

Lucie woke up to the murmur of masculine voices. The hallway door closed, followed by the clink of china. She opened one eye as Max approached with a breakfast tray and grinned at her. Lucie groaned and pulled the sheet up over her head: waayyy too much cheeriness.

"Breakfast, sunshine."

"Uhhnh."

"Sorry?"

Lucie reluctantly crawled out of bed and stumbled to the bathroom as Max poured his coffee. She washed her face, then gripped the edge of the sink and addressed the mirror. "Dammit, girl, you have got to stop dragging that man into your bed."

Trouble was, Max's attentive and imaginative lovemaking was quickly becoming addictive. Lucie groaned again.

Max smiled as he sipped his coffee and waited for her: his plan to win her, intellectually as well as sexually, was proceeding nicely. Lucie responded to him with wild enthusiasm, so he intended to bed her as often as possible, to ensure that *his* was the body she thought about when they weren't together.

And he was fairly sure he intrigued her, so he needed to build the foundation that an intelligent woman required. And not annoy her unduly.

There was only one cause for worry: Emma had hired Lucie through a circuitous route of recommendations which had begun with Michael someone's mother, because Michael someone was involved with Lucie. Max wondered what she intended to do about him. She'd have to do *without* him, if she ever decided she wanted Max: sharing Lucie was not an option.

When she emerged from the bathroom, Max poured the steaming milk with one hand and the coffee with the other, then handed her the cup. They consumed the breakfast of warm croissants, jams, butter and fruit, and Lucie told Max about her time with Sophie. She showed him some of what she'd purchased, they sniffed the spices, sampled the chocolates from a tiny shop down the street, and he admired the dishes and bowls she'd accumulated. The behavior of a couple.

The rest of the day beckoned, so as Lucie got dressed and applied makeup, she called to the bedroom, "So do you *really* like museums? Because if you do, we're going to the Carnavalet and the Rodin." Ah, the True Test, two in tandem. And after a whole evening at the Louvre.

"Oh wow, the Thinker, right?" Amazingly, that was his only question. The man displayed remarkable fortitude. Lucie was suspicious. Even Sophie wouldn't agree to spend that kind of time in museums.

They started with Madame de Sévigné's mansion, and Lucie gave Max a running commentary on the collection that depicts the history of Paris. Max was appropriately fascinated.

Then they headed west on the métro, pausing to

enjoy the performances of several buskers. When they arrived at the Rodin Museum, Lucie showed Max her two favorite sculptures, the full-sized Burghers of Calais, outside, and a much smaller piece, The Cathedral, inside. But Max was mesmerized by The Kiss. He stared at the statue of a naked couple in a passionate embrace until Lucie tugged at him and announced, "I'm hungry, Max. We need to find a charcuterie, um, a French deli, and get some take-out for a picnic."

They searched the side streets for a non-touristy area and were soon gawking at the spectacle in a charcuterie window: a row of split lobster tails, mounds of country paté, terrines of all sorts in earthenware pots, pizzas with unfamiliar toppings, seafood cakes, coquilles St. Jacques, saucissons, things wrapped in other things....

Lucie observed, "These shops always make me feel like Ralphie in A Christmas Story, you know, when he's drooling over the display in the department store window and the narrator says 'cornucopia.'"

They bought small portions of many of the items, picked up a bottle of wine in a grocery store and retreated to one of Paris' many little green areas.

Emma's call came later, just as they were trying to find a reason to hoist themselves off the bench – or an excuse not to. Max nodded and disconnected, then turned to Lucie and told her they needed to meet Emma at the Gare de Lyon around dinner time, that she'd taken the TGV rather than go through the hassle of flying.

Lucie squinted at nothing. "I wish the treasure were hidden in Paris, like in a forgotten métro tunnel, or in the cellar of new building where an old one used to be. I have a book about that."

"Of course you do. C'mon, we need to walk off

lunch." They disposed of their trash in a large wire bin, leaving a bit of food for the squirrel who'd been staring at them, and left the quiet of the tiny park.

***

As Max opened the hotel door for Lucie, she remembered something: "The Train Bleu restaurant is in the railroad station where we're meeting Emma and I've always wanted to eat there."

"Sounds great, anything you want. And we need to get a room for her, by the way."

The new man behind the front desk quickly found several very nice rooms that were currently available, and which would Madame prefer? Lucie chose, let Max pay for it, and retrieved their room key. Max took it and began, "So, do you want me to - "

Lucie sighed in resignation. If he got his own room, he'd just find some other excuse for co-habiting. "You might as well stay where all your stuff is."

A few minutes later, Max was sitting on the side of the bed, staring at Lucie. "So, what's the deal with all the museums? Was it some kind of endurance test?"

"Sort of." She grinned and sat next to him on the bed.

"And did I pass?"

"Well, yeah."

Max pulled her onto his lap and poked at his phone, scrolling through his photos, then held it behind Lucie.

"Let's see, your right leg goes over my left leg and touches my right leg, your left arm goes up around my neck like this." He draped her extremities gently over his body and continued, "My right hand goes on your hip but really, Lucie, we should be naked."

"You're doing the Kiss, aren't you?"

Max grinned.

"What, I owe you for putting up with all those museums?"

"Something like that." He pulled her sweater up over her head.

***

Lucie stood in the curve of Max's body, hanging onto the pole as she peered at the métro map displayed above the windows of the train car. "Let's see, we have one more stop, then a transfer. And I'm hungry. Why did you drag me away from that burger place? I wanted a cheeseburger."

"You don't eat in burger places, ever. And we're going to have an excellent meal in a little while. Be patient." He bent to nuzzle her neck.

"I'm not good at patient."

Max smiled. Good thing the Gare de Lyon wasn't all that far.

***

"Just so you know, I could have stayed in Provence; Jean-Luc certainly wanted me to. But you two are just so entertaining, and I do want to do the Eiffel."

Max took Emma's suitcase and started for the Train Bleu restaurant. "Walk and talk, ladies. Lucie's starving." He turned briefly to ask, "You're on a first-name basis with Gérard's lawyer?" And wound up staring at his friend's grey hair, newly and flatteringly styled to frame her face.

"Well, of course I am, Gérard introduced us and it turns out he's very accommodating, and right now, as we speak, he's poking through Notarial records for us and by the way, Jean-Luc's English is nearly perfect!"

Max almost ran into someone: 'E. Harris' never, ever used entire paragraphs to express herself. Especially ones that involved not stopping to take a breath.

Lucie glanced sideways at her: this ebullient Emma was a little scary.

"And Didier asked the old priest to see if he could find out what happened to Marie and her people, and the priest said he'd contact his friend, the cemetery keeper, who has all kinds of records on the locals. Jean-Luc and I think it's worth a shot."

"So how much does he know about the treasure?"

"The basics, Gérard had already told him about the postcards, and he obviously knows about Gaston."

"So he won't discuss this with anybody. Right?"

"Of course not!"

"Good."

Emma looked miffed. "Jean-Luc is completely trustworthy."

Max stopped abruptly and gaped: the woman trusted *no one.*

Lucie ignored them both, pushed past Max and climbed the curved steps that led to the restaurant.

The opulence of their surroundings halted conversation as they gazed at the somewhat grandiose, yet elegant Belle Époque décor of the main dining room. Then a bored waiter seated them perfunctorily, and ten minutes later Max was filling their wine glasses.

Emma raised hers. "So. A toast to finding treasures, whatever form they take." A cryptic remark, but it signaled the return of the calm, laconic woman they knew. Max and Lucie breathed a sigh of relief as they lifted their glasses.

"So, Lucie Richards, what do you recommend here?"

***

Between mouthfuls, they exchanged stories about recent activities, and what was left unsaid was surmised. Emma told them that Jean-Luc had sent an assistant to search through local records, but that he was handling the French Notarial records himself.

"First of all, you need the name of the notary of the time period, which in Jean-Luc's case is easy, it's been his cousins for generations. But then you have to visit the archives in person, and sift through piles of wills, property transfers, records of marriage settlements – useful documents, but extremely tedious work."

"Long story short?" Max was enjoying his leg of lamb and not the dry details of Jean-Luc's research.

"It's not easy to find genealogical data in France."

"Got it. We still don't know where Marie went after Épinal."

"But we will."

***

No one wanted dessert, so they went back to the hotel to drop off Emma's luggage. By the time they emerged from the métro station, it was already dark in Paris, and the Eiffel Tower was in her glory, doing her every-hour-for-ten-minutes sparkling act. Emma was entranced.

She murmured, "Jean-Luc told me it would be like this."

Max looked slightly annoyed. "You could've googled that much."

She ignored him completely and Lucie snickered.

They bought tickets, and as they exited the first elevator to switch to the one that would carry them to the top of the tower, Lucie told them to enjoy the view, that she'd have a beer and wait for their return.

"You aren't going the whole way up?"

"I hate Up."

As Max and Emma entered the elevator for the third level, Lucie heard Max say, "You know, I'm not all that crazy about going the whole way up there either."

Emma's voice rose with the elevator: "Oh stop being such a wuss. You do *not* have acrophobia."

Lucie purchased a beer from the cafeteria-style bar and wandered outside, staying near the center of the platform where she felt comfortable. She watched the lights of Paris for a while, then found a quiet area to call her sister, who was dog-sitting for her. Murphy was thriving but Lucie missed her little Bichon.

Suddenly she felt, rather than saw, Max near her. He was gazing at the City, careful not to eavesdrop. Lucie looked up and smiled. Max smiled back and reached for her beer. She relinquished it without protest and he drank for several seconds, then told her, "Emma's still up there. She called Jean-Luc to describe the view and she's talking in paragraphs again. And have you noticed, she's wearing different, uh, tan-colored clothing instead of her usual?"

"Uh-huh. Her hair looks good, too." Lucie waited for him to make his point, but he just sighed and returned her drink.

By the time Emma descended from the third level, it was time to go back to the hotel. Goodnights were quick, and Lucie was alone with Max before she realized it. He let her use the bathroom first, and when it was his turn, was careful not to move her toothbrush.

Lucie was in bed when he emerged, and she was wearing at least a tee shirt. “Um, Max, it’s been a long day, I’m tired and I don’t want to, um, wear out the equipment.”

He wasn’t sure whose equipment she meant, but was relieved: Olympic sex with Lucie made him feel young in one respect, but he was really feeling his fifty-plus years that night.

“Wouldn’t want to do that.” With a smile that almost made her change her mind.

“Which side you want?”

“Doesn’t matter, it’s your bed.”

Lucie seemed to like that response and patted the right side of the bed. “We both have nightstands, so you have a place to put your, um, teeth or whatever.”

Max laughed and almost changed *his* mind.

***

It was early when they met in the elegant morning room of the hotel, and as Max poured café au lait for his ladies, Emma told them that she had some business in Paris, so could they wait until afternoon to take the train south?

Lucie pulled a timetable from her pocket and handed it to her. “Choose what works for you, ok?”

Emma glanced at the departures, pointed at one and showed Lucie. “It’s three hours to Aix-en-Provence on the TGV and only 37 kilometers from there to Lourmarin: fastest route, I’ve already rented a car for us in Aix.” Perfuntory Emma had returned.

They arranged to meet at the Gare de Lyon and that Lucie and Max would procure a picnic lunch for the train. Emma took off for parts unknown, leaving her suitcase with Max and Lucie, who appreciated not having to hurry their morning.

Lucie had almost finished packing when the memory of waking up in Max's arms, luxuriating in the warmth of him, returned. Feeling the zing of his closeness, but not needing sex. But not needing - what! She stomped her foot, angry with herself. Their relationship had sneaked right on up to the next level! Suddenly she turned.

Max was leaning against the wall, hands in his pockets, staring at her.

"You ok?"

"Yeah, fine. Just wondering where I put..." 'My resolve' echoed in her brain but remained unsaid.

***

They checked out of the hotel and stopped at a Leader Price store for lunch provisions: crusty baguettes, spreadable French cheese, ham and bottles of water. And Max bought a wheeled tote for the wine.

Emma was waiting for them at the station, and they were soon settled in their seats, which faced each other and had a table in the middle. Lucie looked across the aisle and noticed a cute little dog snuggled on the seat beside its owner; it was barely visible, but stuck its tiny head out when it noticed Lucie noticing. She smiled and was fairly certain she saw a doggie grin in return.

Lucie unpacked her laptop, a notebook and a map of Gérardmer, which she spread across the small table, causing everyone else to hastily retrieve the items they'd put there. Then she accessed her computer file on the Quest, added Emma's recent information, and clicked on another icon.

"Well, well, this train provides wi-fi" was followed by rapid typing and close scrutiny of the screen.

Several minutes later, Lucie poked at Max. "Look

at this: Gérardmer, founded 1048-1070, apparently known for good hunting, had a population of 10,000 before WWII. Hmm, there's a French link here." As Lucie flew in and out of web sites, Max sat back and stared out the window at the passing scenery.

"Em, after I left, did you search the winery property for the treasure?"

Emma looked up. "I did. Even tapped walls and pulled a few floorboards. Nothing."

"Hmm."

Lucie pointed to her screen and read aloud, "Gérardmer est prise le 22 juin 1940 par l'armée allemande - um, Gérardmer was taken by the German army on June 22, 1940, then, faced with the advance of the Allies in November of 1944, they practiced la terre brulée. The entire city was covered by a thick, black cloud while 85% of the city burned: those bastards!"

"It says that?"

"No, I did. I can't imagine almost getting through the war, then, with the end in sight, losing everything. I wonder if the treasure survived all that? Let's see, they moved it there, probably in 1924, at least that's the date on the postcard."

She peered at the map of Gérardmer until Max folded his arms across his chest, having nowhere else to put them, and ventured, "I think I'll make my world-famous chili when we get back."

Emma, who'd been using her phone to text, raised an eyebrow. "You mean the food that took a layer of skin off my tongue? Even Antonio had to run for bread."

Max looked hurt. "Wasn't *that* bad, at least Bruno liked it. Um, Lucie, you're going to take a break when it's time for lunch, right?"

Lucie looked up and blinked, finally realizing that

they were holding their possessions in their laps. "Oh, right, sorry."

As she folded the city map and moved her computer to one side of the table, Emma returned her attention to her phone and remarked, "When you're done there, I have something to tell you."

"Go for it."

"Not now, Jean-Luc is expecting this text."

Max rolled his eyes. "You're going to wear out your thumbs, Emma."

"Whatever." She typed for a while, pressed Send, then got up to stretch. She walked to the end of the car, pushed the button that made the door open in a whoosh, and stepped through to the area between train cars. Max stared at her cell phone for a moment, then stood and followed her. Lucie barely noticed their departure, but all of a sudden, something made her glance at them through the glass door.

That they were discussing something serious was evident: Max was talking with his hands and Emma looked angry. She pointed an accusatory index finger at him, then splayed both hands in exasperation and shook her head.

Max crossed his arms; now *he* looked angry and leaned back against the wall. When he inclined his head slightly, it was evident that an impasse had been reached. Emma pointed through the door, without taking her eyes off Max, and they both turned slowly to stare at Lucie. Eyes wide, she gulped: their expressions were grim and, Lucie imagined, menacing. She quickly looked down at her computer.

Lucie's brain went to overload and segments of various movies flashed before her eyes: an unwitting civilian caught up in an elaborate scheme concerning a treasure and betrayed by partners who were dangerous ex-spies and bound by an enormous secret.

The rhythm of the train swept her into a convoluted Agatha Christie-like plot...

She awakened with a start: the cork being extracted from the wine bottle sounded like a gunshot. Well, sort of. Max was pouring wine into little plastic cups while Emma sliced the baguettes lengthwise for sandwiches. Lucie squinted at them, watching for signs of duplicity. Everything *seemed* normal, but it would, wouldn't it, given their expertise in concealment?

Max glanced at her and laughed. "You were drooling."

"Was not."

Had her mind amplified the situation? No, the bad vibes, the flash of suspicion had been unmistakable. Lucie continued to stare and considered just asking them about it, but quickly abandoned what suddenly seemed childish. If they wanted to share it, they would. They should, if it involved her. Which it did. Lucie frowned.

"Bad dream?"

"You have no idea."

Max asked what she wanted on her sandwich and normal conversation resumed while they ate; Lucie's suspicions were relegated to the room in her mind where the rest of her uncertainties resided.

She was finishing the last of her sandwich when she noticed the little dog across the aisle again: it had crept out from its lair and was staring wistfully at the remains of the picnic. Lucie asked its humans if she could share a bit of cheese and bread, was granted permission, and thoroughly enjoyed the next few minutes, feeding and petting the well-behaved little animal.

When a muffled voice announced that the train would arrive at the Aix-en Provence station in fourteen minutes, Lucie began to gather her scattered belongings.

Emma suddenly sat straight up and glanced furtively at the seats near theirs, seemed satisfied that no one was eavesdropping, and began, in a hushed voice: “It cost me a minor skirmish with the Dark Side, but I found a solid reference to the Krupps and lost gold near the end of the war.”

Max blinked at her. “What? Why’d you wait ‘til now to drop that bomb?”

“Well, I sort of forgot. Ok, I got sidetracked. Jean-Luc has been asking me all kinds of, ah, personal questions, and vetting one’s responses is so labor intensive, especially if you have to text everything.”

Max interrupted her with “Emma, dear, you are beginning to sound like Lucie when she’s off and running.”

“Hey!” Lucie, who was still rummaging, smacked him. “I was only half listening, but I’m pretty sure I’m insulted.”

“You want to hear this or not?” Emma leaned forward and whispered,

“It’s in a classified military report that details the sale of Krupp armaments to Turkey and Bulgaria, who then paid in gold bullion and shipped it to Essen, the heart of the Krupp empire. Only it never got there.”

Max stared.

“And guess who filed that report?”

Lucie looked up and said quietly, “Lt. James Milnar.”

CHAPTER 26

The TGV glided smoothly under the curved expanse of the Aix station, and the continuously beeping tone reminded them to de-board quickly: the TGV waits for no one. Max was off first and the women had barely handed their bags down to him when the train whisked away almost silently.

They were left standing on a platform with a view of parking lots, some buildings, a highway, lots of concrete, and, in the distance, mountains. But no Aix-en-Provence.

Max turned slowly, dumbfounded. "Emma. Where's the town? Did we get off at the wrong station?"

Emma held up a 'just a minute" finger as she ended a phone call. "We're about thirteen kilometers outside of Aix, and the rental will be here shortly."

Lucie gazed at the intensely blue Provençal sky and grinned as the sun warmed her face. "This is *terrific*, just look at - " But Max and Emma, already discussing the logistics of locating a lost shipment of gold, ignored her; so she kept her delight to herself until a diminutive Frenchman hooted at them from the parking lot.

As they dragged their luggage to the rental car, a late model dark blue, leather-seated, über-luxurious Mercedes-Benz, Lucie enthused, "Whoa, nice ride, Emma!"

The little man loaded their luggage into the trunk and Max looked from the car to his former partner, clearly astonished. "This is a rental? I'm impressed, Em. Where'd you find a Benz S600?"

Emma's smile was enigmatic as she took the keys from the Frenchman, tipped him and climbed into the driver's seat. Max protested immediately, "But I always do the driving, and that's a V12 under the hood."

She lowered the windows and bellowed in her Bruno-fetching voice, "Back seat, Max. Today I'm pilot and Lucie's navigator." She motioned for Lucie to get in on the passenger side and handed her a highlighted map. Max grumbled and folded his long frame into the rear, sitting sideways until Lucie moved her seat forward.

The drive to Lourmarin took them through magnificent countryside, and Emma kept the tinted windows partially lowered so they could smell the still-fragrant Provençal air. Their route soon led them under an honor guard's raised sabers: the plane trees that lined the road had grown together at the top, forming a majestic canopy.

They drove to the town center and consulted the French directional signs: attached to a pole, they resembled the 'sticky arrows' that designate where a document needs to be signed.

The local château was listed, along with a discreet hint that a visit was possible. Then, pointing in another direction as though they didn't want to be associated with the château, were all the villages with Saint before their names. And local eateries, designated by a crossed knife and fork. And the Sautier winery, with a shabby little arrow, a wine glass and a suggestion to present oneself for a dégustation.

"They really go all out with the signage, don't they? The leather on the back seat made soft noises as Max craned his neck to see.

Lucie squinted at the map and said, "Emma, I can't figure out - "

The older woman leaned over, pausing to shift her eyes at the face protruding from the back seat.

"Do you mind?"

Max flopped back and mumbled, "Car has a GPS, you'da used it, we'd be there already."

Emma snorted.

***

The bastide, visible as they entered the winery property, was more than an old farmhouse: constructed of warm-beige stone, it flaunted three chimneys, an ancient, noble entrance door and many white-framed windows scattered all over the exterior.

The narrow lane that meandered toward the house was neatly lined with rectangular stones and contrasted sharply with the grounds, which were splattered with a wild explosion of trees: graceful willows, oaks, umbrella pines, the ubiquitous plane trees that looked as though they were in a perpetual state of shedding, and everywhere, the cypress trees that were Lucie's favorites.

As they slowly pulled up to the building, a large, whitish, long-haired dog of obscure origin rose from its resting place by the front door and ambled over to sniff the car. When Lucie opened her door carefully and greeted it in French, the dog responded gleefully, wagging its entire body, then pointed itself toward the house and barked several times.

In a reverse Pavlovian scenario, the door opened and a smiling Gérard emerged. While Max treated the dog to an ear-rub, Lucie ran to hug Gérard and, right behind him, Marie-Françoise; then Kate and Didier appeared, and everyone babbled at once until Gérard called for welcome drinks on the south terrace.

Didier helped drag the luggage inside and upstairs: the guest bedrooms were all on the upper floors, and because the house had been modified many times, there was a large, segmented second floor and a bit of a third. Kate and Didier had a room and bath on the second level, and Emma chose hers there as well.

Max and Lucie wandered up the short, curved stone staircase to the top floor and found a master bedroom with a large bed, en suite bathroom and French doors that opened onto a balcony. Adjoining that room was a smaller, bright bedroom with two twin beds, a writing desk, a window seat alcove, and a sink.

Lucie looked longingly at the room, thinking she'd like to have her own space. She turned to Max, who was watching her intently.

"You know what, Lucie, I think we need both rooms."

The man was a genius.

***

They gathered on the long, arbor-covered terrace that ran the length of the house to share a toast and enjoy the fragrance of plants that grew just beyond: lavender, rosemary, thyme and sage.

Milou, serving in his capacity as the official winery dog, wandered around and under the table as Lucie fed him tiny bits of the appetizer that Marie-Françoise had bought earlier in the village: eggplant dip with goat's cheese, served with crudités.

Gérard launched into a welcome speech, stopping occasionally so that Lucie could translate. He told them that he and his wife had been living in the village center for about a year because the bastide had outgrown the couple, but that they'd temporarily moved back in order to spend time with the treasure-hunters. Then he asked Lucie if she wanted to see their townhouse tomorrow, the one she'd eventually inherit.

Lucie said nothing for a moment, and everyone turned to stare, uncertain of a quiet Lucie. Then she nodded slowly; she'd get to the issue of the Sautiers' will later.

Kate broke the silence with, "Well. Now that Didier here turned seventy-five, he's resigned from the Sautiers' employ." Eyes bright, she folded her hands and nodded at everyone.

"With his savings and severance pay, he can support us for our foreseeable future and – this is for you, Max - has insisted on a pre-nup that keeps my money in a separate trust. But best of all, Gérard and Marie-Françoise have given him the other half of their town house and we've been fixing it up ever since we got here!"

Kate unfolded her hands and slapped them down on the table triumphantly. "So here I am, at my age, going to housekeeping all over again!"

She went on to inform them that they'd put the wedding off until the Three Musketeers found the treasure, which led to questions, until the air turned too chilly to remain outdoors.

Marie-Françoise rose and beckoned them indoors for the meal she'd prepared earlier, Beef Daube. As they settled at the long wooden table in the vaulted dining room, already set with lovely Provençal bowls,

Lucie noted that the air was *not* redolent with the long-simmering dish. Odd.

Gérard produced a carafe of Sautier table wine as Kate and Marie emerged from the kitchen with a huge tureen of the red wine stew and another of noodles, which Didier passed around the table. Marie murmured "Bon appétit" and indicated that they should ladle the stew directly onto the noodles.

Max finished his mouthful before the rest, blinked several times and asked for the large basket of sliced baguettes. He smiled, nodded at his hostess and quickly stuffed several in his mouth, washing them down with wine.

Lucie took her first bite, and her eyes widened as the food assaulted her tongue: the stew, usually hearty and savory, should have included the flavors of garlic, rosemary, and thyme. Instead, she tasted a sea of salt and a forest of harsh bay leaves.

She snatched the bread basket away from Max, gulped a whole glass of wine and groaned inwardly: really good wine would have gotten them through the meal, but the Sautier wine was mediocre at best. Lucie surreptitiously glanced around the table: no one had gotten past the first bite.

Didier noticed the universal reaction to the food and slipped into the kitchen, returning moments later with a gigantic bowl of a mixed-greens salad. As several hands grabbed for it, he motioned for Kate to follow him; they emerged from the kitchen with a platter of local cheeses and a dessert that was above suspicion, having been purchased in the village along with the appetizer.

When Marie-Françoise excused herself to make coffee, Emma, Max and Lucie escaped upstairs to 'freshen up.' Emma followed them to the top floor and closed the bedroom door behind her. Then got the giggles.

"I can't believe it. Marie-Françoise is a really lousy cook! I didn't think that was even legal in France." And started to giggle again as she flopped onto the chair in Max's room.

"You should have warned us!"

"I didn't eat dinner here, Jean-Luc and I ate in the village. What's that noise in the bathroom?"

"Probably Lucie obliterating the taste of that food." Just as he said it, Lucie emerged, toothbrush in hand, scraping her tongue.

"Macth, hbbtichu,"- she extracted the toothbrush – "Max, how about you offer to take everyone out to dinner tomorrow night?"

"Sure, now can I get my mouthwash?"

Emma got up and sighed. "Well, you two are no fun. Meet you downstairs."

***

Lucie wanted to show Gérard what they'd done with his postcards, so after surprisingly good coffee, she spread them on the now-cleared dinner table. She explained their analysis based on chronology, the XOs, and the food notations. Gérard chuckled and observed that it was appropriate for a treasure-hunting chef to be following a food trail.

Then Emma unfolded a map of France that was marked with Xs for the pin locations, and pointed to possible locations for the Legacy. She asked Lucie to explain that they were at a dead end, that they needed additional information about the three whose lives wandered in and out of those cards.

Gérard sat down slowly and rubbed his face, willing the past to return to him.

"I never knew the cards existed until my father was

on his deathbed, after a stroke. He told me to look for an old shoebox in the attic, and guard it, that the family legacy was at stake." He stopped and looked up at them. "I thought he was delirious, an old shoebox! Marie found it, but not before he took its secret to his grave. We did not think anything more about it until we cleared the place out to move to the village last year, and then we decided to present it to Gaston in New York."

He stopped, lost in memories. "My father would not talk about the Great War, you know, not ever. He said those horrors were best buried and forgotten. My mother once told me he was a broken man when they sent him home, but the fire inside him returned when Marie, a childhood friend, came back to town near the end of the war...and then he married my mother in 1922."

"I grew up, and the clouds gathered again, as my father said they would. Another War." The old man, suddenly drained of all remaining energy, finished with, "I am sorry, perhaps in the morning I will remember something that will help you."

He rose slowly and smiled at them. He said simply, "I am glad you are here."

Marie- Françoise followed her husband, pausing to whisper to Lucie, "Thank you so much for coming all this way, it means a great deal to him." Kate and Didier bade everyone goodnight as well, leaving the three of them in the dining room. They stared at the cards for a moment, then Emma got up, stretched and said she had a long call to make to Jean-Luc before going to sleep.

As they climbed the stairs to their rooms, Max spoke quietly to Lucie: "Do you still feel that connection with Gérard, the former life thing?"

"Yeah, and it's starting to creep me out: I mean, I

like it that I get vibes about people, but this is a whole other level of awareness, and it scares me a little."

"Hypnosis could uncover your shared past."

Lucie glanced quickly at Max: his face wore an odd, unsettling expression.

"That's not gonna happen."

"You aren't curious?"

"I am not. There's a reason Gérard and I were put in each other's path in *this* life, and that's all I need to know. Period."

"Well at least stay open to it, Lucie, your instincts are a valuable asset."

She'd just flipped on the light in the small bedroom when Max heard "Milou, what the - !"

A startled Milou shook himself, launching little clouds of white hair everywhere, then ran past them and down the stairs. Max peered into the room: the dog had pulled the sheets from both beds and made a fluffy nest for himself on the floor.

Lucie put her hands on her hips and frowned. "There's dog hair all over this room: I can't sleep here! Why the heck didn't he camp out on *your* bed, I wonder?" She looked at Max suspiciously.

"Because I didn't feed him." Max grinned and put his hand on the back of her neck, drew her to him, and kissed her deeply.

"Looks like you get me for a roommate after all."

"Yeah, well, I still think you two were in cahoots."

***

Max was fast asleep when the sun woke a hungry Lucie, so she slipped into some clothes and went downstairs. She stopped abruptly at the entrance to the kitchen, overwhelmed by the effect of the sun on the ancient Provençal tiles behind the sink and stove, and on the terracotta colored floor. The room was awash in light and warmth and the vivid blues and yellows of the tiles seemed to vibrate.

Then she noticed Gérard at the corner table, studying the postcards. He raised his head slowly, smiled and gallantly rose to pour coffee for her. She returned his smile and thanked him, but grimaced when she saw what he was having for breakfast.

Biscottes. A horrid pretend-food which is not to be confused with Italian biscotti. *Ever.* Lucie had subsisted on biscottes, which look like toast but are really no-flavor, super-dry squares, as a student in France, and vowed never to eat them again.

So she asked Gérard if she could prepare a little something for breakfast, and the old man immediately brightened, telling her to use anything she wanted. Lucie searched the cupboards for ingredients, thinking there was no time to make bread, so it had to be something quick: she pulled out flour, sugar, baking powder and salt. And from the frig, milk and butter.

Lucie made biscuits, coated them with melted butter and baked them to a golden brown. She repeated the procedure until she had enough for everyone, and Gérard brought out jams and fresh fruit.

They enjoyed the breakfast quietly, comforted by the nurturing aroma of baking, until Gérard's attention returned to the postcards.

"Chère Lucie, do any of these cards...mean something to you?"

How did he know? She looked deep into his clear, light blue eyes and then down at the cards. She lightly touched the postcard from Gérardmer.

"Mais je ne sais pas pourquoi." She had no idea why.

"And none of the others?"

She shook her head.

"And why does the Great War speak to you?" Not if, or how, just *why*.

Lucie told him the story of her grandfather, the evocative books she'd read, and the strong connection she felt with that time.

He nodded as he reached for another biscuit, but remained silent.

Lucie said softly, "Gérard, I cannot escape the feeling that I knew you before we met in New York, and I think I understand the gift of the postcards, your legacy. But to make me your sole beneficiary, it is too much."

Gérard gazed far into Lucie's eyes, shook his head and said simply, "No, it is not, petite-fille, and you must accept that." End of discussion, apparently.

Max's voice arrived in the kitchen before he did: "Don't push, Magoo, I'm hungry, too, and shoving me won't get you food any faster."

"It's *Milou*, and he probably doesn't understand English." Lucie grinned: the large dog had decided to attach himself to Max after all.

As Max tried to divest himself of his new friend, Lucie made a place for him at the table and started another pot of coffee. Gérard, meanwhile, gathered the postcards and had just taken them to the dining room when the rest of the household, lured by the aromas of baking and freshly brewed coffee, wandered into the kitchen.

Morning conversation ebbed and flowed, one language overlapping another, until Lucie asked for a tour of the estate before they went into the village. Gérard said he'd be delighted, and half an hour later Lucie was coming down the stone stairs when she saw Max and Emma, deep in conversation by the front door. They stopped abruptly when they noticed her,

Max looked uneasy, which he shouldn't have, and it was the train all over again.

Lucie frowned and continued toward the kitchen, telling herself that she was being over-sensitive; she'd just shared Max's bed, surely she'd know if something were amiss, afoot, whatever. Then she inadvertently glanced outside, through the large windows by the kitchen door.

At the Judas tree that Marie-Françoise had planted herself and pointed out to everyone. Adorned with beautiful pink blossoms in the spring, autumn had rendered it barren, a solemn symbol of betrayal.

A shiver slid down her spine as she heard Max behind her and she turned, ready to confront him. But Gérard and his wife were beckoning from the back door, anxious to show off their life's work: the confrontation would have to wait.

***

The winemaker's house was only partially obscured by a half-hearted group of gnarled olive trees just beyond the south terrace, and as Gérard unlocked the front door, he began, "C'est très confortable" - but they could see that for themselves. The huge, well-furnished living area on the ground floor included a fully-equipped kitchen, half bath and a study with an entire wall of winemaking books, a computer desk sans computer and a disconnected printer.

Marie-Françoise sighed, letting her eyes travel slowly around the room that was bereft of personal objects. "We had hoped that Gaston would someday live here and take over the family business, but he always said that the legal profession was so much more lucrative and that he needed to live in a city."

When Marie sighed again, her husband quickly led

them to the winery, an immense structure that contained all the equipment needed to produce wine, but where an air of neglect hung over the vats. Gérard explained that while 70% of the wine produced in Provence was rosé, his winery had produced blended reds. He pointed to a spigot in one wall, and remarked, with a smile at the memory, that many locals used to come with containers and buy their wine in bulk, exchanging news of the day in the process. Unfortunately, the only Sautier wines that were left resided in the 'cave' in the main house.

A connecting path led them next to the chai – the wine storehouse, with its rows of aging barrels - and it looked just as forlorn as the winery. The remaining building was a tired-looking cottage whose roof sagged a bit on the back side.

But the Sautiers, oblivious to the gentle ruin around them, seemed happy to be walking family land again. Heads bent to each other, arm in arm, they started back up the path to the bastide and suggested that everyone join them for lunch at their favorite restaurant after the visit of the townhouses.

Max waited until they were out of earshot, then turned to Lucie: "Did Gérard mention anything about his father at breakfast?"

Lucie shook her head. "No, and he won't consider changing his will."

***

Market day meant that the village was bustling, and the Sautier townhouse was located very near the central square and the adjacent market area. As Max parked on a side street, he suddenly turned to Emma and Lucie.

"I can't face another one of Marie-Françoise's

meals, so how about we hit this market and get what we need to make dinner tonight?"

Lucie hesitated.

"What's the matter? I know it's what you do for a living, but - "

"It's not that. I just don't want to hurt Marie's feelings: it's her kitchen, her territory."

"Then don't outshine her."

"That's not possible. Besides, they already know what I can do"

"Then keep it really simple."

Lucie brightened. "That's actually a very good idea, and if you help me get what I need, I'll let you be my sous chef."

"Does that involve - "

"Just carry the bag."

The three wandered through the aromas of recently-picked produce, spices, cheeses, herbs, garlic, olives, seafood and fruits of all kinds. So many to choose from, all displayed in endless barrels, buckets and baskets, proud vendors standing watch behind them, some calling out to prospective buyers.

They filled the shopping filet with fresh tomatoes, garlic, local olive oil, basil, herbes de Provence, several kinds of cheeses, pasta, the makings of a salad, and baguettes.

Armed with the certainty of a palatable dinner, they made their way back to the building that housed both the Sautier home and Didier's new apartment.

Kate bubbled with enthusiasm as Didier watched her in adoration. "I'm so excited to have you see our new digs, come on, Didier, show them what you've done so far. And Mrs. Harris, Lucie, I must take you to this little shop down the street, you should see the gorgeous linens and soaps and oils and, oh so much! It's all so lovely."

Their apartment was in various stages of being painted and furnished, so when they toasted to everyone's health, they had to sit on boxes in the living room.

Then Didier chuckled and said he wanted to explain something to Lucie. He told her that Marie-Francoise, when first married, almost killed Gérard with a seafood stew, not knowing that he was allergic to shellfish. And that even though it's illogical, she started to cook only the blandest of foods, enhanced with salt, in case he was allergic to anything else. Didier laughed, and said that her great love for her husband had produced the worst food in Provence.

Lucie translated for Emma and Max, and as they toasted Didier's tale, Max decided that he liked the man: he told a good story and he adored Kate. Not much else was terribly important.

The Sautiers arrived and insisted on showing off their apartment, which resulted in another toast, this time out on the balcony. Gérard pointed to the many cafés and restaurants below them and recommended one for lunch, citing regional specialties. He gazed out on the red umbrellaed tables, the chalk board menus, the sound of dishes clanking against each other, of muted conversation. And smiled a contented smile.

"You see, I do not want my wife slaving in the kitchen all day, so we take most of our meals- (he made a sweeping motion with his arm) – below."

Lucie slid a sly glance at Didier, who was examining his shirt for stains....

***

They lingered over an excellent lunch, and when the Sautiers said they were delighted that Lucie would be preparing dinner, she realized she'd forgotten dessert. Didier promptly offered to take them to his favorite bakery just down the street, so they all poked into little shops on the way while Emma used her cell phone.

Lucie found Babas au rhum and when she bought eight of the tiny cakes, Max pointed out that they only needed seven.

"I have a feeling we'll need eight, just humor me."

Max flipped his eyebrows, but refrained from the 'Whatever' he was thinking.

Kate and Didier wanted to ride in the Benz, so, happily laded with the promise of good food, the five headed for the bastide.

***

They knew something was wrong when they saw Milou pacing, clearly distressed. He started to bark franticly as they got out of the car: the entrance door was slightly ajar. Max told everyone to wait outside, motioned for Emma to take his back, and slowly pushed the door open.

The Sautiers had just pulled up to the front of the house when a grim Max reappeared and announced, "All the postcards are gone, so's the map. The bastards got it all."

CHAPTER 27

As Lucie told the Sautiers what happened, Emma met Max at the front door and announced that she was going to take a walk; Lucie noticed the bulge under her jacket and figured what her 'walk' would entail.

Everyone but Lucie rushed inside, where Marie-Françoise wrung her hands and cried softly as Gérard stared sadly at the bare table. "My father's legacy is lost forever, and I cannot remember - how will you ever find - "

They were startled when Lucie deposited her laptop in front of them with a firm clunk. "Good thing I stowed this in the trunk of the car." She flipped up the lid of the computer and brought up the images of the postcards. "Voilà! Copies of everything!"

She looked at Gérard and said quietly, "The Legacy is still safe. Besides, the cards already spoke to me, remember? I don't need them now." And to Max, "Could you please get the food from the car? We need to banish the violation of this house with good aromas."

Kate found some brandy and herded the Sautiers into the living room while Max dragged the provisions into the kitchen, then took out his cell phone. "I'll help you with the prep in a minute, I have a call to make." The grim expression had returned.

Lucie opened a bottle of wine to put in the sauce and began to scrub the vegetables. And blatantly eavesdropped.

"Why the hell did you move your surveillance to the village?"

Lucie could hear the loud, indignant voice of the operative: "Our instructions were to guard the Sautiers. That's what we did."

"Well, there's been a robbery here at the winery."

"Look, Mick, you did *not* hire us to conduct surveillance on an empty house. You wanted the old folks protected, that's what we did. You wanna change that?"

"No... the original instructions stand. And thanks." He disconnected, put the phone on the counter and frowned. "Hacking at food will probably make me feel better."

Lucie carefully handed him a knife and the garlic, onions and tomatoes. "Knock yourself out."

Max washed his hands and was soon making surprisingly adept movements with the knife.

"Where'd you learn to chop food like that?"

"Watching you." He grinned and leaned over to brush her ear with his lips. Lucie stifled a moan: there was dinner to make.

***

The aroma of simmering marinara sauce wafted throughout the entire ground floor of the bastide, and, along with the brandy, lulled the elderly couples into naps. Emma returned from her 'walk' and reported that the grounds were secure and that Max's surveillance team was in place.

The Three tiptoed out onto the terrace and had just sat down when Max's cell phone rang.

"No, it's ok, good to hear from you." He mouthed 'Dylan' to the women, then listened attentively for a long time.

When the conversation finally ended, Max turned to Lucie and Emma and shook his head. "Can't be the same girl. She - "

He was interrupted as the Sautiers, Kate and Didier joined them and wanted to know what was going on. With Lucie's help, he reported, "My daughter Dylan has made definite plans to run the winery!"

"Hard to believe, but she contacted the placement office of an Oenology School, got some recommendations, and has apparently persuaded a fledgling winemaker to come over here with her."

Lucie asked, "She doesn't want to study the process herself?"

Max grinned and shook his head. "Dylan's idea of studying is finding out who has the knowledge she needs, and hiring him. Her. Anyhow, the guy she's bringing with her is French, he's been studying in California, and the two of them are already talking about sourcing grapes from small growers in this area." His expression of pride was mixed with a soupçon of skepticism. "I told her she needs to be serious about this venture, that a family's heritage is involved."

The Sautiers smiled, clearly pleased at the respect in Max's voice.

"We need to keep an eye on her, though: she called the oenologist a hottie and - "

Max stopped to stare at the distinguished-looking gentleman who'd just appeared on the terrace: of medium build, he wore his receding grey hairline as well as he wore a nicely tailored suit and an air of authority. The wrinkles only added interest to his face.

His eyes darted quickly around the table and had a calculating, shrewd quality about them: 'Lawyer' flashed through Max and Lucie's minds as Emma leaped out of her chair and hurried to him.

"Jean-Luc, how lovely to see you! Oh, and look, you've brought wine!"

Max frowned. "Lovely? She never says lovely."

"Be quiet."

Emma introduced the lawyer to Max and Lucie and invited him to stay for dinner, nodding at Lucie.

"Fine with me, we have a ton of food."

Jean-Luc immediately ingratiated himself by commenting on the wonderful aromas emanating from the house; Max rolled his eyes and snorted.

He flinched when Lucie kicked him under the table and looked annoyed when the newcomer asked, in perfect British English, if he were all right.

Lucie snickered and excused herself to get the meal ready to serve, but her peripheral vision caught Max sneaking a peek at the labels on the wine that Jean-Luc had brought: Côtes-du-Rhône, from what he called an amazing boutique winery. Max scowled and followed Lucie indoors.

As she added some salt to the boiling pasta water, Lucie raised an eyebrow at Max. "What's with you and Jean-Luc?"

Still scowling, he leaned backwards against the counter, arms folded in confrontational body language. "Typical lawyer, thinks he knows – ok, I'll tell you what the problem is, it's Emma: I've known her forever and she's NEVER acted all – girly. She's flirting, for God's sake! So beneath her, so, unsensible."

"People change, Max. Jean-Luc seems charming, and she obviously likes him, but we'll have to see if he's worthy of her. Ok?"

Max growled.

"You jealous?" Lucie squinted at him.

Max turned to stare at her. "Jealous! Me? Don't be ridiculous." He turned away. "It's just that we've been partners for so long, I figured we'd always be there for each other."

"Really. You *do* want her to be happy, right?"

"What!?" Max's head whipped around as though she'd slapped him, and he stared at her as he slowly lowered his face into one hand. "Oh God, of course I want her to be happy. How could I - " He looked up at Lucie. "All I could think of was how Jean-Luc in *her* life would impact mine." He shook his head. "You must think I'm a - a - selfish prick."

"Matter of fact, I do not." She stood on tiptoe to kiss his cheek.

In another life, Lucie had chosen a man who was irresistibly attractive in his maleness. But living with him revealed an alpha male who got bored easily and made it clear he hadn't signed on to 'understand' or 'share' emotions. And who didn't really like the word 'emotions' anyway, it reminded him of PMS.

So. Here was a man who actually *wanted* to share his feelings, someone flawed, but honest enough to admit it. And, at the end of the day, genuine. Then there was the absolute fact that she was having trouble keeping her hands off him.

"Look, Max, I know Emma means a lot to you, and I care about her, too. When I'm not afraid of her, that is. How about I check out his vibes?"

"Check out his *what*?"

"Vibes, Max, remember? I'm good at reading people. If Jean-Luc's a Giles, we'll sabotage him, ok?"

Max looked hopeful. "Yeah, we could do that, couldn't we?" Then he smiled at the Giles-as-scoundrel reference.

"And while we're talking important issues, on the train yesterday, and just a little while ago, what were you and - "

Lucie was interrupted by Milou and a noisy parade of hungry people who wanted to know how soon dinner would be ready.

***

The day's balmy weather had extended into the evening, so Lucie insisted on dining at the long table on the terrace. Dinner was congenial: Max's mood had lifted, Jean-Luc and Emma were animated, and the Sautiers seemed to have put aside their anguish over the burglary.

By the time they'd finished with the fresh marinara dish, crusty baguettes and the huge, simple salad followed by a platter of cheeses, Jean-Luc's wine was just a memory, the empty bottles lined up on the table.

Over coffee and babas au rhum, Jean-Luc began, "Your Madame Harris is a very special lady" and Emma actually blushed. Max opened his mouth, but stopped when Lucie raised an eyebrow at him.

"Now then, your – ah - search généologique." He spoke mostly in English, translating immediately for the French, then sat back and entwined his fingers in typical lawyerly fashion, pausing for effect. Max made a face.

"Because Madame is a brilliant detective and because of the most excellent French Census system, we know that Marie Bottecher lived in Épinal, with a daughter, in 1928."

He paused again and Max started to fidget.

"What we do not know is where she went after that."

Max crossed his arms and said, "We already know what we don't know." Then he leaned over to Lucie and whispered, "I wasn't being rude, I just want him to cut to the chase."

Jean-Luc couldn't hear the whispered remark, but he read Max's body language, and, aware of Max's preeminent position in Emma's life, showed restraint in his response.

"Very true, Max, and I am afraid that the meager amount of information that I was able to acquire today is not terribly illuminating." He paused again, and this time Lucie began to squirm.

"In the Mairie, there is a record of the will of the dead husband of Marie Bottecher. Not much was left to the widow, and there was no mention of offspring. There was no legal activity after that, so I assume that she never moved back to her ancestral home." He sat back with a satisfied look on his face, but frowned when his cell phone rang.

He got up to excuse himself but sat back down, rapidly, listening to the other end and adding only monosyllables to the conversation. He snapped the phone shut and addressed the table in English only, any pretense of grandeur put aside.

"Something extremely disturbing has occurred: my friend at the Mairie, Monsieur Lemieux, has been assaulted and now he is in hospital!" He shook his head in disbelief and continued, "Just after I left today, a man wearing a ski mask demanded to know what records I had accessed. Monsieur Lemieux, of course, revealed nothing and tried to call the police and that is when he was rendered unconscious!"

Max forgot his rancor and asked, "Anything

taken?"

"The original documents were on his desk at the time of the attack, and are now missing." Jean-Luc gave Max a shrewd look. "Stolen, I would think, by the same person who took your cards."

Lucie verbalized what everybody was thinking: "So Gaston now has the Bottechar information as well as the cards: the ratbastard is following us around, letting us do all the work, and now he's escalated from burglary to assault and battery."

Jean-Luc looked thoughtful and said, "Pity we cannot have him arrested: M. Lemieux did not see his face and therefore cannot make a positive identification."

When Lucie threw a quick translation down the table, Didier looked stricken and excused himself. Max watched his mother follow, and observed, "Nothing we can do until Gaston makes another move, and I don't like that at all."

He nodded imperceptibly at Emma and they left together, so Lucie began to clear the table. When Jean-Luc helped her, she accorded him a silent approval point.

***

They were seated at the dining room table, enjoying the glow from the fine cognac that Gérard had proudly pried from his liquor cabinet, when Kate and Didier returned.

Didier took a deep breath, asked Lucie to translate: "My friends, the cemetery keeper and the priest are well." He nodded vigorously, as though that affirmation would keep them so.

"The old priest could not remember anything about the Bottecher family, but he asked his friend Mathieu, the keeper of the cemetery, to search in the records. And we have discovered something quite extraordinary!" He waited for the translation, looking pleased with himself.

"It seems that many years ago, the family of Marie Bottecher gave up one of their family plots, because Marie was already buried - in Gérardmer."

Lucie gasped, Max raised his eyebrows and Jean-Luc, one-upped by a non-legal, stood up slowly and deliberately, as though he were about to address a jury. He announced that he had the connections to access the Notarial records in Gérardmer, and Emma smiled proudly. "I will find her lineage. I - " A shadow crossed his face with the reality of what he'd proposed, and he back-pedaled a little.

"We must hope, of course that Marie did not remarry, that we can trace the name of Bottecher, and that she owned property and that I can discover the name of the Notaire who processed the alleged documents and that the daughter Albertine produced offspring..." He sat down quickly and looked worried.

When he remained silent, Lucie turned to Didier, thinking that this Quest of hers had turned everyone into long-talkers, smiled and thanked him profusely for his help. But she stopped talking abruptly, looked away and then stared down at her hands.

Max noticed. "Lucie?"

"So much of Gérardmer was destroyed in 1944, what are the chances the town documents survived?" She looked up at him. "We need information from the 1930s and 40s and it could all be gone."

"Or not. Let's let Jean-Luc make his inquiries." With just a hint of 'put up or shut up' on his face, Max turned to the lawyer.

Jean-Luc sat up straight. "So. Madame Harris has indicated to me how important this is to her, and to you as well, so it would be my great pleasure to be of assistance." He made a small bow from his seat. Emma beamed.

Confidence restored, Jean-Luc took a small notebook and pen from his suit jacket and began to write. Without looking up, he told them, "We shall assume that the town elders of Gérardmer hid what was important, as Frenchmen did all throughout France: I am sure you are aware of the story of the treasures of the Louvre."

He must have been sure, because he didn't wait for an answer.

"Now that we have an end point for our Marie, I will have the census for Gérardmer accessed. And I will ask my cousin the Notaire to make some calls for Gérardmer, it is much easier to find a former Notaire through the current one, and on to the Notarial records and her will."

Lucie groaned. "Why can't this be like the National Treasure movies, where one clue leads directly to another. This is all so convoluted...and *legal*."

"It's only easy in the movies, Lucie."

***

The two elderly couples disappeared after some fast Bonne Nuits and almost immediately, Max's cell rang. He listened for a moment, then turned to the others and said, "Gaston's been sighted on the outskirts of the winery. And he's got a woman with him." He listened for a moment, then put the call on speaker.

"You want us to bring 'em in?"

"No, we don't have anything that would stick. But don't lose him."

"Uh, Mick?"

Max rolled his eyes.

"We have ears on, and that woman is a nasty piece of work."

"She heavily armed, talking damage?"

"Doesn't have to be, you should hear the mouth on her. When she isn't yelling at the subject for being stupid, she's preaching at him. She just nevvverrr shuts up, but the guy's a tool and we think he's afraid of her. She's a real ball-buster, Mick!"

Max made a wry face. "I know she is. Worked for me for more years than I care to remember. She's why the guy is here."

"No shit? Worked for *you*? Why the hell - "

Max sighed. "Long story. Listen, if they move, call. And thanks."

"Right back atcha, Mick, we appreciate the business."

Max disconnected and said, "We're in good hands, the Brothers are the best."

He got a blank stare from both Lucie and Jean-Luc.

"What? They really are brothers. Anyway, if Gaston and Julia are still watching us, that means they didn't get anywhere with the postcards and the records from the Mairie. So they'll probably just hang around 'til we make our move and then follow us."

Max pretended to yawn and got up. "Emma, could I see you for a minute?"

Lucie narrowed her eyes at him, he caught it, and winked at her. He led Emma into the kitchen and a short conversation ensued while Lucie and Jean-Luc finished their brandies in companionable silence. She gave the man several more points for being cool enough to enjoy not talking.

Emma was smiling as she emerged from the kitchen and motioned for Jean-Luc to follow her upstairs. "See you in the morning, Lucie, we have a lot of calls to make when the government offices open." And winked at her.

What was it with all the winking? Then she noticed Max, arms folded, leaning against the archway to the kitchen. Grinning at her.

"What?"

"The look on your face. C'mon, bedtime." He helped her clear the table of snifters, and, still grinning, leaned to whisper in her ear as she rinsed out the glasses. "Don't you want to know what that was about?"

"Not unless you – yeah, I do."

"I told Emma that I appreciate Jean-Luc using his time and resources on our behalf."

"That's all?"

"Aw, come on, Lucie, that's a huge step for me and I really don't like the guy all that much." Max was indignant until he saw Lucie's shoulders shaking in silent laughter.

He touched the back of her neck lightly and steered her toward the stairs. His touch had the predicted effect on her, and once in their room, she unbuttoned his shirt with increasing speed as her mouth found his.

When he came up for air, Max ventured, "To what do I owe this unexpected pleasure?"

"The ear thing, the neck thing, but mostly all that winking."

"You mean all I have to do is wink?"

"Sometimes."

CHAPTER 28

Soft morning light woke Lucie, who grinned and flung an arm out to find Max; but his side of the bed was empty, so she rose and dressed quickly. Following the aroma of coffee and the sound of laughter, Lucie found everyone in the kitchen, enjoying croissants from the village bakery. Max gave her a sexy smile and got up, indicating a seat beside Jean-Luc. He wiggled his eyebrows, and Lucie remembered her promise to get a read on the lawyer.

As they chatted amiably over breakfast, Lucie paid close attention and discerned what seemed to be genuine affection for not only Emma, but for the entire group. The positive vibes were unmistakable, this was no Giles.

Only negative thing was his cologne: Jean-Luc used industrial-strength scent and Lucie wound up smelling just like him every time she even shook hands with the man. She wondered if using a hand sanitizer would help, or just compound the problem.

***

They agreed to spend the morning working on

Didier's apartment, then go their separate ways: Lucie wanted to shop for Provençal fabric, Emma wanted to go with Jean-Luc while he began his research, and the elderly folks wanted a peaceful afternoon.

On the way into the village, Max glanced sideways at Lucie and asked, "Anything from Gérard yet?"

Lucie shook her head.

Emma turned to Jean-Luc, "Then it's all up to you, mon cher."

Jean-Luc looked worried.

***

Emma and Jean-Luc had just put the finishing touches on the smaller of two bedrooms and asked for help moving furniture back into it. While the men carried the heavy items, Lucie picked up an antique lamp with dangling cut glass circles that clunked dangerously every time she moved.

She entered the room cautiously, but the toe of her shoe caught the edge of a rug; she stutter-stepped for several feet, hurtling forward until Jean-Luc miraculously caught her from behind and pulled her upright.

"Whoa, thanks, Jean-Luc!"

The Frenchman smiled graciously, Max smiled insincerely and an alarmed Kate relieved Lucie of the lamp.

"That does it, I need lunch."

The Sautiers, Kate and Didier went to the adjacent apartment to clean up, Emma and Jean-Luc headed out on their own, and Lucie noticed that she smelled overwhelmingly like the lawyer: serious washing was required.

"Max, I don't think my hand sanitizer is going to work on this much Jean-Luc and it's really bothering me, but I'm starving, so - "

"Just ignore the smell, I'm starving too, and besides, I have a surprise for you." He hurried her outside and into the Benz, then drove to a charcuterie a few blocks away.

"Wouldn't it have been easier to grab a sandwich at a café?"

Max grinned, got out of the car, and as he pushed the door to the French deli, called to Lucie: "I'll only be a minute."

He spoke briefly to the girl behind the counter and emerged almost immediately, carrying an enormous picnic basket.

As he put it in the back seat, Lucie twisted around and flipped the lid.

"Wow!"

"Got everything you picked out when we were in Paris, remember, the day you drag- um – took me to all those museums?"

She smiled at him. "Sure I remember, and thanks, this is really cool. I take it we're going to eat outdoors? Soon, I hope."

"Winery's only a few minutes away, but you can start if you want."

She did, and shared the lobster with him as he drove.

They unpacked the car rapidly and Max led her out to where the olive trees met the vineyards, where the view of the multi-hued Provençal hills was absolutely perfect.

He spread the blanket under a tree and was in the process of removing food from the basket when Lucie's shadow suddenly darkened the area like an impending storm.

"Emma says you can kill with your bare hands. So did you, ever?"

Max blinked several times and looked up at her incredulously. "Why are you asking me that now? That's a middle-of-the-night-in-the-dark question."

"So did you?"

"Just because I can, doesn't mean I ever did." This was definitely not the way the afternoon was supposed to play out.

"That's not an answer."

"Ok, then, no."

"No you agree that's not an answer, or no you never killed anyone?"

"I'm getting a headache."

Lucie put her hands on her hips and dug in.

Max sighed. "No, Lucie, I have never killed anyone. With my hands or anything else." When she continued to regard him with suspicion, he asked, "What now?"

"It just occurred to me that if you had, you probably wouldn't tell me anyway."

Max made a strangled noise and looked up at her.

"Could we please just eat, and look, I'm going to open this nice bottle of wine and I'm sure you'll feel better after you have some."

***

Max was right, Lucie did feel better after several glasses of wine and the excellent lunch. Leaning against the tree, he'd settled her into the curve of his shoulder, and they talked about their families and childhoods until the warmth of the air and the wine made Lucie drowsy. She had almost succumbed to an uncharacteristic nap when something occurred to her.

She sat up abruptly and her eyes darted from the food still on the blanket, then to the wine, then to Max.

"You're up to something. The last time you arranged a superb meal, you wanted, well, you know, and since you already got that, (she narrowed her eyes at him) what is it now?"

Max pulled her back to him. "No monkey business, I promise."

Lucie sat up again and turned toward him. "Because if you were thinking Sex in the Afternoon in the Vineyard, consider that your surveillance team is watching everything and Gaston and Julia are lurking somewhere. And sex has never been a spectator sport for me."

"Good to know."

"On the other hand, if you wanted to find a secluded spot where absolutely no one could see anything..."

"Great idea, hold that thought." Max pulled a tiny red box out of his pocket.

"Um, it's not my birthday." Silently, don't do this, Max.

"It's not for a birthday."

Lucie gulped: her 'Think About it Later' list just hit the fan.

He pulled a tab on the top of the box, and both halves of the lid unfolded to reveal a stunning blue diamond ring that immediately caught the sun and radiated pinpoints of light like the Eiffel Tower at dusk. Lucie's favorite shade of blue, it was set in a wide filigree band of silky platinum, sturdy and elegant at the same time.

Lucie groaned.

Max grimaced. "That wasn't the reaction I was hoping for, but here goes anyhow." He put his large hand on her cheek stared intently into her eyes.

"Lucie, marry me. Please."

"I – I don't want to live in the château and work

out of Long Island, Max."

He lowered his hand from her face and took the ring out of the box, tilting it in the sun so she could see the faceting.

"I may not be living there much longer, so that doesn't have to be an issue."

"What?" Trying not to look at the sparkling gem in his hand.

"That place was my father's idea of a home, not mine. My suite, the library and the main kitchen are the only parts of it where I'm comfortable."

"But I need my own space."

"You're avoiding the issue, my love." He took her hand, put the ring in it and closed her fist around it. "Know what? I think Lucie Richards is commitment-phobic."

Lucie snorted, "Am not, I just don't want to be wife number five." She tried to open her fist to return the ring, but Max kept his hand on hers and ignored the dig.

"Also, you should know that I have loved you ever since Bruno sat on you. Or shortly thereafter, anyway." He smiled and waited.

Lucie tried a feeble smile. "Ever watch Two and a Half Men? This is the part where Charlie usually says, 'Thank you.'"

"Lucie." Max frowned.

"What, you're allowed humor and I'm not? Max, I..." She tried to pull away and couldn't, physically or emotionally. "All right, you know damned well I'm in love with you."

"Good, then put me out of my misery and say you'll marry me."

"But I don't marry everyone I fall in love with. And besides we don't know each other well enough and I still smell like Jean-Luc and we can't have a discussion of this magnitude with me smelling like another man!"

"Forget Jean-Luc. I know everything I need to know about you, Lucie, and you know *exactly* what I'm like - in the morning, in the middle of the night, what I like in bed, my favorite foods, you know my family, you love my dog. So what else is there?"

Lucie just stared at him.

"Is it my past? I guess I could understand not wanting to get caught up in that."

Lucie remained silent as Max released her hand and leaned back against the tree. "So what happens when we get back to the States? We see each other occasionally and spend the rest of the time feeling incomplete, wondering what the other is doing - and with whom."

"Can't we compromise?"

Max suddenly grabbed her shoulders. "I can't share you, Lucie. I don't want you for a sometime lover, I want to grow old with you. And I'll do whatever it takes to make that happen."

Close to tears, Lucie choked out, "I don't want to get married again!"

As she fought for control of her voice, she pushed him away and scrambled to a standing position.

"There is a reason I rely solely on myself, Max, it's like how I bring my own knives to the job: I hate variables, and husbands are variables. You can't count on them because they don't do what they're supposed to. Just when you start to trust them, they rip the carpet out from under you, your world collapses and you have to start all over! " Her speech ended when she choked back a sob.

Max got to his feet slowly and said quietly, "Then you weren't with the right men. They weren't worthy of you." He touched the fist that held the ring and said, "Would you wear it on your right hand, as, just a gift?"

Lucie started to cry. "*Stop it!* I had all that hurt locked away and you just - "

"Dammit Lucie, I have to suffer for all those bastards in your life, and I'm the one who's going to be there for you no matter what."

Lucie stopped crying abruptly and frowned at him. "Wait a minute. That line's from the Goodbye Girl, you didn't make it up yourself."

Max twitched: conversational whiplash.

Lucie shook her head, vehemently: "I can't do this." She turned around and plopped down in the lotus position. "I need to get rid of the negativity."

Max was confused, so he squinted. "Does that mean you want to prune something?"

"GET AWAY FROM ME! We're done!"

Max froze. His ability to annoy her apparently knew no bounds.

Lucie closed her eyes and started to hum.

"Uh, just so we're clear, you want me to pack up, get out of your life?"

The humming stopped abruptly. "What?" She opened her eyes and turned.

He began again, carefully. "You want me to - "

"For heaven's sake, Max, go take a walk or something! *Just GO!*"

"A walk?"

Lucie spoke through clenched teeth. "I cannot restore my inner balance with you standing there!" She clamped her eyes shut, faced away from him again, took a deep breath and waited.

"*You're. Still. There.*" Her voice was ominous.

Max took a chance. "Um, think I'll just go find Kate and Didier."

A growl escaped just before the humming resumed.

She shooed him off with her right hand, and just before he turned to go, Max saw it. The piece of vibrant blue sky that scintillated from her finger.

He blew out a sigh of relief and grinned. There was hope after all. He wasn't banished, not very far anyway, and she was wearing the – his – ring. And her objection to marriage was not due to anything he'd done, other than being born a male. Now, to get her to move it to the other hand.

As he neared the house, Max thought about the hurt in her voice: that had surprised him. Lucie always seemed so sure of herself, but she was clearly still suffering from the emotional devastation of at least one of the marriages.

So Lucie Richards was vulnerable after all.

***

They were seated at the terrace table, drinking wine together and discussing the day. And Lucie's new piece of jewelry. Max and Jean-Luc had supplied the wine, and the lawyer announced that he and Emma would be making supper, since anyone wearing a spectacular ring like Lucie's should not have to soil her hands with food. Ever the charmer, Jean-Luc.

Lucie raised an eyebrow at him. "Considering that's how I earn a living, this ring could turn out to be a major inconvenience." To herself: and I won't be wearing it at all if Max brings up the proposal in front of everyone.

But all he said was, calmly, "She can do anything she wants while she's wearing it, it's virtually indestructible."

Kate looked at him speculatively and murmured, "My my, what a very *practical* gift."

Jean-Luc laughed and motioned for Emma to

follow him to the kitchen. Max suddenly looked worried and glanced at Lucie: “I’ve never, ever, seen that woman cook, so unless *he* has some culinary skills ...”

***

Supper turned out to be a passable salade niçoise, complete with homemade lemon vinaigrette, and lots of sliced baguettes. They enjoyed the meal, and chatted over several more bottles of wine until Lucie started to scratch at her shoulder.

“What’s the matter?” was accompanied by Max leaning over, poking his finger under the neckline of her shirt and peering under it. Lucie swatted him away and frowned.

“I think something bit me out in the vineyard this afternoon” met with uproarious laughter from Max and Kate, even more so when she attempted to explain to Didier. Lucie made a face at them and said she was headed for a shower. Alone.

***

The scent of Max’s shower gel wafted throughout the bathroom as water streamed sensually over Lucie’s body. Then a cold breeze rudely zapped her out of the sensory reverie. A cold breeze that shouldn’t have been there. Lucie shut off the water and cast wildly about for anything that could pass as a weapon.

She shrieked, “Max you sonofabitch, I told you to never bother me in the bathroom, that does it, I’ve got my KNIFE and you are dead meat!” She clunked the underside of her new ring against the shower spigot, hoping it sounded convincing: better to scratch the ring than risk having her body mangled, she reasoned.

Then Lucie crouched and pushed aside a tiny bit of the shower curtain, peering out from the top of the tub. No one materialized, but the cold current of air continued to make its way through the bathroom door. The door that had been shut only moments before.

She hopped out of the shower, wrapped a large towel around her, tiptoed to the door, peeked into Max's room and gasped: the balcony doors were open!

Lucie hurled herself through the bedroom and out into the hallway, nearly falling down the steps. For the second time that day, she stutter-stepped, this time around the corner and through Emma's open door. She threw herself against an interior wall and panted, wild-eyed, "Either of you open the upstairs balcony doors just now?"

Max was on his feet in a nano-second, and Emma went for her bag. As she extracted a gun, Lucie yelled, "Wait just one minute, you're not leaving me alone!"

"Then hurry up and get dressed."

Lucie grabbed Max's arm and dragged him upstairs with her; she threw on a pair of jeans, a light sweater and sandals while he unearthed a gun from under her pillow. Max muttered something about the arsenal they'd brought in the Gulfstream, searched their rooms, motioned for her to follow him closely, then hurried down the stairs and met Emma on her floor. She'd already checked that area, so the three of them descended to the ground floor, where everyone was playing dominos.

The moment Jean-Luc saw the look on Emma's face, never mind the gun, he bolted upright so fast that he sent the playing pieces flying.

"Intruders on the top floor" was the terse greeting she gave him, while Max spoke into his cell phone: "Entry on the top level, through the master balcony doors. No damage. We're going to secure the immediate perimeter, so don't fire on movement near the house. You two take the outbuildings, then sweep the property."

Jean-Luc quickly told the Sautiers what had transpired and asked them two questions. He turned to Max and reported that there was no way into the wine cellar except the door that was in plain sight of their present location, and that the attic door was padlocked from the stair side. And that Gérard had forgotten that Gaston had keys to the house.

Max winced, then nodded and motioned for Emma to follow him out the front door.

Jean-Luc quickly asked Lucie to stay with the elderly couples and excused himself to check the ground floor for prowlers. While he was gone, Lucie helped put the dominos back on the playing surface and made small talk until he returned.

His voice said, "There is no one, you are quite safe," but his eyes told Lucie that he needed to speak with her. Lucie asked Kate to start a new game and stepped into the kitchen with Jean-Luc.

He immediately showed her what he'd found: a thick envelope that was addressed to the Sautiers. His face full of concern, he said, "I think you should open this with Madame Sautier: Gérard is too fragile."

A determined look on her face, Lucie took the envelope: "Whatever this is, I won't let it hurt them." As she strode back to the domino players, Jean-Luc nodded. Another woman of substance.

***

Lucie and Marie-Françoise were seated in one of the many alcoves on the ground floor, staring at the unsigned note and at the scraps of postcards that had fallen from the envelope.

"From Gaston, I am certain." The Frenchwoman shook her head, "And he did not even have the courage to put his name on these despicable threats."

Lucie assured her, "He won't trouble you again: we'll have all the locks changed tomorrow, and Max's people will protect you."

Marie-Françoise bent down to pick up a fragment of a postcard. "He is destroying the Legacy because he does not understand it. All he can do now is bully and threaten, and he will follow you to take what he thinks should be his." She turned to Lucie. "You know this, do you not?"

Lucie nodded.

Her companion slowly reached over to the table lamp beside them and turned it off. She sat back, folded her hands and sighed, staring through a large window and into the night.

"Has your Max been damaged by a war?"

Lucie was surprised by the unexpected question. "No, I don't think so, well, not by a war, anyway."

"That is fortunate for you. It changes men so much... The soldiers return and find they no longer fit back into the lives they left, that their wartime experiences have changed the shape of their being. Civilized society is not always kind to those who have sacrificed to preserve it."

She turned back to the shadows. "Gérard was 'detained' by Maréchal Pétain's men, right after the old soldier agreed to rule the south of France for Hitler. My husband was tortured by his own countrymen, some of whom were childhood friends, and then he escaped to join the Résistance. And all he ever wanted was to make his wine and care for his father, in peace."

"When we married after the war, Augustin spoke to me privately and told me why Gérard and I would never have children." Her voice was brushed with muted anguish, and Lucie waited out the pause, not willing to intrude on her private sorrow.

"The nightmares eventually became less frequent, but never entirely disappeared. I am afraid that the betrayal of Gaston has upset him greatly, enough to bring them back."

Marie-Françoise was on the verge of tears when Kate and Didier appeared to ask why the two women were sitting in the dark.

The Frenchwoman rose slowly and said simply, "Remembering" as she handed Lucie the envelope and made her way back to the dining room. She found her husband sitting with Jean-Luc at the table, his light blue eyes weary when he looked up. Lucie's heart ached for Gérard as Marie tenderly put her arm around him and said she was exhausted. They held hands as they moved slowly to their bedroom.

***

Emma and Max were deep in conversation as they came through the front door, and the last of it sounded like "We have to wait until the asshole and the witch do something we can pin on them, legally: no more direct route to a solution, dammit."

They put the safeties on their weapons, and as they clunked them down on a table, Max announced: "Gaston and Julia have disappeared and the house is secure."

Although he'd brought good news, his face was grim and everyone fell silent. Kate suddenly decided that she and Didier needed to retire, and stood, bidding them goodnight.

When the four of them were alone, Max began, "Jean-Luc, you know any locksmiths?"

"I have already called them, they will be here in the morning." Emma smiled at him briefly and asked Lucie about the envelope she was holding.

Lucie showed them the pieces of postcards and the note, then related an abbreviated version of Marie's story. Jean-Luc nodded. He was aware of Gérard's war experience.

Lucie began, "I'd like to shoot that bastard Gaston in the foot and then slap Julia the Bitch so hard - " Suddenly Lucie turned to Max with an incredulous look on her face.

"Wait a minute; you hid the gun under ***MY*** pillow?"

Max blinked several times, then looked at the others and shrugged helplessly.

Emma observed, "Lucie, I just realized that you convinced the intruder that you were armed. Not bad, for a civilian." She looked over at Max and raised an eyebrow. "I think it's time to suit her up."

Max squinted at Lucie, clearly assessing something, and nodded at Emma. She grabbed her everythingbutthekitchensink-sized purse, rummaged around in it and finally produced a pink stun gun.

Lucie's face fell when the older woman handed it to her, and she turned it over in her hand, clearly disappointed. "A taser? But I'd have to be really close to use it, and I'd probably just zap myself with it." Lucie put down the unwanted weapon, poked at it, hung her head and sighed. It worked.

"Well, she's got a point there, she does keep singeing the top of her ear with a curling iron. Probably be safer with a gun."

"How about the PM9?"

Max nodded and Emma again delved into her portable armory, finally extracting a small Kahr pistol.

Lucie's eyes widened.

Emma held the weapon in front of Lucie. "Now,

please pay attention: this is the safety, make sure it's always on – like this - unless you mean business. Tomorrow we'll teach you how to load and fire it. For tonight, anyone sneaks up on you again, just point it at them, that'll be enough."

She carefully passed the gun to Lucie.

"Wow, this is light, it feels really good in my hand, I can't wait to use it!"

Max looked worried.

"Maybe this isn't such a good idea."

"Oh no you don't." Lucie stuck the gun in her pocket and got up before Max could change his mind.

Emma smiled. "Jean-Luc and I are going to remain on this floor tonight, just in case." She glanced over at the Frenchman, who got up and stood behind her, his hand on her shoulder. "We were planning on some strategy talks anyway."

Max nodded and crooked his finger at Lucie. "C'mon, Annie Oakley. I need to call Dylan, then Antonio, you need to call your sister about Murphy, and Sophie hasn't heard from you and is worried."

"How do you know – oh, never mind." Lucie trudged up the stairs behind him, muttering that one's thoughts and messages should be sacred.

***

Max conducted his calls from the balcony off his room, partly to give Lucie some privacy in her room and partly for surveillance. He was enjoying a wine nightcap when his peripheral vision caught her watching him from inside.

She'd hesitated to join him, not wanting to get dragged into another discussion about marriage, but when he smiled at her and held up an empty wine glass, she opened the door.

As he poured the wine, she observed, "You brought two glasses out here, huh?"

Max grinned.

"Nice." She sat down beside him. This didn't feel awkward at all. "Sophie's worried about our safety, says we don't know what we're getting mixed up in. Probably I shouldn't have told her about my gun, that sorta put her over the edge. Why are you laughing?"

Lucie made a face at him. "Anyway, Murphy's fine, but I really miss my dog."

"Yeah, I miss Phoebe, too. Tried to reach Antonio, but he isn't answering his cell, I'm thinking it has something to do with Jessica. Anyhow, I'll try again tomorrow. Oh, and Dylan. She'll be here with her 'wine posse,' as she calls him, in a few days. We'll see if her attention span survives the flight over."

"Max, why *did* you get married all those times?"

He twitched, but recovered quickly: he was getting used to her thoughts careening all over the place.

"An attempt at normality, I suppose: my childhood in the château was just weird, my job was, well, you know, so I thought getting married would provide the 'normal' in my life. But it didn't because I wasn't with the right woman, er, women."

He turned to her. "My turn: given how you feel about marriage, what advice did you give Sophie on the subject?"

Lucie sipped her wine. "Fair question. I didn't tell her anything for a while, figured I was no authority. But eventually I told her to find the best person she could and marry him. Or her, if that were her persuasion."

Max tilted his head slightly. "So you not wanting to marry me means that I'm not the best person you've found."

"You may well be, but – and this is getting old,

Max, - I do *not* want to get married again. You're just going to have to accept that." Lucie put her glass down on the balcony and climbed onto his lap, facing him. "But know this: you're the most fascinating man I've ever met, and that fact has staying power."

"I - "

Her mouth on his ended the conversation.

∻ CHAPTER 29 ∻

Lucie woke with a start, and, realizing that she was alone, listened for sounds that should not be there. She cautiously left the bed, hurriedly threw on jeans, a tee shirt and a light sweater, and tucked her newly-acquired weapon in her waistband.

When she entered the kitchen, Max grinned at her and pointed at his mother, who was in the process of consuming a pile of French pastries.

"Mother, if you're going to inhale all of those, you're going to have to start some kind of elderly exercise program, and don't bother trying to embarrass me with a story about what calorie-burning activities you and Didier share, bec- "

He got no further because Kate shoved a croissant in his mouth.

Lucie laughed, then noticed something different about Jean-Luc and Emma.

"Anything important happen last night?"

It was probably a bit early for abrupt: Jean-Luc looked startled by the lack of polite prologue.

Emma, however, got right to the point. "If it's all right with the two of you, Jean-Luc will accompany us from here on. I see him as a tremendous asset, considering his experience in the Police Nationale."

"KKccc - ahem. Sorry, choked on the croissant mother shoved in my mouth."

Emma narrowed her eyes at Max. "Anyway, Jean-Luc is good with a gun and we're going to his place for more fire power, right after breakfast."

Max frowned. "You really want to involve him in a potentially dangerous situation?"

"Oh come on, Max, he can handle himself. What's this really about?"

Max thought about sulking.

Emma made a wry face. "Get used to it, partner. Jean-Luc is going to be around from now on, as in, we're all celebrating the holidays together and Lucie's making the turkey."

"I'm what?"

"You don't think *I'm* making Christmas dinner, do you?"

***

Jean-Luc's locksmiths arrived early, worked quickly, and soon Max and Lucie were staring at the Benz, or the blur of it, considering how fast Emma pulled out.

Suddenly Lucie looked apprehensive and pulled her sweater tightly around her. "Max, I have a bad feeling about Gaston, and since Lourmarin isn't giving up any more secrets, I think we need to head north. Soon."

Max looked down at her. "I agree, but Emma is adamant that I teach you to shoot before we leave." He motioned for Lucie to follow him and said, "Might as well get started."

When they reached one of the outbuildings, he lined up some cans on an old stone wall, stepped back and stared at Lucie for a second. Then he pulled out his phone.

"Listen, we're doing some target practice, and I've got a novice here, so you may want to make sure you're not near the storage shed. Yeah, the one with the farm equipment in it."

"Hey! I'm not gonna shoot anybody, why'd you tell them that?"

"I need the Brothers to stay alive so they can protect the Sautiers."

Max winced in anticipation.

Lucie smacked him.

Max sighed and asked to see her gun. He took great pains to show her everything from loading to sighting to two-handed firing, and emphasized keeping the safety on at all times: it was, after all, unlikely that she'd ever have to do more than point it at someone.

The next two hours were agonizing for Max, and after Lucie dropped her firearm on his foot, he tried to instruct her from several feet away. When that proved ineffective, he stood behind her and tried to adjust her dismal aim.

She squinted and turned to him: "Max. If you want me to focus on shooting, you're gonna have to stop touching me." Max grinned at that, but when she finally managed to hit one of the cans, he heaved a sigh of relief and quickly headed for the house.

Lucie ran to catch up, protesting, "We can't quit now, I need more practice!"

Max groaned and told her he'd find her a firing range and a shooting coach, just as soon as he could talk someone into it.

She grumbled as they walked through to the kitchen, where everyone had gathered; Emma and Jean-Luc had procured their weapons and brought back several excellent pizzas, which disappeared almost immediately.

The Sautiers, Kate and Didier headed off for afternoon naps and Max had just picked up the keys to the Benz when Emma's phone rang.

"Yes, of course I'm head of household." She winked at Max and listened for several minutes. "Thank you for informing me. No, not much you *can* do."

Max waved at her: "Ask him how Phoebe's doing."

Emma spoke to Antonio for a moment, then disconnected and turned to Max.

"Phoebe's fine and Roland's dying again."

Lucie gasped.

Max sighed. "What is it this time?"

"Antonio's not sure, but he's said his goodbyes, and apparently not even Juan can talk him out of his funk."

"Has he taken to his bed yet?"

"We're way past that, he's at the inconsolable stage."

"Antonio will expect you to deal with this, so if you don't mind, call Roland and tell him, let me think, that we need him to guard the château, he's the only one we trust, and remind him that his demise would leave Bruno motherless. Or fatherless." Max looked puzzled. "I wonder which one - oh, whatever, it'll keep him occupied for a while."

Emma nodded and turned to make the call as Lucie gazed at the two of them.

"Wow, that's really cold. I mean, the man can be a pain, but - "

Max sighed again. "It's a once-a-year crisis. Sometimes more, if he can find a new and obscure disease to be afflicted with. The one I feel bad for is Juan. This is his first Roland Death Watch, and believe me, it wears you down. Until you realize that

Roland always refuses to see a doctor or go to a hospital." Max made a wry face.

Lucie looked doubtful. "What if he's really sick this time?"

"He's not." He got up. "C'mon, we're going into town for the tablecloths and things you wanted."

Lucie narrowed her eyes at him, suspecting a diversionary tactic. Away from her gun. But she did want the Provençal fabric, so she ran upstairs to change her clothes; they were in the village before she could change her mind as well.

***

They were strolling down a side street, past a little café, when Lucie stopped so abruptly that the shopping bag Max was carrying hit her in the leg.

"Sorry about that."

Lucie didn't move: mesmerized, she was listening to the music that floated out of the café. She slowly turned to Max, her unfocused eyes floating over him, then out to the street, to the plane trees, where sunlight filtered through the remaining leaves, accentuating the white splotches against gray bark.

She inhaled deeply and said softly, "Hear that?"

"You mean the song?" He listened for a moment. "Springsteen."

"Mmmm." Her eyes closed, Lucie tilted her head back and lightly touched her neck without rubbing it. And swayed slightly, listening. "It's Streets of Philadelphia. Wait for the bridge..." Lips parted, she made a soft 'uhhh' noise, until the song ended.

When Lucie opened her eyes, Max was staring at her.

"You ok?"

She smiled a languorous, contented smile at him.

"Wow. That was *incredible!*"

"Uh huh. So, what just happened?"

"A mental orgasm."

Max's eyebrows shot up. "A what?"

"It starts in your brain after a sensory trigger – like that song – and floods through your entire body, and you feel energized and happy, like a million endorphins just shot through you. It doesn't reach the nether regions, but you get the euphoria, and, wow!" She plopped down on a tiny metal café chair and signaled for a waiter. And smiled again.

Max looked uncertain, sat down beside her, and squinted. "Am I supposed to do something about this?"

Lucie started to laugh and didn't stop until two glasses of pastis and ice water arrived. They enjoyed what was left of the afternoon and were considering what to get for dinner when Lucie's phone rang.

Emma didn't bother with Hello. "I think somebody has poisoned Milou. You and Max need to get back here right away."

"He's not dead, is he?" Max shot out of his chair, but Lucie waved him back down, mouthing 'Milou' at him.

"No, he's lying on the terrace and moaning."

"The Sautiers are sure he didn't overeat or anything?"

"They say he's never acted like this before."

"Anything around his mouth, like pieces of stuff?"

"Wait a minute." Emma peered at the dog. "Well, his face is all brown, and I'm pretty sure it used to be whitish."

"Sniff his mouth."

"What?"

"Bend down to his mouth and tell me what you smell."

"Is that really necessary? Oh... very well." Lucie heard 'Nice doggie, don't move now' as Emma snuck up on him.

"Why aren't we leaving?" Max wanted to know.

"Because we may have to kidnap the local vet and take him to the winery in a hurry."

Emma was back. "Do dogs eat chocolate?"

"They love it, is that what you smell?"

"Yes, definitely chocolate. And nasty dog breath."

"Maybe he just got into someone's stash. What you need is lots of hydrogen peroxide. Is Jean-Luc with you?"

"Um."

"Tell him to ask the Sautiers for some, and pour it down his throat until he throws up. The dog, not Jean-Luc."

"Until he – oh, yechhhh." Then Lucie heard, "Jean-Luc, we need lots of hydrogen peroxide here, and tell Didier he has to pour it down this dog's throat."

"As soon as possible, Em: chocolate in large quantities can kill dogs. Milou is pretty big, so we'll hit the local pharmacie for more peroxide, just in case."

She rose and signaled for Max to follow her to the shop with the neon green cross outside, and they were back in the car when Lucie's phone rang again. "That dog is vomiting all over the place, Lucie, it's really disgusting."

Lucie held the phone away from her ear so Max could hear. They both laughed silently, and she told the older woman, "That's good, he has to get the chocolate out of his system."

"Oh, and they called their vet, he said to do exactly what you told us."

"Glad I could help."

Lucie hung up as Max remarked, "You've done this before."

"Oh yeah. Murph steals food every chance she gets."

Emma greeted them as they pulled into the area by the front door, a grim look on her face.

Lucie climbed out of the car quickly: "What's the matter, didn't he get the poison out fast enough?"

"Funny you should say that, we *are* back to poisoning. We found a huge pile of chocolate bar wrappers- big ones – near the terrace. A cheap brand nobody in the household buys, so somebody did try to kill their dog."

Lucie's face flushed reddish-purple and she yelled, "I KNEW IT! He's gone too far this time, Max!"

But Max was already talking to his phone. "I'll transport the four of them as soon as Mango can travel. Mango. The dog. It's a long story - just go secure the townhouses, ok? What? Well, pick a lock, it's not like you don't know how. Then don't let them out of your sight, no matter what. Got it?"

He turned to the women. "We leave tonight."

***

They found Marie-Françoise weeping over Milou, while Gérard tried to comfort her.

Emma stopped abruptly and put her hands on her hips. "Jean-Luc, you did *not* let that dog die while we were out front, did you!?"

Jean-Luc, who was kneeling beside Milou, looked up at her, infinitely patient: "Nooo, his present condition is the result of the tenth bout of vomiting." Milou moaned. Jean-Luc stood up slowly. "Mostly on me."

The spectators uttered a collective eeuuwww when

they saw his clothes, which were dripping brown slime and foam.

"The good news is that I believe the chocolate has finished."

Lucie grinned at his odd English as the lawyer got up and walked slowly to the back door. He turned to them with a small wave: "I will go to wash now." And sighed.

"Max, that man is a saint."

Max grimaced and rubbed the back of his neck. "And then some. Uh, mother, wasn't Didier supposed to take care of Muldoon?"

Kate made a face. "Turns out my husband-to-be is extremely squeamish; when this dog started to puke his guts out - "

"Moth-er!"

" - Didier ran out to the vineyards, where I assume he's being sick himself. Haven't seen him since."

"Well, you have to go find him: we're moving the four of you back to town, where you'll be safer."

Kate huffed and headed for the vineyard. Max shook his head and went to look for dog shampoo.

Lucie put her arm around Marie-Françoise and told her that the worst was over, that Milou would surely recover now. And to Gérard, that no further harm would come because they were all leaving for the safety of the village. They looked relieved and, after Lucie said she'd keep an eye on Milou, hurried into the house to pack.

Emma followed the Sautiers, mumbling that pauvre Jean-Luc most likely needed her help, and Lucie watched Milou until Max returned with a hose, several huge towels and a large bottle of bath gel. "Couldn't find the dog stuff, and anyway, Marlo here needs to smell a lot better."

"Max, I've been thinking, maybe you should tell

Dylan to postpone her visit."

He smiled as he attached the hose to a faucet. "Matter of fact, I just got off the phone, told her I don't want her walking into anything dangerous. And thanks for being concerned about my daughter."

Lucie held onto Milou while Max drenched the large dog, who was too miserable to protest. They scrubbed him vigorously with the gel, hosed him off, and were trying to dry him with the towels when Kate yelled from the kitchen that dinner was ready. They led the bedraggled dog into the house, where the aroma of roasted chicken almost overpowered the smell of wet dog.

Milou went straight to his bed in the corner and flopped into it, too wretched to even beg for the food that Kate was removing from the oven. Lucie helped her with the heavy roasting pan and they set it on the stove top.

"Wow, that smells really good, Kate."

Didier, who was sitting at the table with his head in his hands, moaned.

Kate whispered, "It's just a simple chicken and since everyone else took a turn cooking, I thought I'd dust off my kitchen skills. I'm going to make some plain rice for Didier, though, he looks a little green."

Didier raised his head at the whispering. He *did* look green.

Lucie remarked, "Make some for Milou, too, please: it's really all he should have for a few days. Maybe add some boiled ground beef later."

Didier moaned again.

***

Emma sat down at the dinner table, sniffed at Max

and Lucie and wrinkled her nose. "Peeeuuuu, wet dog."

Before Max could retaliate, Lucie raised an eyebrow and said, "Didn't notice anyone else volunteering for the job."

Max's eyes widened and a forkful of chicken remained poised, halfway to his mouth.

"I was busy with Jean-Luc."

"Jean-Luc can take care of himself, and he only smelled like chocolate you-know-what; we got stuck with chocolate you-know-what plus large-sick-dirty-dog smell."

Jean-Luc stifled a laugh and continued to eat. He loved Women with Attitude.

"Still -" Emma tilted her head to one side, narrowed her eyes and considered Lucie for half a minute. Max held his breath. This was a first on so many levels.

Finally Emma grinned and nodded. "Point taken."

Lucie grinned back and the rest of the dinner proceeded without incident, after which Max and Lucie showered and changed into dry clothes. Then a herd of suitcases appeared magically near the front door. When Milou finally roused himself and walked around sniffing the kitchen, Max announced that everyone except Emma and Jean-Luc should leave for the village.

While Max loaded the cars, Marie-Françoise took Lucie aside. "I am happy to tell you that my husband has remembered something important: early in the War, the Nazis summoned Augustin and forced him to procure wine for the Reich, to find the best vintages and send them to Germany. But Augustin had no intention of allowing the Boches to plunder our national heritage, so he visited the great Châteaux and only *pretended* to take their treasures!"

Marie-Françoise smiled proudly. “My father-in-law actually dared to send bottles of table wine, disguised with Grand Cru labels! Augustin planned on blaming the difference in taste, if ever the non-existent German palate had detected it, on damage due to transporting the delicate masterpieces! The Châteaux were, bien sûr, most grateful.” She nodded, pleased to be of help.

Lucie hugged Marie-Françoise and thanked her as they got into the car with Gérard and a mostly recovered Milou.

They followed the Benz into the village, and as they pulled up to the townhouses, a front door opened to reveal a pleasant-looking, short bald man with a sandwich in his hand. He waved to Max and yelled, “Hope you don’t mind, Mick, we ran out of food on surveillance, and we found some stuff in there.” He was pointing to the houses.

Max laughed as he bear-hugged the man, then turned to Lucie. “George, meet Lucie.” Lucie shook his hand, trying very hard not to giggle. So many Georges. As they unloaded the cars, Lucie turned to Gérard and embraced him, then had trouble letting go after he whispered, “If danger finds you, ma petite, you must abandon our quest. You mean more to me than any treasure, and you must come back to us.”

When Kate noticed the tears in Lucie’s eyes, she poked at Max and motioned for him to bend down slightly. She stared into his eyes and whispered, “Son, do not, under any circumstances, involve Lucie in what you and Mrs. Harris are hiding from.”

Max straightened up. “How could you even think that?”

His mother raised any eyebrow. “Oh please. Just leave Lucie out of it, or you’ll have to answer to me.” She turned on her heel imperiously, as Max’s mouth fell open.

***

The Sautiers, Kate and Didier were secure, the Brothers were pleased to be on duty in the townhouses, and Max and Lucie were on their way back to the winery. Lucie had just told him the story of Augustin's wine procurement job during the war and the dangerous trick he played on the Nazis, not unlike Julia's deception with Max's wine.

"No way the great Châteaux didn't compensate Augustin for taking all those risks on their behalf. Max, I wonder..."

Max's only response was "Hmmm," his thoughts running to the next twenty-four hours.

***

When Max and Lucie returned to the bastide, they found Jean-Luc typing rapidly on Lucie's computer, while Emma stood behind him taking notes. Without looking up, she told them, "Gaston and Julia will be looking for us in the Benz, so he's checking train schedules."

Jean-Luc consulted the screen. "What do you think of this itinerary: we drive to Aix and exchange our vehicle for something less conspicuous, continue on to the Marseille train station and board the Corail Lunéa sleeper train to Paris. The Marseille station is quite large, we are less likely to be noticed there. And we will be rested when we arrive in Paris tomorrow." He glanced up for a reaction.

When everyone nodded, Jean-Luc looked relieved. "Bon. I will reserve a first class compartment with four couchettes, we will have more space that way, and we will be secure."

"Does the TGV run from Paris to Gérardmer?"

"Yes, the TGV Est can take us to Remiremont, the closest station, in two hours and thirty-nine minutes."

Max looked thoughtful, then took a credit card from his wallet and handed it to Jean-Luc. "Solid plan, Jean-Luc. Book the entire trip with this, and then, if you don't mind, arrange for the rental car in Gérardmer in your name. Less noticeable, you being French."

Jean-Luc smiled as Emma patted his shoulder and nodded. Max had finally accepted him.

CHAPTER 30

They waited for nightfall, then used the shadows at the edge of the house to secure their luggage in the Mercedes. Lucie and Max crept back into the house, turned on all the ground floor lights, as well as the TV, then pretended to go out for the evening. Loudly. Lucie stepped through the front door, now well-lit with floodlights, and yelled back to no one, "We'll be back before one, so leave the lights on."

As she slid into the passenger seat beside Max, she asked, without turning, "You two ok?"

A muffled female voice said, "Ok for now, but we're cramped on the floor back here."

Max made the trip to Aix-en-Provence in record time, changed out the Benz for a van, and called his surveillance team. He told Larry, George's brother, that Gaston and Julia would be breaking into the bastide in the middle of the night, and that he should follow them until they left the area, then report to him.

No one chatted as they sped through the night to Marseille: all thoughts were turned inward.

***

Lucie already missed Provence and its slow, gentle rhythm of days stretching out in the sun; heading toward the German border suddenly felt like having a root canal.

And she had to admit she was scared of Julia and Gaston: they were dangerous, and Lucie didn't *do* dangerous. That was the province of the two maybespies and the cop. And having a gun really didn't help matters since she was more likely to shoot herself with it than hit anyone else.

Then there was Max. What to do about Max.

***

Max, for his part, agonized over lapsed 'professional' skills and the possibility that he might not be able to protect those around him. Plus he felt vulnerable: his reciprocal arrangement with Emma was in question, now that he'd been replaced by Jean-Luc.

***

Emma, who feared nothing in her life, now carried with her the image of the biopsy report that had dropped her to her knees when she read it: Cancer. The oncologist she'd consulted in D.C. was reluctant to remove it, the danger of it spreading being greater than leaving it there and treating it. But current approved treatments in the U.S. were dismally ineffective.

So, arriving in Paris earlier than announced and, medical records in hand, Emma had visited a research facility in the city, acquired an experimental drug not available in the U.S, and had begun treatments.

She shared this information with no one, especially

not Max, who considered her infallible. She might not have her health, but she would *not* lose her pride. The medication was, however, affecting her equilibrium and reflexes, and that could prove costly in the coming days.

***

Jean-Luc was primarily worried that his formidable ex-wife would discover that he'd taken a leave of absence from his firm, thus diminishing the amount of his earnings, thus impacting her 'pension alimentaire', thus igniting her powder keg temper. Disaster would surely await his return. If he returned.

He was also worried about losing Madame Harris' admiration. So sensible, so un-French in her direct approach to life, she was depending on him to trace Marie Bottecher. But if his cousin's contacts proved unsuccessful, the Quest would come to a screeching halt, and finding the treasure meant so much to his new love and her fascinating friends.

And he hadn't felt this important for a very, very long time.

***

The sleeper compartments on the night train were more comfortable than Lucie remembered, and she surprised herself by sleeping through the night. She awoke first and slipped out to locate the 'snack and hot and cold drink distributor,' which turned out to be a vending machine. Disappointed and hungry, Lucie stomped back to the cabin, and had just reached out to open the door when it flew open.

Max stood in the doorway, gun in hand and looking grim. He glared at her, tucked the weapon at the small of his back and said, "Don't do that again."

"Go for breakfast?"

"Leave without telling me. And don't be flippant, I'm not kidding." Lucie stared at the man. She'd never heard that tone before, and was pretty sure she didn't like it.

"I can take care of myself."

"No, you couldn't have, if the asshole and the witch had gotten to you in the corridor. They could be anywhere from now on."

"Ok, ok, I get it." Lucie frowned. "You need your morning coffee."

"What I *need* is the knowledge that you're safe." He took the one step necessary to reach her and wrapped his arms around her tightly. When she realized that his entire body was tense, Lucie pulled back and saw the look of anguish on his handsome face.

"If anything happened to you -"

Lucie kissed him lightly on the lips. "I'm sorry. I'll be careful, Max, I promise." To Emma and Jean-Luc, who were stretching themselves awake, "Sorry I scared all of you."

"No problem, Lucie."

"Listen, we arrive in Paris in twenty-one minutes, and we have a two hour layover before the train to Remiremont, so how about we put our luggage in the lockers at the station and have a terrific breakfast and then stretch our legs - "

"Breathe, Lucie!"

"Yeah, ok, but I've got first dibs on washing up." And bolted out of the cabin.

They took turns using the restroom at the end of the train car, and were waiting to disembark when Emma suddenly asked, "What did you say we're doing when we get into the station?" She looked utterly confused, and Max stared at her in astonishment.

She mumbled, embarrassed, "Never mind, guess I need my morning coffee more than I thought." Max, unsure of what he'd just witnessed, resolved to keep a closer eye on his friend.

Minutes later, they stood on the platform with their luggage, shivering in the cold Paris morning. Lucie quickly found the locker area and an excellent café near the station, and breakfast had just been served when Jean-Luc's phone rang.

He smiled at them, listened for several seconds, then panic appeared on his face. He turned away, started waving one arm around, and assault-rifle French ricocheted off the wall behind them. Turning slowly as he disconnected, Jean-Luc gathered himself and announced through clenched teeth, "I must inform you that my cousin Maurice the Notaire, for whom I have performed many favors - " he pursed his lips – "- has not been entirely diligent in his search for the Notaire in Gérardmer."

The Frenchman paused to rip off a piece of croissant and ram it angrily into his mouth. They watched him chew in silence, each of them remembering a similarly ungrateful relative in their own family, until he continued.

"I assure you, however, that he *will* be in possession of the names of all the Notaires of Gérardmer since the end of the Great War, since we do not know the exact date of the death of Marie Bottecher."

He pounded his fist on the table. "Every last one of them."

***

The TGV arrived in Remiremont in the promised

two hours and thirty-nine minutes and Jean-Luc had just negotiated a reduced rate on a car rental when Max's cell rang. He answered and grinned almost immediately.

"Hold on, Larry, I'm putting you on speaker."

"Just like you said, Mick, they broke into the house around three AM, didn't stay inside long, then she tore into him out front. Yelled loud enough for us to hear, like, (he raised his voice an octave) 'This is all your fault, I told you to stay with the Benz! Now we have to waste time finding out where they turned it in and you *do* realize they probably ditched it for something we won't recognize!'" Larry paused to laugh at himself, then turned serious.

"Anyhow, I figure they'll bully the rental agencies in Aix and Avignon, until they get what they want. But that'll buy you a little extra time: Mick, she's a bitch, but she's not dumb, so watch your back, ok?"

"Will do, and thanks."

"And Mick - George spotted some CIA types asking questions about you and Harris this morning. He said to watch your back, too."

Max disconnected and explained to Lucie and Jean-Luc, "The Brothers worked with us on some, uh, jobs."

Lucie suddenly blurted out, "Max, we've got all these people after us, and I'm not sure about using my gun yet."

"There's only one reason you'll ever have to use it, Lucie, and that's if somebody starts shooting at you. And then...*you shoot to kill.*"

No one spoke while they loaded the car with their luggage and located the route that would take them to the end of their journey in Gérardmer.

CHAPTER 31

Their route involved taking the D417 through le Tholy and on to Gérardmer, and in the thirty-two minutes of the journey, Lucie decided she didn't like that part of France at all.

"There's no sun, it's cold, it's drizzly, and that," Lucie nodded at Gérardmer lake, "is ugly."

Max glanced out the window and agreed. The lake was the dead gray of aged hair that has lost the ability of color, but doesn't have the energy to morph into graceful silver.

"And I thought we didn't want to be noticed, so what's with this Renault Scenic? I feel like I'm riding around in an assault vehicle."

Lucie flopped back in her seat and continued to complain until she spotted a beautiful old-world villa nestled in the trees that surrounded the lake. "Finally, something worth looking at. I think we should stay there." And pointed.

***

Le Manoir au Lac turned out to be truly old, built in the last century and renovated to its present elegance. They were delighted when the receptionist informed them that their spacious rooms included balconies that overlooked the lake, and as the elevator delivered them to their floor and adjoining rooms, the four agreed to meet for lunch an hour later.

"Wow, this room is gorgeous and just look at that balcony!" Lucie flung open the large French doors in a flash, then ran back in the room and grinned at Max. "I think there's gonna be some sun, really soon, and I call the first shower."

She grabbed her toiletries bag and was in the bathroom before Max could comment.

***

The sun did make an appearance, and while they enjoyed a late lunch at a local brasserie, Jean-Luc's cell phone rang. Relief spread over his face as he listened.

"It seems that my esteemed cousin has discovered the Notaire who can help us, and I am to meet with him straight away!"

Max clapped him on the back, commending him on the reinstated relative's accomplishment. They finished the meal quickly, and after dropping Jean-Luc and Emma at their meeting, Max and Lucie returned to the hotel.As they got out of the car, Lucie remarked, "You know, Max, a bottle of that wine you've been schlepping all over France would definitely complement this whole lake-experience thing."

He grinned as they walked toward the entrance. "I can think of something else that would complement pretty much anything."

***

By dinner time, the restaurant bar beckoned and kirs signaled the beginning of a pleasant evening together. Emma swiveled on her stool, a smug look on her face. "Unless you two want to discuss how you spent the rest of the afternoon, Jean-Luc and I are prepared to dazzle you with our discoveries."

Max laughed, "Go for it."

As Jean-Luc unknotted and removed the tie he had worn for his meeting, he began, "It has happened that the Germans have, for once in our history, done us a favor: in response to their heinous habit of periodically occupying our country, the townspeople began, over a century ago, to ingeniously and systematically hide their important documents."

Emma interrupted. "So the records we require *do* exist, and Maurice's contact here – Notaires are apparently a close-knit bunch - gave us access to the censuses from 1928 on."

Jean-Luc nodded. "Our luck has held, mes amis, the woman remained a Bottecher all her life." He folded his necktie, stuffed it into the left pocket of his suit jacket, then belted back a kir. Max promptly ordered another.

"Marie died in 1968, survived by only one child, so the records for estates and inheritances should be uncomplicated."

He sipped his second drink and continued, "We are to receive a call when the colleague of Maurice has learned who served as Notaire in 1968 and that person will know the location of the documents that he created."

Jean-Luc's phone bleeped from his pocket. His astonished smile stretched impossibly as he listened, then did the rapid-fire French thing into it and disconnected.

"My new friend the Notaire has spent the hours

since we left him in placing inquiries on our behalf: we are to meet this evening with Alphonse!" Jean-Luc looked triumphant.

"Alphonse?"

"Alphonse, the retired fonctionnaire, who has never taken dinner in this establishment and will be happy to join us, it is all arranged."

Max clapped Jean-Luc on the back for the second time that day and sent him into the dining room with Emma as he signed the bar tab.

Lucie leaned back on the bar and mused, "I wonder what Jean-Luc did to his cousin to produce this avalanche of cooperation from functionaries whose main purpose in life is to tell you It Can't Be Done. And if they decide it *can* be done, to come up with one delay after another. All to prove that they are superior, in every way, to mere mortals."

"Had run-ins with French bureaucrats, have we?"

Lucie made a face.

***

Dinner with Alphonse turned into an ordeal when it became obvious that because the former Notaire's fixed income did not allow for meals of this caliber, he meant to make the most of his present good fortune. He devoured the dishes he'd ordered, then ordered more.

He was well into his third dessert by the time Lucie gritted her teeth and batted her eyes at him, explaining in syrupy French that they absolutely could not complete their project without his invaluable help.

Then she slammed into what she wanted: "We need access to the documents from your tenure as Notaire of Gérardmer."

Alphonse choked on his wine, aghast at her non-

French abruptness.

Max frowned. "What'd you say to him?"

As Lucie translated, Alphonse turned to Jean-Luc, seeking a reasonable French attitude.

"But surely you know it is not done comme ça!"

Jean-Luc stared at him. Intently.

"And we need to see those documents as soon as poss – **tonight**." Now Lucie was staring as well.

Alphonse stuttered, "But – I do not – eh bien, they are with my successor, and the one after and so on."

"But *where*?"

Alphonse registered total astonishment at their collective ignorance.

"In that abominable gâchis on the ground floor of the Mairie, bien sûr! Mon Dieu, the Office of the Notaire had to be moved to the first floor, just to escape the horrid plague of boxes!"

Lucie got close to the Frenchman's face and said, "Ce soir, monsieur. C'est très urgent." Without moving, she told Max, "Please order another bottle of wine. Now."

Alphonse forgot about Lucie's rudeness when the bottle of very good wine was opened, then admitted that he still had keys to the town hall, but to call the present Notaire as a matter of courtesy. Jean-Luc had his phone out in a flash, dialing as Max poured.

***

Alphonse used one hand to brandish his huge metal ring, and the multitude of dangling keys clanked alarmingly against each other. He clutched his stomach with the other hand: gluttony had seized him by the gut and he looked utterly miserable.

"My records were right there, in that corner, no those are not my boxes, Aieeee, mon estomac!" He urped and gurgled, "I will return in a moment." He was out of the room in a second.

The four stared at the doorway.

Lucie squinted. "We can't wait until he feels better, we have to make him show us where his records are. Tonight. Otherwise it'll take forever to get through all this."

A collective groan emanated from her companions and settled on the mountains of boxes like a shroud.

It had barely dissipated when Alphonse dragged himself back into the room and leaned on the door jam. His face ashen, he slowly raised his head and gaped at Lucie.

"You are absolutely certain that this task must be accomplished tonight, Madame?" He wobbled slightly.

Lucie propped him up, noted that he smelled really bad and told him yes, absolutely, tonight.

"Then we must find, urp, my blue boxes."

A quick search revealed nothing but faded beige boxes, so Alphonse took them to an adjacent room; fifteen minutes later they located the blue ones, and within an hour, had found Marie's folder and asked to copy its contents.

Alphonse, who desperately wanted the security of his own bathroom, hurriedly led them upstairs and unlocked yet another area. He pointed to a copier and Jean-Luc got to work.

There were more papers than they anticipated, and Alphonse looked positively gray by the time Jean-Luc was down to the last few items in the folder. He bent over in obvious distress, begging to be taken home. Max flung the man's arm over his shoulder and supported him.

"How much longer, Jean-Luc? I think he's going to toss his cookies again."

"It will just be another minute or two."

"Ok, I'll take him to the bench in the hallway - whoa, he's got it on his shoes, copy faster, will you?"

As Jean-Luc removed the last packet from the folder, he noticed that the point of a long, thin, age-darkened envelope was stuck to the staple on the last sheet. He pulled it from its mooring and placed it beside the copier, then finished with the last of the papers. He was about to open the envelope when Lucie ran into the room.

"Oh man, he just vomited again, we need to leave right now!" As she quickly gathered the documents and the copies, Jean-Luc stared at the envelope.

He knew he shouldn't take it: he was, after all, an officer of the court. But this was for Emma and for his new friends, who valued him for himself, not for the money he earned, nor for his social position. He suspected it had something to do with his handling of the barfing dog, but couldn't imagine why.

Lucie didn't notice when he slid the envelope inside his suit jacket.

***

They sent Alphonse home with a reluctant taxi driver and had just gathered in Max and Lucie's room when Emma suddenly looked weary. She observed that it had been a very long day and headed for the door, Jean-Luc close behind her.

Lucie turned to Max, who held up a cautionary hand.

"Don't start, if you do, you'll be up all night. More to the point, I'LL be up all night because you won't be able to contain yourself when you find something. It can wait, Lucie."

Lucie started to protest, cast a longing glance at the pile of papers, and slunk off to the bathroom. Max was asleep by the time she returned; maybe she could just sneak a peek at the will.

"Don't even think about it."

Lucie jumped, startled. "I thought you were asleep and I had no intention of looking anyway."

"Uh-huh." Max shifted to make room for her. "And I'll know if you get up."

***

Lucie stared impatiently at their only link to the legacy, thinking that if breakfast were not delivered in the next few seconds, she'd start on the documents by herself. Then she heard Max's voice in the hallway, and coffee and food arrived with Emma and Jean-Luc.

While they ate, Larry called and Max put his phone on speaker. He reported that Julia and Gaston had spent the previous morning looking for the Benz, and didn't find it until after lunch. "They harassed the rental agency personnel in Aix until they told them you were dropping off the new vehicle at the Marseille train station. That's where they headed, so I took Didier and followed them."

"Geez, Mick, those two threaten everybody they meet! Before we could do something about it, they badgered the guy at the overnight train window into showing them your whole itinerary, how you reserved on the TGV from Paris to Gérardmer. Then I heard the woman say they were going back to their hotel to grab a few hours of sleep, then drive to the German border."

Lucie gulped, "We need to get through these documents as soon as possible. Jean-Luc, you read the legalese and I'll take notes."

***

By late morning, Lucie's note pad was full. She and Jean-Luc, heads together and speaking half-French, half-English, hadn't noticed when Max and Emma left the table.

"Now where do you suppose - " Lucie glanced out to the balcony and stopped mid-sentence. A familiar wave of suspicion washed over her as she stared at them; the expression on Emma's face was hard, and Max was clearly distraught. Feeling Lucie's gaze, they turned slowly to her.

Muttering "Enough already," she quickly stood up, but Jean-Luc, who had noticed her reaction, rose with her and asked, "Qu'est-ce qu'il y a, Lucie?"

Lucie hesitated and considered an explanation, but decided she'd come off like a whiney, neurotic bitch.

"Just too many croissants, I think, JL." She pointed to the balcony. "They need to see this, don't you think?"

Jean-Luc seemed to like being initialized and yelled for Max and Emma.

Lucie shot them a suspicious look and frowned before she began, "Primarily, it's the will. It involves a property transfer, to one Albertine Brichot, née Bottecher. Bingo, we have her married name. And an address here in Gérardmer: 59, Rue Lucienne. I think we need to go see it, now: if it stayed in the family, that would eliminate a lot of other record-chasing, and even if it didn't, maybe the current owner could tell us about Albertine, it's a little town after all and look, I picked up a map at the front desk, and the house is right off Place Leclerc, pretty much in the middle of things - "

"Breathe, Lucie!"

Emma stood up and said, "I agree, let's go see what the house has to offer."

***

Lucie insisted on driving, and stopped at a charcuterie on the way to pick up lunch items: she contended that when bothering folks at meal time, arriving with food would go a long way to encouraging cooperation. Just look what feeding Alphonse had accomplished!

When they pulled up in front of the lovely old mansion at 59, Rue Lucienne, Jean-Luc leaned out of the car window and gaped.

"Fortunate that this gem was not lost when the Germans burned the town."

Lucie was out of the car first, reaching back in for her purse and laptop case. She walked quickly up the front steps, her mind filled with the End of the Quest. The others were still on the sidewalk as she rang the doorbell; then her eyes slid to the side of the door, to the small gold plaque that announced, "la docteur Monceaux."

Max was behind her on the porch, and remarked, "So the husband is a doctor, whoever lives here."

"Chauvinist. The *lady* of the house is a doctor."

"But it says - wait, I am NOT a chauvinist!" Before he could protest further, the door was opened by a person who seemed only mildly surprised to see them. She calmly noted their appearance and then addressed them in English.

"Can I help you?"

Lucie was staring into the eyes of a woman her own age, sturdy–on-the–way-to plump, with shoulder-length, dark blonde hair, expertly highlighted. She wore a red and white scarf knotted, also expertly, around her neck, and it contrasted nicely with the black coat she was wearing.

"Madame la docteur, we've come about Albertine Bottecher Brichot." Lucie said it abruptly and immediately felt awkward. She'd wanted to make an elegant inquiry, not throw it in the face of a stranger.

Madame la docteur, however, didn't seem to mind; she tilted her head slightly, raised one eyebrow, and stepped back.

"Well, then, you had better come in."

CHAPTER 32

The Frenchwoman opened the door wide and, as they entered, took off her coat. She hung it in the foyer and said, "You have arrived at a good moment: I have just come from a board meeting at the hospital and now my day is free." She motioned for them to follow her and said, "Come with me and we will see what business you have about Mémé."

Lucie gasped, "OhmyGod, Albertine is your *grandmother?!*"

Madame la docteur stopped abruptly and turned. "You did not know that?"

"You'd be amazed at what we don't know."

The rueful look on Lucie's face amused the Frenchwoman, and her chuckle lasted the length of the hallway as she led them to a large, comfortable living room that included a dining area.

Lucie put her laptop and backpack on an end table, turned and extended her hand. "Thank you for inviting us into your lovely home. I'm Lucie Richards and this is Emma, Jean-Luc and Max."

"I am Sabine Monceaux." She indicated that the four of them should sit down.

Lucie continued, "We are interested in your

grandmother because she is the only link we have to your great-grandmother, Marie Bottecher, who is one of three people mentioned on our World War I postcards."

Sabine blinked. "You have postcards that are almost 100 years old, and the name of my great-grandmother is on some of them, yes?"

Lucie nodded.

"You have obviously spent a great deal of time and effort to find my family, and all of that because of," she squinted "an intense interest in history?"

"Because of an intense interest in a Legacy."

The Frenchwoman looked puzzled. Jean-Luc saw an opening and said, "Madame, may we offer you the lunch we brought?"

Sabine smiled. "Mais bien sûr, how very considerate."

As the men started for the front door, Sabine remarked, "What a gorgeous man, the tall American." Her gaze involved speculation.

The tall American chose that moment to glance back at Lucie. Sabine caught the look – and the heat - and sighed, but not in resignation. "And of course, he is in love with you." Then blatantly scrutinized Max's walking-away attributes.

Before Lucie could react to the woman's interest in Max, Sabine glanced at her left hand, then at her right hand and the diamond. "Oh my, and it is a complicated affair." She could have been reading tea leaves.

"Madame, may I show you what brought us here?" Lucie had no intention of discussing her relationship with Max.

"Please."

Lucie pulled her laptop from its case and brought up the images of the postcards, indicating those that mentioned Marie.

"These cards were originally sent to your great-grandmother's friend, Augustin Sautier, in Lourmarin. His only son, Gérard, gave the cards to me a month ago, and told me that they would lead to a family legacy, a thing of great value. The clues on the cards brought us here."

Sabine stared at her, perplexed, and began, "How very strange - " but was interrupted when Jean-Luc and Max returned.

As they distributed paper plates, plastic ware and cartons of food, Lucie remarked, "We realized that the story of a legacy wasn't a hoax when somebody shot at me to get the cards."

Sabine's eyebrows moved upward, but she said nothing as she helped herself to several items, then reached over to Lucie's plate and grabbed her slice of quiche.

Lucie scowled and continued, "The postcards indicate that together, Augustin Sautier, Marie Bottecher, and an American officer, Lt. James Milnar, established this legacy, and we believe that the final clues to its location are buried in the lives of those three."

They consumed the lunch over banalities, then Sabine suddenly sighed and glanced at an adjacent chair with a conspicuously plump cushion.

"I miss my Peugeot so much."

Max blinked. This woman changed gears like Lucie. "Um, did you sell it or was it stolen?"

"Mon Dieu no, that bastard Armand got him in the divorce and I only have partial custody now."

"Of a car?" Puzzled looks all around.

"Of my *dog.*"

"Yes, of course Peugeot is a dog, we do understand, I miss my dog tremendously, and his, too." Lucie pointed at Max. As she thought, 'take that, Madame la Docteur, the tall American and I are on share the dog terms,' Jean-Luc took a small notebook from his breast pocket and wrote in it.

Sabine glanced at the images on Lucie's computer screen and observed, "The person who could have helped you the most was my mother, but she died last year, of cancer. I do, however, know that during the last war, the Nazis lived here, in my house."

"What was your mother's full name, please?" Jean-Luc's pen was poised over the note pad.

"It is Genvième Pouliot." She tilted her head at them. "Tell me, how did you come here, if all you had was the name of my grandmother?"

"We found this address in Marie's will and took a chance that the property was still in the family."

The Frenchwoman nodded. "Yes, that is logical." She frowned and gazed around the room, clearly searching for recollections of the past. Not finding them, she stood. "I am truly sorry, but I do not see how I can be of any help to you. We cannot even search the attic for things like your postcards: there is nothing left, it is all gone. The Nazis looted our home before they left, perhaps believing that our bits and pieces were valuable." She paused and looked down at Lucie.

"The old man's story of a hidden legacy, so vague, so long ago. Surely..."

Lucie nodded reluctantly. Hearing it was a lot worse than just thinking it. Crestfallen, she rose slowly and turned around the room, memorizing it as the Place Where the Quest Ended. She closed her laptop, put it in its case and bent to pick up her backpack. As she rummaged in it for the car keys, she told Sabine what a pleasure it had been to meet her, then yowled and withdrew her hand as though bitten. There was blood on one finger.

"What the?"

Sabine glanced at the wound and told her she'd get the peroxide from her kitchen. Lucie wiped the blood from her finger and carefully dug around in the leather pouch. Her jaw dropped as she slowly removed the culprit: she was staring at the tiny tintype of Lt. James Milnar.

Lucie glanced at Max. "I forgot I put this in here."

The sound of a bottle crashing against the floor turned everyone's attention to Sabine, who stood in the archway to the kitchen.

"Where did you get that?" Her voice was low and intense, eyes riveted on the object in Lucie's hand.

"In the box with the postcards. It's Lt. James Milnar." Lucie extended the tintype to her and said, hope in her voice, "You've seen this before, haven't you?"

"Not since I was a child." She stared at the image. "It was on the mantle for years, but Mémé never told me who it was, and then it disappeared. I always wondered about it."

She finally looked up. "And yet you have the same photo, and you know his name and that he was a friend of my great-grandmother." She returned the tintype and stared at Lucie. Then made a decision.

"We must go and see Mémé."

Four sets of lungs constricted.

"*She's still alive*?"

"But of course. She lives in a very beautiful maison de retraite."

***

Lucie squirmed impatiently while Sabine stopped at a pâtisserie for her grandmother's favorite childhood pastry; she'd explained that her mémé was sometimes liquide, that they could hope for a good day and that the pastries would help with the memories.

They followed her to the nursing home, and as they pushed through the entrance door, Sabine told them, "I am very proud of her, you know. She was the first female physician in Gérardmer, and it was she who encouraged me to become a surgeon."

The nurse at the front desk knew Sabine and told her, "Your Ex is with your mother again," then rolled her eyes. Sabine groaned and hurried down the hall as Jean-Luc translated for Emma and Max. He didn't have to translate the groan.

As they approached Albertine's room, a whiney male voice reached them. It belonged to a thirtyish man dressed in sports gear and he was clearly trying to wheedle something out of the old woman in the armchair.

"Armand! Not now!" Sabine pointed to the door. "I warned you to stop bothering her!"

Armand looked back on his way out and complained, "Why are those people allowed to see your grandmother and I am not?"

"ENOUGH!" Sabine slammed the door and smiled at her grandmother, then opened the door rapidly enough to cause the eavesdropping Armand to fall on the floor.

Max walked over to the prostrate form, folded his arms and stared down at him as Sabine hissed, "I told you, she has no money to give you and now there will be a restraining order!"

"If you ever want to see your precious Peugeot again - "

Max heard the dog's name and from the man's tone, understood the threat. He yanked him up by his shirt and dragged him out the door and down the hall.

Sabine leaned out the door to again admire Max's

retreating form and Lucie made a face: the woman's interest in Max was seriously beginning to piss her off. When Jean-Luc whispered something to Emma and excused himself to make a call, Lucie ahemed and Sabine returned her attention to her grandmother.

She sat down beside the old woman and spoke quietly to her while she opened the box of pastries. Her grandmother squealed with delight and immediately devoured several of the tiny profiteroles, the creamy filling sliding onto her fingers.

As Sabine wiped the frail hands, she heard Max in the hallway and quickly glanced at Lucie, a shrewd look on her face: "If you intend to keep a man like that, you had better decide what you are going to do with him."

Throwdown.

Lucie narrowed her eyes: the remark had hit home, but she damned well didn't want to hear it from Sabine.

Emma looked amused and waited for the return shot.

"So, your divorce must have been painful, considering that you're a good deal older than Armand."

Emma snorted and Sabine glared at both women as Max and Jean-Luc entered the room. Then she smiled sweetly at Max and asked Jean-Luc to translate from that point on since Albertine spoke no English.

Her grandmother, a thin patrician with wispy white hair, pointed to an opcn book on the bottom of her TV stand as Sabine introduced everyone.

The doctor explained that Mémé's visitors, herself included, were obliged to sign her journal, along with a date. When Sabine had entered her name, she asked Lucie for the tintype and told her to sit beside Albertine. She carefully placed the photo into a hand gnarled by arthritis; the old woman blinked and held it close to her glasses.

"Sabine, you naughty girl, you have been in my things again."

"No, Mémé, this belongs to Madame Lucie."

Albertine made a face. "Do not be ridiculous, granddaughter, what would she be doing with a picture of my father?"

Sabine gaped. "Your - ***father***? But you never told me!"

"Of course I didn't tell you, child, he was American and he and my mother never married – a common thing during the wars – and we seldom saw him. There was no reason to tell you about a man I hardly knew, or that I was illegitimate."

Sabine was speechless. She turned to the others and shook her head in amazement. "I had no idea."

Albertine narrowed her eyes at Lucie. "So it was *you* who has been into my things, hein?"

Lucie shook her head. "Mais non, madame, the picture is mine. It was with the postcards."

Albertine frowned and looked at her grand-daughter. "What is she babbling about?"

Sabine gave the old woman a brief synopsis of Lucie's earlier story, and as it unfolded, a veil seemed to lift from the ancient eyes.

"So you need to know about my mother." Not a question.

"S'il vous plaît, madame."

"Well, then I had better tell you a story."

***

"My mother, Marie, was born in Lourmarin and she knew Augustin Sautier because she worked in his winery. That is where she first met James, when he was a student; at least she thought he was a student, she was very naïve at that time."

"Then she married a boy who had moved south from Bussang, and he was killed at Verdun in 1916, so my mother *was* a widow, as we told you." She nodded at Sabine.

"When she went to claim his body, she witnessed first-hand the trenches; she described them to me in horrible detail when I was older, and she was very, very angry, even with the retelling of it."

"Because she had learned English, she stayed in that area to teach in a school, and made no secret of her rage against the Germans. Then fate intervened and she met James again, this time quite near the Eastern Front."

She put her fingers to her lips and tapped. "They had an affair." She lowered her voice to a whisper. "And he recruited her for the intelligence work, because she had good English and because she was brave." Albertine smiled proudly.

"My mother became very adept at the Morse Code and the concealment of documents, but she was very nearly discovered. So she returned to Provence to hide and went back to work for Augustin in the winery. Soon James began to send postcards and packages there, such a kindness to the wounded soldier."

Albertine paused. "But he wrote *in English*, you see." She waited for Jean-Luc to translate, then glanced around to see if they got the implication.

"It was brilliant, really. No one bothered about postcards from an American to his friend, and since Augustin could not understand them, my mother was obliged to translate for him. Comme ça, she could easily take from the packages the information that James sent, and forward it: it had to be so, because his messages were being intercepted at the Eastern

Front and James could trust no one there."

Emma nodded. Her initial theory was correct.

The old woman faded and nodded off, snoring lightly. Sabine asked Lucie to go for tea and told them quietly that her grandmother would be clear and revived after a short nap, it was always so.

A suspicious Lucie dragged Max with her, just in case. An orderly produced a tea tray in moments, they tipped him generously, and as they re-entered Albertine's room, their voices woke the dozing figure in the armchair.

She smiled as Sabine poured the tea and offered her another profiterole. The old woman finished the pastry and asked, "Now where was I?" She hesitated, then continued, "After the war, my mother returned to this area and I was born in December of 1923. Sometimes, when I was growing up, my father would visit us in the grand house...the last we heard from him was just before the Occupation in 1940."

Sabine stared at the old woman. "Mémé, a little while ago you mentioned 'your things.' What did you mean?"

"My treasures."

Sabine looked confused. "Where - may we see them?"

Albertine pointed at a cupboard in the corner of the room and her granddaughter opened it to find an old sewing basket. She turned to her, unsure if that's what her mémé meant, and Albertine waved her hand at her. "Of course my things are in there, and what a good hiding place it has been."

Sabine deposited the box on her grandmother's lap and watched as she peered into it, then carefully extracted a tintype of Lt. James Milnar. She looked confused, so Lucie placed her own picture beside it.

"This one belonged to Augustin, the friend of

Marie and James."

Albertine stared at them until Sabine bent down to her grandmother, touched her face and covered her with an afghan. Then she stood, returned the tintype to Lucie and studied her, deciding.

"The family of Augustin entrusted you with the postcards and the picture of my great-grandfather. These relics from the Great War, making their way back to the present - it cannot be a coincidence that you attract them like a magnet. There must be a higher purpose at work, so although I am a woman of science, I will trust my intuition. That which is here." She patted her midsection and settled into another armchair in the room.

"If we can be of any further help, Mémé and I, please contact me. And now I wish you luck with your quest."

Thus dismissed, they thanked Sabine for her help, and as they filed out of the room, Lucie eyed Albertine's profiteroles. Her hand snaked out toward the box and Max quickly made a show of waving goodbye to Sabine with one arm, while grabbing Lucie's hand with the other.

He whispered, "Lucie, Lucie, Lucie, stealing an old woman's pastries. What am I going to do with you?"

Now in the hallway, Lucie whispered back, "She isn't gonna miss one or two of them, she probably won't even remember having them in the first place."

"Doesn't matter."

Lucie's voice was now full-volume and she was frowning. "I'M STARVING! The good doctor was pointing to her stomach because she has indigestion, not intuition. She inhaled that lunch we brought and kept reaching over to steal mine!"

Max pushed open the door of the building for her.

"So that's why you're grumpy. I thought it was

because you don't like her."

"She doesn't." That from Emma, with a snicker.

"Hey, stealing my food is reason enough to dislike anyone."

***

Dinner was, once again, excellent, and they lingered over coffee until the dining room was empty.

Lucie finally stood and stretched. "So we're stuck. Again." She looked disgusted. "You know, I don't understand why the Three didn't just use the treasure, or spend it, or display it back when everyone knew where it was. I understand keeping it away from the Nazis, but that wasn't an issue after 1945."

She yawned and headed for the elevator. "And right now I'm just too tired to care. Bed, Max."

***

Lucie flailed at Max. She was not fully awake and the noise had startled her subconscious into defending herself.

"Ouch, my eye, stop it, Lucie!"

Max grabbed her arms and suddenly sat up in bed as the knocking sound reached his brain. "What the? Can't be an intruder, unless he's really bad at it. They usually don't announce themselves."

He slid out of bed, his hand finding his gun before his feet hit the floor, and flipped off the safety as he stepped into the shadows.

Lucie groaned, "Tell whoever it is we don't want company." And buried her head in the pillow.

Knocking turned into pounding on the balcony door, so Max crept to the curtains and flung one open at the side. He lowered his weapon and shook his head: "I don't believe this. It's Jean-Luc making all that noise."

"But Jean-Luc isn't noisy."

Max squinted at Jean-Luc.

"He is now."

Lucie turned over and looked at Max, her eyes groggy. He still held the weapon in his right hand.

"Probably you shouldn't shoot him just for being noisy."

Max opened the doors and Jean-Luc rushed in, babbling in two languages.

Max rubbed his eyes and said, "English, JL, English."

Jean-Luc waved something wildly above his head. "I have it, I'd forgotten all about it, it was in my suit jacket!"

Max sank into a chair and groaned. "Could you please cut to the chase?"

"Cut – what?"

From the bed: "Say exactly why you're standing in our room in the middle of the night."

"Oh, of course. It is the deed!"

"That's cutting to the chase?"

Jean-Luc took a deep breath and gathered himself. He held the very old envelope out to Max. "You will want to be fully awake for this."

CHAPTER 33

Max blinked at the envelope and put it, along with his gun, on the table next to him. As he slowly rose and flipped the light switch to the huge chandelier, Lucie mumbled, "What did he say he found?"

"Some kind of deed."

Lucie was out of bed in a second, shouting, "A deed? What deed?"

Jean-Luc held up a finger while he used his cell to call Emma. "Yes, they are now awake, please come over. By all means, use the hallway." He sighed, "Yes, I agree, it is much less dramatic."

He tapped on the envelope. "This was attached to the documents in the Bottecher folder, but there was no time to copy the contents because Alphonse was being sick on Max." He continued as he opened the interior door for Emma, "I could not sleep tonight, so I thought I would tidy our room – tidy, that is the word, yes?" He glanced at Emma.

"Yes." She rolled her eyes. "He's very tidy."

JL missed that one and went on, "As I straightened my suit jacket on the hanger, I noticed something in the inside pocket. And, voilà, another clue has presented itself!"

"So you found a deed to - "

JL smiled proudly. "A grocery store!"

Lucie groaned, "We got outa bed for *that*?"

Jean-Luc took the deed from the envelope, smoothed the old document and held it up. "Property at Three, Boulevard Adolphe Garnier, Gérardmer. Commercial. Purchased in 1919 by Marie Bottecher, James Milnar and Augustin Sautier, subsequent ownership to pass directly to the oldest surviving descendant thereof."

Lucie booted up her laptop, and in less than a minute had a map of Gérardmer on the screen. "Boulevard Adolphe Garnier, main street off Place Leclerc, not far from Rue Lucienne, the Bottecher homestead. Number Three, let's see..." She brought up another screen and squinted. "It's really small." Her eyes shifted over to Jean-Luc. "Like a mini-mart."

"Actually, it was the last paragraph of the document that caught my attention:"

'The family of M. Nicolas Reichert shall operate in perpetuity a grocery at Three, Boulevard Adolphe Garnier, free of rent or taxes so long as the present property is maintained and used as stipulated. The area behind the business (see attached plot lines) is part and parcel of this deed and shall remain free of construction. A stipend shall also be paid in perpetuity, to the family of M. Nicolas Reichert, upon yearly verification of these conditions being met.'

"Then it names a legal firm in Nice, one that my partners have dealt with, as administrator." He raised one eyebrow. "A very unusual document, wouldn't you say?"

Lucie stared at the lawyer and said, "How long before we can go downstairs and get some coffee, do you think?"

***

The hotel provided a very un-French breakfast buffet: cold meats, breads, cheeses, yogurts and cereals. At 6am, they were the only ones in the dining room, and when Simon, their waiter from the two previous nights, brought them coffee, Lucie chatted with him, casually bringing the conversation around to the business on Boulevard Adolphe Garnier.

He told her that the property had been a grocery store for as long as he could remember and had always been operated by the Reichert family, who were, by the way, terrible grocers. And who, oddly enough, paid no rent on the building. The locals speculated that some Parisian who had more money than brains had inherited the shop and forgotten about it.

She waited until they were alone to translate for Max and Emma, and Jean-Luc could hardly contain his excitement. "We must go see this property as soon as possible, yes?" He was half way to the elevator when he turned to them: "This will probably turn into a long day, so you may want to make your familial calls before we leave. I myself am going to call my friend Gérard."

Back in their room, Max and Lucie simultaneously ended cell phone conversations and turned to each other. "The Ghosts are still in Lourmarin, apparently the south of France suits them" was woven into "Sophie's well but says not to get my hopes up – what'd you say?"

Max tucked his gun in the waistband at the small of his back and went first: "We only have to worry about Julia and Gaston, no one else isn following us at the moment. What did *you* say?"

"Sophie is skeptical about the outcome and, well, look, Max, if this doesn't work out today, let's just go back to Lourmarin, get your mother married and..."

"And?"

"And, I don't know. This grocery store thing is just too weird and I think we're at the end of the road."

Max reached for her and nuzzled an ear. "I wouldn't give up just yet if I were you."

"Ok, you gotta stop that now or we'll never get out of this hotel." Lucie smiled slightly and threw her backpack over her shoulder. "Time to suit up."

***

The tiny grocery store at Three, Boulevard Adolphe Garnier, was less than unimposing, it was almost non-existent: the four of them standing in front of the 'Épicerie de Gérardmer' was enough to eclipse it entirely. Plus it was wedged between two businesses that threatened to converge on it: a restaurant's sidewalk tables had migrated toward its unconvincing entrance, as had the neighboring pharmacie's large ads on sandwich-boards.

All of which compressed the large, tiered produce stands that both guarded and obscured what was left of the entry. Even the battered metal pull-down, only partially raised, had run out of purpose.

"So much for Aladdin's cave." Lucie peered inside, which involved standing on tiptoe and leaning over a display of tired lettuces. Straining in the dim interior light, she felt a forceful nudge at the back of her knee and almost fell over.

"Hey, watch it!" was lost on the large, white, dread-locked Komondor that wanted her to move out of its way. Lucie stepped back, thinking it might be a shop dog who took his job seriously.

The dog made a point of sniffing each row of vegetables on the stand, snorted, then shook its entire body, putting hundreds of thin cords in motion all at once like a berserk cheerleader with a pompom overload. Then it lifted its leg and aimed at the second shelf of wrinkled, repugnant cucumbers.

Jean-Luc started to laugh uncontrollably, then jumped back as the stream flowed toward his shoes. From the interior of the shop came, "Allez, sale chien, ou je te - !" in an empty threat. The dog tossed its head and trotted off down the street. Mission accomplished.

Max doubled over in laughter.

Emma looked disgusted.

Lucie sighed and stepped into the store, which consisted of just two aisles in an inverted U shape: one in, one out. She'd only gotten half way down the left aisle when a wizened old man materialized from a back corner and smiled politely. All but invisible in the gloom, he was dressed in layers of dark clothing against the cold of the unheated shop. As he approached Lucie, a much younger man appeared and shoved in front of him, eager to speak English with the pretty American.

"We do not get many foreigners in here - " But Lucie had turned and was out on the sidewalk before he could finish.

Tears welled up in her eyes as she told her friends, "There's nothing in there, not even a back room, it's over."

But Max was staring past her, at the right side of the store. He said, very quietly, "Lucie, go talk to the old man and see if he'll let us go *down there.*" And pointed.

Lucie followed his gaze to the counter just inside

the entry, then to the curtain that hung below it. Her eyes widened and she gasped as Max's priest hole flashed through her mind.

"I know what that is! It's an opening to an underground storage level: one guy goes half way down the steps that'll be right under the counter, and somebody passes deliveries to him!" Excited, Lucie turned to Jean-Luc. "Let's show them the deed, maybe they'll let us search the basement."

He dug the document out of his pocket and handed it to her. "Want me to talk to him?"

"No, I do well with old French guys, I'm going in solo." She darted around the eager young man, who'd been trying to eavesdrop, and walked right up to the older one, who smiled again, pleased at being chosen. He held out a half-gloved hand and asked if he could help her.

Lucie took a chance and began, "Monsieur Reichert," then spoke with him for what seemed like forever to those waiting, and at last brought out the deed. He switched on a lamp, studied it and conferred with his son Pascal.

As Lucie emerged from the mouth of the cave-like interior, the sunlight made her blink.

"Monsieur Reichert said he's been waiting for someone like us to come along and explain the set-up here, that the adjoining properties have been trying to buy this place to expand theirs, but that ownership is buried under thick layers of legalities and this place did survive both wars, it's been here forever like Simon thought, but there's an iron-clad – that reminds me, here, JL, you're in charge of the deed and - "

"Breathe, Lucie."

She told them quietly, "I didn't tell him everything, but I didn't lie, and we get to see the cellar. The old man says it's got sections that nobody's bothered with for a long, long time."

***

As Pascal pushed aside the curtain and climbed down the stone steps, his father, who could no longer make it down to the cellar, exacted the promise of a full description of what the Americans found.

Max followed, then Lucie, backpack tightened around her shoulders, then Emma. Jean-Luc was about to join them when his phone rang; he took the call and bent down to shout to those underground that he had to return to the hotel for an urgent fax.

A subterranean voice yelled back, "Alright, come back as soon as you can. If we find anything before that, we'll call, ok?"

He stood up reluctantly, wanting desperately to be a part of whatever was going to happen. But his pragmatic lawyer's brain took over and reminded him that the document waiting for him was crucial.

The narrowness of the entry area necessitated a sharp left turn when they reached the bottom of the steps, and they found themselves in a large stone storeroom, predictably cold and dank. A single naked light bulb and its umbilical extension cord dangled from a hook in the low ceiling, and the young M. Reichert cautioned everyone to watch their heads.

He took several lanterns from a shelf, and as he distributed them, Lucie gazed around her: shelves lined most of the wall space to either side, and were covered top to bottom with all manner of dry goods: boxes of cereal, canned vegetables and fruit, boxes of the dreaded biscottes, jars of spices that had probably long since lost their potency, tinned meats, jars of jellies and huge jars of Nutella.

Boxes of everything from toothpaste to toilet paper

were stacked against the back wall, almost obscuring the wooden doors at each end.

As Lucie made her way toward the door on the right, she suddenly lurched forward. Max caught her arm and told her, "Careful, the floor's uneven."

Pascal added, "Yes, and it declines rapidly at this end."

"Max, could you move this case, umph, it's blocking the door."

Pascal scratched his head in thought. "I think it is empty in there, but I am not sure."

"We'd better check anyway, we've come this far." Max shifted several cases to one side.

Pascal had to put one foot on the side wall and yank repeatedly to get the door open: the wood had swollen in the damp and was now larger than the space it occupied. The hinges screeched in protest, then a gust of mildew assaulted them. Emma aimed her lantern into the space, but the room contained only cobwebs and more gloom.

Lucie wobbled her way over the irregular stone to the other side of the wall and dropped her lantern on the floor with a thump. She put her hands on her hips and narrowed her eyes at the offensive door.

She attacked it with a vengeance, her foot against the wall as Pascal had done. "Obstinate, (yank) stupid (yank) pieceashit door, (yank), you just won't give it up, will you, you, - "

Pascal backed up slightly, alarmed: the pretty, previously charming American had suddenly turned vicious.

" - sonofa - "

"LUCIE!"

Just as they shouted, the door popped open, sending Lucie flying backwards into Pascal, who yelled. She pushed off him, seized her lantern and strode through the opening.

Lucie held her lantern high as she walked further into the darkness, then stopped abruptly, totally unprepared for the contents of the room: they'd discovered a graveyard for antique wine making equipment!

Max and Emma silently pushed past Lucie and put their lanterns on conveniently placed wall hooks. Pascal initially hung back, having decided to treat Lucie deferentially: she might be a hitter, as well.

As they examined the artifacts, wiping dust off some, moving others to get a better look, Pascal explained that his father had explored this room years ago and tried to sell the outdated equipment.

"But no one wanted it then, so perhaps it was a good thing, because now these are all valuable antiques, non?"

Max's face was suddenly inscrutable as he casually remarked, "So that's why the deed includes the area behind the grocery store, to include all of this down here. Pascal, do you know what these things are?"

He picked up a heavy iron implement and said, "Eh bien, with this, I believe that one would, how do you say, mark the wine barrels."

"A branding iron?"

"Yes, branding. It is very old." He pointed at what looked like rakes. "And those are for scraping the winepresses, and those fancy boxes are for the presenting of the wine."

Lucie gazed at what looked to be a heavy iron tool attached to the edge of an old wooden desk supported by wrought iron legs. "Is this a corker, Pascal?"

The Frenchman took a step toward Lucie, then halted. He decided to view the object from where he was, a few feet away. Just in case. He squinted and said, "Yes, I believe so."

"But it's so ornate. And it's dated, look, it says 1885."

Max joined her to look at it and unobtrusively took his Swiss Army knife from his pocket. He leaned over the object and scraped it gently with a blade, whispering to Lucie, "I was thinking about the missing shipment of gold, and I wonder if it's under here." But further scraping only revealed more iron. "Oh well, worth a try." He put his knife away and smiled down at her. "Don't give up, Lucie, it's here, we just need to keep looking."

Lucie rubbed her hands together. "Has it gotten colder, or is it just me?"

Emma was shivering. She said quietly, "By my calculation, we've descended at least three feet since we started."

***

They continued to search until Max suddenly became very animated. His eyes darted around the room and he grabbed Emma by the shoulders. "Bulgaria, the hidden arms shipment? Whaddya think?"

"You mean the false - "

But Max was already walking the width of the room, counting.

"Pascal, would you do me a favor?"

Pascal nodded.

"Go back up and pace off the front of your store. I need to know how wide it is on the sidewalk. Then pace off how deep it is, ok?"

Pascal raised his eyebrows. Strange Americans. Like this had anything to do with the absentee landlord that he and his father wanted to find. But he did as he was asked.

Alone with the two women, Max explained in a rush: "It's been bothering me, the changes in elevation and the fact that this room is at least four feet narrower than the first room, and I'm thinking that somewhere along this left wall - "

But Lucie was already staring in that direction, at an elegant old wine rack that was actually more of a large flat board with sloping holes. It leaned against the wall, weary with age.

"I saw one of those in an antique shop, and it's called a pupitre, I remember because it's the old fashioned word for a student's desk. But there's something else."

Lucie tilted her head in concentration. "Look at the way that old oil lamp hangs just there, beside it: everything else in here is scattered, but *this* placement looks intentional. As in, look over here, here's some light to help you." Lucie squeezed past cases of empty wine bottles to stand directly in front of it. And then bent down to peer behind it.

"Agh, ptooey, dirt." Then, "Max, Emma, look at this." Lucie's voice shook. "The stone back here looks different from the rest."

In a second, Max had his hands on the wall, feeling the surface.

"*That's because it's concrete!*"

He looked down at her and almost yelled, 'You did it, Lucie, this has to be the portal!"

They pulled the board further down the wall, then Emma handed Max one of the winepress scrapers. "Only thing I could find to bash it in. But first, Lucie, why don't you go check to see what Pascal is doing: we don't want him walking in on us."

"Yeah, where *did* he get to?" Lucie rushed off to the cellar entrance while Max started to batter the wall with the long handle of the tool. The thin layer of concrete was shattering nicely under the blows when Lucie returned, looking puzzled.

"That's weird, nobody's up there." But Pascal was quickly forgotten when the fake wall revealed what it was hiding. A brick wall. A solid brick wall that reached half way to the ceiling.

Lucie wailed. "Nooooooooooooo!"

"Nobody throws up a brick wall and then concretes it for fun, Lucie, it's just another layer of insurance. We're still on the right track." Max looked at it intently, poked at it, then announced, "You know what? This doesn't look very sturdy."

He pushed hard on the wall, and because the mortar was spotty or missing entirely, the bricks fell easily into an opening beyond.

"Look, these are pretty much just stacked, they were put here for easy extraction. C'mon, ladies, pull these out into the room, and be careful, you're going to scrape your hands a little."

They lost track of time as the wall disappeared, revealing a black void beyond. When the opening was large enough to get through, Max turned to the women.

"Mind if I take point?"

"Sure, go ahead. We're right behind you."

He held his lantern out in front of him and stepped into the darkness.

❧ CHAPTER 34 ☙

Four feet straight in, light bounced off a stone wall as Max's lantern swayed in his hand. They followed a tunnel to the right, and as they crept along the wall and pointed the lanterns ahead, no one spoke. Suddenly Max shouted, "Whoa, hold it, don't take another step!"

The tunnel had ended abruptly and was replaced by steps that descended along the left wall. The area on the right was open, which terrified Lucie. She plastered herself against the wall and tried not to think about falling into an abyss. It didn't work.

"I can't do this, I'll - "

"Yes, you can, Lucie. Keep one hand on my back and move slowly."

Lucie gulped and started to shake, but followed him.

They were half way down when Max threw his arm out to stop those behind him. He had pierced the darkness with a beam from the lantern and was now swinging it like a strobe light over an enormous underground room.

No one moved or breathed, transfixed by the sudden, intermittent appearance of hundreds of dusty wine bottles stacked neatly on racks that stretched from one end of the cavern to the other. Lying there, waiting, just below the unsuspecting resort town of Gérardmer. And at one time, right under the Germans' noses.

Lucie sucked in her breath and started to shallow-breathe.

"OhMyGod! It's the –we found– it wasn't the gold – it's - !"

Emma stared.

"Didn't think it was real; what are the odds?"

Max moved quickly to the cellar floor. "Be careful, these bottom steps are slick."

Lucie halted suddenly. "Wait a minute – *don't touch anything!* Booby traps!"

"Only in the movies, Lucie."

Max hung his lantern on the end of the closest wine rack, carefully unshelved a bottle and held it reverently, blowing off the cobwebs. As he brushed off the label with his fingertips, his eyes widened.

Incredulous, Max turned to Lucie and Emma. "IT'S A 1945 DRC ROMANÉE-CONTI!" He replaced it, stepped back and scanned the room.

He spotted a rack with huge bottles and hurried over to it, removed one of the bottles, and yelled, "1945 Mouton-Rothschild. A jeroboam! The equivalent of - "

Lucie took the bottle from him and finished in an awe-struck voice, "Six bottles of some of the best Bordeaux on the whole freakin planet!"

Max's eyes moved as he calculated. "Worth over, mmm, $300,000, and look, there's a whole case of them!"

He darted to another rack, then another: "Here's a row of '45 Latours, and more '45 Mouton-Rothschilds, singles" ...his voice trailed off as Lucie wandered to a far corner, intrigued by several empty racks and by the really grimy bottles next to them.

"1934 Richebourgs over here, the wines are older in this section." Suddenly her voice boomed across the cavern: "I FOUND THE MOTHER LODE!"

She stood motionless, transfixed by the sight of bottle after bottle of very, very old wine. Max was at her side in an instant and took the bottle she was holding. His eyes widened as he read the label: "1864 Bouchard Père & Fils Montrachet. And there are more of them!"

He gulped audibly when he found the double magnums of 1921 Château Pétrus, singles of 1858 Château d'Yquem, jeroboams of 1900 Château Margaux and Romanée-Conti from 1911, 1919, 1923 and 1929.

"Max, look at this." She held out a bottle, her hands shaking slightly. "And there are eleven more just like it." They stared at a three-liter bottle of 1865 Lafite-Rothschild. Lucie finally stammered, "I read an auction report last month, on pre-1900 vintages. Max, I – I think that's worth over a million dollars. Just that one lot."

"Holy shit, if all these wines are still in good condition, there's a colossal fortune down here!"

"Uh-oh. Remember Julia's con?" Lucie sounded suddenly deflated and replace the bottle. "Augustin screwed over the Germans the same way, so what if all this is part of the hoax?"

Emma's firm voice reached them across the wine racks. "I don't think you'll have to worry about that."

She stood beside a wine barrel that, given the three dusty wineglasses joined together by ancient cobwebs, must have been used as a tasting table. An old metal box, the lid open, rested beside the wine glasses, and Emma was staring at the pile of papers she had extracted from it.

"How do you know they aren't fakes?" Lucie rested her lamp on the barrel, illuminating the area.

Emma handed her a sheaf of papers. "Because you now possess an inventory of the contents of this cellar, and it looks like the Great Châteaux have signed off on all of it. I'm thinking this is how the grateful winemakers repaid Augustin."

She smiled and nodded at Lucie. *"You've got provenance, my dear."*

Lucie flipped quickly through the names of the world's most remarkable wines. "A find of this magnitude is - how am I – what do I - " Totally bewildered, she dropped the documents on the barrel.

Then she noticed that Emma was holding several folded sheets of paper.

"What's that?"

Emma said softly, this time, "Voices from the past, I'm betting." She handed them to Lucie. "You'll need to translate for us."

The shadow has once again descended upon us: the filthy Boches invaded Paris in June and desecrated our beautiful Champs-Élysées with their jackboots. We foolishly relied on the Maginot Line to protect us, but it was an empty promise, nothing more than a glorified trench.

And so we are unprepared for the powerful evil of the Nazis. Italy has embraced it. The Swiss help no one but themselves. Les Anglais have been with us since September of last year, so I trust they will not let us perish alone.

My James is certain that this plague will not be

contained in Europe. It will find the Americans. We must hope for their neutrality to end, for we desperately need their resources and their resiliency.

The Boches have requisitioned our lovely house, so Albertine and I must flee south, to the vineyards. James, a phantom in our lives, will continue his vital work while we aid the Sautier winery and Augustin's efforts; because he risks his life for the Châteaux, they show their appreciation with gifts from their cellars, which we add to our old collection.

This Legacy, conceived in the trenches of the Great War and born of the resolve to protect a part of our nation's heritage, has required cunning and audacity. Now it grows into a promise for the future, a sacred and noble thing. We must be worthy of what we are creating, for it shall be the greatest collection of wine in history!

Nous trois, nous nous sommes jurés.

Marie Bottecher, le 30 octobre, 1940

Lucie's hand shook as she pulled out the next letter and continued to read:

1946 Gérardmer

Augustin was right. He said that all of our efforts and the final victories were not worth the millions of lives lost. In the end, they were not worth even one.

I have raised my child alone, and now I wait. My James has not returned from this second war, and only God knows what he has suffered. Augustin is in constant pain.

A lifetime ago, James removed his share from this cellar and sold it to provide for us, his family. Yesterday I took my share. When the time is right, I shall use it to fulfill my vow. Augustin remains adamant in wanting nothing more to do with the Legacy in his lifetime, so I will seal the cellars. There is no longer joy in the Legacy, that symbol of our contempt for the Boches and of our hope for the future.

I leave to our descendants this bitter reminder of hubris, of our belief that we could preserve our nation's precious heritage. But the Boches took from us what was most valuable after all, and we could not prevent that.

I go now to wait.

Marie Bottecher

"How very touching." The acid in Julia's voice was a corrosive that ate through the air. ***"Now hand over your weapons."***

CHAPTER 35

Lucie yelled "Aaaaaaahhh!" and tripped over a lantern, dislodging her backpack on the way to the floor. She instinctively clutched it to her chest and rolled as far from the voice as possible.

Julia approached from the dark area by the steps and sneered at Max, whose hand was half way to his back. "Don't even think about it. Put your gun on the floor and kick it over to me, then go sit on those cases. And no funny business: I'm already pissed off about that fool Gaston getting us lost."

Her eyes glittered as she glanced around the cavern and she bared her teeth in a mirthless smile. "I'll bet you didn't know we've been watching you since last night, did you? Had to drive all over this stupid town, checking hotels, but we found you!"

Meanwhile, Emma, who realized too late that she had left her large purse by the bottom of the steps, had slid behind a rack. She quickly took her cell phone from her pocket, silenced it, pressed Jean-Luc's speed dial number, then, leaving the line open, wedged it between two bottles.

"I know you're back there, Harris, and I already found your gun, so you might as well show yourself."

Hands raised halfway, Emma moved slowly into the open and growled: leaving her weapon out of reach was a rookie mistake, and she was angry with herself.

Julia made a sideways motion with the gun she was holding. "Over there, beside him." With her free hand, she snatched the papers from the barrel and slipped into a row of wine racks, out of the sight line of anyone approaching from above.

As Emma went to sit beside Max, who had his arms folded and looked disgusted, she pointed out, in a voice loud enough for Jean-Luc, "Taking the documents won't make all this yours, JULIA."

"Sure it will."

"How do you figure?" This from Max.

She ignored him and pointed her gun at Lucie. "You, stand up and don't move."

"How do you figure, Julia?" He had to get her attention away from Lucie.

Julia turned to Max and made a face. "It should be obvious even to you that since the postcards belong to Gaston, the documents and the treasure are mine, I mean his, as well."

"No, they're not. Gaston tried to cheat his godfather and Sautier gave them to Lucie."

Julia turned to Lucie and pointed the gun at her. "Your little floozy doesn't deserve them!"

Lucie's brain screamed, JJJJJ! Jeffrey, Julien, Julia! What is it with people whose names start with J? They're all - wait a minute: floozy? She frowned and opened her mouth, but Max got there first.

"What did you do with the old guy and his son?" A diversion, he hoped.

Julia whipped her head back to Max. "What?" She frowned. "Oh, them. Gaston told them your lawyer needed to see them both right away at the hotel, and they swallowed it." The mirthless smile returned. “It’s amazing what people will believe when you have a bit of relevant information.”

Max’s eyes darted to the steps.

“I wouldn’t try that if I were you, Gaston is upstairs, and he’s armed.”

Emma repeated, too loudly, “GASTON IS IN THE GROCERY STORE AND ARMED?

“What’s the matter with you, Harris, you going deaf?” Julia frowned at the older woman, then refocused on Lucie.

“You.” She waved the papers. “Sign the contents of this cellar over to me.”

“Don’t be an ass, Julia, what’s here legally belongs to Lucie. Scribbling on those old documents won’t change that.”

Julia turned toward Max, slowly. She hissed, “*What* did you call me?”

Max lost his patience and rolled his eyes. “For God’s sake, woman, haven’t you stolen enough wine already?”

That’s when she shot him.

***

Terrified, Lucie screamed: target practice was one thing, being part of a gunfight was another.

Emma moved to help Max, but Julia waved her away with the gun and snarled, “Oh for heaven’s sake leave him alone, it’s only a flesh wound.”

Julia glared at them. She needed to finish this quickly, before the lawyer returned with the grocers. Now, to manipulate the chef.

When she turned slightly to the side and narrowed her eyes at Lucie, Max slowly reached into his pants pocket and extracted a nitroglycerine pill. He slid it into his mouth, and as he put his hand back on his arm to staunch the bleeding, his mind raced to find a way to take out Julia.

She attempted to soften her voice as she addressed Lucie: "So, what do you say we just split everything and walk out of here together?"

Lucie cringed at the wicked witch tone, almost hearing 'my sweetie' and a cackle.

"Oh come on, you *really* think the two of them are going to let you keep all this? Think about it. Ever see them whispering to each other, then stop suddenly when you notice? They're always sneaking around, plotting something: they're in this for themselves, and you're a fool if you think otherwise."

The shock on Lucie's face was pure gratification for Julia, and she smirked in satisfaction as Lucie's brain shot into the past: the ominous gaze on the TGV, the abruptly-ended conversation at the Sautier estate, and Emma's hard, unfathomable stare at the Gérardmer hotel.

In a nanosecond, Lucie saw Max and Emma in a new light: partners forever, bound by their shared past, a much stronger bond than her short relationship with Max had forged. And those two had successfully blackmailed the most corrupt US government in modern times and – wait - NO!

She could *not* have read them that wrong!

Her eyes met Max's, and the pain on his face had nothing to do with his wound. Her expression accused, 'Betrayal', his pleaded 'How could you even consider that!'

"Leave her out of this, Julia, this is between you and me."

Julia snarled, "You got that right, bucko, it *was* between you and me - you wanted me that night, didn't you? But would you even look at me the next day? Nooooo, and you just kept marrying those insignificant, brainless bimbos when you could have had me!"

Lucie's eyes widened, she grimaced, then shrieked, *"Oh My God, you SLEPT with her!"*

Max winced. "It was a very long time ago and I was drunk. Extremely drunk, and believe me, I've regretted it ever since."

That's when Julia shot him the second time.

***

Lucie screamed again and hugged her backpack in front of her like a shield as Emma grabbed for Max, who was hit in the leg and bleeding profusely. Julia pointed the gun at her and roared, "Don't touch the bastard!"

"You hit an artery" was shouted for the open cell phone, and Emma fervently hoped Jean-Luc was listening. And reacting.

Julia didn't notice Lucie's head snap to the side when Max desperately mind-texted her: "Use your gun, Lucie. Now. Two-hand it."

Shaking violently, Lucie bent over and made what she hoped was a convincing retching sound. "Ucchhh, I'm gonna be sssssick." And while her brain screamed, 'I can't do this!', she dropped to her knees, inserted her right hand into the backpack she still clutched and found her gun. She fumbled with the safety, attempting to release it without getting caught.

As Julia growled, "Stop whining and get up," Lucie glanced at Max, who was making a supreme effort to remain lucid. But he was clearly bleeding out and wouldn't last much longer: Lucie had never been so scared in all her life.

She took a deep breath; she had to distract Julia and get her out in the open.

Suddenly Lucie stood and screamed, "*She's right, dammit, you two are always talking behind my back! Why did I ever think I could trust a bunch of conniving cutthroats!*"

Julia fixed wild, hate-filled eyes on Max and started to laugh maniacally as Lucie turned slightly and stared at Max, willing him to glance at her.

Then she winked at him.

Max dropped his jaw, then as comprehension hit him, made a face and lurched forward, catching Julia off guard. She frowned, stepped out from the safety of the wine racks, and bent down slightly to peer at him.

In a split second, Lucie crouched, raised her backpack with her right arm still in it and shook it so the contents shifted away from the bottom. Her left hand seized the outside of the soft leather and she bellowed, **"OVER HERE, BITCH!"**

Astonished, Julia turned to face Lucie and saw a backpack pointed at her. "Wha - ?" was interrupted by the bottom of the backpack exploding and bullets whizzing by in rapid succession. Then a sharp pain in her side.

Julia's weapon clattered to the floor as she fell and Emma shouted, "Get her gun!"

Lucie flew across the area between them in an instant. She kicked away the firearm and threw herself on the wounded lunatic, smashing her fist into her face.

"MAAAAAXXXXX!"

"Got him Lucie, you stay on Julia!" Emma had pressed Max's jacket onto the wound in his leg and was now yelling to the phone.

"Jean-Luc!" She heard a faint reply, but didn't leave Max's side to get the phone: he was too weak to keep pressure on the wound himself. She screamed,

"Hurry, we don't have much time. Julia's neutralized, you need to come through the entire cellar area and go through the wall where the bricks are piled!"

"Stay with me Max, look, watch Lucie over there!"

Lucie was pummeling a howling Julia with her fists and spewing forth an unintelligible stream of expletives.

Emma slapped Max's face and commanded, "Max, concentrate, what language do you suppose she's speaking?"

Max struggled to stay conscious. He looked over at Lucie and smiled weakly. "Ralphie."

"What?"

"You know, A Christmas Story, when the little guy has had it and beats the crap out of the kid with the yellow eyes? My favorite part..." His voice was fading to a whisper.

"Max!"

With a great effort, he opened his eyes. "Magnificent, isn't she?" Then he passed out.

***

The paramedics worked on Max in the cellar, then loaded him into the waiting ambulance. Lucie insisted on riding with him; the medics had at first refused, but Lucie was in full warrior mode and not to be messed with. She shoved them aside and muttered "I am not negotiating" as she climbed into the back.

Max briefly regained consciousness and looked up at Lucie, who'd been talking to him non-stop, threatening, "Don't you dare die on me, I do ***not*** want to have to explain to your mother why that whack job shot you!"

He managed, in a whisper, “Wow. You hit Julia right in the gut. I’m really proud of you.”

Lucie frowned. “Yeah, well, I was aiming for her head.”

CHAPTER 36

Lucie, Emma and Jean-Luc sat in the hospital hallway. Waiting. Uncharacteristically quiet, Lucie clutched the ruined backpack that Emma had thoughtfully repaired with the blue duct tape she was never without, and stared at the wall opposite, hating that control of the situation had to be relinquished at the swinging doors to her right.

Emma reached for Jean-Luc's hand and smiled into his eyes. "Your quick response saved Max's life today, I'm sure of it."

Jean-Luc kept her hand in his, unwilling to let go now that he had her safe beside him. "But if I had burst into the cellar, that crazy woman would have killed all of you, and so it was the courageous act of our little chef that really saved everyone."

He glanced sideways at Lucie for a response. None came, and he shot Emma a worried look. She made a rolling motion with her fingers, so he continued.

"I was pleased to be able to deal with Gaston myself; it has, you know, been some years since I was on the force." Jean-Luc snuck another look at Lucie: she had begun to rock slightly, a sure sign of distress.

"And the gendarmes who now guard the épicerie might have gotten the impression that there is an unexploded bomb, yet from the war, in the basement. I can assure you they will not allow anyone near the treasure."

Still no response. Jean-Luc nudged Emma, who awkwardly put her arm around Lucie. Not something she was used to doing. She rubbed her hand briskly on Lucie's upper arm, as though trying to restore circulation.

"Guess what, Lucie. Jean-Luc made some discreet inquiries in Nice and *somehow* the Mafia-types, the ones who hold Gaston's past-due IOUs, have learned of his whereabouts. Just in case he slips through the justice system."

Lucie stopped rocking.

Jean-Luc reached into his pocket and withdrew a large brown envelope.

"I have something to show you, Lucie."

"Another deed?" Lucie's feeble attempt at humor was a good sign.

"No, a fax of a notarized statement from my friend Gérard, stating that, because he was born in June of 1923, he is the oldest surviving descendant of the Three and therefore the owner of the property at Three, Boulevard Adolphe Garnier. Which he bequeaths to you."

Jean-Luc looked suddenly shy. "I experienced some of your, ah, vibes, Lucie, and called Gérard this morning. He felt, as I, that we needed to safeguard your claim."

Lucie's voice was jagged. "Thank you, Jean-Luc, but it means nothing without Max - " She was interrupted as the surgeon banged through the double doors.

A grim Sabine removed her cap and addressed them.

CHAPTER 37

They held their collective breath without knowing it as Sabine began, "Your friend is in recovery; he lost a lot of blood, but we were able to stabilize him and repair the damage. Walking will be painful for a while, but he will regain full use of the leg."

Three sets of lungs exhaled.

"Also, the arm wound was superficial, and the nitro he took prevented further damage to the heart." Sabine tilted her head. "The woman they brought in, the one with stomach and kidney damage. She was the assailant?"

Jean-Luc nodded.

"She knew what she was doing. The bullet tore through his artery, where it would do the most damage."

Lucie shivered.

Sabine squinted. "So who shot *her*?"

"That would be me." Lucie stopped shivering.

"I...see." Sabine raised her eyebrows, then shook her head and said, "No, I do not. What in the world have you people gotten yourselves mixed up in?"

Emma summed it up succinctly: "The assailant attempted to steal the treasure, and in doing so almost killed Max. So Lucie shot her."

Sabine blinked rapidly. "She – you found the Legacy?"

Emma nodded. "Under the Épicerie de Gérardmer. It's an entire cellar of vintage wines."

Sabine's jaw dropped. "I had no idea!"

"Neither did we." Emma's voice bordered on wry.

Sabine refocused and said, "Well, he is asking for someone called Ralphie."

Jean-Luc looked puzzled, but Emma snorted, then laughed and pulled Lucie to her feet. "Go see the poor man, Ralphie. Tell him we're all here and come right back with a report."

Sabine frowned when no one explained, and said, "Only for a moment, he is very weak."

***

Max drifted in and out of consciousness until the day after his surgery, when he awoke and blinked at a dark-haired woman who bore a striking resemblance to Lucie.

He mumbled, "Why do you look like that?"

"Hospital Nazis. I - " A noise in the hall interrupted her and she faded away.

The next day, Max woke to find Emma sitting by his bed, busily texting.

"Did I see Lucie with dark hair, or are the pain meds doing a number on me?"

"You did and they're not. Today she's a redhead. Been borrowing the disguises from me: you know I never travel without that suitcase."

"I know I'm going to regret asking, but why?"

"Hospital Nazis."

"That's what she said. And I still don't get it."

Emma put away her phone and grinned at Max.

“Your Intended has been running amok: it started when she told the kitchen staff that the food here is reprehensible and you couldn’t possibly get well if you ate it. So they barred her from the kitchen.”

“Then she lured the police guard away from Julia’s room and tormented her until she went berserk, wouldn’t stop screaming that a demon was after her, so they locked her up in the psych ward. Julia, not Lucie.”

Max laughed, then winced.

“Anyhow, she’s been barred from the entire hospital complex, just short of a Temporary Restraining Order. She claims Dr. Sabine is behind it all, and… ”

The new, chatty Emma. Max was getting a headache.

***

On the fourth day, Max woke up to an old woman with a gray bun at the nape of her neck. With startling blue eyes.

“Nice disguise.”

“Thanks. It’s the best one yet, I found out no one messes with addlepated old people. I need to work on the wrinkles, though, if I’m going to be totally convincing.”

“Emma says you missed your calling. You’d have made a great operative, except for the weapons part.” Max smiled.

Lucie made a face at him.

“And what you did to get Julia out in the open so you could shoot her, that was brilliant.” Max’s smile faded. “But you believed her when she said I betrayed you, didn’t you?”

“Max, I - ”

"No, I saw it on your face. Lucie, I love you, but there's no future for us without trust; I spent my entire professional life not being able to trust people, and it's a lousy way to live."

"My reaction was entirely justified. On the TGV, when you and Emma were arguing? You both gave me a look that sent chills down my back! Then at Gérard's house, by the front door. Then on the balcony at the hotel, a few days ago. Doing just what Julia the Psycho said: you two deep in private conversation that stops abruptly when I notice. Consider your collective dangerous past, put yourself in my place and *tell me you wouldn't have had the sense to be suspicious!"*

Max was dumbfounded. "What!" He half sat up. "On the train? Wait - were we out in the corridor?"

"Yup."

"That was about Jean-Luc, not you!"

Lucie looked puzzled.

"Remember, you and I had the 'you're being selfish' conversation?"

"Oh. Yeah."

"That's all it was, me being angry about Emma having someone else in her life. Didn't realize we even looked at you." His gaze wandered as he continued to search his memory.

"And the only thing Em and I talked about privately in Gérard's house was your blue diamond, I wanted to know if she thought it was the right time."

Max lay back on his pillow and stared at the ceiling. "On the balcony. Lucie, that's when she told me she's being treated for, uh, serious health issues. I guess we did look suspicious when we saw you watching us, she asked me not to tell anyone." He looked over at her, distressed.

"Emma's ill? I'm so sorry, I won't say anything."

"Lucie, bottom line is that deep down, you'll always doubt me."

Lucie snorted. "You give up too easily."

"What?"

"You've had four broken relationships, I've had two. Of course there's doubt, but it only lasted a second. And then, (Lucie flung her arms wide and raised her eyebrows) *I saved your ass!"*

She sat back and crossed her arms.

Max was incredulous. "So you're saying... we're good?"

Lucie rolled her eyes. "Of course we are." Duh.

Max blinked several times, readjusting his perception of relationships. Then he squinted at Lucie's gray wig and observed, "You know, you wouldn't be having a problem getting into the hospital if you were my next of kin. Legally, they couldn't bar you from seeing me."

"You made that up. Sabine can do whatever she wants here."

Change the subject. "I still can't believe you actually shot Julia."

"What, that I shot at her or that I actually *hit* her?"

Max thought a response might be imprudent.

"Anyway, look what I got for my trouble." She hauled her backpack up on the bed and showed him the blue duct tape.

"I'll get you another one."

"That's ok, I think I'll carry it around like this for a while."

***

Lucie, looking like herself, sat beside Max, who was out of bed and in a chair by the window. She'd been reinstated to full access to the hospital because of Jean-Luc: he'd used his legal connections to obtain a court order that gave Sabine full custody of her little dog, Peugeot. Sabine was grateful enough to lift the ban on Lucie's visits, and even allowed her to bring food from the hotel for Max.

When Emma and her lover arrived, Max stood, slowly, used a cane in his left hand and extended his right to Jean-Luc. The haggard look had somewhat left his handsome features, and his voice had some strength in it. And a lot of sincerity.

"I want to thank you for all you've done for us, JL, from all the legal paths you've cleared, to rescuing me in the cellar. I wouldn't be standing here now if not for you and Lucie." Max pumped his hand so vigorously that the Frenchman winced.

"As a result, Lucie and I want to include you in - "

He was interrupted as the swinging door banged open, admitting a wheel chair bearing Albertine and a picnic basket.

Sabine pushed her grandmother into the room and announced, "Max, you have a visitor!"

Albertine nodded at them, and they all shook her frail hand in turn. Max, for whom standing was painful, sat down as she began, with Sabine translating for them:

"So. You have found the Legacy. I wish to thank you for allowing Sabine to show me the letters and documents. It meant a great deal to me, you know." She folded her hands in her lap.

"You have also solved a mystery: I have always wondered where my mother obtained the funds to donate the children's wing to this hospital, and now I realize that she used her share of the treasure."

She paused for a moment, remembering. "She was a strong woman, you know, one of the first feminists, and when I told her I wanted to be a nurse, she said,

Why not a doctor? It was difficult, I was the only female in my class, but I succeeded and so did my Sabine." She smiled.

"My mother wrote that The Legacy is a sacred thing, and it must be used for purposes worthy of the sacrifices that inspired it." She looked deep into Lucie's eyes and said softly, "And now you, my dear, are the sole possessor of the world's greatest collection of wine. What will you do with it?"

Lucie knelt in front of Albertine and took her hands. "We intend to sell the wine and use the bulk of the proceeds to create a Foundation. And I promise you that whatever we call it, Bottecher, Sautier and Milnar will be part of the name."

A tear escaped as Albertine told her granddaughter, "The basket, Sabine, we must drink a toast."

As Sabine handed them all wine glasses, Jean-Luc explained that the old woman had requested a bottle from the cellar earlier that day, and that Emma was certain no one would mind.

"Of course not, I just hope one bottle is enough." Lucie grinned.

"Emma told me you would say that." Jean-Luc grinned back at her and extracted a magnum of 1945 Mouton-Rothschild.

Everyone gasped as Lucie took the bottle and opened it with the reverence it deserved. She asked Max to pour, winking at him.

They raised the glasses and, in two languages, Lucie offered the first toast: "Aux perdus, to the original Three, to an end to war."

Max continued, "And to the brave, relentless woman who believed in the cards and her vibes. And found the treasure."

His adoring gaze left a scowl on Sabine's face.

***

Visiting hours in the hospital were coming to an end and everyone but Lucie had departed. She eased onto the bed beside Max and cradled her head on the uninjured arm.

"JL was really pleased about being part of the foundation."

"He deserves it, and we need a good lawyer, anyway." Max drew her close. "Know what? I think we should keep some of the wine for ourselves."

"So do I. Plus I'd like to give Gérard and Marie-Françoise a few of the bottles, for having faith in me."

"And I think we should use Acker Merrall and Condit to auction the wine, they have an excellent Hong Kong presence, as well as New York. Um, Lucie, it's going to be a full time job running the foundation. You willing to give up being a chef?" He looked down at her, then nuzzled his face in her hair.

"Are you kidding? The chance to give back, big time, with three of the best people I know? Besides, I can always cook for the four of us and whoever else is around."

They thought about that for a while, then Lucie started to squirm, uncomfortable in the small bed.

"Know what, Max? We need to blow this one horse town."

Max raised an eyebrow.

"I need the Provençal sun and I need sex. Smokin. Hot. Sex."

***

The party of four left for Lourmarin the very next day.

~ CHAPTER 38 ~

The rich, deep-blue sky vibrated with intensity and the Mistral that howled elsewhere in Provence fell silent, granting a dispensation to the inhabitants of Lourmarin: cosmic forces were conspiring to hold the terror of the shooting at bay.

Like contented felines, Max and Lucie lounged in the sunlight on the south terrace, perusing a pile of newspapers and magazines.

"They've all got our story, Max, but I'm only considering Wine Spectator and Vanity Fair for interviews; I mean, we *have* to talk to Wine Spectator, but Vanity Fair! How cool is that?! Oh, and Jean-Luc's wine expert says we're looking at upwards of thirty million dollars at auction."

"That reminds me, JL told me he's leaving his law firm to help run the foundation. Pleased?"

"You know it. But I'm worried about him, Max: he's holed up in the winemaker's house, working 24/7 on the auction. He needs to take a break once in a while."

"He's turned out to be such an asset, I'd put my complete trust in him even if he and Em weren't going to get m –m – "

Lucie whipped her head around. "Going to what?"

Max winced.

"Don't make me get out of this chair, Max."

"She's gonna kill me, they wanted it to be a surprise."

Lucie narrowed her eyes at him.

"Ok, ok, they're getting married tomorrow, along with mother and Didier. It's very unlike Em, but she's made up her mind."

Lucie thought about that for moment and appreciated that Max wasn't pressuring her to join in the multiple nuptials.

Suddenly, the door of the winemaker's cottage banged open, startling them. Jean-Luc waved at them through the olive trees and shouted, "Documents to sign, allons-y, vite, vite, vite!" And banged the door shut again.

Max struggled to his feet and grumbled, "You were right, JL needs to chill."

Moments later, Jean-Luc pushed some papers across the table to Lucie. "You need to sign these, my dear."

Lucie picked up a pen, but stopped and squinted.

"What's this?"

Jean-Luc stifled a laugh. "A list of the Board of Directors."

"I can *see* that, JL, I mean this." She shoved the document back at him, poking at one line.

"It says Max Richards."

"I - " Lucie stopped and glared at the conspirators, who were howling with laughter.

When he could talk, Max said, "You know I've always hated my name, right? I mean, what kind of name is Hamish Tuathal Ethelbert-Meicklejohn for a foundation board member?"

"You're deranged."

"Well, I figured hell will freeze over before you change your name again, so I just expedited matters."

Lucie stared at him in disbelief, which precipitated another round of laughter.

***

The entourage from the States – Roland, Juan, Dylan and Maxime (the young French oenologist who would run the winery with her) - arrived just after lunch and settled into the bastide. The rest of the day was spent readying the house for the wedding, and Lucie had just finished her call to the French caterers when something occurred to her. "You know, Max, we've been to hell and back with your former partner and we *still* don't know her first name. Her real one."

Max shrugged as a shrewd glint appeared in Lucie's eyes.

"I think the priest and I need to have a little chat tomorrow."

***

The mild temperature on the back terrace allowed for a brief outdoor ceremony, and those assembled sat in folding chairs as the two couples stood before Father Moreau.

Kate and Didier held hands and were pronounced husband and wife, then the priest, who'd agreed to do the ceremony in two languages, turned to Jean-Luc and Emma. "Do you, - "

Emma heard the creaking of chairs as the guests leaned forward. She turned slightly to confirm her fears, and hissed at the priest.

"Just skip the name part and get on with it."

The priest glared at her.

No one breathed as he continued, "Do you,

ERNESTINE, take Jean-Luc to be your lawfully - "

Roland leaped out of his chair, emitted an ear-splitting shriek, screamed "OH MY WORM!," threw his hands up to his face and started to giggle uncontrollably. Which startled Milou, who launched a cacophony of barking that drowned out the wedding vows. Which pretty much ended the service.

Max lingered with Emma/Ernestine on the terrace as the guests wandered in to the dining room.

"So." He stopped and gazed at her. "My, my, what *are* we to call you now? Can't use Mrs. Harris, your name isn't Emma, and Mrs. Renaud sounds a bit formal, don't you think?" Max tried to stifle the laughter. "Ernie comes to mind."

She raised an eyebrow and said, "If you want to live to see tomorrow, you'll continue to call me Emma."

Max grinned. "Emma it is."

Emma handed Max an envelope. "Don't open this unless I'm not around to tell you not to."

Max frowned. "Not going all sentimental on me, are you?"

Emma looked surprised. "Me, sentimental?"

"Right. What was I thinking."

"It's for... in case the treatments aren't as effective as promised."

"Shouldn't you be giving this to JL?"

"It's not information that he needs."

Max gave his ex-partner a long look, and finally said, "Ok, if that's what you want."

***

Two long tables accommodated everyone in the dining room, where Didier's friends laughed about the unusual wedding ceremony and enjoyed appetizers and wine until Max and Lucie appeared, bearing two jeroboams of 1900 Château Margaux. Everyone gasped as Max slowly filled their glasses, raised his and began:

"I know that, in honor of the weddings, this should be champagne." He paused to allow Didier to translate for his friends. "But our family has, as you know, recently acquired the greatest collection of vintage wine in history."

"And so I propose a toast to my mother and my new stepfather." Max paused to grin. "I give you Les Roussel." Clapping and 'Santé' accompanied a careful tasting of the great wine.

"And a toast to cherished friends, Monsieur et Madame Renaud."

Another round of clapping and cheers, for the lawyer was known to several of Didier's friends.

"And now to those who are not here to be honored. Marie Bottecher, James Milnar, and," Max bowed slightly to Gérard and raised his glass to him alone, "Augustin Sautier." The elderly Frenchman managed a fierce, proud smile to hide his tears as he lifted his glass with the others.

The meal that followed was superb and soon Didier's friends were enjoying the croquembouche and toasting the newlyweds.

As the guests departed, Max pulled Lucie into an alcove, enveloped her face with his hands and kissed her.

"Mmm, what was that for?" Lucie smiled at him.

"Been waiting to share this with you, and now seems like the perfect time." Max paused for effect. "On the way to Paris, I liquidated a sizeable chunk of my holdings, with the idea of contributing to your favorite charities. But now that we have a foundation, it's all going there."

"On the way – *what!*"

Max grinned. “Meeting you motivated me to do something meaningful.”

Lucie’s eyes widened.

“It’s simple, really: the people I love don’t need the money, and Dylan’s inheritance is the winery, if she commits to it.”

“I never expected this, Max.”

“But I don’t intend to live like a pauper, Lucie, I want us to be able to enjoy the rest of our life together.” He hesitated, unsure of the effect of his last words.

Lucie grabbed the lapels of his suit jacket and pulled his face down to hers. Max winced, but Lucie laughed, her eyes twinkling.

“Max Richards, this is gonna be - GREAT!”

DEDICATION

To Wally, who provided that first laptop. And encouraged me every single day.

To Jen, who got me a subscription to Wine Spectator, and believed. And offered to design the cover.

To Lauren, who gave me that box of old postcards. (It's real.) And who laughed at all the funny stuff.

To Melissa, who gave me the Wine Bible one Christmas. And quoted Dr. Seuss at me: "Why fit in when you were born to stand out?"

To Sharon, who read that first manuscript and encouraged me to publish anyway.

And to MacKenzie.

Translations of foreign terms, for those of you who are annoyed when they appear without explanation!

Allez, sale chien, ou je te - : *Get out of here, dirty dog, or I'm gonna –*
À la prochaine, mon ami : *Until the next time, my friend.*
Bastide: *French country house*
Bien sûr: *of course*
Bifteck au Poivre, cognac et crème: *peppered beefsteak with cognac and cream*
Blanquette de veau: *veal stew with mushrooms, potatoes in a creamy sauce.*
Boches: *slang term for Germans*
Bonhomie: *good will*
Ca, c'est la mienne: *That one is mine !*
Ça, c'est pour toi, Lucie. Notre cadeau contient un héritage, et nous sommes absolument certains que tu le comprendras – et le trouveras :
This is for you, Lucie. Our gift contains a legacy, and we are absolutely sure that you will understand and find it.
C'est pas fini entre nous. Je vais te... *It's not over between us, I'm gonna...*
Chère: *dear*
Comme ça: *that way*
Cornichons: *crisp, tart pickles*
Croquembouche: *French wedding cake, looks like a cream puff tree*
De rigeur: *required, customary*
Eh bien: *well*
Elle me fait peur: *She scares me.*
En famille: *with the family*
Fleurs de courgette farcies: *stuffed zucchini flowers*

Fromages: *an assortment of cheeses, served after the main course in France*
Goûter: *a snack*
Il vous offre seulement trois millions cinq cent mille, et pas même en euros. Ferme:
He's offering only three million five hundred thousand, and not even in Euros. And it's a firm offer.
Je vous remercie, Gérard et Marie-Françoise, mais...
Thank you, Gérard and Marie-Françoise, but...
Konichiwa: *Japanese for Hi*
L'autre Fauvent: *the other Fauvent (a character in Les Misérables)*
Madre de Dios! ¿Qué pasa aquí!?:
Spanish for Mother of God, what's going on here?
Mairie: *town hall*
Mais – *But!*
Maison de retraite: *Nursing home*
Mais pourquoi? Je n'en comprends rien:
But why ? I don't understand any of it.
Médecins Sans Frontières: *Doctors without Borders*
Nous trois, nous nous sommes jurés : *We three swear to this.*
Pauvre: *poor*
Pension alimentaire: *alimony*
Petite-fille: *granddaugher*
Prévu: *planned, expected*
Qu'est-ce qu'il y a, Lucie: *what's the matter, Lucie ?*
Quoi? Mais, j'ai supposé que,enfin, c'etait prevu que - mais...ah, bof: *What ! I naturally assumed...*
S'arrange: *work out, be ok*
Salade niçoise: *Salad originally from Nice, typically with greens, tuna, eggs, tomatoes, anchovies and much more.*
Salade verte: *a simple green salad with vinaigrette*
Salaud! Tu me débectes! *Bastard ! You disgust me!*

Sale petite con!

Con used to be a lot nastier, now it mostly means asshole. But combined with sale, (dirty, literally) the insult is worse, implying a serious character defect.

Sans : *without*

Sûreté: *French National Police Force*

Über: *German for ne plus ultra. The ultimate, super, something that nothing is better than.*

Vin blanc: *white wine*

Vuelve pronto: *come back soon*

CREDITS

Specific source quotes and information:

Chapter 13: The notion that Augustin was granted a delay in the call-to-arms in 1914, because of the grape harvest, came from *Wine and War,* by Donald and Petie Kladstrup, New York, Broadway Books, 2001. Page 14.

Chapter 15: James says he saw vineyards sliced up by trenches, blown up and poisoned by chemical shells that leaked into the soil. The idea came from *Wine and War*, page 18.

Chapter 16: Lucie quotes *The Guns of August,* by Barbara W. Tuchman, New York, The Random House Publishing Group, 1994. (Hardcover edition 1962)

To '*gain ten yards and exchange one wet-bottomed trench for another.*' is from Tuchman's book, pg. 439.

Chapter 25: Lucie's rendition of the history of Gérardmer comes from a French web site that I translated myself, at:

http://fr.wikipedia.org/wiki/Gérardmer

Made in the USA
Lexington, KY
07 March 2015